Kathy George was born in South Africa, and has since lived in Namibia, New Zealand, and Australia. A hopeless romantic, she fell in love with *Rebecca* by Daphne du Maurier as a teenager, and includes *Wuthering Heights* and *Great Expectations* among her favourite books. She has worked as a legal assistant, but her true enthusiasm has always been for writing, and she holds a Masters of Fine Arts in Australian Gothic literature from the Queensland University of Technology. Kathy lives in Brisbane and *Estella* is her second novel.

Also by Kathy George

Sargasso

Estella

KATHY GEORGE

First Published 2023
First Australian Paperback Edition 2023
ISBN 9781867252306

Estella
© 2023 by Kathy George
Australian Copyright 2023
New Zealand Copyright 2023

Except for use in any review, the reproduction or utilisation of this work in whole or in part in any form by any electronic, mechanical or other means, now known or hereafter invented, including xerography, photocopying and recording, or in any information storage or retrieval system, is forbidden without the permission of the publisher.

This book is sold subject to the condition that it shall not, by way of trade or otherwise, be lent, resold, hired out or otherwise circulated without the prior consent of the publisher in any form of binding or cover other than that in which it is published and without a similar condition including this condition being imposed on the subsequent purchaser.

All rights reserved including the right of reproduction in whole or in part in any form.

This is a work of fiction. Names, characters, places, and incidents are either the product of the author's imagination or are used fictitiously, and any resemblance to actual persons, living or dead, business establishments, events, or locales is entirely coincidental.

Published by
HQ Fiction
An imprint of Harlequin Enterprises (Australia) Pty Limited (ABN 47 001 180 918),
a subsidiary of HarperCollins Publishers Australia Pty Limited (ABN 36 009 913 517)
Level 19, 201 Elizabeth St
SYDNEY NSW 2000
AUSTRALIA

® and TM (apart from those relating to FSC®) are trademarks of Harlequin Enterprises (Australia) Pty Limited or its corporate affiliates. Trademarks indicated with ® are registered in Australia, New Zealand and in other countries.

Printed and bound in Australia by McPherson's Printing Group

I stole her heart away and put ice in its place.

Great Expectations by Charles Dickens

What have I done! What have I done!

Great Expectations by Charles Dickens

For Merryl Powell and Rosemary Rust

PART ONE

1

I am not aware of how old I was when I was taken from my mother. I have struggled to recall anything meaningful about her. My strongest memory is of her warm, strong hands and I remember darkness, too, but I do not know if it is my mother's colouring or her shadowy skirts where I buried my face.

I did not go gently when they came for me. I remember that I clung to those skirts, put up a fight. Kicked. But I was taken away and made to stand on a wooden board. My clothes were stripped off me, my face put under a water butt, my shivering body pummelled and soaped and rubbed and rasped and kneaded until I wailed like the child I was.

I was trussed up in undergarments and leggings and a dress, with a white pinafore pulled over my head. My hair was brushed and plaited, boots strapped onto my feet, and I was taken by the hand and led away. Still snivelling. Still whimpering. Still damp behind the knees.

Outside, in the street, the evening was drawing to a close and the gas lamps were being lit. I wanted to pause, to watch how the man on the ladder created his magic, but there was no time. I was lifted into a carriage and shoved far back onto the cold leather so that my legs were off the ground and stuck out like rolling pins in front of me. It was cavernous and gloomy inside. A man all in black sat across from me. His arms were spread out, his angled legs flung before him like some gigantic spider. He grunted at me. He had a large head, black bristly eyebrows and vast hands that seemed to have a life of their own. One took out a shiny pocket watch, large as was everything else about him. He checked the time, then tapped his stick on the roof of the carriage. We lurched forward and the horses' hooves went *clip-clop clippity-clop* on the cobblestones. The man slid the watch away. He bit the side of his great forefinger.

I was too far back on the seat to see out of the window and, after some time, no glow of the gas lamps flashed across the ceiling. There were no further sounds of other carriages, of street sellers, of flower ladies crying *Daffodils!* No longer the smell of chestnuts roasting in barrows. There was only a sooty darkness.

The carriage swayed from side to side in a dull rhythmic manner. The horses' hooves thudded on the ground. The man pushed himself back into the corner, rearranged his spidery legs and closed his eyes. He was not asleep. Every now and then, he peered out at me between a half-raised eyelid. His eye was like the dimly lit fire on the hearth from whence I had come.

Sometime later, a hand on my shoulder shook me and there was a faint aroma of scented soap. 'Wakey, wakey,' the man said. But I could not or *would not* be woken. I did not want to face whatever was ahead of me. The great coat that kept me warm was cast aside, however, and I was scooped up without ceremony in his big arms and carried down and out of the carriage.

I kept my eyes closed. I did not want to wake up to these new surroundings, to these foreign smells, this new world. But I was aware of keys clinking, of a journey across a courtyard—the man's boots tapping the stones—of an odour of mildew, candle-light flickering before us and against the narrow walls, and the length of one long passage after another.

I was dumped upon a bed. Someone unstrapped my boots, dropped them to the floor, and my pinny and dress were pulled over my head. My legs first, then my body, were slipped between the cold sheets and the covers drawn up to my chin. The man—I knew his voice now—entered the room. 'Mind you behave yourself!' he instructed, then he departed, pulling the door gently behind him, and I fell back into the abyss of sleep.

2

In the morning, I was awake before it was light—because that was my custom—and I lay in my bed and looked about me. In the semi-dark, I made out that the walls were wooden and bare, the ceiling low and my room small. I got up and stood at the curtained window. I drew it aside to look out at an abandoned yard shadowy with empty casks and silvery with metal staircases, a place I later came to know as the disused brewery.

A bedside table held an unlit candle in a holder on its surface, and my clothes from last night were folded on the end of my bed. Something strange was propped against the bed post ... A knitted doll! I retrieved her and snuggled back down with her under the covers, holding her close in case someone took her away. She had yellow plaits and a red tartan skirt and I decided that her name would be Poppet. Not long after the light filtered into my room, someone bustled inside.

'Good morning, Estella,' the woman said. She was squat with grey hair half-hidden under a white cap, but her wrinkled face was kind and her brown eyes bright. 'You've opened the curtains.

I hope you slept well? My name is Mrs Butters and I am here to help you dress. I see you found your doll? Do you like her?'

I said that I did. I volunteered that I had named her Poppet, and Mrs Butters said that was a nice name.

She told me that provided I did as she asked, we would get along. She told me that I must *always* do as Miss Havisham asked, that if I did not it would be the worse for me, and I wondered how things could get worse and in what way? Mrs Butters also told me that the last bairn she looked after was Miss Havisham herself.

'Who—who is Miss Hav … Hav …?' I asked as the housekeeper pulled my pinny over my head, but I could get no further than the first syllable of her name.

'You will find out soon enough,' Mrs Butters said.

I was taken to the kitchen and fed tea *and* porridge for breakfast, which was more than I ever had before, and then Mrs Butters took me upstairs to be introduced. She held a flickering candle out in front of her as we made our way up in the darkness, and clutched my hand in one of hers. The house seemed enormous and the passages never-ending and dingy, and I was glad of the comfort of her hand.

Upstairs, she knocked upon a door and pushed it open.

'Miss Havisham,' she called, 'I have brought Estella to meet you.'

We entered the room. It was shadowy, the curtains all drawn, and at first I could see nothing and drew back apprehensively on the threshold. But Mrs Butters took up my hand again. 'Come, Estella,' she encouraged, leading me inside.

A fireplace, with a fire glimmering with sparks and light, was against one wall. Trunks half-packed with beautiful silken dresses lay abandoned on the floor, and a large dressing table strewn with dead flowers occupied one corner. Jewels were scattered upon its surface, as well as a silver-backed hairbrush and a pretty little crystal dish containing hairclips. By degrees, as my eyes adjusted, I saw that a lady sat in a fancy and ornate chair alongside the dressing table. She was slender and her face bony and angular, and she had a mass of untidy hair that resembled the head of a dandelion and was decorated with dead roses.

'So this is Estella?' she murmured, gazing at me.

Mrs Butters nodded. 'Say hello to Miss Havisham,' she instructed.

'Hello, Miss Hav … Miss Hav …' But I could get no further.

The lady was dressed in a long white gown, her legs crossed at the knee, and one foot wore an elegant white satiny shoe while the other was bare. The second shoe, I noticed, stood upright upon the dressing table.

'She seems a little on the small side,' she remarked and jewels around her neck caught the light of the fire and glinted as she spoke.

'She is only three,' Mrs Butters murmured.

I had limited knowledge of the world, but I must, at some point, have gone to church and absorbed some idea of angelic beings, for I let go of Mrs Butters's hand and walked around the back of the lady's chair. Which, in hindsight, was particularly brave of me.

Neither woman spoke until I reappeared on the other side.

'Where are your wings?' I asked.

'My wings?' The lady raised her eyebrows.

'Yes, your wings, for are you not an angel?'

'Oh, Lord,' Mrs Butters said, and stifled a laugh.

'Now, now, Butters,' the lady said, but her voice was kind.

Later, I came to understand that it was Miss Hav's wedding gown, yellowed with age, that she wore, and not some angelic robe, that one white satiny shoe was on and the other oft times off, that the withered bouquet on her dressing table had been her bridal flowers, that the clock in the room together with the hands of her watch had been stopped at twenty minutes to nine. That all the clocks in the house had been stopped at twenty minutes to nine. That some awful event had happened at precisely that time, which had changed her life forever.

On that first day, I glimpsed something immense and deteriorating upon a table in the adjacent room. Spiders seemed to have adorned it with webs and turned it into their home, and when I stood quietly I could hear the scritching of beetles' feet coming and going upon the table. They groped about in a ponderous, elderly way, as if they were short-sighted and hard of hearing and not on terms with the spiders, let alone with one another. And in due course, I came to know that the immense and deteriorating thing heavily overhung with cobwebs was the remains of the wedding cake.

Later still, there were many things I came to understand, but for now my world consisted of Mrs Butters, who clothed and fed me, bathed me once a week, and put me to bed every night, and of the lady, of course. Miss Hav—for that was all of her name I could manage for some time.

3

I spent time with Miss Hav every day. Sometimes, depending on her mood, it was only five minutes. Sometimes it was all morning. Sometimes my hours with her were spent in total silence.

What did I do with myself? In the beginning, when I was very young, I would sit on the floor on a rug at Miss Hav's feet, and we would play Old Maid because it was the easiest and simplest card game for me to learn. If Miss Hav did not feel like interacting with me, I would be relegated to the corner where I had a wooden dolls' house with meagre furniture, and I would have to play quietly on my own while Miss Hav spent long hours staring into the fire, lost in thought. I usually brought Poppet along with me and would put her through her paces, although she was too big for the house and I would have to squeeze her up the stairs. Sometimes I left her sitting up there and propelled two fingers up and down the staircase, whispering, 'Yes, Miss Hav. No, Miss Hav. More wood for the fire, Miss Hav?' as I had heard Mrs Butters say.

Apart from these intervals, the day was my own and I learnt how to amuse myself. Before long I knew the layout of the house and the grounds inside out. Satis House had a dark pitched roof, a barricaded dormer window and a gable, and was once grand, but was in disrepair now. The front door with its leadlight panels and pretty stained glass was never used and was bolted shut. The furniture in the drawing room, the entrance hall and the library downstairs was all covered in dustsheets and the floor was littered with ancient mice droppings. Mrs Butters told me the mice had been so bad they had run across her body at night, and she had insisted that Miss Havisham get a cat. The cat was called Tom and, much as I wanted him to be my friend, he was half-wild. I only glimpsed him every now and then streaking across the brewery.

I did not venture further than the doorways of the bedrooms upstairs. There was something dreadful about them, as if their occupants had lain dead there for some time before their bodies were discovered. My own bedroom was downstairs, not far from the kitchen, which kept it warm, and not far from Mrs Butters's room, which had its own advantages. For when I was sad and lonely and Miss Hav had been particularly difficult, Mrs Butters would let me curl up in bed with her—at least until I was asleep. I always found myself in my own bed in the mornings.

Memories of one's early childhood are not at all reliable—one reason why I do not recall my birth name—but I do remember asking Mrs Butters, not long after I arrived, if she were my mother? (I suspect I knew she was not, but wanted to hear what she would say.) 'Good Lord, no,' she replied. I wondered why she was so strongly opposed to the idea. I liked her, but was I so awful? 'Then where is my mother?' I asked. 'A good question,' she said. But if it were a good question, why was there not a good answer, and why did nobody know where she was? I asked Miss

Hav and she said, '*All the world's a stage, and all the men and women merely players: they have their exits and their entrances.*' I did not know what she meant by this, but I had to be satisfied with this explanation, for when I repeated my request, she said, 'Now, now, Estella, enough of that!' Later, when I was older and repeated my question about my mother, she would not even address it, but would jump to some or other question about arithmetic. 'Three times table, Estella. Quick. Three times one is …? *Quickly*, child.' And she would snap her fingers and smack her palm upon the table.

My favourite place was behind the farthest end of the brewery. There was a garden there, overgrown with tangled plants, and every day, come rain or shine, I walked from one end to the other, making a track of sorts, sometimes dragging Poppet behind me, but mostly on my own. I found a lizard that I poked with a stick until I was satisfied it was dead, then put it in my pocket. Another day I spotted a broken and speckled bird's egg that had fallen from a nest in the trees and I put that in my pocket, too. Later, when I reinspected these treasures, the egg was in fragments and I realised I needed a more reliable container.

'What for?' Mrs Butters wanted to know when I asked for one.

I retrieved the lizard and the shells from my pocket and laid them upon the table.

'Lord, child,' she said, frowning.

'It broke,' I said, meaning the egg.

'I see,' she said.

She gave me a little flat tin with a lid, and I put these things inside, and when I saw something I liked—a butterfly's wing, for instance—I added it to my collection. I learnt that if a lizard was freshly dead and not completely dried out when added, the whole tin soon stank to high heaven.

I climbed the trees in the garden and hung upside down from their limbs. Sometimes Mrs Butters came out to call me for the midday meal and caught me and rebuked me. 'Estella, what are you doing!' she would say in exasperation. 'One day you're going to fall and crack your head open like Humpty Dumpty. Come and help me peel the carrots,' she would suggest, holding out her hand.

In the summer, I learnt to trap the butterflies that flitted between the green and yellow weeds, and took the jars up to Miss Hav's room where she released them. The butterflies seemed to amuse her, flying hither and thither, batting their wings uselessly against the drawn curtains or becoming ensnared in the spiders' webs that festooned the corners of the ceiling. Sometimes she would use the butterflies to teach me the rudiments of biology: how they pollinated flowers and so on, and in what ways they were different to moths, but mostly my education was left up to Mrs Butters. Mrs Butters, I learnt, had been a governess in a previous life, before she had come to Miss Hav's family, and she knew a great deal about many things, including teaching children.

I balanced on the wooden casks in the brewery, jumping one to another, and I grew strong with the exercise. Or I explored where I should not—running up the brewery's light iron stairs and along the gallery high overhead. I learnt to hang from the gallery and swing from beam to beam. I had no fear of heights. I propped Poppet up on a cask, left her there and looked down upon her and the dilapidation from my lofty vantage point. I was her queen and she my subject. And woe betide her if she disobeyed me. I would stamp my foot and shout at her, and I know from whom I learnt that.

Sometimes I fell when I was practising springing from one wooden cask to the next, and I would run in with grazed knees or elbows, crying to Mrs Butters. If my wound was bleeding, she would pick me up and prop me on the kitchen table and make up a poultice and apply it. I loved this little ritual. I loved the herbal smell of the ointments, but most of all I loved the attention.

Mrs Butters would check my wound every day and make a fuss over it, and even Miss Hav would be interested. 'What have you done to yourself now, Estella?' she would ask when she saw me brandishing a bandage, and I was always sorry when the wound had healed and I could no longer garner any consideration or sympathy from it.

The things I learnt from Miss Hav were not easy to put into words. They were behaviours that I observed in her, unconsciously absorbed, and mimicked in order to please her: the superiority with which she carried herself, a haughtiness towards those who were less fortunate, and the scorn she displayed towards those who were poorly educated.

I never saw or heard Miss Hav behave in this way towards Mrs Butters, despite the fact that Mrs Butters was clearly less fortunate and her servant, and in this way I understood and learnt what the meaning of *respect* was. It was clear that the two women had a strong and loving bond, even if sometimes Miss Hav *was* short with Mrs Butters, and I could only assume that it was because they had known one another for ever.

There were other things that I learnt from my adoptive mother. One day, shortly after I had arrived, Miss Hav was sitting in front of the fire and I, playing with Poppet, at her feet.

'Estella?' she said.

I looked up.

'Get up,' she told me, making an impatient motion with her hand.

I did. I stood and looked at her and waited obediently for whatever it was she wanted me to do, as Mrs Butters had instructed.

'Would you go down and tell Mrs Butters I am expecting a letter?'

I nodded.

'Yes, Miss Havisham,' she intoned.

'Yes, Miss Hav-Hav-i-sham,' I repeated.

I picked Poppet up by one arm and was halfway across the room when she called once more to me. 'Estella?'

I turned. She had risen from her chair. 'Come here,' she told me, lovingly holding out her arms.

I came back. But when I was close enough to embrace, she stepped away with an expression of absolute aversion on her face and stuck her hands out before her as if she would fend me off.

'What are you doing?' she said. 'I don't want you, why would I want *you*?' She spat out the word as if I were vermin.

I turned and fled, taking the stairs too fast and almost falling, running to Mrs Butters in the kitchen and burying my teary face in her bosom. 'There, there,' the housekeeper always said, stroking my hair.

4

Mrs Butters, bless her heart, taught me to read when I was about five. The newspaper was delivered every day (although I never saw Miss Hav touch it) and lay upon the kitchen table. One morning Mrs Butters came in and found me tracing the letters of the headline with my finger, and she began to explain the principles of reading to me. We started with Miss Havisham's name. Mrs Butters wrote it out on a tablet and sounded out the letters, and soon I had my tongue around it even if I did say *Hav-i-sham* for a number of days, and could not understand how the letter *I* could have two different sounds.

A book was subsequently delivered to the house. The main character of *The History of Little Goody Two Shoes* was Margery Meanwell, who betters herself through charity and education and spends much of the book teaching spelling through games. Mrs Butters read me a page a day and we practised whatever letter was being taught, sounding it out. *P*, for instance, for *plum pudding* and so on. Afterwards, in the garden, I drew the letter in the dirt with a stick alongside a rough sketch of a plum pudding, and sometimes

I had six or seven letters and sketches all in a row before the rain came and washed them away. I found letters stamped on the casks in the brewery and I ran in and informed Mrs Butters.

'I found a B, I found a B,' I sang out, and thus I learnt at an early age that B not only stood for *butter*, but for *bear* and *beer*, which was confusing since the latter two words sounded so much the same. I also had a little book containing rhymes for each letter, for example: *C. The cat doth play, and after slay* was one that was amply illustrated by Tom's behaviour.

I had favourite letters, too. *B*, obviously—I loved that the letter *B* had two big pillowy bumps in it, like Mrs Butters's bosom—and *E* for Estella. I told Mrs Butters that these were my favourite two letters.

'What about *H*?' she asked. '*H* for Havisham?'

I made a face.

'*H* is a wonderful letter,' she said. 'It looks like a house, Estella, and it helps to remember that it has a short bar across the middle of it, connecting its two walls and providing shelter for your head. Just as Miss Havisham's house provides you with a roof over your head,' she said rather sharply.

Later, when I had the basics of the alphabet, I would sit with Mrs Butters as I often did as she prepared our breakfast or dinner, and she would coax me into getting the gist of the headlines. This took time, of course, but time was something I had plenty of.

The seasons came and went. In Satis House's garden they were marked by the bluebells first appearing, struggling gamely through the weeds under the silver birches. The first time this happened, I picked a bluebell and took it into Miss Hav, and to my delight it pleased her. On Mrs Butters's instructions, I brought up a glass jar half-filled with water from the kitchen and put the bluebell into it and placed it near Miss Havisham. For a number of days, she admired it. Then one day it was dead, of course—it was certainly drooping—and in a fit of anger she lashed out and sent the jar and flower tumbling to the floor, smashing the glass. I went downstairs and told Mrs Butters and she tut-tutted, but did not say anything, as if she were not altogether surprised. The upshot of that, however, was that I never dared to present another flower to Miss Havisham. On that occasion I *did* learn from my mistake.

Mrs Butters taught me the names of the trees in the garden and, in summer, the oaks turned a vibrant leafy green and we had mornings of glorious sunshine and long evenings of twilight. Then slowly, in turn, the beech leaves took on a golden-brown hue and drifted to the ground. Until, finally, all the trees in the garden of Satis House stood naked and shivering in the cold, and the days were short and best spent indoors near the fire.

One morning, Mrs Butters sent me and the newspaper up to Miss Havisham and I read the entire front page for her, although I did stumble over some words. 'Hmph,' Miss Havisham said. But the next week a proper book with leather binding arrived, and reading to her became one of my duties. Sometimes the stories were interesting, but all too often they were dreary. Sometimes I read to her from *The Pickwick Papers*, story instalments in the newspaper written by a man called Charles Dickens that were often highly amusing. We both loved those, and would laugh over the funny bits together.

Something unexpected happened at this time. The cat brought in a dead mouse overnight and left it on the kitchen table, as was his wont. I had learnt to pick the mice up by their tails and carry them out to the garden where the crows and rooks could peck at them. But on this day, the mouse had been decapitated and disembowelled and its innards strewn across the wood, and I stopped to stare in fascination. I took a teaspoon from the drawer and separated the dark-red organ from the grey convoluted sack, and prodded the other bits and pieces, and when Mrs Butters came in, I asked her about them. In hindsight, she was tolerant of my curiosity. She did screw up her nose and say, 'Really, Estella, must we do this?' But I insisted that she tell me all she knew, and the next time we had some or other wildlife that needed disembowelling, she showed me how to use the knife. Forever afterwards, I was given the task of preparing any rabbit, duck or pheasant—any game actually—that we got for dinner. I did not seem to mind being up to my elbows in entrails and, on more than one occasion, Mrs Butters shook her head at me as if this interest of mine were odd.

I was probably seven when Mrs Butters sent me on an errand for the first time. We needed fresh bread apparently, and Mrs Butters's legs—she had varicose veins—were troubling her. The high street contained a number of premises. A large man called Pumblechook, who had flabby cheeks and breathed like a fish, had a shop of a peppercorny and farinaceous character, as the premises of a corn-chandler and seedsman should be, and he would stand out the front in his corduroys and look across the street at the saddler, who appeared to conduct his business by gazing across at the coachmaker, who seemed to get on in life by putting his hands in his pockets and contemplating the baker, and so on down to the grocer and the chemist. The watchmaker was the only one who ever gave the impression of being fully occupied by his profession. Mrs Butters said it was because he was engaged in the business of time. 'He has a better understanding of it and of how it can slip away. Before you know it,' she said, looking exasperatedly at me, 'the day is over and you have accomplished nothing.'

A boy, referred to as *Trabb's boy* by Mrs Butters and Miss Havisham, worked for the tailor. I understood it was the boy's job to carry bolts of material back and forth, and I had seen him sweeping out the front when Mrs Butters and I passed by. But the first time I was sent alone on an errand, she warned me against him.

'Do not get distracted by Trabb's boy,' she said to me in the kitchen as she began peeling onions for soup. 'He is generally up to no good.'

'What do you mean?' I asked.

'He is audacious,' she said.

'Audacious?'

'Cheeky, impudent or disrespectful,' she said and sniffed. Her eyes were flowing freely from the onion. 'You are not to associate with him, Estella,' she told me, reaching for her handkerchief. 'Miss Havisham would not approve. If he addresses you, you are to walk on by. He comes from a lowly background and is not fit company for you.'

'What does *lowly background* mean?'

But she shook her head and said, 'Enough questions. Get on with you now. The bread will be stale by the time you fetch it.'

Of course, telling me all this had the adverse effect for I was immediately intrigued by the idea of *Trabb's boy*. Why, for instance, was he not known by his own name?

In spite of the fact that it was a dismal, cold and blustery day, I was glad to be out of the house. I was too young to understand why Satis House made me sad, only that it did. Outdoors, I felt more light-hearted, even if I could not understand why or put my feelings into words. My hands thrust into my coat pockets for warmth, I walked along the high street. The tailor's premises came some way before the bakery and I paused outside. The door was closed, the curtain drawn across the outside window, but a glow of dim light was visible above the railing. Taking one hand out of my warm pocket, I took a deep breath, knocked upon the wooden door and pushed it open.

A fire burned happily in a grate to my right, and to my left there was a long wooden counter on which lay a gigantic pair of shiny scissors, a tape measure and a stick of chalk. Above the counter, stacked against the wall, were rows upon rows of bolts of cloth of all textures and all shades of blue and black and brown and cream.

A little bell had tinkled above my head when I entered and, by degrees, a man, Mr Trabb presumably, came out from a door at the back of the shop. He left the door open and I saw that it led to a parlour and that he had been sitting at a table dining, for the table was laid and a bright red apple together with a knife were upon a plate. There was a window, too, looking out into some tangled undergrowth and throwing light upon the scene.

'And who have we here?' Mr Trabb dug his long fingers into his expansive waistcoat pockets and wiggled them as he surveyed me. Pins were stuck into his lapels and they glittered sharply in the light.

'Miss Estella Havisham,' I said, as I had been taught to say.

'*Havisham?*' He raised his eyebrows. 'What can I do for you, Miss Estella?'

'I am looking—' I began, when the door opened behind me, the bell tinkled and someone stepped inside.

'There you are!' Mr Trabb exclaimed, looking past me. 'Where have you been? Did they have to go into the meadow to find a cow? Look for a pail? Engage a milker? What other possible explanation can you have?'

I turned. A boy, hefting a jug of milk, stood frozen in the doorway.

Trabb's boy.

He paid not the slightest heed to Mr Trabb—and here I thought fleetingly that I could learn a thing or two from this boy—but gazed at me open-mouthed as if he had never seen a girl before in his life.

He stepped inside and closed the door behind him by raising his boot and pushing backwards on the wood, all the while keeping an eye on me. 'The milk,' he said unnecessarily.

'And what of it?' Mr Trabb demanded. 'Come now,' he said, as if he were bone weary.

'Miss Estella,' Mr Trabb began again brightly, steepling his fingertips together and bouncing them against one another, and forcing me to look away from the boy. 'What was it you wanted?'

What did I want?

I had wanted to meet Trabb's boy, but I could hardly tell the tailor that.

'Buttons!' I exclaimed, remembering that Mrs Butters had an old tweed jacket that was missing the buttons. 'Two brown ones?'

Mr Trabb went behind the wooden counter, pulled out a drawer, folded himself over double and ferreted in it. Trabb's boy, meanwhile, moved across the floor towards the parlour, all the while gazing at me, and when it seemed he must turn his back on me to enter the doorway, he reversed in, still clutching the milk, still staring.

He was dressed in a rough and ready manner. His ginger hair stood up from his forehead as if he had licked his palm and spiked it upright. His trousers ended halfway up his shins, and he appeared to have been squeezed into his garments like a skinny sausage into its casing. By and large, he did not make a favourable impression.

'There,' Mr Trabb said, laying two brown buttons upon the countertop and distracting me. 'These are leather. Is leather what you want?'

I picked them up and inspected them. I thought Mrs Butters would be surprised for they were well made. 'Thank you,' I said. 'They will do nicely. Would you add that to our account?'

I had heard the housekeeper say this in other shops and the words rolled easily off my tongue.

'Havisham?' he said. 'I don't believe you have an account.' He paused and stroked his chin pensively with his spindly fingers.

'But you have one now, miss, rest assured you have one now. Please don't hesitate to visit us again!'

'I won't,' I said, knowing that I most certainly *would* hesitate for there was nothing about Trabb's boy or the establishment that would tempt me to come in again.

'Will that be all?'

'It will be.'

I turned for the doorway.

Mr Trabb whistled.

Before I could reach for the handle, there was a flurry of movement behind me and the boy got there before me. He had gold-flecked green eyes, and he raised his eyebrows in a comical fashion as he opened the door. Together with the spikey hair, he made me want to laugh. Indeed, I began to smile and a giggle started up in my chest and I realised I had not laughed for such a long time that I might have forgotten how.

He stepped out into the street with me and pulled the door behind him so that Mr Trabb was not privy to our discussion.

'What's yer name?' he asked conversationally.

He was four or five years older than me, I thought, and consequently taller, and I had to look up to him. The moth-eaten beginnings of a moustache were on his upper lip and there were freckles across his nose and upper cheeks as if someone had splattered mud upon them.

'What's yours?'

'Ted. And I know yer name. It's Estella. You're Estella Havisham and yer live in that there'—he cocked his head in the direction of Satis House—'mansion.'

'I do,' I said.

He seemed to have recovered from being dumbstruck to being overly familiar in a short space of time.

'Wanna go for a stroll later?' he asked.

'A *stroll?*' I repeated, wondering if there was another, different interpretation of the word. 'Where to?'

He shrugged. 'I'll wait for yer outside the house at three-thirty. But not'—he glanced up at the heavens where the clouds loomed low—'if it's rainin'. Or looking like rainin'. I wouldn't want yer to get wet.'

I nodded. 'Very well,' I said.

'Goodbye,' I said, anxious to get away before I agreed to any further outlandish suggestions.

'Goodbye?' he repeated as if the word were foreign, and raised his eyebrows again.

'*Farewell!*' he declared, as if that were the only word befitting the occasion. Then he looked down and smiled at me. His smile was mischievous, yes, but it was all encompassing and it included *me*.

I skipped down to the baker with a light heart. I felt better about everything. Trabb's boy, I decided, was like that dark stuff that Mrs Butters mixed up in a glass and swallowed with a horrid grimace, but which resulted in her doing an impromptu jig in front of the woodstove: a *tonic*, she called it.

There was no doubt now that he intrigued me. Perhaps on our *stroll* there was a chance he would enlighten me as to the meaning of *lowly background*. Possibly, I would finally understand why I was not to associate with persons of *lowly backgrounds*, although I was beginning to comprehend that the phrase had a great deal to do with the way one spoke, the way one dressed and behaved. I was fairly certain wealth came into it, too.

Mostly, I was fascinated because I had the impression that Trabb's boy was a little like me. He was spirited. He *was* audacious and impudent. For he had no business speaking to me in the way that he had, I knew that much. He knew what my background was and that I came from Satis House. He knew that I could report him to Mrs Butters for insolence and he might get into trouble. He knew all this and he did not care.

Well, I decided, sauntering by now into the bakery, if he did not care, I did not care, either.

5

After the midday meal, I settled myself on the staircase. A bare casement window in the stairwell looked out to the courtyard, and from my vantage point I could watch the sky and the heavy clouds that threatened rain. Every now and then, I would run down to the kitchen and check the time on the old clock on the wall. Two o'clock came and went and still it did not rain, and I began to think about Trabb's boy and what we might do on our *stroll*. Then, at two-thirty on the dot—I was in the kitchen at the time—a few drops of rain pinged against the glass of the window. Turning, I ran back to the stairwell, but by the time I reached it, I could not see out of the window, such was the volume of water that fell from the sky. It was still raining at three-thirty in much the same fashion, making venturing out impossible. And, for what it is worth, the rain did not let up until the following day.

And so I was saved, from myself, and from Trabb's boy.

In the late afternoon I gave up my position of sitting upon the window ledge in the stairwell and forlornly looking out of the rain-streaked window, and went to see Miss Havisham. But she was in one of her moods. When she was in one of her moods, she sat before the fire with her gnarled hands upon her stick and her chin upon her hands and stared into the flickering flames, and could not be persuaded to talk.

I sat down beside her.

'What do you want?' she said in a flat tone of voice, without looking at me.

I was close to tears from disappointment, and they started to my eyes. 'Nothing,' I said, brushing them angrily away. 'I thought … I thought that I would keep you company, that is all.'

She shook her head and continued to gaze into the fire. 'Don't trouble yourself,' she said. 'You are of no use to me today.'

She could be like this. One moment calling me her *darling* and the next despising and belittling me. And I forget the number of times this happened. But they were so frequent that eventually when Miss Havisham addressed me in that loving voice, I ignored her. I pretended I did not hear her. I learnt from experience to contain my feelings. For if I reacted positively when she addressed me lovingly, if I allowed myself to smile and reciprocate, it was a double blow when she shunned me. For she not only cut me to the quick, but she made a fool out of me and I would be so much more distressed. As a consequence, I became strong and hard. I did not react when she was loving or hurtful, or pulled me to her to embrace me, or tried to make me cry.

I thought of Trabb's boy again as I sat there. I did not believe he would ever speak to me in such a hard-hearted way, and I nearly went out in all that foulness to find him. Instead, I went down to the kitchen and sat at the table, and Mrs Butters placed a bowl of peas for shelling in front of me. She could always be relied upon to give me something to do.

After a respectable pause, when the only sounds were the rain dripping from the eaves, the pea pods snapping open and the murmur of the fire in the woodstove, I said, 'Please explain to me what *lowly background* means. Is it to do with the way you dress, speak and act?'

'Yes,' Mrs Butters said, settling herself opposite me with the potatoes, a newspaper for the peels and a knife. 'But that is not all there is to it.

'In my opinion, it is largely connected with money. If you have money, then most of those things—dress, speech, manners, education—never forget *education*—are achievable. Are possible. Your actions, however, stem from the way you have been brought up. You may well be rich, but you might possess no integrity—'

'Integrity? What's that?' I stopped shelling peas to pop a couple into my mouth.

'Hmm,' Mrs Butters said as if she were thinking of the best way to explain it to me. 'The way you behave, whether you are a kind person. For instance, I have just now noted that you have popped a couple of peas into your mouth, Estella. Why did you not offer me any? For that would be the correct thing to do.'

'I see,' I said, sliding a couple of peas across to her, but I do not think that I saw at all. 'But wouldn't that be manners?'

'Yes and no. See, I am from a lowly background and so your not offering me peas would be acceptable, but if you *did* offer me peas it would show that you—that you—' she broke off. Her explanation was complicated and she seemed to have become confused and not know how to complete it.

'But why,' I said, 'are we—am I—not supposed to mix with persons from lowly backgrounds?'

'Because *you* are not from a lowly background. I suppose it is because they cannot, they do not have the means, to do the things that you do, and what is therefore the point of being acquainted with them?'

'I see,' I said again. 'So I could not, for instance, be friends with … with Trabb's boy?'

'Certainly not!' she exclaimed.

The knife paused in one hand, a potato in the other, she looked at me steadily across the table. 'Estella, did you disobey me?'

I picked up a pea pod and broke it open with my fingers. 'Not actually,' I said slowly, 'although I did … I did go to the tailor—'

'You went to the tailor? What on earth for?'

'These,' I said, reaching into my pocket. Bringing out the buttons, I laid them on the table.

'Buttons?'

'For your jacket, the one that's missing two buttons? Do you like them?'

'Lord, child. How did you pay for them?'

'I asked Mr Trabb to put them on our account.'

'But we don't have an account.'

'We do now.'

*

I became strong, and grew tall enough for Miss Havisham to lean on my shoulder, and we completed dull circuits of the room, sometimes for hours at a time. She appeared to go into a trance on these occasions, as if we could have walked all day and all night: from her dressing table chair, skirting the half-filled trunks, through the doorway into the adjacent room, and around the table with the decaying cake and back into the dressing room. The only sounds were those of our footsteps and the hem of her dress kissing the floorboards. The dust settling behind us was noiseless.

We were embarking on one of these circuits one day when she stopped abruptly, laid her hands one upon the other on her left side and said, 'Do you know what I touch here?'

'Yes, Miss Havisham.'

'What do I touch?'

'Your heart.' (Mrs Butters had taught me this; after the mice, we had moved on to human anatomy.)

'Broken!' She uttered the word with a weird triumph and kept her sunken-eyed gaze on me. I knew what she wanted from me; I had learnt much in a short time.

'Who broke your heart?' I asked.

'He did!' Again said with triumph. Then she swayed, her hands fell to her sides as if they were heavy and her gaze became vacant. 'He did,' she repeated in a dull voice. 'He did,' she murmured.

She glanced at me and the steely resolve returned to her eyes. 'But you'll break all their hearts, my pretty. All. Their. Hearts.'

'Yes,' I said, although I was not certain I knew what I was agreeing to.

'Good!' she said with relish. 'Good. Now on we go. On we go.'

She leaned on my shoulder and tapped on the floor with her stick, and off we went again.

This patter about hearts became a part of our walk. Sometimes we had it as many as five times in a day, sometimes days passed before she took it up again. Sometimes we chanted the words together as we went around.

What do I touch? Your heart. Broken! Who broke your heart? He did! He did. He did. But you'll break all their hearts, my pretty. All. Their. Hearts. Yes. Good! Now on we go ... On we go ...

6

It was not long after the episode with Trabb's boy that someone unexpected came into my life. In hindsight, I suspect that Mrs Butters had said something to Miss Havisham about my inappropriate interest in Trabb's boy, and perhaps had suggested that socialising with someone my own age might be a good idea. However, I observed and noted that, strangely, Miss H spent as much time, if not more, *playing* with the newcomer as I did.

I was accustomed to the oddness of the house, to its dismal bricks, walled up windows and rusty bars, to its disused brewery with its high places and wilderness of empty casks, and did not reflect much on its peculiarities and secrets. So one morning, when Miss Havisham sent me to fetch a boy named Pip from the gates, and I walked across the courtyard with the key and found the boy gazing around as if the property was a fantastical place, I was a little taken aback. He stopped when he heard my footsteps and turned to look at me. I thought he had a nice face—a kind face—that was my first impression of him.

The corn-chandler, the large man who breathed like a fish and who was by name Pumblechook, and by nature *bumptious and arrogant* according to Miss Havisham, was with the boy.

'This,' Pumblechook said to me from the other side of the gate, 'is Philip Pirrip. Who we call Pip.'

'This is Pip, is it? Come in, Pip,' I said, opening the gate.

Pip was as tall as I was, but he was awkward. His cheeks were flushed. He twisted the buttons on his coat as if his life depended on them. His eyes, however, were the prettiest, palest of blues—when they could meet mine without sliding away.

The man called Pumblechook attempted to step in after the boy, but I blocked his entrance. 'Oh,' I said, 'did you wish to see Miss Havisham?'

'If Miss Havisham wished to see me.'

'Ah, but you see she does not,' I told him.

I clanged the gate and almost laughed at the indignity that ruffled his face. He said something to the boy, which discomfited him still further, but I locked the gate and led the way across the cobblestones.

Alongside the courtyard, the brewery gates stood open. The wind seemed to blow colder here than outside the main entrance, making a shrill, howling noise, which was almost frightening, and I stopped a moment, perhaps on purpose, to test the boy's mettle.

'What is the name of this house, miss?' he asked.

'Satis.' For the first time, I thought how close this word was in sound to *Satan*, and wondered what I should make of that. Certainly, sometimes Miss Havisham behaved as if possessed by the devil.

'It is also called Manor House,' I went on. 'Satis is Greek, or Latin, or Hebrew, or all three. It means *enough*.'

'Enough House,' the boy said, and the wind blew a lock of his curly fair hair across his forehead. 'That's a curious name, miss.'

'Yes,' I said, 'but it meant more than it said. It meant when it was given, that whoever had this house could want nothing else. They must have been easily satisfied in those days, I think.

'Quick now,' I said, knowing that Miss Havisham was waiting and did not like to be kept waiting. She was, on the whole, very impatient. When she wanted something done, she wanted it done *at once!* Although she was more than happy to keep Mrs Butters, or me, waiting interminably for a decision. The question of what foodstuffs we would order, for instance, seemed to take her an inordinate amount of time, and she had lately got into the habit of waving her hand at me and saying, 'Oh, you do it, Estella.' I did it willingly. Unlike Miss Havisham, I was interested in food. Mrs Butters was, too, and we had some fun concocting menus. Sometimes Mrs Butters would laugh at me and say, 'You can't eat potted rabbit with stewed apricots, Estella!' And I would respond with, 'Why not? Let's try it!' But I digress.

We went into the house by the side door. I took up the candle and led the boy called Pip along the passages and up the staircase and, by the hesitant sound of his gait, I knew he was gazing around with curiosity and I knew that he was nothing like Trabb's boy. I stopped at the door of Miss Havisham's room. 'Go in,' I instructed.

'After you, miss.'

I could not tell if he was being shy or polite. I doubted whether he was being plain cheeky. I would have thought the Pumblechook man would have lectured all the cheekiness out of him.

'Don't be ridiculous, boy. I am not going in,' I said.

I left him then and walked away, taking the candle with me and leaving him in the dark. *Pretended* to walk away. After he had gone in, I put down the candle, tiptoed back to the door and stood there listening, but I did not learn anything I did not already know and, after a while, I went on down to the kitchen. Mrs

Butters handed me some leftover pastry and the rolling pin, and I amused myself at the big wooden table. I made a figure with a skirt and long hair, like I imagined my mother to look, and asked Mrs Butters to bake it along with the pie she was making.

Sometime later, my name was called, the sound echoing faintly down to the bowels of the house, and I took up my candle once more, my light going along the dark passage like a star. Miss Havisham had told me that was the meaning of my name, the meaning of Estella: *Star.* Why did you call me *Star,* I had asked, and she said that I had come into her life when she was in the depths of darkness and despair and that she took my arrival to be like that of a celestial gift from the heavens, lighting her way. It was one of the few times when I felt important, as well as needed, when I felt that in spite of the way she treated me most of the time, I meant something to her.

Miss Havisham called me to her side in her room, and I was patient while she took up her jewels yet again and tried them against my hair and on my exposed chest, murmuring her usual platitudes: 'What a beauty she is, Pip!' 'Isn't she beautiful? Don't you think she's beautiful?'

I did not like it when she draped her jewels over me. It was an altogether different sort of attention, and I did not take kindly to it. The jewels were sharp and cold against my skin and made me shiver, and I could not understand her fascination with them. Yes, they glittered brightly, but so did the stars, and the stars were lovely and gave me pleasure, whereas the jewels were lifeless. They were only pretty when the light fell on them—in contrast to the stars, which needed the opposite, which needed darkness to shine. It was a puzzle, I thought, and made me reflect more on my name. Did I need dingy conditions to be at my best? Was I forever destined to only shine in the dark?

I played with the hairpins in the pretty little crystal dish upon the dresser while the boy stood to one side, watching, as Miss

Havisham ooh-ed and aah-ed. He seemed mesmerised by this little performance, and I could see his reaction pleased her almost as much as it annoyed me.

'Let me see you play cards with this boy,' she said at last.

'With this boy?' I repeated. 'Why, he is nothing but a common labouring boy.'

I was merely reiterating the words she had said to me beforehand. 'He is nothing but a common labouring boy, like Trabb's boy,' she had said when I had asked who was this Pip coming to play? 'Then why is he coming to play?' I had wanted to know. 'He will be the first,' she had murmured. 'The first what?' I asked. But she had tired of my questions and waved me away.

'Well, you can break his heart,' she muttered to me now, in an aside.

'What do you play, boy?' I asked.

'Nothing but beggar my neighbour, miss.'

'Beggar him, then,' Miss Havisham said.

We sat on the floor to play. Before the first game was over, I realised Miss Havisham was right, he was nothing more than a common labouring boy, in spite of being trussed up in a tight and fearful suit.

'He calls the knaves *Jacks*,' I remarked to her, 'and his hands are coarse and his boots thick.'

I thought these observations would please her, but she said nothing.

However, I succeeded so admirably in putting Pip off that I won the game, and he misdealt the next round, filling me with contempt for him, for all that his eyes were such a pretty blue. For where was his courage?

Miss Havisham, who looked on, said, 'She says many hard things of you, Pip, but you say nothing of her. What do you think of her?'

'I—I don't like to say,' he stammered.

'Tell me in my ear,' she said, bending down.

He leaned forward to whisper. This secret exchange went on overly long and infuriated me. I was not only humiliated, but confused. Why was I playing cards with a common labouring boy when I was not allowed to be friends with Trabb's boy? I believe I was a little jealous, too. Miss Havisham was mine—how dare this boy occupy her attention!

I won the next round and threw the cards down in spite.

'When shall I have you here again, Pip?' Miss Havisham asked, no doubt aware that I was not far from an outburst. 'Let me think.'

Pip began to remind her that today was Wednesday. How little he knew.

'There, there! I know nothing of the days of the week. I know nothing of the weeks of the year. Come again in six days. You understand?'

'Yes, ma'am.'

'Estella, take him down,' she instructed. 'Let him have something to eat, and let him roam and look about him while he eats. Go, Pip.'

I said nothing until we reached the courtyard. I told him to wait outside the side-entrance and returned to the kitchen. I came back with some bread and meat and a little mug of beer, and when I opened the door, he was studying his coarse hands as if he were embarrassed by their being a part of his anatomy. I plonked the mug down on the stones, spilling some beer, thrust the plate of bread and meat at him as if he were a dog, and the tears sprang to his eyes. I kept my gaze on him, delighted to find that he had feelings like I did, although he blinked furiously and glared back, restraining the wells of water. Which also made me happy. The boy had some spirit after all.

I left him and went to the window on the floor above. When I looked down, he had disappeared, but the plate and mug were still there, the food untouched, so I waited, and by degrees when he appeared again I could see he had been crying. He sniffed and his face was tear-streaked. I was filled with emotions I did not understand. I wanted to comfort him, but I also wanted to hurt him, to make him cry harder than before. I wanted him to cry harder than before and to come to me in his distress. Then, unlike Miss Havisham, I would offer him comfort. I would give him the kind words that I so often longed to hear from her, but never did. *There, there.* I might *think* about stretching out my arms and embracing him, but, to be honest, the thought was frightening. I had never held another child before and I had no idea how it would feel.

The food and drink seemed to cheer him, however, and I left off watching him and went down to the kitchen to collect the pastry I had made. The little stick figure with the skirt was lying on a wire rack, cooling, and I wrapped her in a napkin and picked up the keys and went out to Pip.

His face was clear of any stains. He had sluiced it under the water butt perhaps. The sustenance had given him courage because he met my eyes at the gate.

'Why don't you cry again?' I asked, taunting him.

'Because I don't want to.'

'You do,' I told him. 'You have been crying till you are half blind, and now you are near crying again.'

'Am not,' he said fiercely.

'Prove it,' I said. 'Look at me.'

He did. He looked steadily at me. His gaze did not waver. I was surprised by how much effort it took to keep my eyes upon his vivid blue ones, and I forgot about his thick boots and his calling the knaves *Jacks*. I thought, then, that there was something to him after all. It was not courage, nor was it spiritedness. It was something else entirely. Something at the age of eight I could not name, but which I know now to be intelligence.

'Here,' I said, abruptly pushing the stick figure into his hand.

'What is it?' He glanced down at the napkin bundle.

I wanted to tell him it was my mother, the mother I did not have, the mother I yearned for. But I shook my head, pushed him out, locked the gate and turned away. I did not trust myself to speak, or to look at him again.

*

Another time when he came, and I had taken him down to let him out, I asked if he would like to go to the brewery.

'Yes, miss,' he said hesitantly. 'As long as we don't get into trouble.'

'Why should we get into trouble?' I asked, but he did not answer.

I led him through the brewery gates and up the first flight of the thin rusty staircases and then the next, and the next, and when I reached the top, I stopped.

'This is my kingdom,' I told him, pointing down below.

'Your kingdom?' He made a noise that sounded like a snort of disbelief and, before I could rebuke him, he said, 'Who do you think you are, a king?'

'I am a queen,' I said with aplomb. 'I am *your* queen.'

Now he really did laugh, and I was so annoyed I smacked him on the arm.

'Stop that,' I said. 'One day you will fall in love with me, with your queen, and then you will be sorry that you laughed.'

'I doubt it,' he said.

I was angry. My eyes smarted. I wanted to box his ears.

I fled down the stairs, running lightly and fast because I knew them well. If he wanted to keep up with me, he might well fall, and then *I* would laugh.

When I reached the first level, I swung first one leg then the other over the railing and jumped down upon the empty beer cask below, which I had done many times before. Then I hopped across to the next one and turned and waited to see if he was following.

He was. Which made me satisfied.

I skipped down a row of beer casks and turned and skipped down another. Sometimes they wobbled if you jumped on them too quickly and misjudged your step, but that added to the thrill. I hoped that they were all wobbling uncertainly for him and that he was afraid. I wanted him to be afraid. I had gone right around the yard when I paused again to see where he was.

Directly behind me!

I interrupted his rhythm when I stopped—for he was about to jump onto the cask on which I stood—and he teetered for what seemed an age, his eyes darting wildly about. Then he overbalanced and fell to the ground and all I could see of him was one leg and its thick boot.

I clambered down, but my dress caught on a splinter of wood and by the time I had freed myself and reached him, he was wiping the back of his hand across his nose.

'Don't be a baby,' I said, presuming he had been crying.

'Am not,' he told me fiercely.

'You're crying again. How can you deny it?'

'Look at me,' he ordered.

I looked. His pretty eyes were clear. We stared at one another for an age until—

'You blinked,' he said.

'Did not.'

'I know you did,' he said patiently. 'I don't care what you say.' He rose then from the ground and bent low to rub at his ankle.

'I ought to go home,' he said.

'As you wish,' I told him, although I wanted to say, 'Please, don't.' I wanted to say *Please, don't* because once he had gone, I was on my own again.

*

One day, after Pip had been, I had it in my head that I wanted to follow him, to see where he lived and what he did with himself when he was not with us.

After I had let him out of the gate, I ducked behind the pillar and waited a little while and then I quietly opened the gate again and followed him.

I remember thinking that I was particularly clever because I managed to evade being seen, but in hindsight it was only because Pip never suspected a thing and did not once turn around on his journey. He crossed the high street before he got to that Pumblechook man's store and walked on the other side, and I was not surprised. Then he crossed back again some distance later. Each time I skedaddled across the street when he did.

It was a mild spring day with enough warmth in the air for it to be pleasant and we walked for some while. After we left the town, it was more difficult to remain inconspicuous. Pip had rounded a corner when I paused behind a fence to let him get ahead, and then cautiously stuck my head around the palings. He was sauntering alongside an open field, his hands in his pockets, whistling. Every now and then, I caught snatches of a tune. In the distance stood a small lowly wooden dwelling with an outbuilding beside it, and from my vantage point I suspected this might be the forge, for I could see a red glow in one of the open windows.

I waited until he had disappeared into the house before I snuck around the corner, but, to my horror, he came out again forthwith.

As luck would have it, he did not glance up the street, but went straight into the forge. I crept closer.

I made a run for one of the forge's outer walls before long, and carefully sidled around the wall until I was directly under the open window. A bush of some kind grew there and I bent low and hid behind it. I could hear Pip and the blacksmith talking, but what with the roar of the fire and the clinking of metal on the anvil, I had no idea what they were saying.

I was about to raise my head to peer in the window when the back door to the little wooden house opened and a woman appeared. She was severe-looking, her hair scraped back from her face and a glum expression upon it. She carried a bucket in one hand and a mop in the other. She plonked the pail of dirty water down outside the forge door, shook the mop vigorously and leaned it against the doorjamb. Then she rolled up her sleeves as if she were going to do battle, stepped inside, and in a forthright manner said, 'What's the boy got to say for himself?'

The clinking of the metal stopped. The boy cleared his throat.

'Well?' she demanded. 'Did you play with flags? How many dogs and what kind? And veal cutlets, were there veal cutlets?'

'I—I—' Pip began.

'Am I to believe a word of this?' she interjected—and there I was in agreement with her. Certainly I did not believe him for we had done none of that. Why had he concocted such a tale?

'What do you take me for?' she demanded.

'Now, now, Mrs Joe,' the blacksmith said.

'Now, now, nothing!' she told him and stormed out.

She returned to the little wooden house and slammed shut the door. The clinking resumed.

I was about to retreat when Pip stepped out of the door.

He kept his eyes fixed upon the dwelling, as if he expected the woman called Mrs Joe to reappear at any minute and was afraid, and lifted the pail. Then, without a glance in my direction, he turfed its contents into the bush, splattering my boots. I had to hold my tongue for I came close to crying out and revealing myself. Putting the bucket down again, he went back into the forge. The blacksmith said something to him and he answered. The clinking continued. I shuffled down along the wall and, when it was safe to do so, rose and scampered back to Satis House like a puppy after its mother, for I had seen and heard enough. To be honest, I was afraid of Mrs Joe discovering me—that would not do! At times, I thought Miss Havisham to be the cruellest, nastiest person I knew, but now I realised that there was someone who was equally as abominable, if not worse.

The following time I saw Pip, I had a new understanding of his background and what life was like for him, and I was not so awful. Or so spiteful. Although, of course, there were always exceptions.

*

It was arranged that Pip continue to come to the house on alternate days. A chair on wheels was sent down from London and Pip's main job was to push Miss Havisham—when she tired of walking with her hand on his shoulder—around the room and across the landing and around the other room for hours at a time. It was my job on the days that Pip did not attend.

I always let him in at the gate. Sometimes we talked, sometimes we did not. Sometimes I would forget where he came from and would be fierce with him, telling him that I hated him to see if I could provoke a reaction. I never did. His skin was fair and he would blush scarlet, but would not say a word. Sometimes we had to play cards for Miss Havisham, and I had to endure her asking Pip if I grew prettier, and her embracing me with lavish (and, I suspected, artificial) fondness, and draping her jewellery over me and murmuring in my ear that I should break their hearts and have no mercy.

I was accustomed to her capricious and contradictory moods. I had come to know and accept them, but it was clear that these intimate occasions when she lavished attention on me as if she were obsessed with me unsettled the boy, and he looked at a loss to know what to do or to say.

For my part, I had built a wall of defence against Miss Havisham and did my best not to let her words and actions distress me. I would grow rigid and think of other pleasant things. I would dream of the future, and of the day when I would grow up and be able to leave her.

On one occasion when I joined them, Pip was pushing her chair around the room and crooning to her. I did not know the song. It seemed to be something that might have come from the forge where the blacksmith worked, for I heard the phrases, *Blow the fire, blow the fire*, *beat it out, beat it out*, and *old Clem, old Clem*. It made a nice change from our patter about hearts, however, and sometimes I would join them, and the three of us would traverse the room in the half-light, murmuring in subdued voices as if we were entrapped in some dream and moved not of our own free will but like spirits of the underworld.

7

There was another boy who came into my life at this juncture whom it would be amiss of me not to mention. His name was Herbert Pocket.

The Pockets were cousins of Miss Havisham's, and the first time I had met them was not long after I had arrived. Raymond, Sarah, Camilla and Georgiana Pocket were their names, and they came every year on the pretence of her birthday, but really it was to ensure they were not forgotten when she died, that when her will was read out there would be something set aside for them.

'And who is this?' the one I came to know as Sarah Pocket had asked when she spied me lurking behind Miss Havisham's chair.

'This is Estella,' Miss Havisham said.

'Estella?' Sarah Pocket put her pince-nez to her beady eyes and stared at me. 'And, pray, what is she to you?'

'I have adopted her.'

'*Adopted her?*' Sarah Pocket dropped her pince-nez.

'Yes,' Miss Havisham said.

There was utter silence in the room. The four cousins gazed one to another in shock and confusion. One even spluttered with indignation.

Then Miss Havisham made some comment about the weather and in due course they took up their mindless conversation, and I was not mentioned again.

The cousins, with much simpering and fawning, at last took their leave and, after they had gone, Miss Havisham rose from her chair and banged her stick upon the floor. Turning to me with an expression of absolute glee upon her face, she said, 'Did you see their faces, Estella!'

She did love her little jokes against the cousins.

And it might have been then, although I was very young, that I began to comprehend that there was much more to my adopted mother than I realised. She had not simply adopted me out of the kindness of her heart; there were other plans afoot.

As soon as I was old enough, she put me in charge of receiving them at the gate and admitting them to the house and, between Mrs Butters and I, providing them with refreshments. Sometimes Miss Havisham made the Pockets wait a good hour or two until she was prepared to see them, and the first time this happened I was probably six. It was not that I grew anxious on their behalf that I went up to Miss H, it was because the cousins wore me down. Sniping, dropping hints, giving me sidelong glances, and asking innumerable questions that I did not answer, for Miss Havisham had told me not to. There was no doubt that the fact that a mere child, who was not even a blood relative, was in charge of when they might or might not see Miss H annoyed them intensely. But, naturally, they did not have the spunk to say so to Miss Havisham's face.

There was also a cousin called Matthew Pocket, who never visited, but who had a son called Herbert, and one year the four cousins brought Herbert with them.

He had never visited before, until now, and he arrived with his books and was installed in the room on the other side of the one belonging to Mrs Butters. He was pale and skinny and had pimples and seemed to be growing at an alarming rate. All elbows and knees, his ankles protruded below his trouser hems as if his trousers, try as they might, would never catch up. It was for this reason that I always thought of him as a *young man*, for although he was my age, he was a great deal taller. I was not sure what the purpose of his visit was. Perhaps Miss Havisham wanted to see how he and I got along. Perhaps she wanted to gauge his reaction to me—to see if I could break his heart? I did not know. I was guessing. Perhaps it was nothing to do with any of those reasons at all, but simply that Herbert could not study at his own home on account of his siblings.

'I have a great many younger brothers and sisters,' he told me one day when I had interrupted his studies to bring him a cup of tea and a warm crumpet.

'How many is a great many?'

'Let me see now,' he said, and began to count them off on his fingers, arriving at seven.

'And you are the eldest?'

'By a long way.'

'What are you studying?' I asked, looking at the several large volumes that lay open upon his desk.

'Accounting,' he told me, and I saw now that his fingers were inky and that he had even succeeded in blotting ink upon the tip of his nose.

'And what will you do?'

'Ah,' he said, and his eyes darted about the room as if he was not certain. 'Shipping,' he declared. 'I think I shall trade until the time comes when I see my opening. Then in I will go and swoop upon it and make my capital, and there you are. When you have once made your capital, you have nothing to do but employ it.'

He sat down again then, dipped his quill into the inkpot and lowered his head. 'Pardon me,' he said. 'I must get on.'

I left him, thinking what a boring young man he was. He had not asked me a single question about my own life or shown the slightest interest.

Herbert and the Pockets, the same four who turned up every year, were with us when Pip arrived one day and, together with his arrival, I had never seen the house so full.

I met him at the gate and took him across the yard and into the dark passage where I picked up the candle. I told him that he was to come a different way today, and proceeded to take him through the house and across the smaller courtyard in front of the brewery's cottage.

I took Pip into the cottage. 'You are to stand there, boy,' I said, indicating the window, 'until you are wanted.'

I was conscious of the Pockets ceasing their conversation to stare at him, but I said nothing to them of who he was or why he was here, which I knew would irk them. I did not like them one little bit. I had never liked them. They had never shown me any kindness and were, it seemed, annoyed by my very existence. They were all toadies and humbugs, each of them pretending not to know that the others were toadies and humbugs, because the admission that he or she did know it would have made him or her out to be a toady and humbug. Normally, I would not give them the time of day—always twenty to nine at Satis House!—but because I was interested in their reaction to the boy, I joined in their desultory conversation. They were discussing Matthew Pocket, Herbert's father, in a most uncomplimentary manner and one of them said he was nobody's enemy but his own, to which Raymond replied, 'It would be much more commendable to be somebody else's enemy. Far more natural.' I give this as an example of the witless conversation they indulged in. They then went on to discuss mourning clothes' trimmings for some poor children who had lost their mother. At least they had had a mother to start with, I thought.

The bell rang distantly at last, and I told Pip we were expected and to come with me, and they all stared at him with the utmost contempt.

'Well, I am sure! What next!' Sarah Pocket said, and Camilla added, with indignation, 'Was there ever such a fancy! The ide-a!' And it was as much as I could do not to laugh out loud.

We went along the gloomy passage, the boy following at my heels, and I stopped all of a sudden and turned and faced him with my face close to his and said, 'Well?'

He, checking himself, almost walked into me. His eyes were a much darker blue in the wavering candlelight. 'Well, miss?'

I stood looking at him and, of course, he stood looking at me. He made an odd movement with his mouth, as if this looking at me was an uncomfortable experience, but, for the life of him, he was not going to look away. *Would not* look away. For to look away would mean admitting defeat. It did not bother me, I have to say.

'*Am* I pretty?'

I was of course referring to the conversation he had had with Miss Havisham one of the last times he was here, which I was not privy to.

'Yes,' he said. 'I think you are very pretty.'

I wondered why he did not lie? I would not have been so honest if I were in his boots.

'Am I insulting?'

'Not so much as you were last time.'

'Not so much?'

'No,' he said loftily.

There was something in the way he raised his head and stared down his nose at me and, before I knew it, I had reached out and smacked him across the cheek. Startled, he recoiled.

'You coarse little monster,' I said. 'And what do you think of me now?'

'I shan't tell you.'

His cheek had gone bright red, his face pale.

'Because you are going to tell upstairs. Is that it?'

'No,' he said, 'that's not it.'

'Why don't you cry again, you little wretch?'

'Because I won't. I'll not cry for you again,' he said through gritted teeth.

I turned on my heel and stalked off, and we met Mr Jaggers groping down the stairs as we were going up. He was Miss Havisham's solicitor and managed all her affairs, and Mrs Butters had told me he was a man who knew what's what. He had an office in London and had been coming to see her from time immemorial. I had bade him good morning earlier, as it was his habit to arrive shortly after nine and be gone by midday at the latest.

He stopped on the stairs. 'Whom have we here?' he asked. Taking Pip's chin, he turned it up to the candlelight to examine his face.

'Hmm,' he said, as if he approved of what he saw. 'Boy of the neighbourhood, hey?'

'Yes, sir,' Pip said.

'How do *you* come here?'

'Miss Havisham sent for me, sir.'

'I have a pretty large experience of boys and you're not a bad set of fellows,' Mr Jaggers observed. He released Pip and bit the side of one forefinger as he gazed at him. 'Now, mind you behave yourself,' he warned.

I left Pip at Miss Havisham's door and went back down and through the house to return to the Pockets. They stopped talking and looked at me expectantly. No doubt they were waiting for a sign that Miss Havisham was ready to receive them, and were bewildered when I failed to give it. But they, the milksops, had none of them the courage to ask me, and by degrees they began to talk amongst themselves again. I did not join in.

Pip called for me at last and, together with the Pockets, I made my way to Miss Havisham's room.

He was walking her around and around, as was my custom, but at least he was fully occupied. The Pockets stood simpering at the door.

'Dear Miss Havisham,' Sarah Pocket said. 'How well you look!'

'I do not,' returned Miss H, 'I am yellow skin and bone.'

Camilla brightened when Sarah was met with this rebuff and murmured, 'Poor dear soul! Certainly not to be expected to look well, poor thing. The idea!'

I did not have the patience for them. Eventually they wore Miss Havisham out with their fawning ways and she dismissed them and instructed Pip and me to play cards again. And, as before, Miss Havisham drew attention to my beauty and tried her jewels against my hair and, as tedious as I found this, I did not say anything.

After some discussion, the day was at last confirmed for Pip's return and I took him down into the courtyard and gave him a drink and fed him, leaving him to wander about. I was on my way to Herbert's room for the same reason—to provide him with lunch—when I heard voices. Herbert, I thought, talking.

He was not in his room. I put down the tray and went over to the window, standing back so whoever was outside would be unable to see me. Herbert had removed his jacket, waistcoat and shirt, exposing his slender ribs that resembled the wishbones of chickens, and was bobbing about. I moved further forward and saw Pip, who looked both puzzled and at a loss. His arms hung loosely at his sides and he was clearly not at all enthusiastic about fighting Herbert. Pip stood so stolidly that I thought if he does not ready himself soon, he will be flattened.

I did not see what happened then, it was so quick, but to my astonishment Herbert was suddenly lying on his back with a bloody nose while Pip gazed in disbelief from his fist to his prone victim. Herbert soon got to his feet again. He sponged himself down and skipped from his left foot to his right, and back to his left, feinting.

And was on the ground again.

Strangely, he kept coming back at Pip and, each time he did, I thought, now you are in for it, boy, and each time Pip managed to knock Herbert down. Finally, when Herbert looked done in and I did feel sorry for him, he threw up the sponge admitting defeat. But there was no doubt; he had been beaten fair and square.

I left them then, feeling weirdly triumphant, and went out of the room, returning to the courtyard to wait for Pip. But instead of taking him to the gate, I stepped back into the passage, out of sight.

'You may kiss me—if you like,' I said, offering my cheek.

Pip seemed taken aback. He paused to look at me, almost as if it were something he needed to think about, and then for the briefest of moments his lips touched my face.

I found it odd. I thought his heart would have been gladdened by my offer. But it was as if there were something more at stake, something that some childish kiss only grazed the surface of.

We did not speak again and I saw him out of the gate. On my return to the house, I thought that if I had gone a number of rounds with Herbert *and won*, I would be buoyed, I would be cock-a-hoop, and a mere kiss would not have impressed me, either. I would have wanted more.

*

I do not mind admitting that sometimes I spied on Pip and Miss Havisham, for I was not accustomed to other children and was intrigued. I would take him up to her room and leave him at the door and pretend to walk away, and once he had entered I would return again and listen out of sight at the door. Sometimes, when they moved from one room across to the other, I would tiptoe inside and conceal myself behind the curtains, all the better to hear.

As Pip became more used to Miss Havisham, and her to him, she would ask him questions such as what he was going to be, and it was thus that I heard he was to become apprenticed to the blacksmith. Pip was not the blacksmith's son nor the son of the woman called Mrs Joe, whom I had seen earlier. Mrs Joe was his older sister apparently, who had taken over his care when his parents had died. Sometimes I heard him admit to Miss Havisham that his learning was sadly lacking and that he wished to improve himself, and I believe he did this in the hopes that she might offer some form of education to him, but she never commented on these admissions. It was as if she did not want him to get ideas above his station, and wanted to keep him ignorant and dumb.

'You are growing tall, Pip,' I heard her say to him on one such occasion.

'Yes, ma'am. And I am sorry to report that this might be occasioned by circumstances over which I have no control,' he remarked, perhaps picking up on the displeasure that was in her voice.

She stopped walking then, to frown and stare moodily at him, as if he had been impudent and had expressed a thought that would have been better kept to himself.

'What about Estella,' she muttered, resuming her walk. 'Does she grow prettier and prettier, Pip?'

'Yes!' he responded.

I blocked my ears then, for I did not want to hear anything more about me and my beauty and, at the first opportunity, I slipped from the room. It was not the first time I was the subject of their discussion and it was becoming tiresome.

Later, when I was called in to play cards with Pip, Miss Havisham embraced me with lavish fondness, murmuring in my ear to 'Break his heart, my pride and joy, break his heart and have no mercy,' and looked triumphantly and greedily from me to him and back again. This so incensed me that I behaved badly, and gloated when I won and belittled Pip when he lost, and then not five minutes later I become contrite and simpered and fawned over him. At times like these, I believe I was like a creature that has no control over itself.

8

The pattern of Pip's visits went on for several months and, on the days he did not come to the house, I was bereft and would moon about with a lacklustre air. And yet on no account would I have admitted it.

Occasionally, I would have to try on dresses that Miss Havisham had ordered from London. Six or seven would arrive at once, full-skirted and beribboned, and I would have to put them on and parade before her. Mrs Butters, too, was usually in attendance.

'Curtsey!' Miss H would instruct from her chair, gesticulating with a bony hand.

I curtsied.

'Twirl!'

I pirouetted on my toes.

'Not so fast, Estella! This isn't a game! That hem, Butters, is it overly long?'

If it were not the right length, I would have to climb atop a chair and Mrs Butters would have to get down on her knees and, with a bunch of pins in her mouth, crawl around me to adjust it.

I sat upright on a chair with my hands in my lap and my eyes fixed on a spot on the wall and practised being still, and I learnt the art of being present but also not there, which came in altogether useful when I became a grown-up. Sometimes Miss Havisham made me walk around the room balancing a book on my head. If the book fell at any time during the course of my walk, I would have to begin again. And again, until I got it right.

All this went hand in hand with the trying on of the new clothes. I endured it all under sufferance, but Miss H often became annoyed with me because I was so disinterested. 'One day, Estella,' she would remark, 'you will thank me for this.'

I did not think so at the time. But, later, when I went to school in France, I thanked her, for I was ahead of all the other girls as far as deportment went. And when I grew up, I realised that she had given me a sound education in what styles and colours suited me—although with my dark looks I could wear almost any colour—and what to wear and when to wear it. How a garment had to be in perfect condition to be worn. Any hint of a frayed cuff or a loose stitch and it had to be set aside to be mended. Which always struck me as odd and grossly unfair since Miss H wandered around in a yellowed, ancient and shabby dress herself, and had no regard for how *she* looked. She was as good if not better than Mrs Butters was with a needle and cotton when I was young, and it was only later when her eyesight faded that she gave up repairing my outfits.

Pip turned up at the gate one day with someone whom I presumed was the blacksmith, and I wondered whether this had something to do with the apprenticeship he had earlier mentioned. Joe Gargery was big and brawny, his suit of dark ill-fitting clothes struggling to contain him. He seemed a kindly enough man, but was inept and clearly ill at ease.

I met them both at the gate and, when I looked the blacksmith in the eye, he averted his gaze to Pip and said, 'Good morning, miss,' whilst looking at Pip. Then he took off his hat and, with a serious calculating expression, weighed the brim in his hands as if he had decided it was far too heavy for his head after all.

He seemed both frightened and in awe of Miss Havisham and who could blame him? I gathered by degrees that I was right, that the reason for the blacksmith's appearance was in order for Miss Havisham to oversee the process of Pip's apprenticeship. Mr Gargery, however, relied on Pip to speak for him, and it shames me to recall that I found the blacksmith's behaviour and the whole process rather amusing and struggled to contain my merriment. I did, however, learn that Pip's parents were both deceased—like mine. I did not know for certain whether my parents were dead. In fact, I did not think so, for then Miss Havisham would have said, *Your parents are dead*, instead of changing the subject. And so I rather thought they were still alive. Pip not having a mother and having to contend with the sister named Mrs Joe did, however, soften my heart a little more towards him.

At the close of events, Mr Gargery, the poor man, was in such a sad pickle that he insisted on going *up* the stairs instead of coming down. Deaf to all my remonstrances, Pip was forced to go after him and bring him back and, when I caught Pip's eye, I had to bite my bottom lip for fear of laughing out loud.

Thus, Pip's apprenticeship with the blacksmith began and his visits to us abruptly stopped. I do not know if Miss Havisham missed him. She would never have said and she was not easy to read. I asked her once why she had arranged for Pip to leave us and begin his apprenticeship; had he done something to upset her?

She shook her head and steepled her fingers. 'He had served his purpose, Estella. I had no further use for him.'

'And what purpose might that have been?'

'You broke his heart—'

'I broke his heart? How do you know?'

'I can see, my dear. I have eyes. I saw how he looked at you, how he idolised you. You should pay more attention, Estella. He was the first, never forget that,' she added.

I know I missed him. I regretted that I had not made more of his visits. My life at Satis House was for the most part run of the mill, and Pip's presence had added some spark to what was otherwise a humdrum existence.

It was perhaps not unexpected, then, that after Pip's departure I felt even more confined and restrained. Where once I had been content with treading the well-worn path through the garden, that was no longer enough for me. My spirit hankered for some or other adventure, some or other company, and I began to explore further afield.

*

Before dusk I would take my cloak and slip out of the house. It was not permitted, but I got into the habit of walking out past the village. I dressed in sombre clothes. I drew my hood over my head. And so quickly did I slip along the village streets it seemed that no-one noticed me. Most of the shopkeepers, including that overbearing man Pumblechook, were far too busy with the business of shutting up shop at this hour, which was in my favour, and for now no-one had reported my presence to Mrs Butters.

Ours was the marsh country, down by the river, and within twenty miles or so of the sea. The marshes, crisscrossed with dykes and humps and gates, were a dark flat wilderness beyond the churchyard, and the slinking slate-coloured strip beyond it all was the river. Scattered cattle fed on the grasses and loomed out of the mist, and the wind rushed at me from the sea and the moisture tipped the ends of my hair. On quiet evenings, I imagined I heard the distant rumble of what I thought must be the surf, but I knew I had an overactive imagination—Mrs Butters told me often enough. Once, I heard a booming and she told me there were prison hulks anchored offshore, ancient, rusted and barricaded ships used to contain convicts, and the booming indicated that a prisoner had escaped and was, in all likelihood, roaming the marshes. I was more careful after that. If I heard the booms coming from the hulks, I cut short my outing and headed home.

I found I loved being on the marshes. I loved the briny smells. I loved the little birds that flew up at my feet when my skirts rustled over the grasses. I even came to like the earthiness of the cow pats. I would let out my hair, pull off my hat and run across the landscape until I collapsed, exhausted, against a hedge. I would laugh, then, at my own antics. I welcomed the presence of the cattle and sheep and called to them 'It's only me' or some such phrase when I saw them. I do not know if they recognised me, but after a time it seemed they were no longer afraid of me, or me of them. There was so much I appreciated, but, mostly, it was the freedom I loved. Freedom from the confines of four walls, from the constraints of duty and responsibility, from the drab dreariness of my everyday existence. Freedom for my soul. For the Estella who lived at Satis House was a different girl to the Estella who roamed the marshes.

I was restless then, at that point in my life, and the atmosphere and raw landscape filled me with fancies. I would return breathless and exhilarated from these excursions to the marshes, shaking off my hood in front of the passage mirror in the house with a wild look in my eyes, counting the hours until I could return again.

On one such evening, Mrs Butters was waiting for me inside the passage. 'Oh, Estella,' she said, her tone full of disappointment, 'where have you been?'

'I—I—' I started, wondering who it was that had given me away.

'Never mind,' she said. 'It is not me who wishes to know, it is her ladyship. Quick smart. She wants to see you. *Now*.'

Miss Havisham was not best pleased.

'Estella!' she cried. She glared at me and struck her stick forcibly upon the floor. 'It is as well that you are going away.'

'Going away?' I was shocked. What did she mean?

'Yes. To France. To school. You will learn there that loitering on the marshes on your own is not fit behaviour becoming a young lady.'

Since I had recently turned thirteen, I was to further my education at a private school in France, apparently, and learn to become a proper lady, and would be away for some time. Miss Havisham had been holding off telling me, she said, but my behaviour had forced her hand.

I was going away. To France and to school. I kept repeating the information to myself, but it took time for it to sink in. At some point, I had known I would grow up and leave Miss Havisham, perhaps when I married, I thought, thus for ever after avoiding her belittlement of me, her capricious moods, but I did not realise it would be so early. So soon. And yet, and yet ... The event I had often longed for was to occur. I was to go away. I was to leave Satis House. How could I not fail to be excited?

Miss Havisham declared she would survive for the ten days or so it would take Mrs Butters to accompany me and return, and it was organised with the village butcher and grocer to make deliveries of fresh meat and vegetables to Satis House while we were away. Not that Miss Havisham ever ate much, or that we ever saw her eat. It was against her rules, the ones she had set in place when her heart had been broken. All I knew was that she roamed the house at night and that during these times she picked at what she could find in the kitchen. Sometimes she came into my room. I knew this because I would wake in the morning and find Poppet rearranged so that she sat at the end of my bed and no longer lay alongside me.

On the evening of the day before my departure for France, I wandered too far on the marshes. I was reluctant, I think, to abandon this place of stark beauty that gave me so much pleasure, and I was returning home late, and made use of a short cut that brought me across a muddied field and into a furrowed laneway.

A small wooden dwelling stood there, which looked vaguely familiar, with a light glowing in the mullioned window and a forge beside it. As I passed by, the flames from the blacksmith's fire leapt and danced and cast flickering shadows against the walls. I stopped. A boy with a blackened face stood to one side, pulling the bellows, and I remembered Pip then, and his employer, Joe Gargery. I had not seen Pip for well over a year, not since that last painful day he had visited Satis House with the blacksmith. Skipping over the ditch, I drew up silently to the open wooden window and peered in, looking into what seemed to be the bowels of hell.

The walls were dark with soot, the fire red and alive. Clinking and clanking sounds rent the air. A man was at work at the anvil, hammering away, and a boy stood there alongside him. And, as chance would have it, he lifted his grimy head and saw me. What a shock it was to fasten my eyes upon Pip's once more, his blue ones made all the brighter by the contrast with his dirty face. But before he could speak, I stepped lightly away. I jumped the ditch and fled down the laneway as if all the hounds in hell were following me.

What it was about his eyes that disturbed me, or what I saw in them, I could not tell you. But haunt me they did. For a long time afterwards, I found myself jolted awake and out of sleep, knowing I had seen his face and his eyes in my dreams. It seemed there was something he wanted to tell me, some knowledge he wanted to impart, and I did not know what it could be, and I did not understand what the relevance was.

9

I left Satis House and Miss Havisham on a miserable day in June. Summer rain fell from the sky as if muslin curtains were being drawn across the heavens, and at breakfast, from my vantage point at the window, I could barely see across the yard. Earlier, I had looked for Tom, who was now an old and decrepit cat, to say goodbye, but had been forced by the weather to give up.

I half-expected tears and regret from Miss Havisham at my departure, but she was in one of her fickle moods when I presented myself for my farewell.

I came forward and stretched my palms out beyond my cape, my gloves in one hand, ready to embrace her, but she waved me away from the chair of her dressing table.

'Off you go.'

'But I do not know when I will see you again,' I remonstrated, and bit my lip.

'You will see me again in a year as I've told you,' she said, 'and until then you are to write to me once a week.'

'Will you miss me?'

She snorted in an unladylike manner. 'Miss you?' she repeated. 'Why should I miss you?'

Her tone was cold.

What had I done to offend her? I wondered. Or was it merely that she was determined not to let me see the effect my going away had on her? She reached for her stick abruptly and tapped it on the boards. 'Remember,' she said with vigour, 'break their hearts!' And I took that as good a leave-taking as any.

Mrs Butters and I travelled by coach, a journey of some three to four hours and a change of horses, and it was early afternoon when the four-horse stagecoach on which we were passengers arrived in Dover. Mr Jaggers had arranged for our luggage and ourselves to be transferred by hackney coach to a reputable boarding establishment in the town, where we would stay.

Once settled, I set out for the white cliffs, leaving Mrs Butters resting in our rooms. She had begun coughing soon after we'd left Satis House and had said that she thought she was coming down with a cold, and she seemed now to be exhausted. I had earlier asked if she would like to accompany me on my walk, but she declined, telling me she would have plenty of opportunity to admire the ocean once she was aboard the steamboat. 'The sea is for fish,' she reminded me. In the circumstances, I was relieved, for I thought it better that she stay behind and rest. My only restrictions were not to talk to strange boys and to be back before six.

There was no sign of the summer rain we'd experienced inland the day before, and the sky was as clean as a slate and bright blue. I left the town's cobbled streets and laneways behind me and crossed to a gently ascending path that wound along the coastline. The breeze was fresh, the undulating cliffs covered in luxuriant grass and the odd wild daisy. In the distance was a ploughed field stretching raggedly to the cliff's edge, the newly turned earth ready for planting. A couple of walkers were out and about taking the air—no strange boys amongst them to my regret—only a woman twirling a parasol above her head accompanied by a man walking a dog. The dog was perfectly baffling. It appeared to have the legs and body of an antelope and the head of a large mouse. They all passed me coming down as I was going up and the man tipped his hat to me and we bade one another good day. They faded away into the distance behind me, leaving the cliffs deserted, which pleased me. It may have been that since I spent so much time on my own as a child, I was forever afterwards more than content with my own company. Which was a blessing, really.

At the highest point of the cliffs, I stopped and gazed down at the phenomenon that I had imagined smelling so many times from the marshes. The sea lay before me like a bolt of pale green chiffon. The tide nibbled at the sand, leaving frilled-petticoat edges, and terns wheeled in the sky, crying disconsolately one to another. Further out, some fishermen manned a rowboat, lurching up and down through the breakers and calling out 'Easy now!' I thought the sea easily the most amazing wonder of nature that I had ever seen. Some part of me seemed involuntarily and physically drawn to it, which I found strange, and I had to take care I did not allow myself to step too close to the edge.

On my way back down I noticed two boys had turned up on the rolling grass of the cliffs and were flying a kite. I stopped to watch.

'Do you want to have a go, miss?' one called.

'I don't mind if I do,' I called back and, picking up my skirts, I made my way over to them. They were younger than I was, I thought. They looked like brothers, their faces freckled and scrubbed clean and it seemed to me that they had been let out of the house only on pain of being scrupulously presented.

'Keep a firm grip now,' the taller one said, handing me the strings.

I had never held a kite before. It bobbed on the breeze and I laughed with delight as it tugged on my hands. It was intoxicating, like controlling a small horse, although that was something I had never done before, either.

'Good fun, isn't it, miss?'

I had to agree. What a life to be allowed to go out and about and do things at one's own whim. To knock about and not have to ask permission for any and every thing. I *was* envious. I glanced at the boys. Their faces were eagerly upturned to the sky and I had a wicked desire to let the kite fly free, to let go and allow the contraption to soar into the air, to see their expressions. But before I could act on my impulse, the taller one seemed to read my mind for he took the strings abruptly from me. 'You'll be getting tired now, miss,' he said.

In the morning, we crossed to Calais, and I had an opportunity to admire the sea all over again. For the first time, I boarded a boat and, a little unsteadily at first, felt the ocean moving under my feet. We were told it was to be a smooth crossing, but Mrs Butters was soon confined to our cabin with seasickness and did not agree. She was no better. I had heard her coughing in the night and she seemed fatigued. Our cabin, warm and comfortable if small, was probably the best place for her.

I remained on deck, buffeted by the wind, braced against the railing. The sea rolled under my feet, the paddles chugged along to their own urgent rhythm and the ocean spray flew back into my face. I felt invigorated. Alive. And ever so grateful that I, too, had not succumbed to seasickness.

In the distance, a hint of land nudged the horizon, and I wondered about the unknown future and the world that lay before me.

*

I had thought that we would go straight to Paris after we landed in Calais, but the school I was to attend was apparently in the countryside, some twenty miles north-west of the city.

Mr Jaggers had arranged for a driver and a coach to meet us and, after our luggage was transferred from the steamboat, we set off. We were to stay at Amiens and I was grateful for Mrs Butters did not look at all well. I had to help her into the carriage. She was pale, her handkerchief at her lips, had a shortness of breath and was unsteady on her feet.

We reached our accommodation at last and I left Mrs Butters in the carriage and went inside to speak to the woman of the house. 'Did she have the sickness before she leave the home?' the woman, who had introduced herself as Madame Dubois, asked.

'*Oui*,' I said. 'But only a cold, not ill like this.'

Miss Havisham had taught me some basic French, but I did not know enough to conduct a conversation, particularly not a medical one.

We were shown to our rooms at length, the coach driver assisting me to get Mrs Butters down from the carriage and into the house. With luck, our rooms were on the ground floor and looked comfortable and pleasant.

'Would you waste no time and call for a doctor?' I asked Madame Dubois.

'*Oui, mademoiselle*,' she said.

I loosened Mrs Butters's clothing. I helped her to the bed, removing her shoes, and covering her with a warm quilt because although it was a summer evening she was all atremble. When Madame Dubois returned, it was to tell me, in broken English, that she had sent a message for the doctor to come, but it was possible he would be some time since he was the town's only doctor.

'Could you please bring some broth?' I asked. Madame Dubois raised her eyebrows and went away again.

I was only thirteen, but I took charge of the situation and behaved as if I were eighteen. I had grown beyond my years, partly due to the fact that I was an only child and had no siblings to be childish with, partly due to the fact that Miss Havisham had been my constant companion and did not address me as a child and treated me as an adult, giving me responsibilities beyond my age. I was accustomed to gauging her moods, to caring for her if she were ill, to making decisions. The question of what Mrs Butters was to order in for food and drink was now left entirely to me, and had been for some time. Miss Havisham no longer even distractedly waved her hand to say, 'Oh, you do it.' And there was the reception and handling of her cousins, the Pockets, which I have already mentioned.

I did not trouble myself unpacking. I was much too concerned about Mrs Butters. I had earlier removed my cape and gloves, and I sat alongside her bed, watching her face. It was pale and she seemed cool to the touch. Clammy, even. Her breathing was shallow, and rapid like a dying fish, and she had begun to cough up greeny mucus. I wondered what troubled her, and where the doctor was? How quickly whatever was ailing her had taken hold.

The broth arrived. It was brought in by a serving maid who handed it to me and then fled as if she were afraid of catching something. I did not think it was the plague. I had heard that, in addition to the high fever, the lymph nodes swelled causing pus-riddled sores, and there was no sign of these. I propped more pillows behind Mrs Butters and held the spoon to her lips, coaxing her to open her mouth and swallow, but after a few spoonfuls she raised her hand to indicate no more.

I perched on the edge of her bed, holding her hand as her breathing grew shallower and shallower. I wondered how long we might be detained in Amiens, and what I would do if she grew worse.

Then she opened her eyes, gazed at me and gasped, 'Oh, Estella, dear.'

Her breathing appeared to stop. I laid my ear to her chest, but all was still. Both lungs and heart quiet. Motionless.

'Mrs Butters,' I said frantically, 'Mrs Butters.'

Her head fell to one side and her jaw went slack.

I thought then that perhaps she had left me, but I had no medical training and no certainty, and I continued to sit and hold her hand. Sometimes I talked softly to her, sometimes I caressed her face.

When the doctor came into the room, I rose and stepped away. He touched her, he laid his head on her chest as I had done, and felt with two fingers on her neck for her pulse. He shook his head then, and declared that Mrs Butters was dead. He said he thought it was pneumonia. His English was fractured and there were other things he said, questions he asked, but I had difficulty understanding all he said.

This was my first experience of death and I was numb. I kept thinking that I had not done enough to prevent her death, and that there ought to have been something I could have done. For I did consider for a time that her death was all my fault. If I had not been going to school in France, none of this would have happened. If I had not been disobedient and visited the tailor and met Trabb's boy, there was a chance Mrs Butters would still be alive.

Later, I wondered if Mrs Butters's death was where my interest in medicine and in healing was first kindled? Or was it with the disembowelling of the mouse? Or as far back as the dead lizards I had collected? Think for a moment of the long chain of events that bind you, make you what you are, and think that perhaps none of it would occur but for the formation of the first link on one memorable day.

I kept thinking that Mrs Butters had been like a mother to me, and I had taken her for granted. I kept thinking that I knew nothing really about her. Miss Havisham had once told me that she had been a governess, but that she had fallen on hard times when she had come to work for the Havisham family.

Mrs Butters was always there. And now she was no longer here. She would no longer call for me down the long passage when she needed me to run errands to the village. She would no longer put her head around my door at night to tell me she was retiring and *Pray the Lord my soul to keep*. She would no longer clasp me to her bosom and to her apron that smelled of lavender and say, 'There, there,' when Miss Havisham had been short and impatient with me and I was in tears, which admittedly had not happened often of late.

A letter was sent to Miss Havisham posthaste, but there was no question of me, or of Mrs Butters's remains, returning to England. I did, however, stay a few more days at the boarding establishment at Amiens, and Madame Dubois did soften and become kindlier towards me. The doctor, an overworked and abruptly-spoken man, instructed her to arrange for Mrs Butters's burial and, accompanied by the French woman, I was the only mourner at the graveside. Some poppies had sprung into life nearby, and I picked a number and scattered them into the grave, the red petals like splashes of blood on the simple brown wooden coffin.

In the morning, I resumed my journey to school alone. And gradually my numbness passed. But it was not easy arriving alone in a foreign place and knowing no-one. The other girls stared at me and thought nothing of speaking about me in my presence, for naturally I could not follow what they said. Well, not until later.

I felt different in France at first. The air felt lighter, the sun warmer. I was not so restrained. Within reason, for the French were particular about things: mealtimes, for instance, and when to have coffee and when to drink an aperitif, and the correct pronunciation of words. Etiquette mattered.

But regretfully, all things considered, my time in France was not a happy one. I did learn to speak French, to ride and to dance, which were all things I loved, but there were a number of times when I was ostracised for my Englishness. There were days when I hated Miss Havisham for sending me to school in a foreign country and felt sure my own mother would never have done such a thing. There were even more occasions when I was awoken at night by my tears, for the wall that I had built to safeguard myself from Miss Havisham continued to grow, brick by brick. Only now its purpose was to shelter me from the other girls.

I decided I did not like girls in general. They were a catty, nasty lot. Individually, they could be tolerated. Individually, they were sometimes kind. But put them in a bunch together and they invariably turned on me. I was proud, apparently, and arrogant, and they told me so to my face. I had seen these traits in Miss Havisham, but it had never occurred to me that I might be proud and arrogant, too, and I did not believe my accusers.

Neither did it occur to me that they behaved towards me precisely as I had behaved towards Pip. Perhaps if that had occurred to me, I might have begun to be a better person earlier. But as it was, I did not learn from my mistakes.

I bit my fingernails, a habit I only took up after I arrived at the school, and anyone guilty of this crime had to regularly press their fingertips into bars of lemon-coloured soap, so that the bitterness reached their tongues next time they put their fingers into their mouths and gave them due warning. Fingernails were inspected weekly. I would go for a considerable time without biting my nails and then, all of a sudden, I might be ridiculed for something I pronounced incorrectly and would again be found with ragged, torn and bleeding nails, and would once more have to endure the soap punishment. To this day, I cannot put my fingers near my mouth without recalling the acrid taste.

I was the only English girl at the school, and sometimes the other girls would gather around me and demand that I pronounce a difficult French word such as *un écureuil*, and subsequently fall about with laughter at my attempts to say 'a squirrel'. In light of this, I studied the language with great care and, by the time I returned to England, my French was near perfect.

I have to a large extent blocked the memory of these years from my mind, for as time wore on, I became more and more homesick. I yearned for a damp English day and the smell of chestnuts roasting in a barrow in the village. I longed for the burst of the bluebells under the bare-limbed birch trees in the garden or the sound of a broad English accent.

It is true that I had only discovered the marshland and its treasures in the year before I went to France, but its impression on me could not be overestimated. In addition, I had been at that age when every nuance and feeling and thought seems not only original and magnified, but fraught with emotion. I had looked at a reed of grass a hundred times before, but it seemed to me that I had never before seen the globule of sparkling dew that clung to its glossy green leaf and reflected my image back at me, upside down. What did it mean? Why was I here? And what was the point of anything?

And so it was these things: the mist on the marshes, the cows looming out at me, the drunken gravestones beside the churchyard and the smell of the wind. Oh, how I missed these most of all!

PART TWO

PART TWO

10

I find Miss Havisham is much changed when I at last return from France for good, but to my relief my surroundings—the house, the landscape—remain unaltered.

I have changed, too, naturally, for I am now eighteen years of age. But my adopted mother is thinner than ever, her skin so pale it is translucent, her purpled veins as prominent as if someone has drawn them in with an ink quill. I observe that she is more subdued, at times almost appearing melancholy, and is no longer steady on her feet or so quick to rise to anger. The latter will probably pass once she adapts to my presence again.

Sarah Pocket is in residence. I do not intend to be unkind, but she is a dry and wrinkled woman with a face that might be composed of dried leaves and a mouth like a desiccated rosebud. Sarah has replaced Mrs Butters and now keeps house for Miss Havisham. I do not approve, and conversation at our first dinner together is stilted, but better the devil you know, as they say.

On my second day back from France, and the earliest opportunity I have of getting away, I am out of the house before dawn.

It seems that the high street is unchanged. The man called Pumblechook, who brought Pip into my life and to whom Pip is in some way connected, still has a seed and grain store in business. I wonder about Pip then, where he is, and what he is doing. Whilst I was in France, I heard from Miss H that his fortune had changed. He acquired a wealthy benefactor, came into money and went to London to reside. 'He thinks I am his benefactor!' Miss H wrote more than once, but nothing further. I wanted to ask if she were his patron, but she would not have told me, and so I held off giving her the pleasure of playing games with me. Secrets and being secretive were two things she excelled at. She did tell me that Herbert Pocket had befriended Pip, and that Pip had been reading with Herbert's father, Mr Matthew Pocket. Herbert and Pip now live together, apparently. How strangely things turn out—the two boys who once fought over me sharing quarters, and Miss Havisham's cousins now friends of Pip's. No wonder he presumes Miss H to be his benefactor.

In France, I was allowed to roam the gardens of my school and the woods beyond at certain hours, which I greatly enjoyed. But once I leave the outskirts of the village and head out towards the churchyard and get my first whiff of the marshes, I know that nothing compares to this. Nor will it ever. I would rather the bleak, desolate and raw marshes any day than a forest of green or a pretty, manicured garden.

What is it in one's soul that decides this? Is it a voluntary choice or an inherent one? It is a little bit akin to—but *not* the same—as finding one man more appealing than others. Nothing to do with looks, but rather some innate response. Sometimes I am not even aware of this attraction; it is only afterwards that it occurs to me, and then more often than not I am puzzled by it.

The morning mist wafts amongst the gravestones when I reach the churchyard, and I am about to wander further afield when I am distracted. To my annoyance, I am not alone. For in the distance, silhouetted by the morning light and on the edge of the dark flat wilderness that is the marshes, a man is standing. A man who has turned to observe me. The movement attracted my eye. Something is standing angularly in front of him. An easel, perhaps? For that is what it looks like.

I am irritated to find someone in *my* place, taking advantage of *my* marshlands, but I cannot withdraw now without looking foolish or, worse still, childish, and I slip outside the low walls of the churchyard and make my way over. I draw closer and see that the man is indeed an artist. In spite of the cold, he is in his shirtsleeves, a pair of embroidered suspenders over his shoulders. A sheet of sketching paper is pegged to the easel and his coat is at his feet, a tin of pencils and charcoal sticks lying open on it.

'Hello,' he says.

An informal greeting, but perhaps it is because we are clearly the only two people here and must be kindred spirits to be out and about before the sun has risen. He glances across at me, then studies the tip of the pencil caught between his fingers. His shoulder-length light-brown hair is wavy and loose around his face, and he is clean-shaven except for a narrow moustache that gives him a dashing air.

'Hello,' I respond, aware that in my haste to get out the door this morning, I have not tied up my hair and no doubt appear a little dishevelled.

'Beautiful morning to be out and about,' I say.

'Hmm,' he says. The pencil is poised in front of the paper and he stares ahead. He is concentrating.

The lumps and bumps of the marshes, traversed by the dykes and scattered with grazing cattle, lie before us. The light falls over the landscape, accentuating the mist meandering between its dips and ditches, and it is altogether pretty—if the marshes can ever be considered as such.

'Don't mind me,' he murmurs, as the lowing of an animal reaches us, and still he does not draw a thing.

This is a gentle hint for me to depart, I think. I tiptoe around him and head out to the left, in an attempt to stay out of his sight, out of his picture, and I do not look back.

A number of matters cross my thoughts while I ramble. But I have also got into the habit of attempting to keep my mind clear and open while I walk, to appreciate the sights and sounds that are all around me rather than get distracted by the detail of my life. By the fact that Miss Havisham, for instance, told me yesterday that she has made plans for me to go and live in London in a number of months, to get to know the right people and begin the social circuit. I have to admit it is not something I am anticipating with any degree of joy.

There is no wind and I walk for half an hour, maybe more, until I smell kelp coming from the sea. The only sounds are the rustling of the grasses and my skirts, the twittering of swallows, flitting high above my head, and the odd bellowing of a bovine. No booming from the hulks. No escaped convicts, poor wretches, today. I do not know what the time is when I turn to retrace my steps, only where the sun is in the heavens.

The mist has lifted and it is a bright, sunny day when, at last, the churchyard is in my line of sight. From a long way off, the outline of the artist and his easel is evident, and I have the opportunity to study him without appearing to stare. He seems slenderly built, but is not effeminate, his shoulders are solid. From the movement of his arms and hands, he is hard at work. I decide to stick to one side as before, so as not to disturb him, but as I draw closer, surreptitiously edging around him, he glances up as if he has known I was there all along.

'Miss?' he calls.

I go over.

He lifts his head as I reach him, and for the first time looks directly at me.

He has high cheekbones and deeply set brown eyes. By the lines on his face, I surmise he is perhaps ten years older than I am. He raises his eyebrows inquiringly and steps aside, and indicates that I should look at what he has done.

He has exchanged his pencil for a stick of charcoal, and the marshes and the reeds and the low leaden line of the river lie upon the paper. The mist is a series of faint lines that have perhaps been rubbed with a sleeve to form a blur. Three cows, to the right of the scene, are beautifully and accurately depicted and, on the left, further afield, is a figure of a woman, a woman gazing into the distance, into the light that rises from the horizon.

I turn to him and find his eyes upon my face. I swallow. 'It's me,' I say.

'It's you,' he agrees.

'It's lovely,' I say.

'It's not bad.'

He tosses his stick of charcoal into his pencil box, unpegs the sketch from the board and slides it into a big black folder made of stiff fabric.

'If you wait a moment, I will walk with you,' he tells me.

He packs away his materials. The pencil tin together with the pegs go into the fabric folder as well. The easel is dismantled and folded up and he props it against his leg while he bends low for his coat, and in doing so disturbs the easel.

I lunge forward to prevent it falling at the same time as he does. Our heads bend one to the other, our hands touch. Warmth emanates from his body and I smell the faint muskiness of his breath.

It is all I can do to let go and pull away, to stand erect and step back.

'My apologies,' I say.

'Oh, no, the fault is all mine.' He leans over, clutching the easel to one side, and gazes up at me.

My heart cartwheels in my breast. My pulse quickens as blood hurtles through my body, and I find I am breathless. What is happening to me? I do not recognise these symptoms.

Is this ... Is this what I think it is? Is this what falling in love at first sight is?

He smiles suddenly, dimpling both cheeks, and, coming upright, slings on his coat and hoists the easel and folder under one arm.

'That was close,' he says mischievously.

He is playing with words, of course, and I turn away because of the blush that creeps up my neck, because of the desire to laugh.

We walk back to the village together. It is a companionable walk. We don't talk at first, but the silence is not uncomfortable. I feel that there is either nothing to say or there is an overwhelming amount. For now, I think, I prefer ignorance. For now, I do not want to know the name of the man at my side, or his history, or his future—I only want to hold on to this moment.

'Do you live in the village?' he asks at last, turning to me.

I shake my head. 'Yes and no,' I say. 'I live outside the village. Satis House. Do you know it?'

'I believe I do.'

'And you?' I ask. 'I do not think you are from these parts.'

'You'd be right. I am not—'

A depression in the road catches him unawares and he steps awkwardly, his coated arm brushing against mine. I glance at him and he looks steadily back at me. I feel faint with some emotion I don't know the name of. I want time to stand still. To be here forever. Trapped with him in this moment.

'I'm from London,' he says. 'I have come down for a few days to paint and draw. I am staying at the Blue Boar.'

'Are you now?'

'Yes and no,' he repeats my words back to me. 'I am in residence but my heart is not in it.'

'I am not surprised,' I say.

I have never been to the Blue Boar, but it has a reputation. Mrs Butters used to say that it was a fine place to be laying your head if sleeping beside a hedge was your only other option.

'Shall I walk you home?' he asks as we near the village.

'Thank you. That's kind of you, but it would be better if you did not.' I do not say the obvious, that I am not meant to be out and about alone. 'In truth, it will make things easier for me if I slip through unaccompanied before anyone notices,' I add.

'Perfectly sensible,' he agrees.

We draw closer to the high street. I turn to say farewell and be on my way, but he stops me with a hand on my arm. He puts his index finger to his lips. He does not want me to say goodbye or he does not want me to speak. Which is it?

Our eyes meet and his gaze lingers on mine.

Before I am tempted to do or say something foolish, I draw my cape over my head and turn to hurry silently along the street.

11

The following morning I am out again before dawn. I tell myself I am out because I need fresh air, liberty and the exhilaration that the marshes bring, but I know this is not entirely true.

I am out because I want to see *him* again.

To my regret, the weather has changed. The wind gusts through the town, throwing up leaves and detritus, forcing me to draw my cape tightly around me. I reach the churchyard and the clouds have amassed in anger above my head and raindrops are beginning to spitter down on my hood. It is either going to pour or the wind is going to chase the rain away.

My artist friend is absent. I am not altogether surprised. I stand in the lee of the entranceway to the church vestry and wait, but there is no sign of him or his easel near the churchyard and I cannot see into the distance for the weather and the gloom. The morning's light has been blighted. I do hope he is not further afield because there is every chance he will get soaked.

Even as I watch and wait, the heavens tear apart. Rain begins to bucket down, falling freely, fast and hard. The earth runs with water. Puddles form alongside the gravestones and raindrops streak their grey surfaces. My hands are cold, my boots spattered and I am damp to the touch. But I do not object. I find it exhilarating. I am wondering at what stage the weather will break and I can make a run for home or whether I am stuck here for the duration, when there is a noise behind me.

Startled, I turn.

In the dim light of the vestry, well behind me, is my artist friend. His easel and equipment are leaning against the wall.

How long has he been standing there studying me?

'Good morning.' I have to speak up to be heard above the noise of the rain.

'Atrocious morning,' he announces, coming forward to join me.

'Have you been here all the time? Why did you not make yourself known?'

'I was practising my craft,' he says. 'Observing. Indelibly marking the scene before me in my memory.'

'It was not kind of you,' I respond.

'I do beg your pardon.' He dips his head, but there is no smile about his lips today. He seems sombre.

'So there'll be no sketching?' I ask.

'I doubt it. But it could lift, the weather. I intend to wait and see.' He pushes his gloved hands into his coat pockets. 'And you?' He raises his eyebrows. 'What about your walk?'

'Oh, there is always tomorrow,' I say.

'It is raining steadily now,' he remarks, looking out at the weather. 'You will get drenched returning to Satis House.'

'It won't be the first time,' I tell him. 'Or the last.'

'Forgive me,' he says, 'but you wouldn't be Miss Havisham, Miss Estella Havisham?'

A little taken aback, I turn to him. 'I am.'

'The man at the Blue Boar spoke of you, I believe, yesterday evening. He said you had recently returned from France. *Est-ce vrai?*'

'*Oui*. It is.'

'This'—he puts out a hand to indicate our surroundings—'must be decidedly boring to adjust to after Paris.'

I shake my head. 'Not at all. *This* is what I live for … And I wasn't in Paris,' I add. 'I was in the country. I do not miss it.'

'You are not like other young women, then,' he murmurs.

'And how would other young women be?'

My question makes him uncomfortable, for he shifts on his feet. 'Oh, you know, going to balls and parties. Being seen out and about by the right people.'

'No, I am not like that. But that doesn't mean it isn't something I have to do.'

We turn our attention back to the elements. The rain is easing, but whether the break in the weather will see me safely back home I do not know.

'If I am going to make a run for it,' I murmur, 'now would be a good time—'

'Don't go,' he says suddenly. 'Would you … Would you pose for me?'

'Pose for you?' I glance at him. 'Where?'

'Anywhere …' His eyes dart about. 'There,' he exclaims, throwing off his scarf, pulling off his gloves, unbuttoning his coat. 'Where you were when you first arrived, looking out to the weather.'

'But the light,' I say. 'There is no light.'

He does not reply. He moves quickly, setting up his easel, ferreting in his bag for his pencil case.

I try to remember the way I stood in the lee of the entrance to the vestry, but I have never done this before and am uncertain of what is required.

I wonder if he has begun to sketch when the pressure of a hand on my waist surprises me. Startled, I turn to look into his eyes. He is so close I can make out the individual hairs of his light brown moustache and a number of freckles on his cheek. He has a small mole at the side of his mouth.

'Forgive me,' he says, 'I need you to move a little more to the left.' And placing both hands on my hips, he manoeuvres me into place. 'There,' he says.

I dare not move. I strain my ears to hear the scratchy sound of charcoal on paper, but the recommencement of falling rain obliterates everything.

I think of the landscape beyond me, of the cows whose hides will be sodden, of the air steaming from their nostrils, of the ditches that will be awash with water. I consider the hulks and their prisoners, and their wretched lives. And I think of the man behind me and wonder about his life in London, where he lives, what he does with himself when he is not sketching.

The rain has completely stopped and I have been staring into the distance, wondering if it is safe to turn my head, when he says, 'You should go while you can.'

'Have you finished?'

He has not. He continues to rapidly sketch. I hear the scratch of pencil or charcoal on paper.

'I have done sufficient for now, and I do not wish you to get wet.'

I pick up my skirts in one hand. 'Will you come tomorrow?'

'That depends. Will *you* come tomorrow?'

I tilt my head to one side. 'You are playing with me,' I say across the distance between us.

'Perhaps. Then again I may be serious,' he says, and continues to work on his sketch.

'*Au revoir*,' I call, when it is clear he remains preoccupied.

He glances up. My gaze meets his, and I must drag my eyes away. The flutter in my heart is foreign, my breathing uneven.

'*Au revoir, Mademoiselle.*'

He steps aside from the easel and does a mock bow. Then he blows me a kiss, making me laugh. Before I can change my mind about going, I make a dash for it, skipping across the puddles, and I am halfway home before I realise I still do not know his name.

*

On the third morning, when I reach the marshes, he is waiting for me, empty-handed—no artist's paraphernalia—in the church graveyard. He is in his great coat, but it is unbuttoned and he is bare-headed.

'Hello,' I murmur, attempting to maintain my composure when I want to smile—nay to dance—with delight.

'Good morning,' he returns.

'Do you not feel the cold?'

'Oh, I do,' he tells me. 'But it is exhilarating to feel *something* and I intend to make the most of it. Shall we walk?'

His hands are bare, too, and it is as much as I can do not to reach out and take one in my own as we set off. But I cannot. I must not.

'Why are you not sketching today?' I ask as we skirt the low wall of the graveyard and head out onto the marshes.

'Who said I am not sketching? I am always at work—it is only that today I'm at work in my head.'

I smile. 'Where do you want to walk?'

'Wherever it is you go.'

'It is far,' I warn.

'I am not afraid of distance,' he says.

Yesterday's rain has refreshened the world. It is boggy underfoot and water trickles between the marsh grasses. The cattle's white and brown coats are vivid with colour, and they lift their heads to slowly gaze after us. The birds twitter and, from the east, the light eases over the land as bits of cotton fluff drift in the heavens.

We talk about his work. He tells me he has an exhibition in three months' time in London, that he is terrified for he has not accumulated enough work—

'You, terrified?' I tease. 'I find that hard to believe.'

He nods. 'I am easily terrified. Especially by my work. You never think you are good enough,' he says.

'Earlier, you said that it was exhilarating to feel *something*. Why did you say that?'

He shakes his head and glances at me with pain in his eyes.

'Forgive me,' I say, 'that was impertinent of me. You do not have to answer. Where is your exhibition to be held?' I ask, and bring the subject back to safer waters.

'It's a private showing,' he says. 'Someone has funds and has taken pity on me in an attempt to earn me some money.'

'I see,' I say. I do not know what else to say. I forget that appearances are deceptive and that not everyone is as well off and comfortable as I am.

We walk for some time before he says, 'And you? Will you remain here, in this backwater?'

'No. I am soon to take up residence in London, to be shown to society and society shown to me.'

'I pity you,' he says.

I sigh. 'I pity myself. I do, for this reason, often wish I had been born a man.'

'A man?' He puts his head back and laughs. It is a charming laugh for it sounds like the low peal of a bell.

'If you were a man, you would have responsibilities, you would be continuously trying to get ahead. If you were a man, I would in all likelihood not be walking here with you. Did you think of that? Do you mind that I walk with you?' he asks.

'Mind? Why should I mind?'

'It is not the done thing,' he says in a low voice. 'You do not know me; I do not know you. Etiquette forbids it.'

I stop. I want to blurt out that I do know him, that I feel it *here,* and put my hand on my heart. That mostly I feel it.

He stops, too, then, as if he knows what I am thinking. There are two bright spots of colour on his cheeks as he reaches for both my hands.

I gaze into his eyes. I have forgotten myself, and where I am. I want to kiss him—oh, how I want to kiss him—and I cannot.

'Miss Havisham,' he murmurs.

I am conscious again that I do not know his name. But the truth is that I do not want to know his name. Knowing his name will take away the dreamlike quality of our encounter. Diminish it. Knowing his name will bring reality crashing around me.

The boom from the hulks is frighteningly loud. It startles us both. We drop one another's hands. I realise I can smell the sea, and we have perhaps walked too far.

'What was that?' he says, looking about.

'Come,' I say, 'we must hurry.' I rapidly pick up my skirts.

'But what does it mean?'

'It means—' I start, but I turn to head home. I dodge puddles and hop over rivulets. I have long had a fear of finding a man, a convict, lying in a ditch, of gulls pecking out his eyes, and am too out of breath to continue my line of conversation, unable to get the words out. Perhaps I am overexcited. Overstimulated. Call it what you will.

Another thought occurs to me. Is it because I have caught myself in time from behaving improperly and I am running from what is happening between us?

I am almost at the churchyard and panting with exertion when I stop to check if he is following and find that he lags some distance behind, and continues to glance over his shoulder.

'Why the hurry?' he calls.

'A prisoner has escaped,' I tell him. 'From the hulks that are moored offshore. It is not safe,' I say, turning again to continue homeward, 'to remain here while the poor wretch is at large—'

'—Miss Estella, wait.'

I pause, my skirts in my hands. He has said my name as if he has always known it. As if there are no barriers between us. I glance back. 'What is it?'

'I want to stay. I want to see what happens. If anything. Is that peculiar? Do you mind? I think you will be safe now, and I can look after myself.'

Bemused, I shake my head. 'As you wish.'

His brown eyes are steady on mine as we gaze at one another through the light thin air.

'Will I see you tomorrow?' he calls.

'Will I see *you* tomorrow?' I call back.

He smiles, and a butterfly, *un papillon*, takes up residence in my heart, or my soul, I know not which, and flutters wildly about.

'*Au revoir*,' I call.

'*Au revoir*,' he returns.

I set off for home, passing the low wall of the churchyard. I am disappointed that our time together has been cut short, but there *is* tomorrow. But how will I stand the hours until tomorrow comes?

I am wondering how many more days I have with him when there is a rush of movement.

I turn and he is here beside me!

His face is flushed, his eyes bright from running to catch up to me, and he appears breathless.

He catches at my arm and, before I can say a word, he draws me to him and kisses me.

*

If my heart and soul were on the marshes and with *him* in the days before, it now seems as if my very body roams and wanders the terrain.

I drift about the house in a daze. Even Miss H comments on it. 'What troubles you this morning, Estella?' she asks. 'You're not pining for some sallow-faced youth in France, are you?'

I shake my head. I sit on the floor at Miss H's feet in front of the fire, my knitting lying untouched at my side. 'Perhaps I am tired?' I suggest. 'Perhaps the journey home took it out of me?'

'Perhaps,' she agrees, but I can tell from the way she stares into the flames that she is thinking. Miss Havisham thinking—plotting—is always a dangerous thing.

12

I am wrong. Alas, there is no tomorrow.

When I return in the morning, there is no sign of my artist. I spend some time waiting, walking out as far as the cattle in the mist, doing rounds of the graveyard to pass the minutes, peering into the far reaches of the vestry—no-one there—but he does not appear.

I return home with a heavy heart. On the way, I pass the Blue Boar. Although it is still early, a boy is out sweeping the street in front of the establishment, and he doffs his cap to me. I pause.

'Do you know ...' I begin, and falter.

'Do I know what, miss?'

'Do you know if an artist has been staying at the Blue Boar?'

'Yes, miss, he has. He left yesterday afternoon, miss. He caught the last coach. I helped him with his luggage. He had that many things. The sketches, you know, miss?'

I nod. 'I know. Thank you,' I say.

'No trouble, miss,' he tells me, and resumes his sweeping duties.

I skip breakfast. I have lost my appetite, but I know better than to avoid my time with Miss Havisham. She will smell a rat if I do.

On the way upstairs, I pause to stare out of the window. My initial sadness has been replaced with resentment and anger. Why did my friend leave without an explanation? Without saying goodbye? In such a hurry? What does he know that I do not? Or am I clutching at straws, and the simple explanation is that he left because he overstepped the mark and was afraid of doing so again?

Outside the window, the mist has lifted and it has become a grey day, echoing my state of mind. But I take a determined step forward. I must put on some façade of, if not happiness, at least contentment.

We sit in Miss Havisham's room. Her hands are crossed upon her stick, her chin resting on them, and her eyes are fixed on the fire. I am nearby, on the floor at her feet. I pick up the white shoe, yellowed now, that has never been worn, to distract myself and turn it over in my hands. What a waste. For if there is one thing my time away has highlighted, it is the differences between Miss H and me. I have returned from France full of worldly knowledge and eager to see and experience more, and here alongside me is a woman who was once my age and no doubt was vivacious, still is intelligent, and surely had much to offer. But never left this room. Never achieved anything. Never did anything worthy—

There is a tap on the door.

'Pip's rap,' Miss H tells me.

'*Pip*? You have invited Pip to call?'

'Of course.' She turns to me with bright eyes.

Before I can recover from my astonishment, she calls, 'Come in, Pip.'

The man who enters the room is dressed in a coat and tails, a top hat under his arm. He is very handsome, and I can scarce believe it is Pip, but for his eyes. They match the paisley cornflower blue of his cravat; they light upon mine and dart away. He is still shy, then.

'Pip, come in. How do you do?' Miss H doesn't take her eyes from the fire. I know what she is attempting to do by not drawing attention to herself. She desires his focus on me.

'You may kiss my hand,' she says carelessly, sticking it out at an angle.

'I heard, Miss Havisham,' he begins tentatively, after he has kissed her hand and after his gaze has slid from mine again, 'that you wished me to come and see you, and I came directly—'

'Well?' she says.

'*Well!*' she demands when he does not respond.

The poor boy. He is forced to look at me once more and recognition dawns in his eyes.

'Estella!' he murmurs.

I give him my hand and he says something about the pleasure he has in seeing me again, but I am not really listening. I gaze into his face and his pretty eyes and wonder how it is possible that the boy with the once tear-stained face has turned into this elegant and attractive man.

'Well, Pip. Is she much changed?'

Miss H strikes her stick upon a nearby chair, indicating that he should sit.

'When I came in, Miss Havisham, I thought there was nothing of Estella in her face, but now'—he breaks off to glance at me—'but now I see it. I see the old—'

'You are not going to say the old Estella, are you?' Miss H interrupts. 'She was proud and insulting,' Miss H goes on as Pip settles himself, 'and you wanted to go away from her. Do you remember that?'

'That was a long time ago, Miss Havisham, and I knew no better.'

'I probably was very disagreeable,' I say.

Pip looks down at me from his chair and I see that same flicker of expression in his eyes that I saw for a long time in my dreams.

'Is *he* much changed?' Miss H asks me.

'Very much,' I say.

'Less coarse and common?' Miss Havisham asks and reaches out to play with my hair.

I laugh. I avert my eyes from Pip's, look at the shoe in my hand, laugh again. I put the footwear down and gaze back at Pip. He is still watching me, and I twist my mouth into a mischievous smile and am half-inclined to offer him my cheek and suggest he may kiss me, if he wants. But I do not.

He enquires when I returned from France, and so on, and soon it is settled between Miss H and me that he should remain with us for the rest of the day and return to the Blue Boar tonight after dinner.

'Now go out and get some fresh air,' she says, 'the two of you.' Which usually means she is tired and needs some time alone. 'And when you come in again, Pip, you can wheel me about as you did in the days gone by.'

We go downstairs and along the passage, and I remember stopping here with Pip on more than one occasion. Sometimes I was kind, sometimes I was not. And I half-want to stop again, to pause and say something heartfelt, but I cannot think what to say.

We take a turn in the garden, with my arm threaded through his for the cold wind buffets us, and pass the place where Pip and Herbert had their boxing encounter so long ago.

'I must have been a singular little creature to hide and see that fight you had with Herbert that day, but I did, and I enjoyed it very much.'

'You rewarded me very much.'

'Did I?' I ask as if I have forgotten. 'I remember that I had a great objection to your adversary, for it seemed to me that he was brought here only to pester me with his company.'

'He and I are great friends now.'

'I recollect that you read with his father?'

'I do.'

'Since your change of fortune and prospects, you have changed your companions, I presume?'

'Naturally.'

'And what was fit company for you once would be quite unfit company for you now?'

'Of course.'

'You had no idea of your impending good fortune, in those times?' I ask, signifying with a wave of my hand the time of the fight.

'Not the least.'

I do not know what I intend by my interrogation. It seems to me that I cannot help treating Pip as if he were still a boy, and a poor boy, at that.

We go around the garden once or twice, but it is worse than it ever was, and too overgrown for walking in. We come out into the brewery yard amongst the casks, and he reminds me that it was here that I gave him his meat and drink, and here that I made him cry. I tell him I do not remember, but it is a lie. I remember all too well. I merely do not want him to know how well I remember it.

'You must know,' I say, 'that I have no heart—if that has anything to do with my memory.'

'I doubt that,' Pip says. 'Surely there could be no such beauty without a heart?'

I glance at him and he is all earnestness and gravity when I want to laugh.

'Do not flatter me, Pip. Surely you know me better than that? Oh, I have a heart to be stabbed in, or shot at, I have no doubt. And if it ceased to beat, I should cease to be. But you know what I mean. I have no softness there, no—sympathy—sentiment—nonsense.'

Liar. Liar. Liar!

We pause. Pip looks at me and I at him, and I see again that look in his eyes. What is it? Does he know I am lying? And why do I lie? Is it because I do not want him to become attached to me? I believe it is. I am attempting to keep him at a distance. I do not want to give him any ideas.

'I am serious—' I declare, to break the moment. 'If we are to be thrown much together, you had better believe it at once.'

I stop him when he opens his lips to speak. 'No, I have not bestowed my tenderness anywhere. I have never felt any such thing.'

The Lord strike me dead! For I know this not to be true. My heart has recently longed to bestow tenderness, yearned to belong to another, raced at the thought of *him*.

We stop at the foot of the brewery stairs and I change the subject, pointing a finger upwards. 'I do recall this bit. Running on the staircases, you following, and falling when we were upon the casks, do you remember that?'

'Do you remember that you gave me a pastry wrapped in a napkin?'

'Did I?'

'I still have the napkin,' he tells me. 'Not upon me now, but at my lodgings.'

'Ah, Pip, so I am not always cruel then, am I? Sometimes I have been kind? Now, give me your shoulder to lean on and let us make our way back to Miss H.'

We go in, then, and while Pip pushes Miss Havisham around the room, she tells us that Mr Jaggers has come down to see her and will return to the house to join us for dinner.

When I leave them in the late afternoon to dress, Miss H kisses her hand to me with such ravenous intensity that I wonder what to make of it. Is this all show for Pip?

We dine together, Pip and I and Mr Jaggers and Sarah Pocket. Sarah is put off to such a degree by the sight of Pip in the house again that her dried-out rosebud mouth looks as if a worm has been nibbling at it. Afterwards, we all, except for Sarah, go up to Miss H's room and play whist. And while Pip shuffles the cards, Miss H insists on putting some of the beautiful jewels from her dressing table into my hair and about my neck and arms. It continues to vex me, this making a show of me, as it did when I was a child. Certainly, my feelings about the jewels and their cold beauty have not changed in the interim. But I bear it with good grace, although Mr Jaggers looks at me from under his thick eyebrows, and even lifts those beetles a little. I do not know what he is thinking. I never have been able to tell. I know what Pip is thinking. He raises his pretty blue eyes to gaze adoringly at me, and there is nothing I can do about it.

*

In the morning, I am awake before dawn. I have been dreaming of my artistic friend and I cannot stay away from the marshes.

The weather is miserably raw and the landscape deserted as usual, although the cattle are always there, wafting in and out of the mist and lifting their big heads to stare at me. I walk as far as I can towards the sea before it becomes too soggy underfoot, and in the distance I make out the low line of the river, and on the horizon a column of men with shackles about their legs. They are attired in grey convict garb with great numbers on their backs and a keeper with a pistol at the ready is with them. I do not know what it is they are doing, so far from their prison, and whether this is exercise or punishment. And, picking up my skirts, I turn hurriedly away to head home. But one of them catches sight of me and a shout goes up, followed by coarse laughter. Then a whip cracks and one of men cries out in pain.

The wind is at my back now and I flee home as best I can. I am not far along when I am stopped by a shout. 'Miss!'

It is the keeper with his pistol. The gang of men are huddled distantly together on the shoreline and are staring after us.

'Miss, I need to warn you—' The man breathes hard, his face flushed by exertion.

'What is it?'

'We have one on the run, miss. The night before last. You should not be here. It ain't safe.'

'What, and you haven't found him yet?'

'No, miss. He's either dead, he is, or he's gorn. But do keep a lookout, please. I would so hate for anything to happen.'

I nod. 'I'll be quick,' I say, and turn once more, setting off hastily.

'Thankee, miss,' he calls after me.

My boots are smeared with grime, my fingers frozen from clutching onto my skirts, when a huge cow lumbers out of the ditch in front of me. Great big jaws and saliva looping from her blunt mouth and her bellowing with fright at the sight of me.

I clutch my hand to my heart, step sideways, backwards, in an attempt to dodge her and her massive bulk. Trotting with fright, steam rising from her flanks, she passes by. A squabble of seagulls rises behind her, squawking and keening with alarm, and I am stopped. My breath catches in my throat, for I see why it is the beast and the birds have been in the ditch.

A man lies there. The thing I have dreaded. A convict with a number on his back. Curled over into himself with his face half in the mud, his hands are tucked up into his armpits. He does not move. The manacle on one leg has chafed at the bone so furiously that the skin is bloody and the gulls have pecked at the wound until it is raw and ragged. I think the man is dead. In fact, I am certain he is dead. The skin of his lower leg, where it protrudes below his trouser cuff, is white and bloodless.

I do not linger. It is my duty to inform the police, but I do not. Wretch and wretched he may well be, but what will telling the police achieve? Rather let his body lie here under the vast and open sky—at peace now—than be lumped up onto a cart and trundled back and turfed into some frigid and unwelcoming hole in the ground.

*

I am in a sombre mood when I return to Satis House. After breakfast I go up to Miss Havisham and sit at her feet as before, with my knitting. The candles which light that dark room of hers are high off the ground and burn with the steady dullness of artificial light in air that is seldom renewed. I look around at the clock stopped at twenty to nine and the desiccated flowers upon the table, and at Miss Havisham sitting upright in her chair with her eyes fixed greedily upon the fire, her hands clasped over her stick. Thrown high up upon the ceiling and the wall is her ghostly, ghastly shadow. Across the floor in the next room, the mildewed wedding cake lies upon the table, and the cobwebs fall like muslin, the spiders crawl and the beetles' tiny feet come and go scritching upon the floor, and the mouse droppings litter the cloth—I see all this and I see a gloomy and unhealthy house and a life that has been hidden from the sun. Far rather to be a man who has done something with his life, albeit the wrong thing, and now lies at peace upon the open marshland under the vast sky!

'What is it, Estella?'

Miss Havisham is watching me. Has she noticed the conflicting expressions upon my face?

'I …' I begin, but trail off.

'You what?' Her curiosity is piqued now, and I know the moment will not be allowed to pass by unheeded.

'Do you not think it is time—and a good idea—that you told me—told me—'

'Told you what?'

I put aside my knitting and make a gesture with my hand. 'How you came to be in this situation? You have never explained it fully to me.'

'Aah,' she says. Her gaze returns to the fire. 'But why? Why should I?'

'In London …' I hesitate, choosing my words. 'In London, there may be talk, of my family, my origins, of you, and I would like to know the truth. It may be a good thing if I know the truth.'

'Perhaps.' She remains staring into the fire.

I sigh and pick up my knitting. It does not seem I am going to get any answers today. I have resumed twisting the wool around my finger when she says, 'It is simple, Estella.'

She turns to glance at me. 'A man said he loved me, *adored* me, and would cherish me for ever … And I loved him. I loved him with all my heart, with that love that has no reason, no rhyme, no explanation, only that it is here!'—she bangs her fist upon her chest—'and all for naught. For he was lying. *Lying*,' she hisses. 'He did not love me at all.'

'Why—?'

'Why!' She turns to me again, her face distorted with hatred.

'Why did he do that to you?'

She moans as if it is painful to continue. 'I had a brother,' she tells me, 'a half-brother who, I know not for what reason—perhaps it was because my father left the bulk of his estate to me, perhaps it was because my father loved me more? Be that as it may, he despised me. He could not keep a shilling upon himself but that he would spend it. He moved amongst thieves and forgers and con men, and inevitably fell in with one such man—the man who broke my heart. And between the two they concocted a scheme to get my money. *My money*, which I had meticulously looked after. Before my marriage, I was persuaded to buy the *brewery*'—she flung out her arm in its direction—'which my half-brother had inherited. Once the funds were safely deposited into his bank account, the man—the man I loved—wrote me a letter telling me he would not be present at our wedding. He gave no reason. The letter was short and to the point. It was only later that I found out—Mr Jaggers found out—who and what he was. May he burn in hell.'

'Do you still have the letter?'

'What? The letter? Of course not. Why would I keep it? I threw it into the fire.' Miss Havisham's stick knocks agitatedly upon the floor. 'There now, dear child, I am tired,' she says. 'Will you please leave me?'

I stand to go and, on an impulse, put my arms around her neck. She smells of dust and old things.

'What is it?' she asks. 'Why this show of affection?'

'What do you know of my mother?'

'Estella,' she rebukes me gently.

'Please tell me.'

'I have told you since you were little. I know nothing of your background. Jaggers is the one to ask. Surely you know this already? Surely you remember that he brought you here all those years ago?'

13

It is decided that in due course I am to take up lodgings with a Mrs Brandley and her daughter in Richmond, Surrey. Miss Havisham informs me that Mrs Brandley is an old acquaintance and a lady of some station, but being a widow with a daughter only a few years older than I am, is not averse to the extra income my lodgings will provide. Mother and daughter are in a good position, and visit, and are visited by, numbers of people, Miss H says. The right people. My understanding of the whole arrangement is that they are as necessary to me as I am to them.

Miss H tells me that Pip will meet my coach and accompany me to Richmond. I need only write to tell him. I duly send him a brief note. *I am to arrive in London on Wednesday by the midday coach. Miss H tells me that you will meet me. In any event, she has that impression. She sends you her regards. Yours, Estella.*

When I first arrived back from France, I was loath to leave Miss H and Satis House, and most of all reluctant to leave the marshes, their magic, and the salt air that I sometimes imagined was borne on the wind. But my heart has been heavy, weighted with remembrances of *him*! And not a day goes past when I do not recall his face and his passionate kiss and his laughing eyes, and it is as much as I can do not to cry out in anguish. With every passing day, I have a real terror that I may find myself joining Miss H on her silent night-time prowls, for that is when I dwell on my situation, when my mind is not occupied and sleep eludes me.

I am ready for something fresh and different. In any event, my presence at home is a constant reminder to Miss H that her plans are not proceeding. Recently, I knocked at her door prior to entering and she did not even glance up at me nor greet me, but remained staring fixedly into the fire. Later in the day, the expected letter from Mrs Brandley arrived, confirming the arrangements, and the change in Miss H was remarkable. She was at once energised and full of orders, and practically skipping around the room, although that did not last long.

'You are to take the emerald necklace, Estella,' she reminds me. 'Has it been packed?'

'Naturally.'

'And the floral brooch with the diamond centrepiece?'

I nod.

'What about the amethysts? Have you got them? Bring me my jewellery box, Estella.'

I dutifully bring Miss H her jewellery box, and she goes through the jewels once again until she is satisfied that every precious stone that I can possibly make use of—not that I will, for I do not care two hoots about them—has been given to me.

'There,' she says, closing the lid. 'I believe you are set. When is your coach?' she asks me for the umpteenth time.

'Early,' I tell her. 'Before you are up, which is why I will bid you farewell this evening.'

That is not strictly correct, for Miss H is always up. I have never seen her sleeping. But I do not intend to disturb her so early in the morning.

'Hmm,' she says distractedly, as if she is already imagining me gone, and I know better than to ask if she will miss me.

'I will write,' I tell her.

'Hmm,' she says again, and returns to staring into the flames.

Our farewell is in much the same vein, only with the added urge to remember to *break their hearts*, and I have no desire to detail it here. Suffice to say, I am concerned that I will not see her again, that she will not last the winter, although I know my reception in London and my activities there will be of great interest to her and will keep her intrigued, if not in her own life, then in mine. I must therefore revert to the habit I developed in France, of making a routine out of writing to her.

*

By the time I reach London, I have put the misery of leaving Miss H and the landscape behind me and am in much better spirits.

The misery of *his* disappearance never leaves me, but I keep a firm lid on it. I keep a steady hold on my emotions and what might have been, but that does not mean I do not spend a great deal of time dwelling on him. My latest thought is that perhaps the man is married? This would explain his speedy departure. Oh, please, let it not be so!

Here is Pip, come to meet me! As the coach draws to a halt, I catch a glimpse of him hovering impatiently and raise my hand in greeting and smile. The effect on him is instantaneous, breaking out as he does into a happy grin.

It has been a while since I have seen him. The last time was when he came to pay his respects on my return from France and was a welcome distraction. I have almost forgotten how charming and sweet-natured he is, and how pretty his eyes, which linger on my own for altogether too long a time. Poor boy, will he never learn?

We stand in the inn yard while I point out my luggage to him.

'Where is it that we are going?' he asks, once it has all been assembled.

'I am going to Richmond, Surrey,' I say. '*Not* Richmond, Yorkshire. The distance is ten miles, Miss H tells me, and I am to have a carriage, and you are to take me.'

'How *is* Miss Havisham?'

I nod. 'Frail,' I say.

'This is my purse,' I tell him, handing it over and changing the subject because I have no wish to discuss Miss H at length. She makes for miserable subject matter. 'And you are to pay the costs out of it.

'Oh, but you must,' I insist when Pip looks as if he is going to refuse it. 'We must do what we are instructed, you and I, we have no choice. We are not free to follow our own whims.'

From the hopeful expression on his face, I realise that he thinks there is an inner meaning to my words, and that he remains convinced we are fated to be together. I must do better to guard my tongue.

He says that he will send for a carriage and asks if I would like to rest in the meantime, and I tell him this is the arrangement: I am to drink tea and he is to take care of me. I wind my arm through his while he instructs a waiter to show us a private sitting room, and I can tell by his confident tone that my arm in his gives him a great deal of pleasure.

The waiter and the premises are sadly lacking, although not in the same respects, and, after some to-ing and fro-ing, we finish up in an overlarge and cold room with no fire in the grate, only a scorched page of a copy book. The air smells as if the room might once have been a stable and then became a place for making soup-stock. Still, we are here and have to make the best of it.

'Where are you going to in Richmond?' Pip asks, after he draws out a chair for me and we sit alongside one another.

'I am to live with a lady there, at great expense, who has the power—or says she has—of introducing me to the right people, of showing me to people, and of showing people to me.' I proceed to take off my gloves and lay them on the table.

'I suppose you will be pleased by the change, by the admiration?'

'Pleased? The admiration? To be honest, I do not care.'

'You do not care?' He knits his brow. 'Why do you speak of yourself as if you were someone else?'

'How do you come to know how I speak of others? Come, come,' I say. I am feeling wicked. 'You must not expect me to take lessons from *you*. I must and will talk in my own way. How are you getting along with Mr Pocket?'

'I live contentedly there,' he begins. 'At least I ...' He trails off and looks mournful.

'At least you ...?'

'Live as contentedly as I could live, anywhere, away from you.'

'Oh, you silly boy, Pip. Do not talk nonsense. Your friend, Mr Matthew, I believe, is superior to the rest of his family?'

'Very superior indeed. He is nobody's enemy—'

'Don't add but his own,' I put in, 'for I hate that type of man. But he really is disinterested and above small jealousy and spite, I have heard?'

'I have every reason to assure you that is the case.'

'You have not every reason to say so of the rest of his family,' I tell Pip, nodding. 'You will remember what Raymond, Sarah, Camilla and Georgiana are like, I trust? You surely remember that time when you came to visit and they were in attendance and how put out they were by your presence? And the last time you visited, when

Sarah Pocket behaved as if she had swallowed a lemon. Oh dear, you can scarcely comprehend the hatred these people feel for you.'

'They do me no harm, I hope?'

I laugh heartily. It is as much as I can do to contain my amusement. If only he knew.

'I hope, dear Estella, that you would not be entertained if they did me any harm?'

When he is worried, a little crease appears between his brows, as it does now. It is truly endearing.

'No, you may rest assured on that subject. I laugh so much because they fail to impress either Miss H or me. Oh, if you only saw—well, you have seen it once, I believe?—the torment they undergo.' And I laugh again.

'They have no idea,' I tell Pip. 'And what pleasure it gives me when they are made ridiculous. You have some inkling of my situation, but you were not brought up in that odd environment from a baby—I was. Do well to remember that. You did not have your wits honed by their conspiring against you under a mask of sympathy and false friendship and all that is soft and charming. You did not experience opening your baby eyes bit by bit to the discovery of a woman who remembers and stores every little incident, who calculates day and night how to wreak revenge on the world—I did.'

Pip's face tells me I have said too much. 'Two things I can tell you,' I say to him, trying to make amends. 'These people will not damage your standing with Miss H—never in a hundred years, never in any particular, great or small—and secondly, I am grateful to you as the cause of their petty-mindedness and meanness, for if it were not you, it would be *me* they would be fixated upon, and there is my hand upon it.'

I give him my hand in play, and he holds it and puts it to his lips, gazing at me with his pretty eyes.

'You ridiculous boy,' I say, 'will you never take warning. Or do you kiss my hand in the spirit in which I once let you kiss my cheek?' I smile. 'Do you remember?'

'How could I forget?' He pauses, his eyes still on mine. 'May I kiss your cheek again?'

I shake my head, despairing of him. 'If you want to.'

He leans across and touches his lips to my cheek as I keep my face motionless. And, oh! I cannot help but think of that other man who touched his lips to my skin.

'Now,' I say, 'remember we are to have tea, and then you must take me to Richmond.'

I remind him of this and of what must be done, to not only steer him back to the present, but to distract myself.

Pip rings for tea, then, and it arrives eventually, after a number of other appliances and bits and pieces of crockery and of cutlery, some of which relate to tea and some of which do not, are brought to the table, and are at first an amusement, and then by degrees an irritation.

The tea is dreadful, as I have expected—nothing more than twigs in hot water—and the bill abnormally large judging by the amount I see Pip part with. However, at length it is paid, and with some relief we board our post-coach and are driven away.

We trundle down grim and unfamiliar streets. It is all strange to me, shadowy and sombre in the fading light. After the freshness of the country, the highways are greasy and grimy, and Euston Road throngs with horse traffic. There are piles of squalid buildings, clustered rooftops and chimneys vomiting forth black smoke. Their rank smell catches in the back of my throat and I wonder why anyone would choose to live in the city. We pass a dark and forbidding-looking establishment, much stained by the elements and here and there hung with fetters and chains, outside which a number of dismal and dreary-looking people are waiting, it appears, to be let through the gates.

'What place is this?' I ask.

Pip ducks his head to look out of the window. 'Newgate Prison,' he tells me.

'Poor wretches,' I say.

'Mr Jaggers,' he says, 'has the reputation of being more in the secrets of that dismal place than any man in London.'

'He is more in the secrets of every place, I should think,' I say in a low voice.

'You are accustomed to seeing him often?'

'Ever since I can remember, I have been accustomed to seeing him at uncertain intervals. But he is a singular man, and I know him no better now than I ever did. What is your experience with him? Do you get along?'

'It took me a long while to adjust to his distrustful manner, but that accomplished, we do very well.'

'Are you friends?'

'I have dined with him at his house.'

'I fancy it must be a curious place,' I say, and I cannot help the shiver that crosses my body in thinking of the type of dwelling Mr Jaggers must inhabit.

We arrive into a sudden glare of gas, alight and alive, animating the air, and when we are out of it something from my past hovers in the back of my mind, something concerning the gas lamps in the street, but I cannot recall what it is.

Pip, too, is quiet, as if the incident reminds him of a forgotten memory as well. Some fragment from the forge, perhaps? I want to ask what it is, but I think perhaps it is best left alone. Some memories are too painful and best not brought up.

We begin, then, to discuss the neighbourhoods, and what areas of London lie along our route. I tell Pip the great city is new to me for I have never left our village, only when I journeyed to France, and even then I did not go to London.

'Does Mr Jaggers have any charge of you while you remain here?' Pip asks.

'God forbid!' I exclaim and by the tug of his mouth I can see my response amuses him.

When we reach Hammersmith, Pip points in the general direction of where he currently lives with Mr Matthew Pocket's family. 'It is no great distance from Richmond, Estella, and I hope that I will see you sometimes.'

'Oh, yes. You are to see me. You are to come when you think proper. You are to be mentioned to the Brandley family. Indeed, you are already mentioned.'

I go on to tell him the little I know about Mrs Brandley and her daughter, and he says, 'I wonder Miss Havisham could bear to part with you so soon after your arrival.'

'It is all part of her grand plan for me, Pip,' I say.

I sigh. He does not seem to understand that Miss H has plans, no matter how many times I mention it.

'I am to write to her and keep her informed, and regularly return to Satis House to see her and report on how I am proceeding. I and the jewels, for they are nearly all mine now.'

'You know that when and if you go to Miss Havisham to see her, I would be only too happy to accompany you. It would be my pleasure. You need only to let me know.'

'I will,' I say. 'And thank you for offering.'

We arrive at last in Richmond, and at my destination: a staid old house, which is not without its charms, opposite the Green. The fence of the house is draped in a climbing rose, and the grounds are well-cared for. A number of larches, now dropping their leaves, form a guard along the perimeter with the neighbouring house and a bird bath occupies centre stage of the sprawling lawn. There are cannas and lilies and dahlias in a garden bed although the approach of winter has them all looking unkempt and scraggly.

Pip knocks upon the front door and two maids attired in cherry-red uniforms come fluttering and tripping out to receive us as if my arrival is a great event. My luggage is soon brought in and absorbed into the house. Matilda, one of the maids, informs us that Mrs Brandley and her daughter send their sincerest apologies. They have been unavoidably detained, but hope to meet me for dinner.

I give Pip my hand at the door and say goodnight, for it is late and I believe we are both tired; I am certainly weary. He takes my hand, but kisses it with such a woebegone expression that after he has departed and the door is closed behind him, I fervently wish that he does not love me so.

Soon after I have been shown my room and my luggage brought up, Matilda appears at my door to help me dress for dinner. I am in the habit of managing on my own, but having a maid to assist me is expected and I will soon adapt. In any event, though, I tell Matilda the journey has wearied me, to send for a tray of tea if she would, and to give my apologies to the ladies for my absence at dinner.

'Would you like me to help you dress for bed, then, Miss Havisham?' she asks.

'On this occasion, that will not be necessary, Matilda, thank you,' I say. 'I am quite used to managing on my own.'

She looks crestfallen at this news, as if she has waited all day for me with much anticipation, and is now being denied the delight of not only serving me, but of seeing the dresses and so on that are in my trunks.

'Well,' I say, reneging, 'if you really would like to …? The dresses in the first trunk'—I indicate the largest of them—'do need airing. They can be taken out and put away.'

She smiles; she cannot hide her pleasure.

I sit in the little sitting room and watch her through the open door. She is as fair as I am dark. Her long hair is plaited and tied up behind her head, and she has a pert little nose and is attractive in her own way. She is around my own age, I think. She appears well-trained but habitually bites her fingernails. Which does not fail to bring back unwelcome memories.

When her task is completed, I mention the nail-biting to her, and she blushes and hides her hands behind her back. 'Sorry, miss,' she says.

'Never mind, we will work on it together,' I say. She seems both doubtful and pleased, and we part on good terms.

14

I meet the Brandleys the following morning at breakfast. Mrs Brandley's surprise that I did not come down to greet them when they arrived home, and her regret at not meeting either Pip or myself the evening before, are so sincere and so well intended that I fear I may not have set the best example. It is clear she was most disappointed. I explain that the journey from the marshlands was long and wearying, that we were overtired by the day's events, and she seems to accept my explanation. I can see that I will have to try harder to make up for my lapse in manners.

Mrs Brandley is Kitty, and her daughter, Daisy, but suffice to say I do not intend to address them as such. Miss H made it clear to me before my departure that the arrangement between us is not that we will become lifelong friends, but rather that we will be of some use to one another. Miss H said that I am on my way up and, in all likelihood, they are on their way down. Callous of her, but I have come to expect such behaviour.

Daisy seems too sweet a name for someone who looks as old as her mother looks young. Mrs Brandley is vivacious and her complexion fresh and pink, while her daughter wears glasses, her eyes are sunken in their sockets and her skin is sallow. Poor girl. I wonder what her history is, and if her father was of some Eastern extract, and I do learn later that indeed he was. Sadly, he died when his daughter was but an infant, so we have that in common, both of us being fatherless. Although, for all I know, my father could be alive.

I learn that Mrs Brandley is always up for frivolity, eager to accept invitations to balls, parties, plays, operas and the like, while her daughter remains pious and serious, and all too often pleads a headache. The mother is keen for the daughter to marry, that much is clear, but I rather think it will be the other way around, that Mrs Brandley will marry again before her daughter. I cannot imagine that anyone would want to marry Miss Brandley.

My bedroom is spacious. It is upstairs in the front of the house and looks out over the garden. This, I later come to appreciate, has the advantage of enabling me to see who is calling to pay their respects and, if necessary—I hate to admit it—to feign illness. The room has bay windows and a window seat with a pretty floral cover, the material of which is echoed in the cloth that covers my bedside table. Several prints of hand-drawn flowers—petunias, bluebells, hydrangeas—hang from the walls, and my furnishings are perfectly charming. Adjoining my bedroom is a small sitting room for my use only, with rose-pink chintz-covered chairs and a Persian rug. Again, another agreeable benefit. Mother and daughter's rooms are further back along the passage, but neither has the privileges nor the outlook that I do. My quarters, in all likelihood, have been occupied by Mrs Brandley until recently and she has given them up for me. Understandable, since it is in her interests that I am comfortable and happy.

I am to share Matilda, my maid, with Miss Brandley, but I understand that I have first call upon her if the need arises. Mrs Brandley, of course, has her own maid. There is also a cook, a housekeeper and a gardener.

In the morning, breakfast takes rather longer than what I expected as the Brandleys and I have much to talk about. They know, of course, about Pip, Miss H having already written to inform Mrs Brandley that he will be a regular visitor.

'Is it impudent of me to ask whether Mr Pirrip is one of your suitors, Miss Havisham?' Mrs Brandley ventures.

I shake my head. 'Not for want of wishing on his part though,' I tell her. 'I have known him since we were children, and I think of him as a sibling more than anything else.'

Mrs Brandley asks me what I have planned for the day, and when I ask if it is convenient for Matilda to unpack the rest of my belongings, she assures me it is.

'I have accepted an invitation to cards later this afternoon on your behalf,' she says. 'Do say you can come? The Wrights are old and firm friends and are anxious to meet you.'

'That would be delightful,' I say. 'And now, if you will excuse me?' I push back my chair. 'I will go up and give Matilda instructions. Lunch is at noon, would that be correct?'

'It is indeed,' Mrs Brandley says.

*

What with the unpacking of my trunks and the putting away of my things, there is not a great deal of time left to work on Matilda's nail-biting habit. I do, however, discover that the horse-and-carriage driver for our neighbour has his eye on her, and she on him. I go out of the room to fetch a pair of scissors from the kitchen—strictly against protocol, but why should I not, I am not engaged in the physical act of unpacking—and when I return Matilda is standing at the window staring out.

I sneak up on her and give her a little start—

'Oh, miss!' She puts her hand to her throat.

Outside in the street, a man on a horse is paused, looking intently up towards my window. He is dressed in rough-looking clothes, but has a kindly and attractive face. When I make an appearance, he immediately continues about his business.

'Who is he?' I ask.

Matilda blushes. 'Albert, miss,' she tells me. 'He is employed by Dr Oliver, our neighbour.'

'I see,' I say. 'And do you like him?'

'Yes, miss.'

'Very much or a little?'

'Very much.' She blushes again.

'We will have to work on those nails, then, Matilda. For I do not believe a ring would look pretty upon your hands in their current state. Hold them out,' I instruct.

She does so. Several of her nails are bitten down to the quick and the skin is ragged around the edges.

'Tomorrow morning,' I say, 'after breakfast, let us polish them and see how you fare with that. It may be enough to stop you. Then again,' I threaten in a mock-authoritarian voice, 'it may not be and we will have to resort to other more severe measures.'

Matilda grins at me impishly.

*

Mrs Brandley and I set off at around three for the Wrights. As I suspected might be the case, Miss Brandley does not accompany us.

Mrs Brandley advised me at lunch that the house has no transport as such, but that she has an arrangement with Dr Oliver, the neighbour, provided she notifies him in good time. Once a medical doctor, he is now an elderly widower who lives a secluded life, she told me. He is not often out and about and, from the time that the Brandleys took up residence, some six months ago I understand, he kindly told her that his horses, carriage and his driver, Albert, were at her disposal.

It is a crisp autumn day and Mrs Brandley and I share a knee rug. If it were not for her, I would beg Albert to stop so I can collect the gloriously coloured leaves that drift from the trees and swirl to the ground, but, as it is, I have a hard time concentrating on anything, let alone making any observations of Matilda's sweetheart, since my host keeps up a continuous chatter.

'Mr and Mrs Wright and Miss Havisham and I are old acquaintances,' she begins, soon after we set off. 'The Wrights have an extensive property outside Richmond known as Wright House, with tenanted land. Mr Wright inherited Wright House when he was but eighteen, and Mrs Wright has money of her own, so between the two of them they do exceedingly well. They have a daughter, Eliza, who is roughly Daisy's age. Eliza is pretty and talented and plays the piano, sketches and sings and there is nothing, it seems, that she cannot do.' I detect a note of jealousy here, but say nothing.

Mrs Brandley pauses to draw breath—her cheeks are rosy from speaking—and pats the rug. 'Forgive me, I have been talking without pause. What do you excel at, Miss Havisham? Do you play an instrument?'

'Sadly, no,' I say. 'I knit and embroider and do modestly well at both, but cards, as it happens, are my forte—'

'Cards!' Mrs Brandley says. 'Excellent. I do look forward to a round of whist with you.

'I have to tell you, my dear,' she begins again on what I assume is a new topic, 'that Daisy has struggled to find common ground with Eliza and I was dearly hoping that my daughter would accompany us this afternoon so she could learn a thing or two from you.'

'Oh, Mrs Brandley, you give me credit where none yet is due. I do not know that I will fare any better.'

'I am sure you will, my dear,' she tells me, 'you have such a charming way about you that the Wrights are all bound to be totally captivated.'

I laugh. 'I would not put money on it, but then I am not a gambling person—'

'No, of course, not,' she interrupts. 'We must not forget—' And here she lays her index finger across her lips.

'Tell me,' she says, whispering, 'is she, is Amelia, unchanged in this respect? Has she come out of it?'

'No,' I say. 'Miss Havisham remains the same.'

'How sad,' Mrs Brandley says.

'Quite,' I agree.

'What are the subject matters that interest Miss Brandley?' I enquire in an attempt to change the subject. 'Is she a reader, does she embroider, or play a musical instrument?'

'Reading!' Mrs Brandley says emphatically. 'This is the thing that has her attention. She reads copiously and widely, and gives herself headaches. I do believe she was up most of the night—' She breaks off.

'Oh, my!' she gazes about. 'We are arrived. Here is the avenue and these are the willows lining it. They are quite something when they are awash with greenery, my dear. Not so pretty now, of course, but do look.'

I murmur something appropriate to Mrs Brandley in appreciation, for we have already begun to meander down the driveway that is bordered by the willows. Many of the leaves are yellow, and a number of the trees have already lost their finery, but they do seem to curtsey before us as if we are royalty.

In the distance, set atop a substantial flat mound, is a large and considerable building made of stone and with mullioned windows, the panes of which twinkle in the afternoon light. The sun catches the lawns of bright green that tumble from the sandstone patio all the way down to the miniature lake at the bottom of the property, and the lake is surrounded by a garden wherein some pastel rose petals still bloom. It is altogether breathtaking.

While our carriage makes its way along the driveway, we see a horse and rider disappearing into the woodlands at the back of the property. His shirtsleeves are billowing and he rides at such a hefty gallop that he is hunched forward in the saddle as if he were Paul Revere himself. Mrs Brandley turns to me. 'Do you ride, Miss Havisham?'

'I do,' I say. 'I learnt in France.'

'Of course,' she says. 'I recall Amelia telling me now that you spent some years in France. I wonder at the French though, do you find that they are—'

I never do discover what the French are—it is no doubt uncomplimentary; it is no secret that the English despise the French—for Mrs Brandley breaks off again, and says, 'Here we are!'

We have arrived at the entrance. The Italians call it a *portico* and I like the word. It has such a distinctive sound to it. A manservant emerges to help us alight and lead us inside.

Mr and Mrs Wright and their daughter are waiting to welcome us in the library. The room is well furnished, but it is not ostentatious, one entire wall—floor to ceiling—being composed of shelving and books. Miss Brandley would be in her element and I wonder why she did not accompany us. The library has been laid out with card tables, and the other guests, a Mr and Mrs Hathaway, who I understand live close by, are in attendance.

'How are you enjoying your return to England, Miss Havisham?' Miss Wright asks, hovering at my shoulder.

'It is good to be home,' I say, turning to her. 'It is also good not to have to think overmuch about what I say and how I say it.'

'*Oui*,' she says, and smiles.

Miss Wright seems both delightful and delighted by my company. She is becoming. Her blue eyes remind me of Pip's, but whereas his are all too often serious, hers are alive with merriment. Curly fair hair frames her radiant face and she is slenderly built, but does not appear weak in disposition. I take to her straight away, in that incomprehensible manner that one is sometimes attracted to another without any foreknowledge, and we fall to talking about France and the French. She visited Paris the year before and is eager to tell me all she knows and to compare recollections.

'Will you be attending the ball at Waverley Manor, Miss Havisham?' Miss Wright asks me as we settle into our card game and she shuffles the deck. 'It is still some time away but—'

'My dear child,' her mother says, interrupting. 'Miss Havisham only arrived yesterday. Do give her a chance to settle in.'

Miss Wright glances at her mother. 'Sorry, Mama. But, Miss Havisham, if you haven't an invitation, I will ensure you receive one. The Waverleys hold a ball every year and it is quite the occasion.'

I thank her for her concern, and Miss Wright deals and we proceed to play. The afternoon passes pleasantly enough, though I have to admit I am out of practice at being social for so long a period. We are served light snacks and refreshments around five. I have settled myself opposite Mrs Hathaway and taken up a cucumber sandwich when, at my elbow, Miss Wright says, 'Would you like a tour of the grounds, Miss Havisham?'

'That is kind of you,' I say, putting my sandwich on my plate. 'I would love to.' The fresh air will do me good, I think, and go some way towards reviving my flagging spirits.

*

Outside, the light is fading. A golden glow lies over the land and the lake at the bottom of the property shimmers in the last of the sun. It is a fetching vista. If this outlook were mine, I would want for nothing, although I have to admit I would pine for the marshes.

'Let us go down to the garden to begin with,' Miss Wright says. 'And let us link arms,' she suggests, extending her arm to me, 'as the grass can be uneven.'

I remark upon the golden lining of the clouds and the twilight that softens everything in its path, and Miss Wright says the grounds are indeed lovely and she is fortunate.

'I will be sad when I leave.'

'When you leave?' I glance at her. 'What do you mean?'

She colours. 'Forgive me, I have spoken out of turn. I am to marry James Waverley in the near future. We have been promised one to another.'

'Indeed? And how do you feel about this match?'

'It would make me happy. I am fortunate in that he is an admirable man.'

'How is it that you and Mr Waverley are acquaintances?' I ask.

'James and I have known each other since we were'—she breaks off to indicate a lowish height with her gloved hand—'so high. Our parents are old acquaintances.'

Miss Wright pauses. 'Do you have a friend like that, Miss Estella? That you know practically as well as you know yourself?'

'I know someone whom I have known from when we were children, but I do not know that I can say with certainty that I know him as well as I know myself.'

'It is a man?'

'Yes.' I glance at her. 'You sound surprised?'

'It is uncommon, that is all—'

'My upbringing was uncommon.'

'I see. I have heard something of your background from Mrs Brandley. Then you do not have a lady friend?'

'No, but I am anxious to make one.'

Miss Wright glances at me again. 'I would deem it an honour to be your friend, if you would like to be mine?'

'That would please me greatly,' I say, 'but are you certain? Surely you have many friends and even more acquaintances?'

'Oh, I do! But I have few intimates. To be absolutely candid, Miss Havisham, I am easily bored by women my own age.'

'Then there is nothing I would like better,' I tell her. Indeed, I do already feel a kinship with the lady at my side.

'Then you must call me Eliza. And may I call you Estella?'

'Of course! I would be delighted.'

We have come through the garden and along the path that radiates from the little lake and reached the lake's edge. The late afternoon light is reflected in the water, turning it into a cloth of silver at our feet, and I think about the marshes and about how at this time of the day the little birds would fly up from my feet, the grasses would be rustling and the sky would be sluiced in pastels.

And then I am aware of Miss Wright—Eliza—gazing at me, for we have both fallen silent.

'Penny for your thoughts?' we say at the same time and Eliza smiles, dimpling her cheeks.

'Tell me about your Mr Waverley,' I suggest.

'James?' Her blue eyes dance with pleasure as she glances at me. 'He is the most agreeable companion I know. He manages somehow to be eternally grateful to not only be alive, but for each day and, in truth, his enthusiasm sometimes wears me out.' She laughs. 'And your friend? Tell me about him.'

'Pip?' I shake my head 'There is not a great deal to tell. He is handsome and kind, but he is also more than half in love with me, which is a trial.'

'Oh? Then you are not in love with him?'

'Not at all. I am of the opinion that surely there is more to life than simply falling in love and getting married.'

Eliza laughs. 'What do you propose, Estella? It's my view that we do not have much choice.'

'You are right that we do not have a choice, but I intend to at least live a little before I marry.'

'I see.' My companion glances at me. 'What would you say if I tell you that I have tried that and been unsuccessful?'

'How so?' My interest is piqued.

'I tried to convince Papa that I could help him with the running of the estate, but both he and Mama are adamantly against it. I have been told it does not befit my position.'

'That is indeed a shame!'

'I am fortunate that James does not feel the same way. He intends for me to become involved in certain aspects of Waverley Manor such as housing for the tenants, and I am keenly anticipating the challenge.'

She pauses. She turns to consider me.

'What is it?'

'I am thinking,' she says. 'James has a brother, an adopted brother, Laurence. Captain Laurence Waverley is a soldier in the Dragoon Guards and'—she pauses to give her words weight—'devilishly dashing. I would love to introduce you, if I may?'

'Certainly,' I say. 'There will be no harm in an introduction, will there?'

'Harm?' She laughs. 'That is for you to decide once you have met him!'

'If he is'—I pause as Eliza did—'*devilishly dashing*, why is he not yet betrothed?'

'Between you and me, he is fussy. He says he is seeking someone with *joie de vivre* and he has not yet found her.' Eliza glances at me. 'I believe you have spirit, Estella. I believe this is something you have been blessed with.'

'Is that right?' I raise my eyebrows with amusement.

She nods. 'I am serious,' she says. 'And well pleased. And now we should return to the house or Mama will have something to say about me keeping you out in the cold.'

I nod, and we turn and link arms once again.

'Do you think that if you were in love, you would feel differently about *living a little* before you marry?' she asks as we walk. 'Forgive me, but you are not in love, are you?'

'In all honesty, I do not know if I would feel differently, but perhaps there is some truth in that,' I say, sidestepping the question of whether I am in love. Living with Miss Havisham for so long taught me to be circumspect and I am not going to admit to anything, least of all a love affair with an artist!

I think of the young lady at my side and how she knows with certainty where her life is headed. And I think of Pip, and of my artist friend, and of Miss Havisham and how she wants me to *break their hearts*.

Surely she does not mean me to go on breaking their hearts forever? Surely there must come a time when I can say *Enough!*

And then, what is it I really want?

The truth is, I do not know. The truth is, I am confused. With my upbringing, is it any wonder?

15

The invitation, the first of many, arrives in the post at lunchtime the following day and is brought up to me on a silver platter. *Lord and Lady Waverley request the pleasure of the company of Miss Estella Havisham at the annual Waverley Manor Ball*, etc.

It is a couple of months hence, in November, and I reply favourably to it, then put it to one side, although it does cross my mind to wonder if Pip is going. I should find out.

The weather is unusually warm for this time of the year, and I take the opportunity of a walk around the Green across from the house before dinner.

The air is cooler there—all that greenery and shade, perhaps—but it is invigorating. The grounds are pretty just now with the colours of autumn, and it seems I cannot go five steps without picking up yet another rust or ruby-coloured leaf until I have made a fan of them.

I am so lost in thought that I do not notice the elderly gentleman under the oaks until I am on the third round of the Green.

Rising from the bench where he has been sitting, he raises his hat and says, 'Good afternoon.'

I stop. 'Good afternoon,' I respond. I hold out my leaves. 'Are they not ever so delightful?'

He nods. He is warmly dressed, considering the current climate, with scarf and buttoned up coat. 'You must be Miss Havisham,' he says.

'I am,' I tell him. 'How did you know?'

'I am Dr Oliver, your neighbour. Mrs Brandley and her daughter have spoken these preceding weeks of little else but your arrival. Would you like to sit down, my child?'

I take a seat on the bench alongside him. 'It is unseasonably warm for this time of the year, would you agree?' I venture.

'It is indeed.' He pats the front of his coat with his gloved hands, perhaps indicating his lungs and his warm attire. 'Sadly, I cannot take any chances. If I am ill again this year, my doctor will not be best pleased.'

'I am sorry to hear that,' I say.

'I believe you have come up from the lowlands, and prior to that you were in Paris?'

'Not quite,' I say, thinking to myself that Mrs Brandley *has* been busy. 'I was in France, not Paris.'

'And now you are being presented to the world?'

'Not quite,' I say again, laughing. 'Merely to Richmond.'

'Ah,' he says, 'but it won't be long before news of your beauty spreads and soon you will be the talk of London town.' He has a head of white hair under his hat and his bright eyes twinkle with amusement.

'You flatter me,' I say, laughing again.

'Tell me,' he says, 'will Miss Brandley be accompanying you on your social outings?'

I shake my head. 'I do not know. I only know that she would far rather stay home and read than be social.'

'She is a singular girl.'

'You have spoken with her?'

'When I can. When I see her. We have sometimes discussed books. I have told her and her mother, mark you, that she is at liberty to borrow from my extensive library, but she seems reticent. I wonder …' He pauses and rubs his chin with the gloved fingers of one hand.

'You would like me to encourage her? Why don't I bring her over?'

He turns to me. 'You read my mind. Would you? I feel that once she has visited, she will not hesitate to come again. She needs only to break the ice.'

I nod. 'Shall we say tomorrow afternoon at three?'

'Splendid,' he tells me.

There is something about this elderly gentleman with his white hair and his sharp mind that inspires me, and I know instinctively that I can trust him.

At dinner, I tell Miss Brandley that I have accepted an invitation on her behalf for both of us to call on Dr Oliver the following afternoon at three.

'You have?' Miss Brandley replies. I cannot make up my mind whether she is annoyed or surprised.

'I met the good doctor in the park this evening and we had quite the discussion. It appears that he would like to show us his library, and would be honoured if we borrowed a book or two, or three. I took the liberty of telling him I thought you would be most pleased.'

Miss Brandley pauses, fork in one hand. A small smile creeps upon her usually serious face. 'Thank you, Miss Havisham,' she says.

'I regret that you were not invited to accompany us, Mrs Brandley,' I say, looking at the older woman. Her daughter bends her head to her meal again, and I wink.

She is quick on the upkeep, Mrs Brandley. She smiles as if she is also in on whatever arrangements I have made to draw her daughter out of her reclusiveness, then remembers there is nothing comical about this and hastily puts her hand before her mouth.

'Yes,' she says. 'It is regrettable, but in fact I must go through my wardrobe and make up my mind what it is I am going to wear to the ball. Have you decided what you are wearing, my dear?' she asks her daughter.

'The ball is two months away, Mama, and I am not sure that I want to go.'

'Oh, Daisy,' her mother says. 'Perhaps Miss Havisham'—she glances across at me—'will help me to change your mind?'

'Perhaps,' Miss Brandley echoes.

*

Before three the next day, Miss Brandley and I make our way over to Dr Oliver's house. The dwelling is old-fashioned and dark and without a woman's touches of prettiness and femininity, but the library makes up for everything.

It is a large room with wall-to-wall books, and skylights that let in the light. In the centre is a heavy wooden table and chairs. A sofa and two comfortable armchairs for reading in sit to one side, and a fire burns merrily in the grate. A jug of coffee, cups and saucers, and a delectable-looking arrangement of petit-fours have been laid out on the table and, as the maidservant has left the room, I take it upon myself to pour the coffee. It also means that while I am thus engaged, Miss Brandley has no option but to converse with Dr Oliver.

They begin, of course, in typical English fashion by discussing the weather and how unpredictable it is at this time of the year. But then Dr Oliver shows a book to my companion and asks if she has read *Oliver Twist*. She shakes her head and pushes her glasses back up her nose. She looks paler than usual and begins to wind the fringe of her shawl anxiously between the fingers of her hand. I do wish there was something I could do to set her at her ease.

Dr Oliver proceeds to tell her a little of *Oliver Twist*, of its themes of good versus evil, poverty and alienation. Of how Oliver forever changed his life by being so bold as to *want more*.

He places the book on the table and pats its cover.

'You are welcome to borrow this one,' he tells her. 'Do you read Dickens, Miss Havisham?' he asks me.

'I have not yet had the pleasure of all of his novels,' I tell him. 'I read so much and so widely in France that I am yet to catch up with what our English writers have been penning.'

'Ah,' he says. '*The Count of Monte Cristo*, Flaubert, Victor Hugo.'

I nod, and smile. 'Among others,' I murmur.

'Voltaire,' Miss Brandley suddenly volunteers, and colours.

'*Candide*? You have read *Candide*?' Dr Oliver asks.

'I have,' she says.

'And tell me, what do you think?'

To my relief, Miss Brandley gives her opinion. It is clearly a subject on which she is informed and, although she stumbles a little in the airing of her views, I am gratified to see her confidence blooming. It is strange how this small thing does my heart good.

I leave them and wander over to the far corner of the library where I distract myself by picking out titles and studying their contents. Some of the books are ancient, their covers moth-eaten, some are French. A great number are medical tomes. These are the ones that interest me. I find the human body and how it all works in symmetry quite enthralling, and I have not forgotten where my interest all began: with the little mouse on the table in the kitchen at Satis House. In the background, the low murmur of the conversation of my companions continues and I allow myself to read page after page on the subject of an ailment known as *phossy jaw*. In short, workers (mostly young girls) employed as matchmakers develop abscesses in their mouths from working with phosphorus. This often leads to facial disfigurement and sometimes brain damage, for the abscess creeps up into the head, and it crosses my mind that I have seen girls with deformed jaws such as this in the street. I am in wonder at their bravery, for the journal reports the condition is unbearably painful.

Sometime later, the maid returns with a tray to pick up the coffee cups and what remains of the little cakes, and I realise it is dusk, and that we should take our leave.

The afternoon has gone better than I expected, and I am pleased. As for Miss Brandley, it appears to have done her the world of good for she is vivacious at dinner, and even volunteers an opinion or two, and her mother looks at me across the table with grateful eyes.

*

Miss Brandley is late for breakfast in the morning, but it is an opportunity for her mother and me to talk alone. Mrs Brandley bends low to whisper across the table.

'In your opinion, Miss Havisham, what would be the harm of us nurturing Daisy's friendship with Dr Oliver?'

I bend low to whisper back. 'You are thinking of a match between Dr Oliver and Daisy?'

She nods. 'I am.'

'You are not keen on Dr Oliver yourself?'

She shakes her head. 'I have been tempted, but the man is too staid, too reticent. We would get on one another's nerves after a time.'

'The doctor is old enough to be Daisy's grandfather,' I venture. 'If I may say so?'

'I am aware of that,' she says, 'but their minds seem to be so compatible. Who am I to stand in their way?'

'Has Daisy indicated that she is romantically interested in Dr Oliver?'

Mrs Brandley shakes her head. 'Sadly, she does not appear to have a romantic bone in her body.'

'Well,' I begin, but I am forced to break off, for a movement over my shoulder tells me it is no longer safe to continue our conversation. It is as well, for Miss Brandley pulls out a chair opposite me.

Her mother has the foresight to begin a conversation about expected showers later in the day and we are brought back to safe waters.

I write to Miss Havisham after breakfast and tell her in great detail of my visit to the Wrights, of Eliza, of the forthcoming ball, and of Dr Oliver, our neighbour, and my little attempts at matchmaking. The latter will amuse her, if nothing else. And then I write to Pip to ask if he is going to the Waverley ball. Although the ball is not for some time, it will be of comfort if I know someone else who is attending apart from the Wright family, the Hathaways and Mrs Brandley. Although, admittedly, I will soon be acquainted with Eliza's James and be introduced to his brother, the Captain. I wonder about Captain Waverley. Certainly, my interest is piqued. I have had little to do with soldiers and soldiering, this is true, but from what I have heard they are not well off financially. *Estella,* I think, *you* are *being hypocritical! How can you dismiss Captain Waverley on the grounds of impoverishment and yet want to become involved with a penniless artist?!*

The difference is that I am more than half in love with my artist. The difference is who said anything about *marrying* him? And I return to my pet topic, of speculating where he lives in London. How I can find him.

Matilda knocks at my door. She wants to show me her nails. She has not bitten them since we polished them and is proud of the fact. It is a welcome distraction. I am so relieved, for I could not have brought myself to resort to the soap.

Another welcome distraction arrives in the early afternoon. A letter from Eliza, hand-delivered by a messenger apparently waiting at the back door for an answer.

Estella, I trust you are well. Would you like to ride this afternoon? Please say you would, for the weather is perfect for the moment. If you would like to, please give your answer to the bearer of this letter and I will send a chaise-cart to fetch you at two. Yours, Eliza.

Thank you! I would love to, I scrawl on the bottom of the letter and, giving it to Matilda, I ask her to return it to the man waiting downstairs.

*

Eliza is waiting for me when I arrive at Wright House, and comes out to meet the chaise-cart. Her curly fair hair is tucked up underneath a riding hat adorned with a blue ribbon. She embraces me warmly and tells me the horses are saddled and ready to go, if it suits me.

'Oh, it does,' I say, 'let's not waste this glorious weather.'

'I have taken the precaution of giving you Dora,' Eliza tells me as we walk around to the stables at the back of the property. 'Dora is my horse from days gone by. She is reliable and, dare I say it, a plodder!'

'And what will you ride? Wait, let me guess. I predict that you will be upon some feisty stallion. Am I right?'

'Absolutely. Bolt. Named for his tendency to, er, bolt.'

We smile at one another.

The groom is waiting with the horses standing alongside one another and the contrast between the two animals could not be greater. Bolt, his black sheened coat rippling, and the gentle but old brown lady, Dora, at his side.

We mount our horses, settling ourselves. Eliza sits astride Bolt like a man, I note, while I have been given a side-saddle.

Her steed prances ahead and Dora plods along obediently behind as Eliza leads us onto a track that winds through the back of the property and into the forest. Roughly ten minutes later, we emerge out of the woods, halfway down an extensive field of bright green. We stop to take in the view. Dora immediately drops her head to graze while Bolt stands tall and magnificent, ears pricked and tail flicking. Beyond the lush grass, the land falls away and melts into undulating purpled hillocks. On the right, a field of hay is being harvested. Windrows lie in the sun and straw-hatted workers move between them, rhythmically bending and scything.

'Are those lands yours?' I ask.

'They are.'

'I harvested hay as a schoolgirl in France,' I say. 'The smell of grass, the sunshine, the satisfaction of labouring—have you done this?'

'No. But I will take your word for it,' she says.

'You ought to try it some time.'

'If I am permitted, which is doubtful,' she says. 'Incidentally, did you receive your invitation to the ball? I know you have only been here a matter of days, but I do hope you will come?'

'I did, and I will,' I say.

'That makes me happy.'

Bolt is restless and Eliza allows him to canter on and loop a circle before she reins him in and brings him back to my side.

'Why not let him run?' I suggest.

She looks dubious. 'I do not want to leave you—'

'I have an even better idea,' I interrupt. 'Could I … May I … May I ride him?'

'Hmm,' she says, shaking her head. 'I do not advise it, Estella. Bolt is not an easy mount. Mama and Papa were dead against me having him and it has taken me months to train him to my liking.'

'Please?'

'I don't know that I can allow it. If you met with an accident I would be in so much strife—'

'Oh, please trust me, Eliza! I have done this before, and it is my wish. I have been living with all due care for far too long.'

'All right,' she concedes. 'But if you mount him and he shows signs of not accepting you, I must insist that you give up the idea.'

'As you wish.'

I lower myself from Dora while Eliza dismounts. I have to rely on Eliza bending low to make a step for me with her hands—because of Bolt's height—before I can put my boot into the stirrup, fling a leg over his back and heft myself into the saddle.

She gazes up at me open-mouthed when I have done so, as I ride astride as she did. That I have taken her by surprise is obvious.

'I learnt to ride like this in France. It is far safer.'

'I could not agree more,' she says.

Bolt shifts uneasily, utterly alive beneath me. He puts his ears back, swings his hindquarters. I glance down and Eliza's anxious face stares up at me. 'Please don't worry,' I tell her.

'Don't worry?' she repeats. 'That's easy for you to say, Estella.'

'It's all right, boy,' I murmur to Bolt, and lean forward and run one hand through his mane. He pricks his ears in response, which fills me with confidence. He knows how to listen.

I press my calves into his sides and let him take the lead, and we head uphill where he has to labour and cannot dominate.

We pause at the top of the field. Shaking his head in impatience, ruffling his mane, he whinnies.

'It's all right,' I say again. 'It's all right, boy.' Then I hunker down behind his head and we surge downhill, thundering across the open grassland. The wind is in my face, and it's as much as I can do not to shout with rapture.

My skirt billows out around me. My hat flies off. My clips come loose and my hair takes flight.

I almost lose my nerve at the lower end of the field. I have a feeling Bolt wants to clear the hedge and continue into the distance, and I have to persuade him otherwise. 'We are going to turn, Bolt,' I murmur. 'We *are* going to turn.' Not that he is going to listen to verbal instructions! It is a matter of me adjusting my weight in the saddle, pulling on the reins, stiffening my back, flexing my thighs—in other words, giving him all the cues.

I have the briefest second to notice that some of the straw-hatted workers have stopped to watch our progress, and I cannot help thinking it would serve me right if Bolt baulked at the hedge and I went flying over.

'Whoa,' I say. '*Whoa!*'

At the last minute, he veers from the hedge. He wheels uphill. Then we ride like the devil himself is after us, all the way back up.

We reach Eliza and I rein in her mount. Bolt is breathing hard and I am laughing.

Eliza has retrieved my hat and holds it in one hand as she stands and stares at me. Then she snorts with enjoyment, to my relief. Not very ladylike, but completely natural in the circumstances.

'Forgive me,' I say, pushing my hair into some semblance of order, but I need not worry for she seems lost for words.

We change horses once more and return to the house. Eliza is quiet. I think she is still in shock, though when I catch her eye she erupts into giggles.

Walking around the back of the property, we approach the stables. There is a clatter of hooves and a rider, hunched in the saddle, emerges at full tilt from the open doors. I believe it is the man we saw on the day we came to play cards, but I am not entirely certain. He barely has time to call a greeting to Eliza and touch his fingers to his hat as he gallops by. I get a fleeting impression of dark looks and a swarthy face before he disappears around the corner of the house and heads into the forest.

'Who was that?' I ask.

'Mr Bentley Drummle. He has an arrangement with Papa. He keeps his horse here.'

Eliza glances at me. She seems at once sombre. She also seems a trifle annoyed, either by the encounter, my curiosity, or the man's manners. Or perhaps it is all three. 'You are sure to meet him in due course,' she adds.

16

If the staid old house at Richmond, which is not without its charms, should ever come to be haunted, it will be haunted surely by the ghost of Pip! For it seems to me that in the first months that I am in residence, he never leaves my side. Though, clearly, he must return home nightly to sleep and to refresh himself.

Indeed, my two meetings with Eliza are rare occasions when Pip is not present, and although these observations about Pip may seem trivial and petty, they are important to note alongside what comes later, when he seems to despair of me and disappears from my life.

I do not grow weary of his company, however, or of his ideas to amuse me, for he can be funny, droll and also kind. He is regularly at Richmond and I see him often in town. He seems to enjoy most the occasions when it is only Mrs Brandley and me and he makes a habit of taking us out on the water, rugged up against the cold. He has strong arms and is a good rower and he seems content, rowing easily and ably, and I do not tire of watching him pull at the oars. The three of us go on picnics and attend fête days, plays and operas and all manner of pleasures, until I begin to think that his invitations are more about keeping me away from other admirers than about entertaining me.

Gradually, however, I grow acquainted with people and am independently invited to parties and the like. And when I attend a party or an occasion where Pip and a number of my admirers are present, he does not cope well. He seems either as miserable as a wet summer's day or as prickly as a hedgehog. I believe he is jealous. I believe he thinks that since he has known me for far longer than anyone else, no-one else has the right to my attention. I do find this tedious. I am short with him, and later take pity on him because he is so woebegone. Usually it is when the night is drawing to a close and we are saying our farewells, which is admittedly probably the worst time to encourage him.

During these months, I do not see as much of Eliza as I had hoped. She does, however, write to apologise and to say that her plans to introduce me to Captain Waverley have for the moment been foiled. The soldier is away on manoeuvres with his regiment and cannot be contacted. As far as she is aware, though, he has promised to be present at the ball and she assures me that he is not a man who reneges on his commitments. I have to admit I am becoming more intrigued by Captain Waverley by the day!

I have not forgotten the ball, of course. Indeed, Matilda does not talk of anything else in the days leading up to it.

In the afternoon I find that she has laid out two dresses for the ball on my bed: one that I earlier gave instructions for wearing, and another.

'What?' I say, teasing her. 'You mean me to wear both at once?'

'No, miss,' she says, laughing. 'But I do so like this one.' She touches its hem. 'I think it will suit you more on this occasion.'

'And why is that?'

'Because it is ivory, and with your hair and your eyes ...' She trails off. 'Because you are new there tonight, miss. And you should make an entrance.'

'Is that what you think?' I raise my eyebrows.

'Begging your pardon, miss, I do.'

So I wear the ivory dress with the tulle-capped sleeves and the heart-shaped neckline, and the pearls suspended from its hem. Matilda puts my hair up, using hairpins from Miss Havisham's pretty little crystal dish upon the dresser, and adorns it with droplets of pearls threaded upon a filigree. She hangs two fat and glistening pearls from my earlobes. I wear nothing around my neck, for she says my neck is like a swan's and to fasten jewels around it would distract from the beauty of my face. And there I am in agreement, for my feelings about jewels have not altered.

Matilda is so excited, teetering on her tippy-toes at the doorway and waving Mrs Brandley and me off, that one would almost assume she is the one attending the ball and not I.

Miss Brandley is not accompanying us. It has been arranged that she will have supper with Dr Oliver, and that he will escort her home before nine. These things are proceeding as planned, if a little faster than Mrs Brandley and I anticipated.

*

James Waverley has a lovely home, and the ball is well attended.

James is not what I was expecting. He is not conventionally handsome, nor particularly striking, and yet there is something about him. He is young-looking, almost boyish, and has a kind, pleasant face, but it is his bright and charming personality and his sincerity and good-naturedness that make him what he is.

I suspect that, having known one another since they were both little, the bond of friendship between Eliza and James is particularly strong. But it is more than that, for he gazes upon her with adoration in his eyes, scarcely leaves her side all night, and when I look at them they are laughing or talking animatedly to one another. She leaves him to come across to whisper that it is regrettable but Laurence, the Captain, will be arriving late. She seems particularly excited about introducing him to me.

I know only a handful of people: Eliza, obviously, her parents, the Hathaways, Mrs Brandley, Pip, and Herbert Pocket. I have not seen the latter since he visited Satis House at the time of the boxing incident, but it is clear he has no inclination to pursue our association for he barely has the manners to be polite. I wonder what he says of me behind my back?

Each time I turn, there is someone wanting to be introduced to me or staring at me, and it becomes tedious. I try to escape by dancing, but even so the hours are long before I can embark for home.

The crush of guests, the men in their pressed finery, the women in their bejewelled dresses, the tapping of shoes, the colourful swirls and whirls of the dancers as they spin around the floor, the fragrances of various pomades and perfumes: musk here, floral there—I feel overwhelmed. I behave more badly than I intended and torment and torture Pip and it would appear I am well on my way to breaking his heart. Miss Havisham would be well pleased, I think. If one less than awful thing comes out of it, it is that I am introduced to Mr Bentley Drummle.

I do not know what it is about Mr Drummle that I find alluring, for he is hardly handsome. His face is dark, his eyes so black and so deep they are like grottos. Solidly built, with a squarish head and overly long arms and legs, he seems to sprawl in a chair rather than sit. Perhaps the attraction is that he does not fawn upon me?

He takes note of me from the moment we are introduced, but rather than linger by my side and pester me to dance, he stands apart and observes from a distance, as if I am a wild creature and he is devising how best to capture me. For every time I look his way, I find his eyes upon me, deep in thought. I understand that he comes from family and money down in Somersetshire and is in line for a baronetcy. Pip also lets slip that Mr Bentley Drummle came to Mr Pocket for tuition when he was a head taller than that gentleman and half a dozen heads thicker than most gentlemen.

I think I can safely say that Mr Drummle is not a man whose heart I can break, for I believe his heart is not fragile—if, indeed, he has one. Out of all the men I have met since I came to London, he is by far the most singular. Note: I do not say charming or attractive. And, for the moment, I put him to one side, not to ignore but to reflect on when the mood takes me.

I dance with Pip several times and when I am not dancing, which is rare, Pip remains at my side and I shower him with affection, call him by his first name, which appears to madden my other admirers, touch him on the arm, such that the poor boy is in a state—though whether it is of delight or confusion is debatable. He looks exceedingly handsome this evening. He wears blue with those pretty eyes, and a number of ladies have bestowed looks upon him that, sadly, he has ignored.

It comes to a head when we go out onto the patio for a breath of fresh air and Pip and I stand back in the cooling shadows of the house.

'What is your opinion of Eliza?' I ask, for naturally I introduced Eliza to him.

'Who?' Pip says.

'Eliza,' I repeat.

'She is quite lovely.' He answers absently as if he is distracted.

'She appears to be well suited to James, don't you think?'

'How long have they known one another?'

'Since they—' I break off, for beyond Pip's shoulder, lit up by the light streaming from the ballroom, Mr Bentley Drummle appears on the balcony. More than likely, he is searching for me.

'Pip,' I say, 'I do believe there's an insect caught in your hair.' I gaze up at him. 'Keep still,' I instruct, for it occurs to me he means to take advantage of my uplifted face and kiss me.

My hand drifts near the edge of his face.

'Do you have any idea how exquisitely beautiful you are?' he asks.

'There!' I say, pretending to capture the insect. Pretending to toss it to one side, out of sight.

Pip clutches at my fingers and brings them to his mouth to kiss them. 'Oh, that I were that insect,' he murmurs.

'Estella?' His eyes are dark and troubled.

'What is it? What's the matter?'

I bring myself up close to whisper while Mr Drummle hovers in the background.

'You don't mean this, do you?'

'Mean what—?'

'This kindness, this affection you show me tonight.'

I lean ever nearer so that our breath mingles and our faces practically touch, and shake my head. 'No, I don't.'

'You are cruel, Estella.'

'Do you think I do not know this?' I whisper angrily. 'How many times have I told you I have no heart.'

'Will you never have a heart as far as I am concerned?'

'No,' I say.

I cut him to the quick, for he drops my hand. Mumbling something about refreshments, he retreats. Not to re-enter the ballroom, but across the patio and out into the darkened garden. To lick his wounds, no doubt.

Leaving me exposed. Leaving me to Mr Drummle. Who shambles up.

'Why do you waste yourself on that fellow?' he asks.

'Who? Pip? He's my childhood friend.'

'Hmph,' he says. 'Dance with me,' he instructs. 'The night is almost over.'

He holds out his hand. I could be churlish and refuse. Instead, I reluctantly take his hand and he leads me back into the ballroom.

Pip is waiting for Mrs Brandley and me at our coach at the end of the evening. He has taken it upon himself to accompany us home, but makes no reference to what transpired earlier. He is subdued and speaks little, and I feel his despair. If Mrs Brandley notices, she is discreet and says nothing.

At the Richmond house, she bids us farewell and goes in first while I linger.

'Will you never take warning?' I ask Pip at the garden gate.

'Of what?'

'Of me.'

'Are we not meant to be together?'

'I don't know, are we?'

'Estella,' he moans with exasperation.

I do believe that he thinks that in spite of everything, Miss Havisham means him to have me. Means us to marry!

'You wrote and asked me if I were going to the ball, you led me to believe—'

'I led you to believe nothing, Pip.'

I turn my face from him and stare into the night, at the few stars that are still strung across the lightening sky.

'Miss Havisham,' I say abruptly, 'wishes me to visit. Would you take me the day after tomorrow?'

'You know I will take you,' he murmurs. 'You know I will do anything for you, Estella. *Anything!*'

'You are to take the charges—'

'—out of your purse and provide you with tea and so on.'

'Exactly. We must obey our directions.'

'What does this mean, obeying our directions?'

'It means what I say. Nothing further and nothing less.'

I touch his hand briefly and leave him, and go up the garden path, calling 'Goodnight, Pip.'

*

I rise shortly before lunch the following day and, after the meal, the time stretches interminably before me. What to do with myself? I wish that I drew or painted—*painted!*—that I had matters such as a man does which could occupy my mind. Here I remember that my introduction to Captain Waverley did not eventuate the previous night. Something must have happened to detain the man. No matter, I am sure I *will* eventually meet him. It is only a matter of time. And I wonder if, after all this hullabaloo, I will be disappointed in the captain.

I take a book and stretch out on the chaise longue in my sitting room in a patch of sunlight and read … But I do not take in a word, for the mention of *painted* has reminded me of a certain, other man. Yes, I return to the marshes and to *him*. I recall his mischievous tone when he said *that was close*—implying quite a different interpretation—and how his hand held me firmly around the waist. The feel and taste of his lips against mine when he kissed me. Why did he leave in such a hurry? Was he protecting me, afraid of what might occur the next time I saw him? Surely, he is meant for me? How can I find him, I wonder. I should ask Mr Jaggers to track him down, but, in all honesty, I do not want that man to be involved in my affairs more than I can help.

We go down to Satis House in the morning, Pip and I, and join Miss Havisham in front of her fire and take up our habitual positions. And I see from the way Miss H hangs upon me, from the dreadful greedy look in her eyes, from the manner she claws upon my person, that my letters have been sustaining her, feeding her, yes! But that she wants more.

Since I returned from France, I have realised that I am easily annoyed by Miss H, and she appears to have developed the ability to bring out the worst in me. When I am away from her, I miss her and seem to feel love for her, yet when we are reunited I feel nothing but exasperation. Indeed, right now, I am vexed and irritated by her manner and would like nothing more than to give her a good, hard smack.

I am forced to sit beside her with my hand drawn through her arm and clutched in her own trembling one in the presence of Pip, and to go through the men I have mentioned in my letters, their names and their situations. At one point, I consider making a stand and refusing to go on, but I dare not, for Miss Havisham does not take kindly to being rebuked or being refused. I am being disloyal, but she has always had everything she desires—except for the man she loved, of course—and she is accustomed to getting her way. She sits now with her other hand on her stick and her chin on that and her pale bright eyes flickering between Pip and the fire. And every now and then she says, gloatingly, to him, 'How she does use you, Pip. How she does use you.'

I wonder how the poor man can stand it.

Eventually, I tire of this and detach my arm and rise to stand alongside the fireplace and stare into it, as miserable as I have ever been.

And instead of understanding the situation and taking pity on Pip, Miss H flashes her eyes upon me and says, 'What? Do you tire of me already?' And I realise that my recountings have put her in a high state of agitation.

'I tire only of myself.'

'Speak the truth.' Miss Havisham strikes her stick upon the floor. 'You are tired of me, are you not?'

I want to tell her then, that it is not her that I tire of, but this fixed, *relentless* preoccupation with me and the men in my life. But again, I do not want to provoke her.

I gaze down into the flickering flames and wish I could be anywhere else.

'You cold, cold heart!' Miss Havisham exclaims.

'What?' I say mildly, for I have run out of patience. 'You reproach me for being cold? You?'

'Are you not cold?'

'You should know, for I am what you have made me,' I say, and hope that that will be an end to it.

But Miss H cries out to Pip, 'Oh, look at her, look at her! So hard and thankless on the hearth where she was reared. Where I took her into this wretched breast when it was first bleeding from its stabs, and where I have lavished all my tenderness upon her!'

'Tenderness?' I repeat. 'I do not know the meaning of the word. Now tell me what you would have me do? You have been good to me and I owe you everything, but what is it you want from me?'

'Love,' Miss Havisham says.

'You have always had my love.'

'I have not. Not love as I know it should be given.'

'And did you give me love as you know it should be given? Answer that if you can.'

She is quiet then, and I ought to hold back and wait to see if she continues this ghastly conversation, but she has set off something in me and I cannot hold back.

'Mother by adoption,' I say, knowing the term riles her. 'I owe everything to you. I have said this. All I possess is freely yours. Beyond that, I have nothing. But if you ask me to give you what you never gave me, my gratitude and duty cannot oblige. They cannot do impossibilities.'

Miss Havisham turns wildly to Pip again. 'Did I never give her love?' she cries. 'Did I never give her a burning love, inseparable from jealousy at times and from sharp pain, whilst she speaks thus to me! Let her call me mad—'

'Why should I call you mad?' I say, speaking again in a steady voice. 'I, of all people? Does anyone live who knows what purpose you had half as well as I do? Does anyone live who knows what a memory you have half as well as I do? I, who have sat on this same hearth on the little stool that is even now beside you there, learning your lessons and looking up into your face, when your face was strange and frightened me!'

'Soon forgotten,' moans Miss Havisham.

'No, not forgotten,' I say. 'Not forgotten, but treasured in my memory. For when have you found me inconstant to your teaching, unmindful of your lessons? When have you found me giving admission here'—I touch my bosom— 'to anything that you excluded? Be fair.'

'So proud, so proud,' moans Miss Havisham, pushing one hand through her mass of grey hair.

'Who taught me to be proud?'

'So hard, so hard,' moans Miss Havisham again.

'Who taught me to be hard? Who praised me when I learnt my lesson?'

'But to be proud and hard to *me*!' she shrieks.

She drops her stick to stretch out her arms to me. 'Estella, Estella, to be proud and hard to *me*!'

I look at her and remember how she taught me to be proud and hard. I cannot forget it. I do not think I will ever forget her behaviour when I was a child, when I was at my most vulnerable. The defence I built around myself, however, is still there ... I can retreat behind it ... It will protect me.

'I begin to think,' I say coolly, 'that I almost understand how this comes about. If you had brought up your adopted daughter wholly in the dark confinement of these rooms, and had never let her know that there was such a thing as daylight by which she had never once seen your face—if you had done that, and then, for a purpose known only to yourself, had wanted her to understand *daylight* and to know all about it, you would have been disappointed and angry?'

Miss Havisham perches forward on her chair with her head in her hands, moaning and swaying. She does not speak.

'Or,' I say, 'which is nearer the case, if you had taught her from the dawn of her intelligence, with your utmost energy and might, that there was such a thing as daylight, but that it was made to be her destroyer and her enemy and she must always turn against it, for it had blighted you and would blight her—if you had done this, and then for a purpose known only to yourself, had wanted her to take naturally to the daylight and she could not do it, you would have been disappointed and angry?

'So,' I continue when my adopted mother does not answer, 'I must be taken as I have been made. The success is not mine, the failure is not mine, but the two together make me.'

As if I might have pushed her, she slips from her chair and onto the floor and sways like an animal on all fours amongst the faded relics, the withered flowers, the tattered bridal ribbon strewn there.

And for a moment, I despise her for being weak, for not rising above the tragedy of her life, for indulging herself in lifelong self-pity.

Pip, poor boy, has been standing to one side not saying a word, and he cannot take any more. He rises abruptly and with a rough gesture of his hand leaves the room.

I move from the fireplace, then, and help Miss Havisham to her feet and guide her back to her chair. Saying nothing, I take a needle and thread from her basket and sit at her knee and begin to patch her dress where it is coming apart, and by and by her claw-like hand comes forward and covers my own. When I glance up at her, her eyes are fixed upon the fire, her lower lip trembling.

I ask myself if this vexation that I feel for her is because we are too similar? Has she taught me so well that I am now just as scornful and derisive? Equally arrogant and proud? Just as capricious? These thoughts cause me so much anguish that I prick my finger, but manage to catch my gasp of pain before she hears it.

Thus Pip, his face still bearing the emotion of the evening's distress, finds us when he returns. We play cards, as before, but neither of us is inclined to talk and the evening wears away. Pip says goodnight and he is restrained and sombre and cannot look me in the eye—as if this is all my fault, as if I should have been kinder to and more patient with my mother by adoption. But I am weary of always being the one who makes allowances, who acquiesces to Miss H's every whim. Has he so soon forgotten how she belittled him in front of me?

He goes to bed in the building across the courtyard, and I go down to my old room. But I cannot sleep. I am saddened by the events of the night and I am restless. Noises disturb me. Candlelight flickers past my closed door. Miss Havisham is sleepless, too, I think. I reflect on what I said to her and consider whether she is right and there is no love in my heart. But there must be! I know I am capable of love, for how can I feel the way I do about the marshlands, about nature, without love in my heart? How can I feel the things that I feel for *him* without love? And I *am* fond of Pip, too. I know I am. But being fond of and being in love with are two different things, and I cannot profess to love him in that all-encompassing, blindly devoted way.

Once, I get up and go to the bottom of the staircase and look up and see Miss Havisham's light pass on the landing above and hear her low moan. I think about my own mother, then—there is another example of someone I love! And I wonder where she is, and whether—if she were alive and I knew her—I would love her differently? Surely I would?

17

It is not long after this incident that Pip and I are together at yet another party where Mr Bentley Drummle is present.

We are partnered at cards, as it happens, Mr Drummle and I, and must of necessity converse. It appears that we are good at playing together, for we win handsomely, but then I have to suffer him doggedly lurking about me. I would not mind so much but that he would say something. But he is either silent or utters something inappropriate. As I have said before, he is a singular man.

I am waiting alone with Pip at the end of the evening, for it is his habit to accompany Mrs Brandley and me to and from these events, when he says, 'Are you tired, Estella?'

'Rather,' I say.

'You should be.'

'Say that rather I should not be, for I have my letter to Satis House to write before I go to sleep.'

'Recounting tonight's triumph?' he asks. 'Surely a poor one, Estella.'

'What do you mean? I was not aware there had been any.'

'Estella,' he murmurs, 'do look at that fellow in the corner yonder, who is looking over here at us.'

'Why should I look at him?' I return, with my eyes on Pip. 'What is there in that fellow in the corner yonder—to use your words—that I need look at?'

'Indeed, that is the question I want to ask you, for he has been hovering about you all night.'

'Moths and all sorts of ugly creatures hover about a lighted candle,' I reply with a glance at Mr Drummle. 'Can the candle help it?'

'No,' Pip responds, 'but cannot the Estella help it?'

'Well?' I say, laughing. 'Perhaps. Yes. Whatever you like, Pip,' I say, for I *am* tired.

'Estella, don't be flippant. Do let me speak. It makes me wretched that you encourage a man so generally despised as Drummle. You know he is despised.'

'He plays a good hand of cards.'

'You know he is as ungainly within as without,' Pip goes on. 'A deficient, ill-tempered, stupid sort of fellow.'

'And what of it?'

'You know he has nothing to recommend him but money, and a ridiculous rollcall of addle-headed predecessors?'

'Well?' I say, widening my eyes in mock curiosity. 'And what of it?'

'*Well? And what of it?*' Pip repeats. 'That is why it makes me wretched.'

'Pip,' I murmur, 'don't be foolish about my encouraging others. I may intend it to have an effect upon them, but not upon you. It is not worth discussing—'

'Yes, it is,' he says, 'because I cannot bear what people should say about you, throwing away your graces and attractions on a mere boor, the lowest in the crowd.'

'I can bear it,' I retort.

'Oh, don't be so proud and inflexible,' Pip says.

'Call me proud and inflexible,' I say, '*and* reproach me for stooping to a boor?'

'There is no doubt you do, for I have seen you give him looks and smiles this night such as you never give—you never give to me.'

'Is your memory so short that you have forgotten the ball from a few weeks ago? Do you wish me to behave such as I did that night again? Is that what you want—more deception and entrapment?'

'No,' he says miserably. 'But tell me, are you serious about him? I couldn't bear it if you were serious. Or do you deceive and entrap him, too, Estella?'

'What do you think? Of course I do, Pip—all of them but *you*!'

'And why *me*?' he asks. 'Why am I spared?'

I pause. 'Why do you think?'

Mrs Brandley appears then, still talking animatedly to our host, but prepared to depart, it seems, and my conversation with Pip is cut short. Thankfully, so.

*

The round of parties, picnics, fête days, plays and so forth continues.

And still I do not get to meet Captain Waverley, or ascertain anything more about my artist!

More often than not, Pip accompanies Mrs Brandley and me. At one occasion, *Richard the Third* at Covent Garden, Dr Oliver and Miss Brandley join us and it is clear from the lively discussion between them at the intervals that they are much suited to one another. On our way out of the theatre, Dr Oliver takes me aside and tells me that he would like to see me—*on a private matter*—if I have the time to meet him in the park the following day, weather permitting.

We are both rugged up when we meet. It is not raining or sleeting, but winter has set in and the cold wind blows right through me. It rattles the limbs of the trees and shuffles the dead and brittle leaves along the path, occasionally hurling them up to the sky for sport.

'Is it wise for you to be out?' I ask Dr Oliver as we settle ourselves on the park bench, our hands tucked into our pockets and sitting close together for warmth.

'It will not harm me provided I do not dally,' he tells me.

'Well, come straight to the point, then,' I say, patting his knee. 'I will not object and I have half an idea what it is you wish to discuss with me.'

'You do?'

'Miss Brandley. Daisy,' I say, for that is what he calls her.

'Ah,' he says, smiling, 'you are one step ahead of me, then. You know I am old enough to be her grandfather?'

'I know.'

'And what, you have no opinion on this?'

'My opinion is that you may well be old enough to her grandfather, but it is evident that you are both admirably matched. You have made a world of difference in her life. She has gone from a dull, quiet girl to someone who is animated and has an opinion on almost everything.'

'Thank you, my dear.'

'And if—mark you, I say *if*—you are contemplating marriage, for I believe you are, I see no harm in it. In fact, I think it will be the making of Daisy.'

I glance at my companion. He is quite touched for his eyes are watering, unless, of course, it is the wind. It is blowing about our feet now and gusting up into our faces.

'I know this seems rather rushed, but time is not my friend,' he tells me. 'You do not anticipate any objection from Mrs Brandley?'

I shake my head. 'We have already discussed the possibility, if you will forgive me for saying so, and Mrs Brandley is much in favour. Though what Daisy will say is quite another question. Has she given you any indication of her feelings?'

Dr Oliver shakes his head. 'To be honest, my dear, I have been afraid of frightening her away and have given her no indication of *my* feelings.'

'Ah,' I say. 'Very wise in the circumstances. Why not let me broach the subject with her when we have some time together alone, and report back to you?'

'Capital,' he says, his eyes shining.

'You should go in now,' I tell him. 'Come, take my arm, and I will see you safely to your gate. The path is icy in parts.'

I find the opportunity to talk to Miss Brandley alone in the morning. Mrs Brandley has an early fitting at the dressmakers, and has a rushed breakfast before she leaves us both sitting at the table.

'Daisy,' I say. In spite of Miss Havisham's instructions to stick to formality, I have taken to calling Mrs Brandley and her daughter by their first names. I do not see the harm in it. 'Have you plans to spend time with Dr Oliver today?'

She glances up from buttering her toast. 'I do, Estella,' she says. 'How did you know?'

'I didn't. I am guessing.' I smile encouragingly and push the marmalade across to her. It is her favourite. She has it on her toast every day without fail.

'Only you are spending a great deal of time together,' I say, picking up my cup and sipping at my coffee. 'Forgive me for asking,' I go on, 'but do you like the man? Are you fond of him? Or is it purely a mutual interest in books and literature that keeps you so interested?'

Poor child. (I am aware she is older than I am, but I cannot help but refer to her as a child; she seems so helpless so often.) She blushes furiously. 'Oh, Miss Estella,' she says.

I put my cup back in its saucer and lean forward confidingly. 'If you must know, he's very taken with you—'

'He is?'

'To be candid, Daisy, he wants to marry you, but is afraid of what you will say, what *others* might say—about how much older he is than you. He does not wish to cause you, or your mother, any embarrassment, you understand.'

'Oh,' Daisy says. She pauses with her knife loaded. Drips of marmalade fall onto the tablecloth, but she does not notice. Her eyes are big.

'So you would have no objection ... if ... if he did ask for your hand in marriage?'

'Not at all.' A smile creeps upon her face. 'There's nothing I would like better, in fact.'

She puts down her cutlery and pushes her glasses back up her nose. 'Imagine ... all day and all night with all those books at my fingertips!'

'Well,' I say, smiling now, too, and reaching for the coffee jug to refresh my cup, 'perhaps it won't be quite like that, but certainly the library will compensate for a great many things.'

After breakfast, I go straight to my sitting room and write a brief note to Dr Oliver. *All is well*, I write. *Rest assured, she is positive.* I place it in an envelope, seal it and ask Matilda to deliver it next door. She is only too happy to oblige for this gives her an opportunity to see Albert.

*

I have many admirers at this time, but my two most ardent are Pip and Mr Bentley Drummle. Though it hardly seems fair to call Mr Drummle *ardent*, since his attentions towards me are more like dogged pursuit. Imagine a large dark rottweiler set to guard a small fluffy toy Pomeranian and lumbering after it every time it moves. Thus he holds on. Wherever I am, there he is. Not saying anything, not doing much, on occasion only doffing his hat, but always within sight. Always watching. If there is one word to describe him it is *lurking*. He is always lurking about. Sometimes I find it insidious. At other times it amuses me. And so I play accordingly with him, openly despising him, or the reverse—encouraging him, flattering him—and the next occasion pretending I have no idea who he is. And still, in spite of these setbacks, he keeps on.

On more than one occasion, Pip flares up and expresses a wish to flatten Bentley Drummle to the ground, and I am obliged to talk him out of it. It is clear that he loathes the man.

Pip's presence in my life is a constant, for he verily believes that it is only a matter of time until I return his love and affections, no matter how many times I tell him that it is unlikely to happen. I am fond of him, yes, but I cannot easily forget his background. He is kind and generous, admirable traits, but he is my dear friend, nothing more.

The friendship between Eliza and I grows and, one chilly December afternoon, I am at Wright House at her invitation. We are wandering arm-in-arm down to the lake, our hands embedded in muffs, when she blurts out, 'Oh, Estella, cannot you please fall in love with Laurence, with James's brother! It would make me so happy if you were my sister-in-law.'

'I can hardly fall in love with him when I am yet to meet him!' I tease. 'What happened at the ball? Did he turn up? I did not see him.'

'Yes,' she admits, 'but it was too late. I was otherwise engaged and I believe you were fully occupied fighting off Mr Drummle.' She smiles, dimpling her cheeks.

I remain silent for a moment or two. 'I would like to be your sister-in-law,' I say quietly, 'but I have yet to meet Captain Waverley and there is always the chance I will take an instant dislike to the man. I cannot force feelings of love where no love is, Eliza.' She seems to accept this, and I believe it is because she is in love with James Waverley and knows what true love is.

'Have you *ever* fallen in love?' she asks.

'Once,' I say.

'And ...?' she encourages.

But I laugh. I say, 'When are you expecting James to ask you to marry him?'

She cannot help it, she blushes. 'At Christmas, I hope. He and his parents are coming to spend a few days here.'

*

I suffer from a touch of fever at Christmas and am not well enough to go down to Miss Havisham or attend any festivities. Pip is good to me during this time. He calls every day and is most put out because I do not allow him to come up to talk to me.

Eliza writes now and then and laments the chance to call on me (she is forgiven since I know she has a house full of guests) and bemoans the fact that Captain Waverley is now home, but I am indisposed. Mr Bentley Drummle calls most days, too, but Matilda always gives him the same message: *Miss Havisham is not well enough to see anyone.* One morning, I hear his response floating up to me from the front door. 'Confound it!' he says. It is as much as I can do not to laugh. (Laughing, of course, is dangerous, for it sets me off coughing.)

On one occasion, when I am almost better, Pip stands below on the garden path with his bright face looking up at me. I am wrapped up with a thick scarf around my neck and feeling more perky, and I open the window and call out my greetings.

'Dr Oliver is lending us the horse and carriage this afternoon,' he tells me. Pip has become quite friendly with the good doctor, and the doctor has taken it upon himself to look in on me and prescribe medication. 'He thinks you are well enough to have an outing, provided you are warmly dressed. Please say you will come, Estella?'

'I would be delighted,' I say huskily. I would be. There is no doubt that the four walls of my room and the stale air have become tiresome.

'I have an even better idea,' I say, glancing back at Matilda hovering behind me. 'Why not let's take Matilda with us? She can sit up front with Albert and keep him company.'

Matilda mimes clapping her hands and begins to hop up and down with excitement, and this small gesture on my part fills me with unexpected happiness.

Pip raises his shoulders and spreads his gloved hands in acquiescence. 'Splendid,' he says. He glances at his watch. 'I will see you at two o'clock.'

I nod, wave to Pip, and step back.

Matilda leans forward and closes the window. 'He is a kind gentleman, Mr Pip, isn't he?'

'He is indeed,' I say.

I know what she is intimating, that I ought to consider him as a match for myself since he is both caring and generous with his time, and she glances at me, perhaps to gauge my feelings, but I turn my head for fear she will see my face.

I am not in love with Pip. Nor will I ever be. I have said this before. I will reiterate it. My feelings for him are merely those of fondness. I have known him for a long time, but I cannot forget that he comes from the family of a lowly blacksmith. I *cannot* marry him!

The four of us take a turn around the park in the horse and carriage in the afternoon and it is altogether a happy occasion. From my vantage point inside, I am able to observe the looks that

Matilda and Albert give one another, and how one of his hands often drifts across to the top of her thigh, and how she quietly pushes it away.

Sitting opposite me, Pip gives me longing looks. But there is something else that I cannot put my finger on. Something troubles him that he wants to say, but cannot. I am reminded of the years when I woke from sleep with his image in my dreams, and that same expression in his eyes.

'What is it, Pip?' I ask, more than once.

But he shakes his head and turns his face away.

He is pretending, this time, that it is about us and his desire for me, but I do not believe that it is.

Something troubles him. Something he would like to discuss, but cannot. Or dare not?

18

Eliza announces her engagement to James shortly after the new year begins and I am jubilant, since what little I know of the man I like, and I believe they will be happy together. Eliza writes that the two families are naturally overjoyed and she does hope I am now fully recovered, for an invitation to her engagement party will soon be arriving in the mail.

When a letter addressed to me in a flourishing hand arrives at the breakfast table, I expect it to be the engagement party invitation, but I am wrong. All the same, it is a gilt-edged card. It says:

Mr James Waverley has pleasure in requesting the company of Miss Estella Havisham at a private showing of artworks: 10th January at 4:00 pm. A light supper will be served. Please RSVP, etc.

I put the invitation down alongside my breakfast side-plate and stare at it thoughtfully.

I can't help thinking of *him* and wondering if they are *his* paintings. But there is no mention of the artist's name, although it would not help me if there was.

'Is everything all right, Estella?' Kitty asks.

I nod. 'Yes, thank you. Have you also received an invitation to—' I break off to indicate the card—'a private showing of artworks at Mr Waverley's?'

She shakes her head. 'No, but then it is probably only for people who have the funds. Sadly, we are not in that category—'

'Not yet,' Daisy puts in and we all smile.

Her mother and I have been expecting a proposal from Dr Oliver since before Christmas, but things seem to have stalled and, more than once, I have wondered whether I should find out why.

'I wonder who the artist is?' I say.

'Is there nothing further in the envelope?' Kitty asks.

I pick it up and peer inside. I have missed a separate thin sheet of paper. I retrieve it and unfold it. *Estella, Edward Pevensey is a talented but struggling artist. Your charming presence will give him a welcome boost of confidence and greatly add to the atmosphere and I would be most pleased if you could see your way clear to accepting this invitation. Thanking you in advance! Yours, James Waverley.*

I write to Pip after breakfast and give him the details of the invitation and ask if he knows anything about one Edward Pevensey. Then I reply to James, telling him I would be delighted to come.

I also write to Dr Oliver and ask if he could spare the time to see me briefly in the early afternoon, and Matilda brings his answer back upstairs: *Yes. It would be my pleasure.*

'I will be out this afternoon,' I tell Matilda. I realise I have been preoccupied and have forgotten to check her nails since Christmas, when I was ill.

'Let me see your nails, please?' I ask, reaching for her hand.

She holds them both out proudly. 'Look, miss,' she says. She cannot help beaming.

'I am so pleased,' I tell her, for her nails have grown well. They have been cut recently, and she has filed and shaped them. They are short but pretty. 'Well done,' I say.

'Thank you, miss,' she says, blushing. 'Now all I need is the ring.'

I smile. 'I am sure that won't be long,' I tell her.

Matilda leaves my sitting-room and it crosses my mind that everyone is getting engaged or married or expecting proposals except me. Still, I am not anxious about marrying. It is much more important to find the one I love—if only I can track *him* down.

*

My meeting with Dr Oliver is reassuring, but also sad.

'My heart, this time, has been playing up,' he tells me, patting his chest. 'I have told myself I need rest, but it is difficult when there is so much to discuss with Daisy. Additionally, I have been concerned by the excitement that a proposal of marriage will generate, all bad for my health, which is why I have held off.'

I nod understandingly. I have no advice for Dr Oliver. He, after all, is the doctor and knows what is best for him, but I do propose that he excuses himself when Daisy next comes over. I suggest that she quietly read while he does the same. He says he will consider it. Much as I hope for the financial security that Daisy's marriage will bring to her and Kitty, there is nothing I can do. It is out of my hands.

Before we part on his doorstep, I ask Dr Oliver if he knows anything about art. 'I have been invited to a private showing,' I say, 'by the artist, Edward Pevensey. Does his name mean anything to you?'

He shakes his head. 'I am sorry, my dear, no. My head is all too often in books and not enough out of them.'

Pip's response a day later to my letter with the same query is in the negative and, not only that, but it is abrupt. And I wonder again what it is that troubles my friend.

*

The days drag until the event at James Waverley's, and I keep myself busy by going up to London, ordering two new dresses and returning a second time for fittings.

On another day, I am in my sitting-room writing to Miss H when I hear the doorbell ring, followed by a male voice saying, 'Good afternoon.'

I tiptoe to the window. 'Is Miss Havisham in?' the voice asks.

I have taught Matilda to say she is not sure, she will find out, which she does, and a minute later there is a quiet knock at my door.

'Who is it?' I whisper.

'It's Mr Drummle, miss.'

'Oh, god,' I say.

Matilda looks as if she wants to laugh. I put my finger to my lips. 'I suppose I had better face him,' I say. She nods in agreement.

'I will come down in a moment,' I tell her, 'if you would show him to the drawing room?'

'Shall I light the fire, miss?'

'Yes, please. Thank you, Matilda.'

I tidy myself and my hair, draw a shawl over my shoulders and make my way downstairs. I find Mr Drummle restlessly pacing the drawing room. He has not put his hat down, but is turning the brim agitatedly in his fingers.

He takes my hand— 'Miss Havisham'—and kisses it. He appears swarthier than ever. Perhaps it is the new style of sideburns that envelop his lower jaw?

'To what do I owe the honour?' I say, taking a seat near the fire.

'I—I—' he breaks off.

To my horror, he kneels at my feet. And continues to fiddle with his hat. 'There is no other way of expressing myself, Miss Havisham—Miss Estella. Will you … Will you marry me?'

'Mr Drummle! Please.'

I rise from the chair to distance myself. And the man gets up and pursues me!

I move further away to the window. I put out one hand to fend him off. He appears not to notice.

'Miss Estella, I have loved you from the moment I saw you,' he says.

'I—I—I cannot say I have not noticed.'

'I can make you very happy. I am—I am, as you recall, one away from a baronetcy.'

I nod. 'I do recall. But Mr Drummle—'

'Perhaps this is too sudden?' he suggests. 'Perhaps we should wait until the spring? How do you feel about a spring—a spring—?'

I feel sure he is about to say 'wedding' when an ember from the newly lit fire jumps upon the hearth mat. Matilda has forgotten to replace the fender!

'Mr Drummle,' I say, pointing to mat. 'Quick!'

He turns. To his credit, he sees at once what the problem is, grabs the tongs and turfs the culprit back into the fire. Putting to bed any lingering ashes, he stamps on the hearthrug.

'Oh, thank you,' I say. I put my hand to my chest and feign distress. 'I can't tell you how grateful I am.'

He does not respond. He looks blankly at me. I do believe the incident has made him completely lose his train of thought.

I will have to tell Matilda later how eternally grateful I am to her for neglecting the fender and her duty!

Mr Drummle is still staring at me. He is resolving how best to return to his subject, I think.

'That has quite frightened the wits out of me,' I murmur. 'In fact, I feel faint with shock. Would you please excuse me, Mr Drummle?'

I leave the room. I do not look back. I do not give him any opportunity to pursue me, or the subject.

Matilda tells me later that he waited for some time in the room before he departed. I do not think he entirely comprehended what had happened. I know it took a while for me to come to terms with what he said—nay, asked.

Marriage to Bentley Drummle? *The ide-a!* As Camilla Pocket once remarked.

*

Then two things happen in quick succession. They say it never rains, but it pours.

Matilda comes to me before breakfast, smiling and holding out her hand. 'Look,' she says.

I expect to again see her new and nicely formed nails and indeed I do see them, but it's the thin gold band inlaid with a small gem on the finger of her left hand that gets my attention.

'You're engaged!'

'That I am, miss.' She beams.

'Oh, Matilda! How wonderful.'

I take her hands and lead her into a little jig around the room. I am still in my nightgown and my plait of hair swings against my back and over my shoulder.

'Miss!' Matilda says, almost in admonishment, but she laughs all the same.

'When is the date?' I ask, pausing breathlessly.

She shakes her head. 'We haven't put a day on it, miss. We must first ask permission from Dr Oliver to live together in Albert's quarters.'

'He'll surely have no objection?'

'I don't know, miss. Seeing as Dr Oliver hasn't been himself... Albert is almost too afraid to ask him, miss.'

'I see. Do you want me to say anything—?'

'No, miss. That won't be necessary.'

At breakfast, I am about to tell Kitty and Daisy Matilda's good news when I notice Daisy gazing at me in a sort of stupefied, loving way. Which astonishes me. Normally, she has her head down, attending to piling copious amounts of marmalade on her toast.

'Is there something you want to tell me, Daisy?'

She nods. She smiles demurely. I glance at Kitty, her mother, on her other side, who has paused in the eating of her egg and is biting her lip, watching me. They are both agog. What is it!

Aah. I am slow this morning, still thinking of Matilda and Albert. I lean across and look at Daisy's hands. They are both spread out at the sides of her plate, which should have alerted me earlier, and on the fourth finger of her left hand is a soft-gold ring. It is similar to Matilda's, only bigger and wider, and the large inlaid sparkling gem is without a doubt a genuine diamond.

'Oh, Daisy!' I clap my hands together in excitement. 'Really?'

'Really,' she confirms, colouring.

'When?' I ask.

'He asked me yesterday evening, and we haven't yet settled on a date, but he says he would like it to be earlier rather than later.'

I nod. This doesn't surprise me. The good Dr Oliver has clearly decided to throw caution to the wind.

'We are thinking of a small and intimate wedding,' Kitty says. 'At Dr Oliver's. You will come, won't you?'

'Definitely.' I nod again. 'Decidedly,' I say. 'I'm so happy for you both.'

I reach for the coffee pot, then, and pour myself a cup. While I am adding cream, I ask Daisy what she intends to wear, and we begin an animated discussion that goes on all through breakfast.

Matilda's news can wait for a day or two, I think, and Daisy and Kitty can have their happiness and their day all to themselves.

When, at last, I return upstairs to write to Miss Havisham and tell her of the latest happenings, I cannot—selfishly—help thinking of myself. When will this happen to me? This joy, this jubilation, this happy day. When will I find the man I seek, and is he the one called Edward Pevensey?

The final elation of the day arrives in the afternoon in the form of Eliza's invitation to her engagement party. It is in three weeks' time, and I put it to one side and continue to dream of my artist friend. And of Edward Pevensey. Whoever he may be.

19

Alas, a second letter from James Waverley arrives with the first post in the morning. it is written with haste. *Dear Estella, Forgive me, but various responsibilities have forced me to defer the showing of the artworks. We do, however, have a new date.* He goes on to tell me it is now set to be held *after* the engagement party and apologises again. I sigh with annoyance, but there is little I can do. The engagement party for James and Eliza must, of course, take precedence.

Before breakfast, I ask Matilda if she has had word from Albert regarding their future accommodation and she tells me that she has.

'Dr Oliver has been kind,' she says. 'If you ask me, miss'—she lowers her tone— 'he is quite beside himself with Miss Brandley's decision.' She smiles mischievously. 'In any event, he's given permission for me to share Albert's quarters.'

'Do you now have a time and a day for the ceremony?'

'I do.' She nods. Her face is aglow with happiness. 'The fourteenth of February at ten in the morning. In two weeks, miss.'

'The fourteenth of February?' I repeat. 'That's Valentine's Day!'

'Why, so it is, miss.'

She looks at me as if there is something she wants to add, and puts her hand up to her mouth. I pull it down again. She giggles.

'You wouldn't be there, would you, miss? I would so like it if you could? If it's not too much trouble, if you weren't doing anything else of importance? If—'

'Of course, I'll be there,' I tell her. 'I wouldn't miss it for anything.'

*

St Valentine's Day dawns and I can't remember when last the fourteenth of February was such a glorious day. February is known as the cruellest month of the year. It is dreary and dark. Christmas is over and there is little to look forward to. The coldest day of the season often occurs in February, but it is as if the sun and the season and Zeus have all come together to behave with decency and kindness on Matilda and Albert's special day.

Matilda looks enchanting. Her fair plait is wound at the back of her head and she wears a ring of tight pink rosebuds and maidenhair ferns on her head. Her dress, which we chose together and which I gave her as a present, is creamy white and caught underneath her bust with pale pink ribbon. She carries a modest bouquet of the same pink rosebuds and maidenhair ferns.

As we set off in Dr Oliver's horse and carriage, I can see from the looks given to us by Kitty and Daisy, standing at the doorway waving us off, that they are extremely jealous they have not been invited as well.

Albert is driving us. I attempted to persuade him otherwise, but his mind was made up. He said that it would be an absolute honour and a pleasure to drive Matilda, whether she was marrying him or not, but that he was especially pleased *it were 'im*. He wears a suit of tails and a grey waistcoat and a top hat, and looks most handsome. I believe the suit has been borrowed from Dr Oliver's wardrobe. It is a little on the short side because from where I am sitting I can see Albert's exposed ankles. In spite of the sunshine, they must be chilly.

One of Albert's friends is the best man and has the privilege of looking after the ring. My task is to hold the bouquet while the couple say their vows and Albert slides the ring onto Matilda's finger. Albert's parents are both deceased and he has no idea of the whereabouts of his siblings, while Matilda, who has had some schooling, became an orphan recently. She has siblings, but none of them are able to make it to the ceremony for reasons of employment. Which means it is only the four of us and the officiating minister in the chapel. I have to say, however, that I take great pleasure in the intimacy of the quiet affair.

Sometimes I have wondered what it must be like to have siblings, although, to be fair, I often think of Pip as a brother. He is someone I saw consistently through a great deal of my childhood, but I dare say he is not of the same opinion.

After the ceremony, the four of us go down the road to an establishment for a glass of ale in celebration. *The White Cross* is situated on the Thames, and I cannot help thinking of Pip again, and his house which I know to be further downstream.

After a respectable interval, I take my leave of Albert's friend, and of Mr and Mrs Findlay. They have been most kind to me, but will far better enjoy themselves without my company. The latter are going on to an establishment in the country for a couple of days that has generously been paid for by Dr Oliver. I address them as *Mr and Mrs Findlay* when I take my leave, and their expressions are a joy to behold. They laugh self-consciously, gaze at me, and then at each other. In truth, they can barely take their eyes one from the other.

Two souls bound and fettered together in harmony make for a love that is as profound as it is deep.

*

I reach home to find no less than five Valentine's Day cards have arrived in the post. There are also flowers, red roses naturally, from an anonymous admirer. I recognise Pip's handwriting on one of the cards, but the other four are a mystery. One, no doubt, comes from Bentley. Then, again, perhaps the roses are from Bentley. Or the roses *and* the card are from Bentley. But who are the other cards from? Could one be from Captain Waverley? I have not, of late, given the soldier in the Dragoon Guards much thought, for it seems we are destined never to meet.

I think that surely this going around and around the suitability of one admirer opposed to the other is not all there is to life? That surely there is something more to occupy my mind and my time than endless thoughts of finding a husband? Then again, if I desire something more meaningful to engage me, perhaps it is up to me to find it.

These reflections and these happy marital occasions do, however, help to pass the time until the showing of the artworks at James Waverley's. The following event is Daisy and Dr Oliver's wedding, also a small affair, though, naturally, not to the same degree as the previous one.

I was not aware of this, but Dr Oliver and his first wife had no children. The only guests from his side, therefore, are a long-time friend and his wife. On Daisy's side, her mother and I are the only two representatives. The day before, Kitty admits to me that she has a sister, only she has not invited her to the wedding. She fears her sister will conclude Kitty has come into money and begin to harass her for funds. I nod knowingly, thinking of Miss

Havisham's cousins, the Pockets, and how they continue to plague her. What is it with families and money?

It is clear Dr Oliver is not altogether well. He has a coughing fit at one point and has to sit down and sip at a glass of water before the reading of the vows can continue.

We have an opportunity for a quick tête-à-tête after the ceremony, which is held in the warmest room in the house. Dr Oliver had to apply to the authorities for special permission to have it in the library, since the laws about marriage and where it can take place are strict. He tells me somewhat ruefully, 'I am not getting any better, and I could not have left Daisy waiting any longer.'

Daisy wears an ivory gown with a bustle, a train, a close-fitting veil and long gloves, while Dr Oliver dons a morning suit. Daisy's dress seems a little staid and old-fashioned, and I cannot help but unkindly compare her attire to Matilda's. But Daisy *is* marrying someone who is twice, nay three times, her age and maybe sedateness and respectability are called for.

I do think they will be happy, for I see them murmuring to one another when refreshments are served afterwards. They are not honeymooning, they tell us, for reasons of Dr Oliver's health. Perhaps they will do so in the summer, they say. I do hope there will be a summer for the good doctor.

It is strange to return to the house in the late afternoon and not find Daisy there. She has been so much a feature of the place ever since I arrived. I almost miss her. I wonder about Kitty, alone now, and what she will do once I marry?

I cannot imagine myself married. It seems so unlikely. And yet what am I destined to do with myself?

*

Last, but not least, is Eliza and James's engagement party. It is a glittering and distinguished event. A far cry from the previous two happenings, but fitting that it be so, and I would have expected no less.

There appear to be upwards of two hundred guests, but neither Pip nor Herbert Pocket are there, and I cannot help worrying about my dear friend. Bentley Drummle is in attendance, no doubt because he is one away from a baronetcy, and he makes a beeline for me.

'Miss Havisham.' He takes my hand. It appears that he has put the last occasion he saw me from his mind.

'Mr Drummle,' I respond.

'How are you? It seems to have been overly long since I last saw you. Did you by any chance receive roses?'

'I did indeed.'

'I am pleased to hear they arrived safely.' He lets go of my hand and stations himself beside me.

'They were from Pip,' I tell him, lying because I want to see his face.

'From Mr Pirrip?'

'Yes.'

'You did not receive roses from me?'

'I don't believe so. The roses I received had no card accompanying them, but I am quite certain they were from Pip.'

'Oh.' He looks crestfallen. The corners of his fleshy mouth turn down. The roses that he paid a fortune for have been accredited to someone else, somebody he is not particularly enamoured with.

'Why are you so sure they were from … from that Pip fellow?'

'Pip has his heart set on me, didn't you know?'

'Ah—but—but,' he blusters. 'I believe things are not altogether well with the man. Have you heard this, too?'

'I have not.'

'Aah,' he says, mysteriously. He glances at me and raises his eyebrows.

'Do you always believe everything you hear, Mr Drummle?'

He flashes me another look. 'When I have sufficient grounds to, Miss Havisham.'

I have upset him and it pleases me.

I spot Eliza's face then, in the crowd, and say, 'If you will excuse me, Mr Drummle,' and make my way over to her.

'Estella!' She claps her hands with delight at the sight of me.

We embrace. She is radiant in buttercup yellow. Her curls, pinned up behind her head and decorated with small yellow daisies, cascade down her back. She is effusive and happy. As an engaged woman should be. I do envy her.

We have five minutes together. Five minutes to say no more than 'How have you been?' 'Well, thank you. And you?' 'Perfect,' she says. 'I have missed you,' she adds. 'When this'—she twirls one finger in the air—'has all settled down, you must come and visit.' 'I would like that,' I tell her. And just before she is whisked away, she says, 'And guess who is here?'

A waiter hands me a glass of champagne and I turn to find Bentley Drummle hovering behind me. My first thought is that I do not think this is the man Eliza means.

'Mr Drummle,' I say.

'Miss Estella,' he repeats, as if we have not already met.

'I must …' I raise one finger of my free hand. 'If you will excuse me?'

'Of course.' He bows and stands aside.

'Persistent, isn't he?' a voice says as I make my way out of the ballroom.

A man I have never seen before and to whom I have to raise my head, since he is a great deal taller than I am, is at my side.

I stop. 'Have we met?'

He shakes his head. 'Laurence Waverley,' he says, taking my hand and kissing it. 'You must be Miss Havisham?'

'I am. Waverley?' I ask, pretending puzzlement, for one cannot allow a man to think he is so important that one already knows all there is to know about him. 'Are you the brother of James?'

'That I am. His adopted brother.'

The captain's eyes are an astonishing green. Straight dark hair juts over his collar and a solid moustache of the same hue lines his upper lip. He looks nothing like James. Which should not come as a surprise. Eliza, I recall, described him as *devilishly dashing*. She was not wrong.

He relinquishes my hand. But I am not ready to let him go. Moving away, I draw us both behind a pillar where we can better converse.

'How is it I have not met you before, nor heard much of you?'

He laughs. 'Hah. I am something of a mystery. Firstly, I am adopted and, secondly, I am in the Royal Dragoons and seldom at home.'

For a moment, I have a vision of him in uniform, in a splendid red jacket. He is mounted on a horse, long black boots in the stirrups, a lance in one hand. It is an altogether pleasing image.

'I see,' I say. 'Then we have something in common, you and I.'

'Yes. I had heard that you, too, are adopted.'

'How is it that you seem to know a great deal more about me than I do about you?'

He smiles. When he smiles, his expression is captivating and I cannot help smiling back. His face with those green eyes is altogether striking, but when he is serious it bears a look which is almost haunting. There is something exotic about his looks. I wonder if he has foreign blood. Russian, perhaps? I am letting my imagination carry me away.

'I would be lying if I did not admit that I have wheedled everything James knows about you from the moment I saw you.'

'You have seen me before? I don't believe I've had the pleasure of …'

He shakes his head. 'You are right. We have never been introduced, but I caught a brief glance of you at the ball our father gave late last year—only I couldn't get near you. Do say you will dance with me tonight?'

'I would be delighted,' I tell him.

I tilt my head to one side enquiringly. 'It wasn't you who sent me a Valentine's Day card, was it?'

He lowers his gaze. 'Possibly,' he says coyly, teasing me.

The first violin starts up and I look away from him and into the ballroom. The dancers beginning to line up are a swirl of colour. James and Eliza have taken their place at the head, waiting to lead the first dance.

'Shall we?' Laurence extends his arm.

I wave my half-full champagne glass uncertainly in the air. 'What shall I do with this?'

He takes the flute from me, downs the remainder and places the empty glass on a passing tray. 'There,' he says.

A decisive man. I like that.

Although Laurence is tall, he moves with ease and grace on the floor. Each time I pass him, he looks into my eyes, and I find it hard to drag my gaze away. I am mindful that he is aware that he has set out to captivate me. Oh dear. The shoe or, in this case, the boot is on the other foot tonight!

It is never easy to talk on a dance floor, but I discover that Laurence Waverley has been in the Royal Dragoons for a year, is yet to see active service, and was given special dispensation to be here tonight.

'I expect to be given my orders in the next week or two,' he tells me, in passing. 'And should you not hear from me or see me, it is entirely because I am unable to do so—'

'You seem sure that we will remain in contact—' I say at the next opportunity.

'I *am* sure.'

I raise my eyebrows.

He murmurs, 'Only wild horses would keep me away—' at the next turn, and I cannot help smiling.

Four dances go by before we are interrupted and I am claimed for the fifth by some admirer that I scarcely know.

'May I?' the man asks.

'If you must,' Laurence Waverley responds, but it is not said with bad grace.

My new partner leads me away, but out of the corner of my eye I am aware of Laurence waiting in the shadows for the dance to come to an end, and to claim me back again. Which he does.

The interruption alters the atmosphere between us. We pass one another in a flurry of colour and a rhythm of sound, and I raise my eyes to his. His expression is earnest, his gaze fixed on mine, and our connection deepens. He means to have me, I think, to capture me, heart and soul. And he may well do so if I am not careful.

Sometime later, I run into Bentley Drummle a second time. He practically clutches at my hand in his agitation. 'Miss Estella?'

'Yes?'

'Could I—?'

'I'm afraid not,' I say. 'I am spoken for, for the remainder of the evening.'

His look turns stony. His eyes are almost black with anger.

'He will tire of you,' he mutters, 'and then you will return to me. Take my word for it—'

'Mr Drummle,' I say. 'I think you forget yourself. I never was *with you* in the first place.'

I turn away, feeling smug, feeling secure and confident that Bentley Drummle is mistaken about Laurence.

At the close of the last dance, I say goodnight to the captain. He lingers over my hand and kisses it with intent.

'If you do not hear from me,' he tells me, 'it is because duty calls. But I *will* see you again, Miss Havisham, rest assured of that. If I can, if it is at all possible!'

'I don't doubt it,' I tell him and smile. He returns my look with shining eyes and dimpled cheeks, and there is no doubt in my mind that Captain Laurence Waverley is an extremely attractive man. I get the impression, too, that he is spontaneous, that he would be fun to live with.

It is after midnight when I lay my head on my pillow. Under the covers my feet continue to dance, swirling and gliding around the floor, and above my head Laurence's green eyes gaze steadfastly down into mine.

I do believe he has enchanted me. How have I allowed this to happen?

20

My first thought when I awake shortly before eight is that I was beguiled the night before. Beguiled, bedazzled and *enchanted*.

It is all transparent in the daylight. Quite logically so.

All notions of my artist and the marshes were swept from my mind. I gave not one thought to my friend, Pip, his absence and what torments him. I mislaid my manners, for I did not politely interact with any of the other guests. Only a fool could have missed seeing that I was wholly distracted.

And yet apart from Laurence Waverley's looks and his charm, what does the man have to recommend to him? No title, no property and, I suspect, little income.

With this thought uppermost in my mind, I call for Matilda and tell her I am rising.

I am sitting in front of the bedroom mirror as she does my hair when we hear shrieking. It starts in the distance and grows louder as it comes ever closer.

Matilda darts to the window.

'It's Miss Brandley—Mrs Oliver,' she says, turning to me. She looks concerned.

I join her at the windowsill in time to see Daisy stagger through the garden gate. She clutches her neck and looks close to swooning.

'Quick, go down,' I tell Matilda, 'and see what troubles her. I will finish my hair.'

It does not take me long to jam in a few extra pins. I pull a shawl over my shoulders, pick up my skirts and hurry downstairs.

Daisy, her head thrown back, is sitting in an armchair near the fire when I reach the breakfast room. Her hair is awry. She is still in her dressing gown with the hem of her nightgown peeking underneath.

'What is it, Daisy?' I ask.

She does not answer. Her eyes are closed. She appears incapable of speech. I look at Matilda, who raises her shoulders in bewilderment.

'Where is Mrs Brandley?'

'She's out, miss. She left directly after breakfast and said to say she would see you this evening.'

'One of us had better go round and see what has transpired,' I say. 'You stay here, Matilda, and look after Miss Brand—Mrs Oliver. I'll go.'

'But miss, what if it's an intruder? What if it's dangerous?'

'I'll find Albert first,' I tell her. 'Where will he be at this time of the day?'

Matilda puts her hand to her mouth. 'Oh, miss, I've just remembered. He's with Mrs Brandley. He will have taken her wherever she was going, and waited. Miss—'

But I am already on my way.

The front door of Dr Oliver's residence is wide open and the air in the entrance hall is frigid. I ring the bell, stand at the threshold and call out.

'Hello? Hello, is anybody there?'

One of the maids comes through, one I met the first time I went to the library. 'Good afternoon, miss,' she says. She appears calm and unaware of any mishap, perhaps only mystified by the open door.

'Something has happened,' I tell her.

'Happened, miss?'

'Yes. Mrs Oliver is at our house in a state. Have you seen Dr Oliver this morning?'

'No, miss. He has not come down yet. Neither had Mrs Oliver.'

'I need to go up and check that Dr Oliver is quite well under the circumstances, do you understand?'

'Yes, miss. I think so.'

I go inside and mount the staircase. Behind me I hear the maid closing the front door and the sound of her footsteps retreating to the kitchen.

'Dr Oliver?' I call.

It does not take me long to find Daisy's bedroom because the door is flung wide. As I imagine Daisy left it when she exited in a panic.

'Dr Oliver?' I say, at the doorway. 'Dr Oliver?'

The good doctor is lying on his side in the bed and appears unconscious. He is certainly not responding to my voice.

I move closer and put two fingers to his neck as I remember seeing the French doctor do with Mrs Butters. I have to move my fingers around a little before I find a pulse, but I do find one although it is faint. I lower my ear to his open mouth then, and check that Dr Oliver is breathing. He is.

I cover him warmly with the bedding, tucking the covers in around his neck for the air is cool, and then I run quickly downstairs to send for a doctor.

*

What with Dr Oliver's near escape from death and Daisy's hysteria, there is little time to think of anything else. The doctor who attends Dr Oliver, another of his old friends, congratulates me for my quick thinking and actions and asks if I have trained as a nurse? I shake my head and smile, and wonder what Miss Havisham, who brought me up to be a lady, would say.

A nurse is engaged to attend on Dr Oliver since he requires close watching for the next week or two, at least until he is stronger. And after a day spent recovering with her mother by her side, Daisy returns to her own home. I understand from Kitty that her daughter presumed her new husband had died, and was in shock, and given that she has led a sheltered life, I now understand her behaviour a little better.

I spend the following morning catching up on various little chores that have been awaiting attention. There is no word from Mr Laurence Waverley—or should I call him *Captain* Waverley?—but I am not altogether surprised. I have an idea that Captain Waverley is quite accustomed to leading young women by the nose like lambs to the slaughterhouse. Shortly after lunch, I begin a letter to Miss Havisham. I have scarcely written *Dear Miss H* when I pause in my writing, for horse's hooves are coming at a gallop down the road outside the house, which is unusual in itself.

'Whoa!' someone says. The horse comes to a stop, or rather the sound of its hooves cease and, all too quickly, the garden gate squeaks. I have time to rise and cross to the window and glimpse the back of a red-coated man, before there is a knock upon the door.

I catch a vision of myself in my dressing table's mirror with my mouth agape, for I believe it is possibly Captain Laurence Waverley.

I tidy myself quickly, pinching my cheeks to put some colour into them, and head downstairs and meet Matilda coming up.

'Captain Laurence Waverley is here to see you, miss,' she says. Her eyes are big. 'The captain is in the drawing room, miss.'

'Thank you, Matilda.'

I cannot fathom it, but my knees knock together and my heart has taken off like a wolf pursuing prey. For goodness' sake! What is wrong with me!

At the doorway, I pause, for the captain has his back to me. He is looking out of the window. He is in full regalia, although he has taken off his hat—that strange metallic affair with the plume of black horsehair—and his hands are clasped behind his red-jacketed back. He is taller than I remember, standing erect, the backs of his long shiny black boots almost but not quite touching.

I do not say anything; to be honest, the sight of him has made me lose my tongue for the moment. Then he turns and looks directly at me as if he has sensed my presence.

'Miss Havisham.'

'Captain Waverley.'

In three long strides he crosses the carpet, picks me up, holds me close against his chest and spins me around the room. It is as much as I can do not to cry out.

'Forgive me,' he says when he puts me gently back down upon the floor, but his eyes are laughing as if he is not genuinely seeking forgiveness.

'I was—I am—I have unexpectedly been granted time away from my post. I did not even have time to change out of my uniform or, rather, I did not want to waste time changing. I wanted to be with you as soon as I could. I hope I am not intruding? Please say I am not intruding. Could you—could we—?' He breaks off and stares down at me. His face is animated, his dark eyebrows raised, his green eyes vivid with life. I half expect him to kiss me!

But I must bear a look of disapproval on my face, for he releases me and says, 'Please accept my apologies, Miss Havisham, I do not know what came over me.'

I swallow. I smooth down my bodice, pat the back of my hair. I try to be serious, but I cannot help the smile that spreads across my face.

'Ah, excellent,' he murmurs. 'You are not cross with me.'

'How could I be?' I respond.

'Can we go somewhere,' he asks, 'somewhere where we can talk? I have a short time, an hour at a stretch. We can take my horse or we can simply walk? I can leave Scout here and we can—'

'There is a park across the road,' I tell him, interrupting. 'If you will wait while I get my coat?'

'Of course.'

Thus it is that I find myself on the Green with Captain Laurence Waverley. I am not entirely certain how we reach the Green, for it feels as if my feet are not on solid ground and that I float across. I only know that he asks me to take his arm, and that once we are out of the garden gate, he introduces me to his horse.

Scout snuffles the palm of my hand with his damp nose, looking for food, and I pat his neck. I remember these details, for horse's hair feels coarse and quite different to anything else. 'How long have you had Scout?' I ask.

'Since I was seventeen. I brought him with me from Waverley Manor. He is—he is very special.'

Then we are sitting in the park, in a patch of dappled light, with the worn wood of the bench under my hand, a slight chill at the back of my neck and the leaves fluttering above us.

The captain seems unable to sit still or straight, but that he must half turn so that he looks at me.

'Estella?' he says. 'May I please call you Estella?'

'Let me see now,' I say. 'May you call me Estella? On what grounds do you ask?'

'Do not tease me,' he says. 'I have only an hour. On the grounds that we are to be friends, nay, more than friends.' He pauses, then runs on again. 'Estella, I want to know everything about you. Who is Miss Havisham and what is she to you?'

'Miss Havisham? Miss Havisham is my mother by adoption,' I say, and proceed to tell him all about her and how she took me in when I was three, and how I have little recall of the time before.

'Who is Pip?' he asks, when I pause.

'Pip? Where do you hear this name?'

'I have seen the man with you. I arrived late, but was in time to glimpse both of you at the ball, and James tells me he is an ardent admirer and a childhood friend of yours. Are you in love with him?'

'Captain Laurence!' I cry.

'I am sorry. Please forgive my impertinence. And please call me Laurence.' He pauses. 'Would you please say my name,' he asks, 'would you please say Laurence?'

'No, I don't believe I will,' I tell him.

He turns away from me then, and throws his long booted legs out and folds his arms. 'I deserve that, of course.'

I say nothing at first. To be honest, I am altogether taken aback.

'You are highly agitated today, if I may be so bold as to say so,' I venture, for the calm and collected soldier I met at the ball is nowhere in evidence. 'Why would that be?'

'I cannot tell you. All I can say is that we have received our orders.'

'Aah. You are going away?'

'I am going away,' he repeats solemnly, turning his sombre green eyes upon me once again. 'I do not know when yet. It may be tomorrow, or the day after, or the day after that.'

'Are you afraid?'

'No, I am not afraid. Not of fighting. I am only afraid of losing you while I am away!'

'This Pip fellow,' he says, 'do I need to be concerned about him?'

'He is a friend, nothing more.'

Oh Estella, so callous, so unfeeling.

'I see. You are certain about that?'

He gazes at me, his straight dark hair brushing the edge of his collar. His eyelashes are sooty and on his cheekbone under one eye is a small scar. 'Would you write to me, darling Estella, while I am away?'

'I would. I will. But I will need an address.'

'I will send you an address. I will write to you before I leave, you have my word.'

Without thinking I reach out and touch his cheek, finger the small scar. He does not flinch. 'What happened here?' I ask.

'I fell when I was little and split the skin. It is nothing.'

He glances away. 'I have to go,' he says. 'Will you walk back with me?'

I nod and rise to take his arm.

I do not speak as we return to his horse. I am concerned that he will hear the beating of my heart. Anxious I may say too much. Possibly he is anxious about the same thing, for he is silent as well.

We reach Scout all too quickly, and he takes my hand and, gazing deeply into my eyes, kisses it. 'Estella.'

'Laurence,' I murmur.

'Laurence, Laurence, Laurence,' I say, gazing up at him.

I cannot adequately describe the look that passes between us, only that it is a moment of significance.

Then he glances away and, without further ado, unhitches the reins from the fence, settles his hat on his head, puts one foot into a stirrup and swings himself over Scout's back.

He does not look at me again. He does not look back. He does not even glance over his shoulder.

I believe it is because he cannot trust himself.

I feel sure of this. I feel sure because I cannot trust myself, either. I feel sure that were he to look back, I would relinquish all control of my senses and run to him.

21

It comes as no surprise to find the captain occupies a great deal of my waking moments, as well as my sleeping ones. I try to distract myself by ordering a couple of new outfits, including a dress for the showing of the artworks, and going up to London the next day to fetch them. I write to Pip beforehand, at the address of the house down by the river, and say I am coming up to London if he would like to dine with me, but do not receive a response. Which puzzles me. Where is my old friend and why is he being so difficult to reach, so elusive?

The fittings go well, although one outfit needs further work, and I will have to return another time to fetch it. But it all takes less time than I have allowed for and, on a whim and because I have time on my hands and need to occupy my mind, I think of calling on Pip unannounced. I know that he and Herbert reside in the Temple Chamber, for that is the address he gave me to write to him. Perhaps he can be persuaded to talk and tell me what troubles him.

In the early afternoon, I alight from a hackney coach outside the last house in Garden Court. It is a lonely area, exposed to the Thames and the shoreline of reeds, and a ferocious wind whirls up the street. It bats at the coach's canopy and ruffles the horse's mane, and I have to hold onto my hat and draw my coat closer around me as I ask the driver to wait.

I am about to approach the front door of the house when St Paul's and all the many church clocks in the city—some leading, some accompanying, some following—strike the hour. Three o'clock. The sound is ominous, flawed as it is by the wind. The peals of the bells roll down the river like iron balls of the kind that convicts wear, and reverberate back up again, making me stop in my tracks to listen.

'Can I help you, miss?' someone says, behind me.

It is the caretaker. He has stepped out from the adjacent lodge and is also grasping his hat.

'Mr Pirrip,' I say, 'he lives here?'

'Yes, miss, but he ain't here now.'

'Oh,' I say. 'Very well.'

'His uncle's here, miss. Do you know his uncle?'

'His uncle?'

'Yes, miss.' The caretaker screws his eyes up, clutches his hat still tighter and sways a little against a sudden gust. 'You wouldn't like to step inside, would you, miss?' he says apologetically.

I do so and he closes the door behind me. It is immediately calmer, but the wind continues to buffet the little house, dashing against the walls and juddering the foundations as if cannons are being discharged somewhere nearby. It all reminds me a little too much of the marshes and the hulks, and I half expect to see cattle looming in at the window, or hear the booms.

'His uncle arrived a few days ago, miss.'

'I don't know the gentleman,' I say, shaking my head and frowning. Indeed, I had no idea Pip had an uncle. Unless …

'Is the uncle called Pumblechook?' I ask.

'No, miss. I think the name were Provis.'

I shake my head again. The name means nothing to me.

'Can I give Mr Pirrip a message, miss?'

'No, don't concern yourself, thank you. Don't even tell him I was here.' If Pip knows I called and he missed me, it will distress him still further.

'As you wish, miss.'

I leave the caretaker and the lodge. The wind propels me along, blowing my skirts out in front of me, and I reel back to the carriage.

From the safety of the interior, I look up at the house's top floor, where I understand Pip lives.

It is dark and shuttered. No light shines from any window.

I bring my gaze back down and am about to call out to the driver that I am ready to depart when I notice the door on the ground floor slowly closing. Someone stands behind it—a figure, shadowy and obscured. I cannot make out who it is. All I can think is that I have been observed. And I wonder who it is that is resident in Pip's house, and why he is reluctant to come forward and meet me?

In the night I have a vivid dream.

I am walking on the marshes. The wind rushes at me from the shore and the salt-laden sea, and mist wafts in and out of the flat wilderness. The afternoon is bleak and raw, the silver light ricocheting across the landscape. I walk without knowing where I am going, criss-crossing mounds, side-stepping cattle, fording rivulets.

At the edge of my sight, a figure walks together with me, but apart. I know this to be Pip but, try as I might, I cannot go to him nor him come to me. *Estella*, he calls across the distance. *Pip!* I return, *Pip!* But we are each on our own trajectory, our own orbits, and like planets, we cannot deviate from the path laid out before us.

Then, suddenly, as things in dreams happen, we come within touching distance and he reaches for my hand. I'm not wearing gloves and his skin is warm and comforting against mine. Before us is a ditch. I know what lies in its depths and I clutch Pip's hand harder in anticipation.

'Don't be frightened, Estella,' Pip says. 'I am with you, and I love you—you must know this.

'Don't be afraid of the darkness,' he goes on. 'For you are in everything I do and touch. You are in the river, on the marshes, in the light and in the gloom. You are in the wind, in the woods and the sea. Remember you cannot choose to step out of my life, only I can allow that. Remember you cannot tell me to forget you, nor to forsake you, only I can permit that. Remember you will forever be a part of me … Remember that …'

He fades from my sight and, unwilling as I am, something forces me to step to the ditch's edge. Oh, the horror. The horror. For I know what is in the ditch. I know what I will find.

But …

No man, no prisoner, no convict lies dead and decaying in the ditch. In the ditch, in its depths, strangely clean for all the mire and mud, is a small bundle of white swaddling.

I peer closer, for it seems to me that the swaddling moves. I peer closer and a baby's face, calm and blue-eyed, gazes back at me.

I wake then. I am drenched in sweat and trembling with fear.

It is no surprise that I cannot return to sleep, and I lie awake for hours wondering what it all means.

22

Within days of being with him on the Green, I receive a letter from Captain Laurence Waverley. He has been on my mind. In fact, he is often to be found at the edges of it, most often in uniform sitting astride Scout and looking terribly dashing and brave. How ridiculous my imagination can be at times! *Laurence, Laurence, Laurence.* I do not know what to make of the man.

The writing paper is gritty under my fingers, soiled with mud, I believe, and I imagine the captain dressed in his red coat and perched on a rough camp bed in a tent. One hand is running through his black hair, the other holds his pen while his green eyes scan the words he has written. The candlelight flickers in the evening breeze, the canvas flaps damply. Horses nicker, and the air is thick with the smell of grass and newly-stirred earth and of gunpowder. Someone has been firing a musket.

My dear Estella, he writes. *I do not know where to start this epistle and using your name is, without a doubt, of comfort to me. It was for the same reason that I asked you to say mine, so that I could imagine you saying it in my ear. But you must have guessed this?*

I want you to be aware from the outset that I have never, I repeat never, written a letter such as this one in my life. I know—actually I do not know, I am presuming—*that your opinion of me does not rate highly. I could see it in your eyes on the night I met you, on the night of my brother's engagement party, and I had hoped that my second meeting with you would act as reassurance. I want to be honest with you, for honesty is a trait that I value highly. I believe that we, you and I, are similar beings, and that we recognised each other for what we are, for what we were about. Each intent on capturing the other. But whereas you returned home on that night and no doubt smiled over my feeble and unsuccessful efforts to win your heart, perhaps chastised yourself a little for failing to completely bewitch me, and then subsequently and promptly forgot about me, I had a different experience. An experience that was altogether rare. An experience which demanded that I meet with you a second time in order to put my mind at rest. And of course it did precisely the opposite.*

In short, Estella, I have been unable to put you from my mind. You have no idea what you have done to me. I don't believe you have any idea of your own exquisite beauty, either. Which is a rare gift. It is why men become jelly-legged in your presence—believe me, I have watched them. I cannot eat, sleep (particularly sleep) or drink, but that I see your lovely face before me. I am quite beside myself. I do not know how to adequately describe my state since I am not familiar with the effect you have had on me.

Bear with me. I have told you I was adopted. And, perhaps, therefore, you will understand this better than most. I was five and an orphan when Lord Waverley found me wandering the streets and showed me compassion, returning with me to Waverley Manor. The servants took me off for a scrubbing and an extensive soaping before I was dressed in some of James's clothes, and met by both James and the woman who became my mother. I slept, at first, in James's bedroom, but sadly I began to suffer from night terrors and, in an effort not to disturb James, I was given my own bedchamber. However, this worsened my terrors, for I would awake in a state of fear and find myself completely and utterly alone. Several nights passed in this fashion before I plucked up the courage to walk from the room when I woke shuddering with horror. The servants would find me asleep in the most unlikely places when they began work in the mornings. Once, I let myself out of the house, crossed the yard to the stables and slept with the horses. Lord Waverley knew, naturally. There was little he did not know, which, incidentally, is still the case, but he never said anything. Perhaps he thought I would get over it in my own time, and I did—it simply took longer than anyone anticipated. By and by, as these things happen, Lady Waverley got wind of my night wanderings and one morning at breakfast, as I was passing her chair, she surreptitiously passed me a small note with a map of the house drawn on it and an arrow showing the location of her room. I slept alongside her bed after that. I would come in at all hours and quietly settle myself on the floor, and within a few seconds a pillow and a soft rug would appear, and her hand would reach down and hold mine until I went to sleep. This kindness was one of the sweetest experiences of my life.

I mention it here, dear Estella, because when I think of you, I remember this kindness. My greatest desire is for your hand to hold mine at night, every night, until we are both asleep. Until we are old. Until the poets have run out of verses. Until I can no longer remember your name, only the touch of your hand.

Returning, as I must, to my wretchedness and my distress, the fact is the simple opportunity for me to declare my love in person is, at this moment in time, beyond my control.

We leave for the Balkans in a matter of days. I had thought it was earlier, but it was not.

If there is anything you can say that will allow me to hope that you return my love—for I love you truly and deeply—please write to me soonest, care of James. He will know where to send the letter.

I remain yours, dear Estella, forever,

Laurence Waverley.

I am in my sitting-room when I receive the letter and read it, and I put it to one side and steeple my fingers.

I could be happy with Laurence Waverley. It would mean that I could remain close to Eliza, for she would become my sister-in-law.

In an effort to win me over, he has shown me his soft and gentle side, and I believe that he would love me, and care for me with the greatest affection. And, if I am honest, I admit that I am more than half in love with him.

On the other hand, the simple truth is that the man has no property and little income, and he would be absent, off soldiering, a great deal of the time. Furthermore, if I am to be fair, soldiering is a dangerous profession and I have no wish to be a widow so early in life. Should I become a widow—God forbid, but it is something I must take into account—it will be so much more difficult to find a second husband. Nobody wants to marry a widow. They do not fit in at cards or other social gatherings because they are single. They are in a class, and a lowly class at that, of their own, unless they are exceptionally wealthy and, alas, I will not fall into that category. They are—how shall I put it?—spare parts. Unkind of me, I know.

Thus do I deliberate whether or not to respond to the Captain's letter ...

His epistle is beautifully written and the part that continues to tug at my heartstrings is the description of his early years at Waverley Manor. It is plainly told, and all the more poignant for its simplicity, and I am sorely tempted. But I cannot afford to be sentimental. In addition, my artist friend is always lurking in the back of my mind. I cannot commit to anything until I have solved that dilemma.

In the end, I write to Laurence to refuse him. I am not unkind. I do not mention his lack of prospects. I thank him for his kind offer of marriage, but say that regretfully I must decline. I do not give a reason. The Captain is not slow-witted; he will work it out.

I address the letter to his brother, as requested, and try to put Laurence Waverley—and the kindness and sincerity that has shone through his words—from my mind. But now that I have begun to think of the man and his dark hair, of his bewitching green eyes and honesty, it is difficult.

23

The day of the showing of the artworks is the following one. *Finally!* The event is at four in the afternoon and I can hardly contain myself until then. I try to fill the time with reading, only I read a page and have no idea what I have read, and must begin anew. In the end, I take out a gown, the hem of which caught on something and ripped, that needs mending. Usually this would be Matilda's task, but I am desperate for something to occupy not only my fingers but my mind, and this takes up some of the morning.

When I previously attended James Waverley's house for the ball, the surrounding estate was in darkness when we arrived. But this afternoon, I come unexpectedly upon Waverley Manor in the daylight and it is an altogether pleasurable experience. The dwelling is on two levels and made of pale grey stone. Large and stately, it is set on flat hectares of green, dotted by masses of snowdrops. The nearest woodlands, dark and deep, are some distance away and nothing detracts the eye from the mansion's beauty. The grey roof of the house is pitched, the windows are casements. At one corner are French doors leading out onto a stone patio. The patio has the prettiest little fountain and cherub at its centre. And all this to be Eliza's when she marries James.

I think about Laurence again, my Royal Dragoon Guards captain. I have to admit my thoughts have strayed to him all too often since his letter. I had determined not to think about him, but it has been difficult. He seems honest and honourable and sincere. Did he take up soldiering, I wonder, because he knew that he would not inherit the estate? It seems unfair, does it not?

The manservant who greets me at the door and takes my coat leads me through the library at the left and into a room beyond. I recognise it as the ballroom, only now it is filled with an array of paintings on easels and, in the far corner, a gathering of guests.

James detaches himself from the group and comes over to take my hand. 'Estella.' He has taken to calling me by my first name because of my friendship with Eliza.

'It is good of you to come,' he tells me.

'It is my pleasure,' I say, endeavouring to concentrate on his words rather than gaze frantically about for a sighting of *him*.

'Feel free to wander amongst the art,' James tells me. 'Refreshments will be served at five, followed by Mr Pevensey talking a little about his work, and then we will have supper.

'If you are looking for Eliza'—alas, my gaze *has* been distracted!—'sadly, she is not well and sends her greetings and hopes you will not miss her too much.'

'That is too bad,' I say. 'I do hope she will be well soon.'

He smiles good-naturedly at me. I thank him, and he leaves me to tour the room and the paintings in my own time.

I move around quietly, not wanting to draw attention to myself, for I have found that art is something best studied on one's own and without interruption. The paintings appear to be a mixture of materials, but chiefly they are oils. The vast majority are pastoral scenes from the country—Wiltshire, perhaps? Hayricks and harvesting and wagons stacked with offcuts of wood, and so on. Then there are a total of three paintings from the marshes. *My* dark flat wilderness, with the low leaden line of the river in the distance. They are not inspiring, these pictures. There are no cattle or people in them and they seem lifeless and insipid. And I begin to doubt that Mr Pevensey is the man I seek.

I leave the paintings at length and join the other guests and take up the glass of champagne offered to me. Apart from James, there is no-one here that I know, which is always tedious, for I have to make an effort and appear not only interested in my companions, but interesting. And on this occasion, I have to keep the tension out of my voice. The gathering is mostly men, although one or two wives are also present. Mr Edward Pevensey is not here. Not yet.

I stand back a little, out of sight, behind but between the shoulders of two men, and it is as much as I can do to stop trembling while I wait. James eventually enters the ballroom from the library with a bearded fair-headed man trailing at his heels. The man is unkempt, for his trousers are baggy and his jacket patched at the elbows, but from the titter in the crowd I know this must be the artist: Edward Pevensey, a man I have never seen before in my life.

James introduces him and tells us a little of his work, but I am not listening. All I want to do is leave, depart. Flee. But I am stuck between two men.

Stuck between two men! How ironic.

I think about pretending to faint, but that would draw unnecessary attention to myself and my glass would no doubt shatter. Then I think I will not have to *pretend* for I feel quite light-headed. The alcohol has gone straight to my head and behind my eyes black shadows come and go.

I concentrate on Mr Pevensey. He appears a trifle nervous. One hand twitches at his side, the other touches his beard a little too frequently. He begins to talk, welcoming us, thanking us for coming.

'I was—I was fortunate enough to have some days on the marshes south of our great city,' he says. 'And you can see I made full use of my time. I find the light down there otherworldly.'

He may have found the light otherworldly, I think, but it has not inspired his work.

A guest near the front engages Mr Pevensey in conversation, but I am too far away to hear what is being said. The gathering breaks up, however, and the guests mingle once more, chatting amongst themselves. Some take a fresh opportunity to cross the floor and revisit the artworks, and I find myself standing alone.

On the pretext of visiting the powder room, I absent myself. I remember where the powder room is from the time before and return to the entrance hall, which is empty.

Darkness has fallen outside. I retrieve my coat and make my escape. Albert is waiting for me with the horses and carriage and there are enough guests present that James will not miss me.

For which I am grateful. If he were to see my face, I believe he knows me well enough to detect my disappointment and distress, and he would be left wondering.

24

The following day, I go up to London again to fetch the outfit that required further work. I do not have to go today, but I need to be diverted. I need to escape thoughts of how much store I put by meeting Mr Pevensey. I should have known that it would not happen so easily. These things never do.

In all truthfulness, Captain Laurence Waverley also awaits my attention at the back of my mind. I have not been able to banish him or his green eyes and dark hair, for he is now vying for attention with my unknown artist. I long to settle that, one way or another. It has been so long since I was on the marshes with my artist friend that half of me is beginning to think I imagined it all.

Because of this, I ask Albert to make a detour with the horses and carriage and drop me outside the National Gallery. Since I have no notion of how long I will be, I let him go, telling him that I will return home by chaise-cart. I am not sure what I hope to achieve by visiting the gallery, but at least I am making an attempt to find *him*.

The National Gallery, a neoclassical structure with several columns soaring loftily into the air supporting the entrance, is in Trafalgar Square and is an altogether stately building. Inside is a small collection of oil paintings, and while they are attractive and interesting, I can tell at a glance that I have wasted my time. For one thing, none of them are of the marshlands, for another, their styles are old-fashioned, if I may say so.

I leave the gallery and commence making my way to my dressmaker on the edge of Mayfair. I travel part of the way and walk a fair bit of it. Walking and the distraction it brings eases my state of mind!

One of the establishments I walk past is Brown's Hotel in Albemarle Street and, on a whim, I go in and order tea in the hotel's drawing room. I have not been here before, although I have heard that even Queen Victoria is fond of taking tea here, and once I am inside I am not surprised. It is an elegant establishment. I am taken with the dark-wooden wall panelling, the light that slants across the tables, the chairs sumptuously upholstered in hues of ruby and royal blue, and the pretty *petit fours* upon the cake stands.

I take a seat in the middle of the room, order tea and gaze around. Paintings are hung upon the wooden panelled walls and I turn to study each one in turn, for I have now become a little obsessed with art. And stop in shock.

One of the paintings is of the marshlands, of my flat wilderness, the land intersected with dykes and mounds and gates, the cattle looming out of the mist, and the graveyard with its small lozenges of rain-stained graves. A figure stands at the edge of this painting, a female form wearing a dark hooded cloak and facing away from the artist. The hood of her cloak is barely pushed back and her face not visible as she gazes out at the landscape before her, but I know with certainty that the figure is me.

There is a signature at the bottom of the painting, but it is not distinct.

'Do—do you know who—who painted that scene?' I ask the serving girl when she brings my tea, stumbling over my words in my excitement and indicating the picture.

'No, miss,' she says, curtseying politely. 'But it is new. It were hung only last week.'

'I see,' I say. 'Thank you. Do you think you could find out for me who the artist is, and where I can find him?'

'I will try, miss,' she says.

Such is my agitation that I burn my tongue on my first sip. I play with the teaspoon until I am in fear of knocking the cup over, and at least one of the ladies sitting near me glances curiously in my direction. I cannot resist looking towards the door every ten seconds to determine whether the girl is returning.

Finally, I see the maître d' making his way over to me.

'You are the one that enquired about the painting, miss?' he says, tilting his head towards the picture.

'I am. What can you tell me?'

'I believe the artist is a Mr Theo Whittaker. If you would like, I can locate his address?'

'I would be grateful,' I say.

'I will attempt to find it now, miss, but I will have to look up the details and it may take me longer than five minutes.'

'No matter,' I say. 'I will wait.'

Theo. It is a lovely name. I believe it is Ancient Greek, meaning *Gift of God*.

I attempt to sit patiently and not fiddle, and persuade myself that I do not need, let alone want, a second cup of tea. Five minutes turn into ten, but eventually the maître d' returns and hands me a slip of paper neatly folded into two.

'Thank you,' I say. 'I am much obliged.'

I open the paper and find an address in a none-too salubrious area. But there is nothing for it, I think, as I rise from my chair.

Only wild horses would keep me away. Quote: Captain Waverley.

I hire a hackney coach to take me, and I cannot describe how we get there or what occurs on the journey since my mind is in turmoil. Finally, I am to meet with my artist! I am to meet with Theo. *Theo*: the gift from God. I can scarcely believe it.

We stop outside a row of run-down tenements which are similar to something that might be out of *Oliver Twist*. It is a poverty-stricken area. The air is thick with smoke from the factories. Grey sheets spattered with soot are strung across a courtyard. The lower window of the dwelling is bricked-up, and a grubby urchin sits on an untidy pile of logs out the front playing in the dirt with a stick. I ask the driver to wait, pick up my skirts, navigate the muddy yard and make my way up the staircase that smells of urine.

By this point, I am half in doubt that this is where I will find Theo Whittaker. It seems so unlikely. He was not in penury when I saw him, but he was to have an exhibition, and there is always the likelihood that things have not gone well for him. To attempt to make a living from art of any kind is tricky and unpredictable, this much I know. Upstairs, I pause outside the worn wooden door and knock upon it.

The woman who opens the door is clearly with child. At a glance, I would say the infant is not far off from coming. Her skin is reddened by the cold, her lips chapped, her long hair bunched up behind her head. In spite of this, however, there is a glimmer of prettiness and wholesomeness in the woman's face.

'Yes?' She looks at me curiously. She does not address me as *miss* confirming my opinion that perhaps she has fallen on hard times only recently, that perhaps she was a lady in another life.

'Who is it, love?' someone calls out.

The woman widens the door to admit a man, a man that I at once recognise in spite of his torn coat with the frayed cuffs, his overlong hair and his paint flecked trousers. There is no mistaking the deeply set brown eyes, although his face is gaunt now and his cheekbones bonier than ever.

Theo Whittaker looks at me and has a split-second of hesitation. It is the slightest start that can escape a man, and the most carefully repressed and the soonest checked, but it does cause him to stumble over his words. 'How—how can I help?' he says, averting his gaze from mine.

His thin line of moustache trembles and his cheeks begin to flush. He appears to look past me, away and down the murky staircase, as if this situation is the most awkward in the world.

I think of how I imagined meeting him again, of his gaze settling upon mine, of his laughing eyes and teasing manner, and his hand resting upon my waist, and I could not agree more.

I put one gloved hand against the doorframe to hold myself up.

'I ... I appear to have make a mistake,' I get out. 'I was looking for—' I break off. 'My apologies. It scarcely matters whom I was looking for. I clearly have the wrong address.'

'No matter,' the woman says. She folds her hands over the top of her belly, and I notice the ring on the fourth finger of her left hand. She is staring at me now with a puzzled expression upon her face, for my hair is done in much the same way as it was when the man in front of me painted me, and I am wearing my hooded cape. She recognises me and yet she does not.

I turn away from the door. I leave without another word. I cannot find the phrases even to bid them both good day. Clutching onto the rough brick wall for support, I make my way downstairs, cross the courtyard on shaky legs and half-fall into the hackney coach.

'Where to, miss?' the driver asks, and I manage to form the words, to tell him where I live.

When I reach home, Matilda takes one look at me. She leads me upstairs, undresses me as if I were a child and puts me to bed.

A doctor is called for. He says I am overwrought, and prescribes bed rest for a number of days. If I am not feeling more like myself in a week, he leaves instructions that Mrs Brandley should send for him again. He will bleed me then, he tells me.

I fall into lethargy, and although I am not asleep I am not of this world.

I have been betrayed and, not only that, but I have been made a fool of.

How could I have not considered that such a charming, good-looking man should not already be married?

I recall that I did once think this, but dismissed the thought.

I believe I know why. I believe arrogance is one of my traits. Not to mention presumptuousness. And conceit.

It would appear that I have had a lucky escape, but instead of feeling anger I am empty.

If I feel anything, it is disappointment in myself and in my behaviour.

25

Dr Oliver pays me a visit. I suspect he has been kept informed as to my condition by Mrs Brandley.

I have not seen him since the day I found him unconscious, and the first thing he does is to warmly kiss my hand and thank me for saving his life.

'I did not save your life,' I say. 'You were alive when I found you.'

'But I might have died had it not been for your quick actions, my child. Besides, did no-one ever teach you that when you are given a compliment to accept it graciously?'

I smile. 'Thank you,' I say.

We sit in my sitting-room. The sun comes into my quarters upstairs in the mornings and it is altogether the most pleasant room in the house in the winter.

Matilda brings us a tray of tea.

Out of habit, I suppose, Dr Oliver takes my pulse and nods. 'Satisfactory.' He resumes his seat. He is looking well in spite of the recent event. His white hair has been recently cut, his beard tidied and his face has a healthy rosy glow. It would appear that married life agrees with him.

'My child,' he says, taking up his cup. 'Would you like to tell me what ails you?'

I shake my head. 'It is nothing, really.'

'Come,' he says. 'It must be something.'

When I do not respond, he goes on.

'It is most unlike you to be confined inside, and I can see from your face, which is normally so bright, cheerful and, dare I say it, impudent?—that you are still far from being well.' He pauses. 'Or,' he murmurs, 'should I say, content?'

'I am discontent,' I say, moodily tugging at the tassels of my shawl. 'I cannot tell untruths there.'

'Good,' he says. 'We have established something then, have we not?'

He sips at his tea and replaces the cup in the saucer, where it wobbles precariously, for his hands are none too steady.

'It is something to do with a man?'

I nod.

'And has this man wounded you?'

I nod again. My lips are closed tight. My eyes begin to fill with tears. My expression must be one of wretchedness, I fear.

'No surprises there,' Dr Oliver remarks. He puts his shaky cup and saucer back down, to my relief.

'Do you think, my child, that you are the first woman in history to have been wounded by a man?'

'No,' I burst out. 'No, of course not!' I continue. 'But I do not know—I do not know how to proceed. I do not know how to go on,' I grind out, and the poor tassels of my shawl receive several more hard tugs.

'Hah,' he says. 'That's more like the spirited girl I know.'

He pauses again, covering the endings of his chair arms with his wrinkled and liver-spotted hands. 'Let me ask you a question,' he says. 'What happens when you fall off a horse?'

'You get back on again,' I say miserably.

'*Précisément.*

'And,' he adds, 'if you are Miss Estella Havisham, you ride like the devil to make up for lost time.'

I laugh. I cannot help it.

He smiles. 'It's good to hear your laughter,' he says.

Matilda is clearly of the same opinion, for she comes to the door on the pretext of refilling the teapot, but her arched eyebrows tell me she, in fact, wants to know what has caused the merriment. I will tell her later.

Dr Oliver wipes his eyes and rises. 'Good day to you, my dear child,' he says, taking my hand.

'*Merci, mon ami,*' I say.

'*Tout le plaisir était pour moi,*' he responds.

*

After Dr Oliver has departed, I tell Matilda that I wish to dress, and that I am going out.

Her standard reply to any request of mine is usually *as you wish, miss*, but today she looks at me strangely. No doubt she is curious as to my sudden change of demeanour.

'We are going out, Matilda,' I repeat.

'Right, miss,' she says.

When she has done my hair, I ask her to slip next door and see if Albert is free to take us both to Hyde Park.

'Hyde Park?' she repeats.

'Yes, Matilda. Dr Oliver has prescribed fresh air and sunshine. And look,' I say, pointing out of the window, 'it is a brilliant day and we must make the most of it.'

At the park, I leave Albert and Matilda with the horses and carriage, noting that Albert has already slyly reached for his wife's hand, and walk.

I go as far as the Serpentine. My gloved hands are in my pockets and I have on coat, boots, hat and scarf, but for all that I shiver with cold. It is invigorating, though.

The trees are bare, reaching their bony fingers up to the sky, and an icy frost from the night before sparkles on the grass in places. The swans glide over to me out of curiosity, their webbed feet paddling the shadowy water. I have heard that all the swans in London belong to the Queen, but I do not know that I believe this. It seems unfair towards the swans. I have nothing to give the white feathery creatures with their long elegant necks, and I withdraw my hands from my pockets and hold them out to indicate they are empty. My hands are like my heart, I think.

While I am communing with the swans, I smell chestnuts roasting and I look around to find the street seller with a barrow. Fortunately, I have some coins in my pocket and I make my way over. I buy three packets and return to Albert and Matilda, giving them one each.

Then I wander off again, eating hot chestnuts straight from the paper and squinting into the weak sunlight. Some children have gathered at the lake's edge and with much hilarity they are sailing, and more often than not sinking, paper boats. I stand and watch their bright faces and think that although I am not exactly happy, I am more content than I have been for some time.

26

I am upstairs. It is not yet ten. Sitting in the feeble spring sunlight that enters my rooms, I am writing to Miss Havisham once more. I have a mind to tell her about Captain Waverley's proposal, but not about the contents of his letter, for I fear she will make fun of his sincerity.

I pause in my writing, for I again hear horse's hooves coming at a gallop along the road outside the house.

My heart leaps into my throat when the horse comes to a stop as before. Has my captain taken leave and come to plead his case? How will I be able to refuse him now? Indeed, I do not think I will refuse him ... Indeed, I believe I am as excited as a schoolgirl at the thought of seeing him again.

All too hastily, the garden gate squeaks, but before I have time to rise and cross to the window to confirm the identity of the visitor, there is a *rat-a-tat-tat*—an urgent knock if ever I heard one—upon the door.

Someone opens it and a voice carries up to my window.

'Mr James Waverley to see Miss Havisham, please.'

James, not Laurence.

The maid comes running upstairs. Not surprising, since the tone of James's voice indicates he is extremely anxious to see me. It is not Matilda; it is Mrs Brandley's maid and, before she is halfway, I step out of the room and tell her to let Mr Waverley come up.

Puzzled, I wait in the doorway and watch as James takes the stairs two at a time.

'Estella,' he says, reaching me and taking my hand.

His hand is cold and trembles in mine. His normally bright and happy face is sombre and I am concerned by how pale his cheeks are.

'What is it?' I ask, leading him into my sitting room.

'Can I offer you tea or coffee?' I add, out of politeness.

He shakes his head.

'Won't you sit down?' I say, for he stands stiffly behind one of the armchairs.

'I cannot.'

'James,' I say, putting my hand on his arm, 'has something happened to Eliza?'

He shakes his head again, but now he blinks rapidly for tears have appeared in his eyes.

'You wrote,' he begins, 'you wrote to my brother, to Laurence—?'

'I did. Only recently. He told me to send the letter care of you. He said you would be kept informed of his whereabouts and would send it on.'

He pulls a crumpled envelope from his pocket. The envelope has been opened and I glimpse a folded letter inside.

'I give you my word I have not read it,' he says, handing it to me. 'Is this the letter?'

I nod, recognising my handwriting on its front. 'It would appear so. But I do not understand.'

'I only know that my brother wrote to me. He wrote saying he intended to ask you to marry him—we have no secrets—and I presume this is your reply.'

I nod again. 'It is.'

He runs one hand feverishly across the back of the armchair like he is possessed, then jerks his hand back to his side. 'I have no right to ask for the contents of your letter, Estella—'

'James,' I murmur. 'What is it? Please tell me?'

He looks at me, his eyes awash now with tears and his throat working.

'Estella, Laurence was killed late yesterday afternoon,' he says.

27

Laurence Waverley is buried on the Waverley Estate in the family graveyard on a cold but bright sunlit day. Only the family and close friends, an exception being made for me, are present. His unit, the Royal Dragoon Guards, has already departed for the Balkans and there is not a soldier in sight. There is not a soldier in sight, but there is a horse. Scout. He stands at the side of his master's grave, twitching and tossing his mane, but otherwise silent. It is almost macabre.

Laurence touched my life briefly and fiercely like a firefly in the dark, and I have no words to describe my grief. No phrases to detail the loss of such a noble and honourable man. The words, the phrases I do have, are those he uttered to me: *Only wild horses would keep me away; I wanted to be with you as soon as I could; I want to know everything about you; would you please say my name, would you please say Laurence?*

But more than this ... Oh, so much more than this is the way he looked at me ... From the moment we met.

Oh, what have I done? What have I done?

The man with the black hair and the bewitching green eyes has forever left my life. I cannot take it in. I cannot comprehend that I will never see him again, that he will never ask me to say his name again. *Laurence, Laurence, Laurence.*

I have been told by James that his brother intervened between two of his men who were having a fight. One drew his pistol and, in the confusion, Laurence was shot and died at the scene from his wound. My letter, apparently newly received, was found on his bed by one of his men and returned to James along with his other personal effects.

James spares me any comment, but the family must know what the contents of my letter—my answer—to Laurence was. They *must*. For surely, if I had accepted Laurence's proposal of marriage, I would want to share that with them? I *would* share it with them. I would tell them that I had wanted to marry their son, that I loved him in return. And I did, I did!

Then again, perhaps James has not divulged that information. He has not told them that his brother requested my hand in marriage. Can this be the answer? Is this why the family continues to talk to me, and why I have been allowed here today?

I cannot help but ask myself if Laurence's intervention between his men was deliberate. That after my news, he no longer cared for or valued his life. I will never know, of course. I have since gone over and over the appalling, offending letter. Oh, if only I had said this and not that. If only I had been more sincere and less abrupt. If only I had taken his lead and spoken from the heart. If only I had been less callous and more caring. (What is wrong with me that I am so unfeeling?)

If only …

It is now burnt, the letter. I could no longer bear to look at it, to be in the same room. It is enough that I must live with my words for the rest of my days.

After the last of us has thrown a handful of soil on the coffin, and we have each in turn patted Scout upon the nose, and Lady Waverley has stooped to drop a dozen red roses on its top, we return to the library. Tea, coffee and refreshments are served. James talks softly to Mr and Mrs Wright. Eliza and I murmur one to another. Lord and Lady Waverley appear to be encapsulated in their grief and only speak when spoken to.

At an opportune moment, I cross the floor to Lady Waverley's side. She has sunk into one of the sofas, cup of tea in one hand, and stares into the distance.

I sit down beside her.

She looks up, glancing across at me. She has tried to disguise it with powder, but under her eyes the skin is bruised. Nights of broken sleep. I, too, am suffering from sleeplessness. But I am not a mother, and I cannot presume to understand her anguish.

I extract the piece of paper which I previously folded and inserted into the long black sleeve of my mourning dress, and hold it out to her. It is a cutting from the original letter which Laurance penned to me.

'Laurence wrote me this shortly before he died. I think you should have it,' I tell her.

She blinks at me. 'Are you sure? Is it not something intimate?'

'It is personal,' I tell her, 'but it concerns you.'

'Me?'

'Yes.'

'Would you read it to me, my child?' she asks. 'I'm not sure I know where I have placed my spectacles.'

I read to her. I have begun the words about Laurence being rescued by Lord Waverley when the others drift, one by one, over to us, and Lady Waverley stops me with her hand on my arm and asks me to begin again so that they might hear, too.

And so I read again the words I know by heart now. The phrase about sleeping with the horses. The sentences about the map and the arrow; the pillow and the soft rug; the kindness of Lady Waverley. My voice is stilted. I have to make frequent stops. But by the time I reach the place where her hand would reach down and hold Laurence's until he fell asleep, there is not a sound in the room.

*

Over the following days, I cannot take control of the state of my mind.

Or of my heart.

I cry needlessly. Tremble for no apparent reason. I am not accustomed to these emotions, and I do not understand them. I also find myself staring into space for hours and forgetting where I am. It is not like the previous time when I was persuaded to get back on the horse and ride like the devil—now I only wish I did not exist.

How am I to continue with my life as I know it? How am I to resume the rounds of parties, balls and theatre visits. How am to find my gaiety again?

Something has altered within me. This much I know. I cannot take up that old life again.

One evening, Matilda finds me lost in thought, sitting on the park bench in the cold.

'Miss! We have all been wondering where you are. Won't you please come in?'

'Miss,' she says again, when I look at her as if I do not know her. She touches my hands, curled tightly in my lap. 'Miss, you're frozen.'

Taking my arm, she brings me to my feet and, with her help, I cross the Green and return to the house. Kitty wants to call the good doctor, but I refuse. What will he think of me coming to pieces for a second time?

Something weighs heavily upon my mind and I write a note to James Waverley asking if he will see me, and he writes back to say he has an hour free the following day and will call upon me.

When he arrives, Matilda brings him up to my sitting room.

He is pale and gaunt-looking, and his boyish face seems to have aged ten years. Sadly, his being here reminds me of when he called to inform me of his brother's death. That thought is certainly not far from my mind, and I am certain it is not far from his, either.

He sits at my request. Perches, actually, on the edge of the chair. He is not at ease, this much is clear.

Matilda asks if she should bring tea or coffee, but James declines both. I would not be surprised if, like me, he cannot bring himself to eat and drink.

When Matilda has left, I indicate that we talk low-voiced, for I do not wish anyone to overhear our conversation, and he understands and has no objection. It also appears he has half an idea of why I have asked him to call.

'Estella,' he says, before I can broach the subject, 'you must know that I have told my family nothing, that is, nothing of Laurence's request for your hand in marriage. I only told them that he spent a great deal of time in your company at the party, and they would have seen for themselves and formed an opinion of how he felt about you.'

I nod. 'I thought so. It would explain their acceptance of me the other day.'

I pause, fidgeting with the stiff cuffs of my dress. Dressed in mourning clothes, in black, I cannot imagine a time in the foreseeable future when I will once again wear colours: pink, or scarlet.

'Oh, James,' I burst out, in distress, 'I can't tell you how much I regret my letter.'

'So you did refuse my brother? The other day at the funeral, I was not convinced, but your face this afternoon tells me everything. Why, Estella? Why did you refuse him? Forgive me if you would rather not answer. It is, after all, none of my concern—'

'I refused him for financial reasons. I presumed that he had little or no income. I did not know how we would manage on my inheritance alone. I am financially well off, but I am not immensely wealthy—' I break off, for I am not being completely truthful and in addition James is shaking his head with a pained expression on his face.

'What? What is it?'

'You were not to know, Estella. My father had set aside funds for him. It is true he would not have inherited the estate, but he was to be given a portion equal to its value.'

'No,' I say, 'no!'

If I were beside myself with grief before, I have no words for how I feel now.

'Do not blame yourself, Estella,' James says. 'We don't know that your letter had anything to do with his death.'

'I have made a fine mess of things,' I say. 'First …' I begin. 'First—' But I break off. 'No, I cannot tell you that.'

For I cannot, I cannot speak of Theo Whittaker without harming his career *and* his marriage.

'Everything I touch seems to crumble before my eyes. Am I cursed, I wonder?'

James leans forward in his chair, his elbows on his thighs.

'Don't say that, Estella. If Eliza heard you, she would be most distressed. Forgive me, but why is it you have brought me here today?' he asks gently. 'Surely it is not simply to put your mind at rest?'

'No,' I say, 'it isn't.'

I pause.

My rigid hands are like claws, clutching onto the ends of the chair's arms as if I am trying to hold onto life itself.

'I have come of age,' I explain, 'and I do not have to ask permission of anyone.' I pause again, for this is hard for me to elucidate. 'James, I have it in my mind to marry someone else to put me out of my misery, to call a halt to this endless cycle of parties, dances and the like.'

He nods and smiles faintly as if this is welcome news.

But I shake my head. 'I do not love this person.'

'And?' he says, tilting his face to one side. 'You want my blessing? Is that it? What exactly do you want?'

'Your advice. You are objective, dear James. Not to mention rational and sensible.'

'Can I be open with you, Estella?'

'By all means.'

'Is this person Mr Pirrip?'

'No.'

'No?'

He is taken aback. 'But why would you not marry Mr Pirrip?' he asks. 'Supposing he asked you? He loves you, Estella. Surely you are aware of that?'

'I like him, I am exceedingly fond of him, but I do not love him,' I say sorrowfully. 'And he is aware of this. He deserves someone to love him from the deepest depths of their being, as if their life depends upon it. He deserves the love that you and Eliza bestow one upon another. He believes I will grow to love him, but I do not think so. I love him as a friend and as a gentleman, but I am not *in* love with him. There is a difference. You do understand, don't you, James?'

The tears spring to my eyes and I blink rapidly.

'I do,' he says. 'For it is only after this has happened to oneself that one understands it.'

'*Exactement.* I worry that should I marry Pip, we would grow to loathe one another. He would know, you see, that my love for him is platonic. I have known him for so long, and he me, since we were children, and, in spite of the way I treat him, our bond is strong. I am fond of him, but he knows that I do not *love* him, not in the true sense of the word, and he would begin to despise me—I know it!—and I could not bear it. I have ruined one man's life, let me not ruin another!'

No, I could not endure that, I think, for Pip has been the one constant in my life, the one thing I can rely on, and can count on as lasting. And although I profess not to love him, I am uncommonly fond of him.

'Rather let me agree to a marriage of convenience,' I go on, 'and marry a man who does not love me, and whom I do not love. And in that way ... that way nobody need be hurt, nobody need suffer needlessly—'

James leans back in his chair and crosses his legs. 'Estella, I do not know what to say.'

'But you see my point?'

'I do. Would you like to tell me who it is you have in mind?'

'You will despise me.'

'Drummle,' he says flatly, smacking his palm against the chair arm.

I nod my head in misery. 'Oh, why did I think you would not guess?'

James bites at his lower lip. 'I do not advise it, Estella.'

'But I cannot go on like this. I must do something with my life. This endless, tedious round of parties and dances and men fawning over me is wearying and I am tired. I am so tired of it all.'

And Pip waiting ever hopefully in the shadows, too, I think, but do not say. Let me release the poor boy from his misery once and for all.

James nods as if he understands, but I wonder if he does. My attitude towards these social events is not like most young women he knows. It is singular, I am aware of that.

But I wonder if he realises that Laurence's death weighs heavily upon me, that I feel I must atone for it?

And surely, once I am married to Bentley, I will be able to put the past behind me and start over? I will become capable of finding a purpose and a design to my life?

Surely, my restless, guilty heart will at last settle?

28

I pen a note to Mr Drummle, short and to the point:

Mr Drummle, if your feelings towards me are unchanged, please do me the favour of calling upon me tomorrow afternoon at 3:00 pm, when I will give you an answer to your previous request. Estella.

When I have written the letter, I seal it in an envelope, address it, and dress warmly to take it down to the post office.

For all that it is March, the weather continues to be damp and the wind cold. But in some trees, tiny pink blossoms have appeared and the first sprigs of green. Small birds hop from one branch to the other, chirping and twittering, as if they have something to be content about. I envy them.

I finger the edges of the envelope in my pocket as I walk, dog-earing them. I reach the post office and still I hesitate. Returning the letter to my pocket, I walk to the end of the village street and back, and the second time I pause before the office, I force the contents of the letter from my mind. I think about the seasons and how spring is the mark of new beginnings. I think about the small spotted dog who is even now cocking his leg against the lamp post and urinating, and about how life goes on. *Must* go on. And I go inside and post the letter.

I tell myself that I am doing the right thing, that there is no alternative. Well, no immediate alternative, and I cannot face another round of balls and dances and suitors fawning over me. It is time to lead a quiet life; it is time to settle. I cannot, in any event, face the gaiety of balls and dances. Bentley and I will lead amicable but separate lives. No hearts will be broken, no suffering endured by any persons, for this is a marriage of convenience: a business arrangement, if you will.

It is thus that Estella Havisham agrees to marry Bentley Drummle.

When the news that I will marry him if he so desires is given to him, and his astonished and subsequent toadying response suffered and endured, I retire to my sitting room to write to Miss Havisham to tell her the news.

Someone knocks at my door. Matilda.

'Miss? Miss, the kitchen maid … the kitchen maid overheard you tell Mr Drummle that you agree to marry him. Is that right, miss? Have you?'

I would be a fool if I did not hear the incredulity in her voice.

I put down my pen.

'I have, Matilda.'

'Oh, miss.'

'It's not what I would have desired, Matilda, but Mr Bentley is wealthy, he has capital and the marriage will benefit us both.'

'Yes, miss.'

I pick up my pen once more, but I am aware Matilda has not left the room.

'Begging your pardon, miss?'

I look up. 'Yes, Matilda?'

'When miss goes away, when miss marries, er, Mr Drummle … I'll … I'll go with miss, if miss would like?'

'And what of Albert?'

She raises her shoulders. 'I don't know, miss.'

'Thank you, Matilda. I will talk to Mr Drummle and see what I can arrange.'

I look back at my letter, but she remains in the doorway.

'What is it now?' I say with exasperation.

When I gaze back up, her face has gone pale and one hand has slipped up to her mouth.

I have been unnecessarily harsh, but I cannot now retract my words and those fingernails remain a temptation.

'It's nothing, miss.' She shakes her head. 'Nothing.'

She backs out of the room and I hear her retreating down the stairs. Her footsteps are slow and heavy. Ponderous.

29

After I agree to marry Bentley, things proceed rapidly, for he seems anxious to make it official as soon as possible. Perhaps he is worried I will change my mind?

We go to Somersetshire in order for me to meet his family. Mr and Mrs Drummle seem nice, if a little distant. My impression is that it does not concern them *who* Bentley marries, as long as he does marry, and marries well. He has two younger brothers who are like him in every way, down to the custom of observing me as if I am a zoological exhibit in Regent's Park. No love is lost between them. The brothers spend the days continually sparring with one another and, on one occasion, a stable hand is forced to step between them to avoid a physical confrontation. It is most unpleasant.

On the return trip to Richmond, I tell Bentley that it is only fair that I now take him down to Satis House to meet Miss Havisham.

'That would be the proper thing to do, Estella,' he says.

'Might I suggest that while I reside with Miss H, you take a room at the Blue Boar?'

He nods. 'I will make a booking. I'll enquire about riding, too, while we are down there.'

In response, I tell him that he is free to ride whenever he wishes, but my sole reason for going down there is to see Miss H and to make the necessary introductions between them, and that he should not forget this.

We set off on the early morning coach before it is yet light. By the time the day crawls in, shivering like some vagrant clothed in rags of mist and whining for sustenance, we are already out on the open country road. It is a drizzly journey and I spend a great deal of it staring out of the window at the landscape. The weather reminds me a little of the marshes, and I wonder if I will get an opportunity to slip away. Alone. I do not wish to take Bentley. What is the point? He will not understand.

We converse little on the journey. I have found that Bentley is not talkative unless he has had a few drinks and then he is positively garrulous. He speaks only when he has something to say. I do not mind this. In fact, it suits me. The coach is full, as it often is at that time of the day, which means there is little opportunity for any personal discussion between us. But I do so want to tell him a little bit about Miss H. *Warn* him. Is that too strong a word?

As it turns out, I have a brief opportunity at the Blue Boar to mention how things will be. We stop there to offload Bentley's luggage and for some quick refreshments, although nothing at that establishment is ever done with any haste. Over coffee and a late breakfast I tell him of Miss Havisham's eccentricities, her mode of dress, the reason for the way she is. He listens attentively, but does not comment.

'You do not say anything?' I remark, reaching for my coffee cup.

'In truth, Estella, I am already aware of these things.' Bentley pauses with a knife in one hand and fork in the other. 'And have been for some time. Mr Jaggers,' he says.

'And how is it you have been in conversation with Mr Jaggers?'

'I was invited to dine, along with that *Pip* fellow.' He spits the word out like it is distasteful.

'I like Jaggers,' he says decisively. 'And he seems to like me.' He leans forward. 'Apparently, he calls me *the Spider*.'

'The Spider? Why would he do that?'

'I don't know. Perhaps I am cunning? What do you think, Estella? Have I woven a web for you and entrapped you?'

I laugh. I cannot help it. 'I think it's more likely to be the other way around, Bentley.'

'Do you now?' he says.

*

Miss Havisham is unchanged since I last saw her. She seems neither impressed nor disappointed by Bentley. For his part, he is the perfect gentleman, and I expected no other behaviour. Sarah Pocket, who grows more wizened and pinched-looking every time I see her, brings us a tray of tea and we have it in Miss H's rooms. Bentley appears to take everything in his stride.

'And what is it you do?' Miss H asks him, turning her head from gazing into the fire and staring at him, as is her wont. 'Are you employed, or a man of leisure?' She has always been straight to the point.

'A man of leisure, Miss Havisham. My family have acres down in Somersetshire, and I am in line to a baronetcy, but one. But what is one?' he adds, and laughs as if this were neither here nor there. Bentley is not modest, but he is what he is, and it is my experience that it is hard to find a man who is without pride or arrogance—although, of course, I have known one. Nay, two. They do exist.

It is decided that Bentley and I will ride the following morning and that he will attend Satis House for dinner in the evening. After tea, I accompany him downstairs to see him out.

He does not pause to look at me or talk to me in the passage like someone else I remember, which disappoints me, until we are at the gate when he takes my hand to kiss it.

'Until tomorrow,' he says.

He appears a little indifferent. He does not look back as he departs. He is probably already thinking of riding out this afternoon and where he will go. I am fond of both horses and riding, make no error, but I am not obsessed. With Bentley, riding hard and riding fast is a matter of pride and not to be taken lightly.

The weather in the morning is foul. It is not only cold and raining, but the wind blows sideways, and I send word to Bentley at the Blue Boar that I will not be riding today.

After breakfast, I join Miss H in her room and we sit before the fire. I have brought my knitting. I am not much of a knitter and to improve my skills I am making Bentley a scarf. We sit companionably. We talked well into the afternoon yesterday, and this morning there is no sound but the fire crackling, the rain at the window and the occasional whine of wind down the chimney.

When there is a knock at the door, Miss H turns her head from the fire and glances at me. I know what she is thinking; it is Pip's knock.

I raise my eyes and look across the room and I see a man in the doorway who is both Pip and not Pip. For this man looks older and thinner—I am almost inclined to say haggard. I glance at Miss H. He is changed, we say silently one to another. Something has happened.

'And what wind,' asks Miss H, 'blows you here, Pip?'

'Miss Havisham. I went to Richmond yesterday to speak to Estella, and finding that some wind had blown *her* here, I followed.'

Miss H motions for him to sit down and he takes the chair by the dressing table and brings it forward.

'What I wanted to say to Estella, Miss Havisham, I will say to you in a few moments. It will not surprise you. It will not displease you, either. But I am as unhappy as you can ever have meant me to be.'

Pip's words make me anxious. He has skipped all the niceties of polite conversation and is being downright candid, and who can blame him? For that is the way Miss H operates. But I do not look up. I do not wish to see the anguish—yes, that is the word—on his face. I continue to knit, my fingers working the grey wool, but at the same time I attend to what he says.

Or doesn't say. For he has taken off his hat and turns the brim around with his fingers, and it reminds me of the first day I met him and how he twirled the buttons on his coat as if his life depended on it.

'I have found out who my patron is,' he says with finality. 'It is not a fortunate discovery, and is not likely to enrich me in reputation or station or fortune. There are reasons why I must say no more. It is not my secret, but another's.'

My mind is agog. This is clearly what has been disturbing him these last few months. So Miss Havisham is not Pip's benefactor? How is it I have been mistaken? I felt sure that she was. I felt certain that her master plan was to allow him to fall in love with me, endow him with funds, then disallow him from having me—break his heart, as hers was broken.

'It is not your secret, but another's,' Miss H repeats. 'Well?'

'When you first asked for me to be brought here, when I belonged over there'—he gestures with one hand, indicating the forge and his childhood home—'the place I wish I had never left, I suppose I really came here as any other boy might have come, as a kind of servant, to please you, to gratify a whim, and to be paid for it.'

'Aye, Pip,' Miss H replies, steadily nodding her head, 'you did.'

'And that Mr Jaggers—'

'Mr Jaggers,' Miss H interrupts, 'had nothing to do with your coming here. And what's more, to my knowledge, he knew nothing of it. His being my lawyer and his being the lawyer of your patron is mere coincidence. He does the same for any number of people.'

'But when I fell into the mistake of thinking you were my benefactor and remained so long in that mistake, you led me on?'

'Yes,' Miss H says, nodding steadily again. 'I let you go on—'

'Was that kind?' Pips interrupts, with desperation in his voice.

'Was that kind?' Miss H repeats. '*Was that kind?*'

She strikes her stick so violently upon the ground that I glance up in surprise.

'Who am I,' she cries, 'who am I, for God's sake, that I should be kind!'

'I cannot help my words,' he murmurs. 'Do forgive me.'

For all Pip's apology, Miss H is annoyed. She glares at the fire and the embers positively tremble.

'I was generously paid,' Pip begins again, 'for my attendance here, and in being apprenticed to Mr Gargery, and I raise these questions only for my own information. What follows has another purpose. In humouring my mistake, Miss Havisham, you practised on, punished—perhaps you will supply whatever term expresses your intention—your self-seeking relations?'

'I did. Why, they would have it so! So would you. What has been my history, that I should be at the pains of entreating either them or you not to have done so! You made your own snares. *I* never made them.'

'I have been thrown among one family of your relations,' Pip resumes after a moment as if Miss H never made this outburst, 'and have been constantly among them since I went to London. I know them to have been as honestly under my delusion as I myself. And

I should be false and base if I did not tell you, whether it is acceptable to you or no, whether you are inclined to give credence to it or no, that you deeply wrong both Mr Matthew Pocket and his son, Herbert. Do not suppose them to be otherwise than generous, upright, open and incapable of anything designing or mean.'

'They are your friends,' Miss H murmurs.

'They *made* themselves my friends,' Pip says. 'Not like, not like ...' But he does not finish. He means the rest of the Pockets, Raymond, Sarah et al.

Miss H looks at Pip. 'What do you want for them?'

'Only,' Pip says, 'only that you would not confuse Mr Matthew Pocket and his son with the others. They may be of the same blood, but believe me they are not—never—of the same nature!'

'What do you want for them?' Miss H repeats.

Pip flushes.

'I am not so clever, you see, that I could hide from you that I do want something. If you would spare the money to do my friend, Herbert, a lasting service in life but which must be done without his knowledge, I could show you how.'

'Why done without his knowledge?'

'Because I began the service myself more than two years ago, without his knowledge, and I don't wish to be betrayed. I cannot explain why I fail in my ability to finish it. It is part of the secret I mentioned earlier, which is another person's and not mine.'

Miss H stares into the fire again, and for a long time there is no sound but those noises I mentioned earlier—the fire crackling, the wind in the chimney—and the clicking of my needles.

I do not look at Pip, although I am aware that every so often he looks at me. I am aware that deep in my heart I yearn to go to him to comfort him. And I must not. His heart is already in little pieces. If I go to him, if I offer him solace, he will again begin to hope that there is something between us.

The collapse of some red coals in the fireplace rouses Miss H. She looks towards Pip again. 'What else?'

'Oh,' Pip cries, 'why did I know you would not be satisfied? Why do you want more from me?

'Estella.' He turns to me now. His voice is trembling. 'You know I love you. You know that I have loved you long and dearly.'

I glance at him, at the distress in his face, but I do not respond. What am I to say? There is nothing to say. I continue to knit.

'I should have said this sooner,' he goes on, 'but for my long mistake which induced me to hope that Miss Havisham meant us for one another. But I will say it now. I *must* say it now.'

I shake my head, silently asking him not to, but he says, 'I know, I know. I have no hope that I shall ever call you mine, Estella. I am, in fact, ignorant of what may become of me soon, how poor I will be, or where I will go. Still, I love you. I have loved you ever since I first saw you in this house.'

I shake my head again, *Don't*, I think. *Don't*. But he goes on.

'It was cruel of Miss Havisham to prey on the susceptibility of a poor and innocent boy, and to torment me through all these years, but I do not believe that she once reflected on the gravity of what she did. I think that in her own suffering, in the endurance of her own trial, she forgot mine.'

My attention is distracted by Miss H putting her hand on her heart and holding it there, and looking between Pip and me. She is moved. *At last* something other than her own predicament moves her.

'It seems,' I begin, holding myself in check and speaking calmly. If I do not speak calmly, there is no knowing what I will say. 'It seems you have sentimental fancies, Pip. Call them what you will, I am not able to comprehend them. When you say you love me'—I shrug—'it means nothing to me. I have tried to warn you of this, have I not?'

'Yes,' he says in a miserable manner. 'Yes.'

I put down my knitting. 'But you would not be warned, for you believed I did not mean it. Now, is this not so—?'

'I thought and hoped you could not mean it! You, so young, untried and beautiful. Surely it is not in nature—?'

'It is in *my* nature,' I return. 'It is in the nature formed within me. I make a great difference between *you* and all other people when I say so much. I can do no more.'

'Is it not true,' Pip goes on, leaning his arms upon his thighs and looking steadily at me, 'that Bentley Drummle is in town here and pursuing you?'

'It is quite true.'

'And that you encourage him, and would've ridden out with him this morning had the weather allowed it, and that he dines with you this evening?'

'Quite true,' I say. How is Pip aware of this? I can only surmise that he has bumped into Bentley at the Blue Boar.

'You cannot love him, Estella!'

'What have I told you? Do you still think that I do not mean what I say?'

'Do you love him, Estella? Would you marry him?'

I glance at Miss Havisham, but she is not looking at me. This is my decision, after all, not hers, and I pick up my knitting again.

'Why not tell you the truth?' I say. 'I *am* going to be married to him.'

Pip drops his face into his hands. I look at Miss H and her features bear such a ghastly expression, part horror, part dislike, that I wonder at my decision. Am I making a mistake?

'Estella, dearest Estella,' Pip whispers, 'do not let Miss Havisham lead you down this awful path. Put me aside for ever and bestow yourself on some worthier person than Drummle. Among those men that truly love you, there may be one who loves you as dearly as I, though he has not loved you as long. Take him! For your sake. And I can withstand it better.'

'I am going,' I say in a gentler, kinder voice, for this is almost more than I can bear, 'to be married to him. The preparations are already underway. And why do you unfairly bring Miss Havisham into it? It is my own decision.'

'Your own act to fling yourself away upon a brute?'

'On whom should I fling myself away?' I retort. 'On a man that I do not love, on a man who will know that I took nothing to him? Do not answer that. I shall do well enough with Bentley and he with me. And if you must know, Miss Havisham would have had me wait and not marry yet, but I am tired of the life I have led, which has had few charms for me of late, which has been difficult, and I wish to change it.' I shake my head. 'Say no more, dear Pip. We shall never understand each other.'

'Such a mean brute, such a stupid brute?' he cries in despair.

'It is a marriage of convenience,' I say. 'Nothing more and nothing less. Come, take my hand, and let's part as friends? Please, dear Pip?'

'Oh, Estella.'

He is crying, for tears fall upon my hand.

'Even if I remained in England and could hold my head up with the rest, how can I see you as Drummle's wife?'

'You will get me out of your thoughts in a week,' I say.

'Never,' he grinds out. 'Out of my thoughts? In a week?'

'Oh, Estella, you are part of my existence, part of myself! You have been in every line I have ever read since I first came here, the rough common boy whose poor heart you wounded even then. You are in everything I do and touch. You are in the river, on the marshes, in the light, in the darkness. You are in the wind, in the woods, in the sea. You cannot choose to step out of my life, only I can allow that. You cannot tell me when to forget you, only I can do that. You will forever be a part of me …'

I cannot remember where I have heard these words before, for they seem vaguely familiar. I do not how he gets them out, such is his despair.

He stumbles to his feet, takes my hand and kisses it and, with tears in his eyes and a look that lingers longingly on my face, he leaves the room.

I stand looking after him in fearful wonderment.

What have I done? *Oh, what have I done?*

After some time, I notice Miss Havisham. Her hand remains on her heart, but her face is a ghastly stare of pity and remorse, and even as I watch, she turns that macabre visage upon me and I flee from the room in fright.

PART THREE

PART THREE

30

Bentley and I marry on a blustery summer morning. The sun is out, but weak and, as I step out of the carriage, gusts of wind batter my bouquet of pink camellias and gypsophila. The wind snatches at my lacy dress, blows its ruffled skirt hither and thither and shivers run down my spine. The trembling is not caused by the cold. I am apprehensive.

The Pockets are present: Sarah and Camilla, Raymond and Georgiana. Not Mr Matthew Pocket nor his son, Herbert. Not Miss Havisham, who was unfit to travel the distance. Not Mr Jaggers, who was invited, but pleaded a prior engagement. Not Pip, for Bentley refused to allow me to invite him. I think of Pip often and remember the haunted expression he last wore, and the shadow, the stranger, in the doorway. Who was that? Was it his uncle, or his benefactor, and are they the same person? And why does it gnaw at me so?

Bentley's family is present. His mother and father, naturally. His younger brothers. Some aunts I have not met before, and two or three family friends. All in all, it is a low-key affair.

Eliza and James Waverley were sent an invitation, but they replied with their apologies. In the circumstances, and considering James's advice not to marry Bentley, I would have been surprised had they accepted.

Matilda and Albert are present, but sit in the back row of the church. They have been invited to the ceremony, but not the wedding breakfast. Still, when I turn from the altar on Bentley's arm at the close and walk down the aisle as a married woman, Matilda's happy face is the one I notice the most. Instead of the joyousness I should feel on my wedding day, I am heavy-hearted. But perhaps this is what marriage is: a knuckling down and an undertaking of duty and routine. And isn't this what I want? What I deserve?

We honeymoon in Rome. I have not been to Rome before and am taken with its history, its antiquity, and wish to see everything and experience anything. Bentley has been before. Several times. He spends the first day trailing after our guide and me as we visit the Trevi Fountain, the Sistine Chapel and St Peter's Square. At dinner, he suggests that since he has already seen almost everything on my list, that he ride the following day while I continue to sightsee.

Incidentally, as regards the consumption of food. He shovels it in as if there is no tomorrow, scarcely giving time for one forkful to be savoured before another is waiting in line. Strange. Why? I ask myself. Was the man starved at some point?

I had anticipated that our honeymoon would give me an opportunity to get to know Bentley better, to understand him, but within the first day it becomes apparent there is not a great deal more to be understood. We spend the remainder of our honeymoon largely apart. We are together most nights, of course, except when Bentley leaves early to play cards and returns late, which allows me some respite from his attentions.

I do not want to but I feel I must elaborate on that awkward subject. I was not ignorant of what to expect on my wedding night; my education in France saw to that. Or, I should say, my time in that country, for it was not only the study of Michelangelo's David that enlightened me but also the talk amongst the girls. What I was taken aback by on my wedding night was obviously the pain, which was far greater than I had anticipated, but also Bentley's lack of tenderness, his clumsiness, and his need to *mount* me—as he put it—several times that first night. As if I were a new and headstrong filly that must be dominated and subdued.

I lay awake after each time, unable to sleep for the throbbing between my legs. I lay awake and the tears welled in my eyes. It came to me by degrees that I had, as Pip had predicted, made a terrible mistake. One I had brought upon myself. But it was too late now. The deed was done. If I had wanted to punish myself for the death of Laurence, I had indeed done so by marrying Bentley.

My bed was made, however, and I must lie in it.

*

The Drummle family owns a house near Hyde Park and it is here that Bentley and I return to from Europe and make our home. *Make our home* is a misnomer, for the home is already made. It is on four levels with our quarters on the top floor, the library, dining and drawing rooms one up from the street, the kitchen and so forth on ground level, and the servants' quarters below. The townhouse is beautifully furnished and expensively and extensively decorated. There is nothing wanting. Nothing of mine that I can bring to the dwelling to make it my own. And so from the moment I step inside I feel like a stranger in my own house. And it is not my own house, in fact, as I later discover.

Before my marriage, I did as I had promised Matilda and insisted to Bentley that I be allowed to keep my maid and he acquiesced, for which I am grateful. But I had a lengthy battle to retain Albert. I argued that the couple should not be parted, and that Albert would be useful in various capacities. I was, at last, successful, but I have an idea that as soon as my back is turned Bentley will find a reason to dismiss him. I mean to keep an eye on the situation. Bentley's manservant, Jarvis, has been with him since he was a child and, according to Matilda, Jarvis regularly attempts to score points off Albert. Jarvis is tall and so skeletal that his uniform flaps around his arms and legs. His large hooked nose appears to have a smell underneath it at all times, and he is neither friendly nor jovial. He takes his duties towards his master with the utmost seriousness. I have tried, but I cannot take to the man.

Not long after we have taken up residence, I ask Matilda and Albert to rearrange some furniture in the drawing room for me. We push the chintz-covered sofa and the two armchairs around until I am satisfied with the new arrangement. I believe that the sofa against the window blocks out the light and the outlook to the garden and it now faces the window, and the two armchairs look into the house instead of the other way around.

In the evening, Bentley and I dine together, and afterwards retire to the drawing room. Me, to take up my knitting, he, to peruse the newspaper.

'What have you done here, Estella?' Bentley says upon entering the room. He stops in the doorway. 'Whose idea was this?'

'We rearranged the furniture to better advantage,' I say, coming in behind him. 'That is all.'

He taps the newspaper impatiently against his trouser leg. 'It must be restored to the way it was,' he tells me. 'Tomorrow. At the earliest. Mama will have a fit if she sees it like this. Whose suggestion was this, may I ask?'

'Mine,' I say.

'Are you sure?' he asks. 'From what I hear, those two that you brought into the house are extraordinarily persuasive.'

'Matilda and Albert? Nonsense,' I tell him. 'Who told you that?'

'Never you mind.'

'I thought the house had been given to us, Bentley?'

'No,' he says abruptly. 'Nothing is mine until it is bequeathed. You'd do well to bear that in mind.'

He turns to me. 'Talking of possessions, Estella, I bought a racehorse yesterday. A fine filly. Now we shall see how we fare with that!'

He speaks with relish. His eyes are aglitter, almost fiendish, which disturbs me.

*

I attempt to take up my friendship with Eliza and James once more. I write to Eliza suggesting that we meet, and she responds by explaining that sadly her time is at present taken up with preparations for her wedding.

I wonder what this is about, for surely she has time to meet with an old friend? I wonder if it is regarding what happened between me and Laurence—have they discovered the contents of my letter and blame me for his death? Or is it about my marriage to Bentley?

I take matters into my own hands. I order the horses and carriage and ask Albert to drive me out to Wright House and to Eliza.

It is a lovely summer's day, and the willows lining the avenue leading up to Wright House are awash with bright green as Kitty once said they would be. I feel guilty at the thought of Kitty, and Dr Oliver and Daisy. I have not seen them since I left to marry Bentley. I have wanted to, but Bentley told me I should not. He does not think it a good idea to maintain my friendship with them. I have a mind to go against his wishes, but I must find an opportune moment when news of my visit is unlikely to reach him.

The house is looking particularly pretty in the summer light, the miniature lake sparkling like a gem, the rose garden abloom with colour. I remember the happy time I had here with Eliza and wonder how it has all gone so awry.

The manservant who answers the bell tells me that Miss Wright is out riding, and Mr and Mrs Wright are currently not in residence. It appears I have two options: I can either return home, or I can track Eliza down. I am a believer in confronting issues, however, and I leave Albert with instructions to bide his time and walk around to the stables.

The stable hand is inside mucking out, and I ask him to saddle up Dora, Eliza's childhood mare, for me. The man is not exactly willing, but he does not refuse. Naturally, he reaches for the sidesaddle. I cannot object. I am a married woman now and must behave with decorum. I mount Dora with the help of the stable hand and set off. He has given me a rough idea of where Eliza might be, and I head in that direction. It is adjacent to the side of the hill where I previously rode on Bolt.

I reach the top of the mound and look down at the workers' cottages abutting one another on the perimeter of the field, and the sheep dotted across the meadow, and spy Eliza. She is coming up the hill on Bolt at a gallop, her fair curls streaming back from under her hat. I presume she is returning for the midday meal or some other engagement. She reins Bolt sharply in when she sees me.

'Estella!'

She cannot keep the surprise out of her voice.

'Hello, Eliza,' I call.

Swinging Dora around, I urge the mare to turn back, which she does at her own plodding pace.

'What brings you out here?' Eliza asks. 'I hope nothing untoward has occurred?'

I shake my head. 'Shall we ride back together?'

'Certainly,' she says, reining Bolt in beside me. 'To what do I owe the honour?'

'I wanted to see you.'

'And what is it you wanted to see me about?'

I glance at her, but she will not meet my eyes.

'You are avoiding me,' I say. 'And I want to know why.'

'Succinct as ever, I see.'

'If you must know, I learnt from a master.'

'Miss Havisham?'

'The same.'

She does not respond. Her gaze remains on the ground in front of her. My being here is clearly troubling her.

'Your avoidance of me. Have you nothing to say in response, Eliza?'

'It is no longer fitting that we meet,' she says, and flushes.

'According to whom? I thought we were friends?'

'Why did you marry Drummle?' she asks, low-voiced.

'There are many reasons why I married Bentley, but let us not argue and go around in circles over something that cannot be changed.'

'So be it,' she says. 'But I cannot continue my friendship with you. James has advised against it.'

'Advised against it? I am affronted,' I say.

'It is not *you*, Estella! It is Mr Drummle.'

We say no more and arrive at last at the stables. We both dismount, and Eliza's face is pale and as deeply unhappy as I have ever seen it.

Oh god! I do not know what to say, what to do, how to change the situation between us.

'Give me your word that you will not seek me out again?' she says.

'If that is what you wish, I will not,' I say, 'although it pains me to say so. I am, in fact, hurt to the quick.'

Eliza closes her eyes briefly. She looks anguished.

'Tell me,' she says, at last looking at me. 'Are you happy with Mr Drummle? Estella?' she asks again when I do not respond. 'Are you happy?'

'I am not,' I manage to get out.

'Oh, Estella,' she says. 'If only there was something I could do or say, but there isn't.'

I bite my lip. 'Let us not prolong this,' I say stiffly. 'I will take my leave of you.'

'As you wish.'

'Goodbye, Eliza,' I say.

'Goodbye,' she echoes.

We do not look at one another.

I walk from the stables. I do not look back.

Around the corner of the house, I reach low to break off a long stem of wild grass and swish it angrily through the air.

Damnation!

31

A lonely, restless period of my life ensues. It seems I am cut off from all my friends and must make do with my own company.

Bentley's and my days and nights fall into a pattern, common, I suspect, in other marriages. My husband rises late. Sometimes he rides. Sometimes he is gone for hours on some or other business. I no longer ask. More often than not, he dines and spends the evening at his club. But the outcome of all this is that I spend a great deal of time on my own. I did not think this was how marriage would be—this is not a simple business arrangement as I said it might be, for it suits Bentley but not me—but there you are.

*

Bentley requests that I accompany him to the races. His new obsession, his filly, is running. Horse-racing is not something I am partial to, however, I am prepared to accept his invitation in the spirit of nurturing my relationship with him.

The race is at Epsom Downs and we go down the afternoon before and stay in one of the many establishments offering accommodation.

Bentley's filly is called Desdemona. She is two, he says, and has great potential. Not only for racing, but for breeding. Bentley tells me all this in the coach and, when he mentions the word *breeding*, he looks awkward and ill at ease.

'You're not ...?' He leans forward confidingly and lifts one finger in an enquiring manner.

'I'm not,' I confirm.

'I see,' he says.

'We have been married less than six months,' I point out.

He sniffs. 'No time like the present, madam,' he murmurs.

'What races will Desdemona run?' I ask in an attempt to distract him.

'The Oaks. The course is a mile and a half. She runs best at a mile and this will no doubt be a challenge.'

I want to enquire how much he paid for Desdemona, but I do not. I have no wish to start a quarrel this early in our time away together.

Ask the question of any Englishman and he will confirm English weather is notoriously unreliable. We have had two days of sunshine and perfect calm; however, the day of the race dawns and it is pouring with rain.

I put aside my elegant black-and-white gown with the long lacy sleeves, and my parasol, and my white summery organza hat with the sweeping brim, and dress warmly and sensibly. I wear my flat-soled boots and a warm woollen suit. My black cape is over my shoulders and I carry an umbrella. I go down to meet Bentley in the foyer and he looks at me in astonishment. 'Why have you not dressed for the occasion?'

'In this weather, in that outfit? Are you mad? I will catch pneumonia.'

He shakes his head. 'I'm not accompanying you unless you change. You will look out of place in that get-up.'

'Well, then, I won't go.'

'*You won't go?* Did I hear you correctly?'

I nod. 'You did.'

'The Devil take you, woman,' he mutters.

It is my first act of wilfulness with Bentley, but by no means my last.

I spend the day in our chambers. A good fire burns merrily in the grate. In addition to a copy of *The Lancet*, I have a novel and my knitting and every now and then I move to the window and look out. The ledge is cold to the touch, and damp. It continues to rain. Droplets dribble down the glass pane and the sky is bruised with clouds. Pedestrians with their coat collars up scurry along the walkways and huddle under umbrellas. Carriages, their moving wheels spraying out water, and horses with limp manes and saturated skins lying flat to their ribcages, pass along the road beneath the window. I am truly glad I am not out and about.

Bentley does not return at dinner and I eat alone. I complete the sleeve of the cardigan I am knitting and read about techniques regarding amputation. Blood loss, shock and how to deal with the excruciating pain remain the obstacles to successful recovery from surgery, although it is reported that a certain Scottish doctor, James Simpson, whose most significant contribution to obstetrics is the Simpson's Forceps, is experimenting with the effects of chloroform and there is hope that he will soon publish a paper.

Bentley does not return at bedtime and I retire alone, leaving a light on for him.

In the early hours of the morning, he comes in. He makes an infernal racket, fumbling with the door, so that it is difficult for me to continue to sleep, or even pretend to sleep.

He throws himself face down upon the bed, and I start up from the pillows. His suit is drenched, his hair dripping with rain. 'Oh, Estella,' he groans. 'Oh, Estella.'

'What is it?' I ask, since this appears to be more than an instance of over-imbibing.

'Desdemona,' he cries. 'Gone.'

'What do you mean *gone?*'

'Gone. Dead. Died. Put out of her misery.'

'How—?'

He rolls over and sits up. 'How do you think, woman?'

'I don't know, I wasn't there.'

'Well, you ought to have been!'

He wipes his nose with the back of his hand. 'Undress me,' he says, snivelling like a child. 'I'm cold,' he says. '*Please*,' he says finally, when I remain unmoved.

At noon the following day, when Bentley at last rouses himself, sneezes and sneezes yet again, and complains bitterly of a sore throat and announces he will spend the day in bed, I discover what happened.

Desdemona, who was in second place and had less than half-a-mile to run, slipped in the mud at the corner. Both horse and jockey went down and were trampled by a number of horses following behind. The horse that won the race was apparently a rank outsider. Desdemona's jockey died at the scene from his injuries, while the filly was shot in kindness later in the afternoon.

I do not ask how much money we have lost. It is clear from Bentley's distress that it is a great deal.

I look up the meaning of Desdemona. It is from the Greek and means *ill-fated* or *unfortunate.*

Why, I wonder, would anyone purchase a horse called Desdemona and, for that matter, why would anyone christen *anything* Desdemona?

*

In the midst of this misery, something gratifying and wondrous happens.

I am in the city one day for some or other errand, I forget what—it may be that I wanted to escape the house—when I walk past a building and someone I know is emerging from its doors and down its steps.

I stop. 'Dr Oliver!' I say in delight.

'Miss Havisham!' he says as he reaches me. 'But you are no longer Miss Havisham, are you?'

I shake my head and hold out my hand. 'I am Mrs Drummle. How are you? And Daisy and Kitty? Are you all in fine health?'

'We are very well indeed, thank you, my child. Kitty has moved in with us and we have a contented household, although we miss you and Albert and Matilda.' He turns to look up the stairs. 'Are you going in?'

'Going in?' I laugh. 'I do not know what building this is.'

'This is the London Library. I assumed perhaps you were outside because you were going to borrow a book.'

'The London Library?'

He nods at me encouragingly.

'It sounds like a capital idea,' I tell him. 'Would you be so kind as to take me in and introduce me?'

'I'd be delighted to. Come, take my arm,' Dr Oliver says.

Inside, the smell of old books, leather and paper is intoxicating. I gaze up in wonderment. The room is cavernous and filled wall-to-wall with novels, volumes, publications, reference books and anything at all that can be printed on paper. Thin and light access railings run along the upper reaches of the book-lined walls, and set upon the floor are a number of wooden reading desks topped with softly glowing lamps. A number of mostly white-haired gentlemen are at the tables, bent over their books or murmuring softly to one another.

Dr Oliver introduces me to the clerk at the desk who completes the necessary paperwork and gives me a little card bearing my name and stating that I am a member of the London Library. I cannot help smiling and feeling pleased with myself.

'What are you interested in reading, my child?' Dr Oliver asks.

I blush a little. 'You might think me precocious if I tell you, but it's medicine. I have become quite intrigued by the subject.'

He shakes his white-haired head and smiles. 'Medicine? Well, I never. That is absolutely marvellous. Come, let me show you where all the books on medicine are kept.'

They are housed on the ground level, which is fortunate, for the idea of Dr Oliver ascending the ladder to the upper level makes me nervous. Here, I find papers by Louis Pasteur and publications on antiseptics by Joseph Lister. There is so much to choose from I do not know where best to begin. The good doctor is of great assistance in advising me, and places a copy of Quain's *Elements of Anatomy* into my hand.

When we part company, he to return to Daisy and Kitty with my felicitations, he tells me he is at the library every Wednesday morning, should I have need of his ear, or of his advice, or of anything, really.

Thus do I renew my acquaintance with Dr Oliver and become a member of the London Library.

Thus does a whole, new, other world open up to me.

And thus do I find a refuge from Bentley. The importance of the latter cannot be over-exaggerated.

*

It is after two when I return from this excursion in good spirits, but enter the house only to hear raised voices.

I go down to the kitchen. It is empty. It is not my domain; however, there are occasions when it is necessary to put in an appearance and by the ferocity of the voices this is one of them. Clearly, whoever it is, they are not aware that I have arrived home.

Albert and Jarvis are jostling on the back doorstep. I believe it is their figures I see through the glass panels of the upper door. I tiptoe stealthily over and abruptly open the door.

'What is the matter with you two?' I ask, startling the pair of them.

'Jarvis—' Albert begins at the same time as Jarvis says, 'Albert—'

I put up my hand. 'Is this some childish quarrel?'

'It is indeed, miss,' Albert says. 'Jarvis refuses to allow me inside. Matilda and me are low on sugar, miss.'

Jarvis does not respond. He purses his fleshy lips, looks down his nose and folds his arms.

'Jarvis? What's the meaning of this?'

'Stealing, Mrs Drummle,' he says.

Albert opens his mouth to protest and I put up my hand again. 'Wait,' I say. 'Who's been stealing, Jarvis, and what proof do you have that it is Albert?'

'The cook, missus, has reported foodstuffs disappearing. I am merely ensuring that Albert is aware—'

'You was not!' Albert puts in.

'I was, too,' Jarvis says.

'Stop,' I demand. 'That's enough. Step away from the door,' I say to Jarvis, gesticulating with my hand. 'Albert, come in and get your sugar. I will wait while you do so.'

'Thank you, Mrs Drummle,' Jarvis says obsequiously, and bends his head with undue politeness before he steps away, as if I have agreed that Albert is up to no good and needs to be watched.

I shake my head. 'That's not what I intended,' I call out, but Jarvis is already walking across the backyard and pretends not to hear.

'I am sorry about this, Albert,' I say, as he reaches for the sugar canister. 'I am not sure what the remedy is.'

'Thankee, miss,' he says. 'I don't believe I know, either, miss.'

32

Bentley and I are abroad in Paris when a letter from Miss Havisham's surgeon arrives. He regrets to inform me that Miss Havisham has been caught in a fire at Satis House and is not so badly burnt as suffering from shock. She has been made as comfortable as possible in the circumstances, but the surgeon has no idea how long she will last. *It may be days, it may be weeks*, he writes. *If you could see your way clear to return to England and to Satis House without delay, it would be much appreciated. Her mind has been wandering,* he closes with, *and not five minutes go by without her mentioning your name.*

Bentley has come in from riding when I find him in his dressing room. He is sprawled across his chair, his shirt half undone, a brandy in one hand. Perspiration has pooled at the base of his neck and he smells earthy, as if he might have taken a tumble in the rough. Green stains, in fact, mark his shirt.

'Did you fall?' I ask, pointing them out.

He gazes down. 'Oh,' he says, 'I might have. I forget.' He laughs. But it is a forced laugh, as if he is attempting to divert me. There are blades of grass in his hair, too, but I try not to dwell on this and how they come to be there, and hold the letter out to him instead.

'The most frightful thing. Miss H has been injured in a fire. The surgeon has written to me. Apparently her clothing caught fire. She is in shock, and he wants me to return home. She needs me, he says.'

Bentley sits forward in his chair. He is at once sober.

'Estella,' he says with concern. 'You must, of course, go. There is no question of you not going. Regrettably, I cannot accompany you. I must stay—I do not know for how long.' He raises the brandy to his lips. 'I have a number of business ends I must tie up before my return, you know this,' he tells me before taking a mouthful.

Hmm, a number of card games, and an even greater quota of horse races, I think, but I know better than to say anything.

'My train is at six in the morning,' I tell him. 'I see no point in disturbing you before I go, but will you have dinner with me this evening, since it is my last night?'

'Confound it,' he says, tapping the tumbler on the dressing table in irritation. 'I cannot, my darling. I have a prior engagement, one from which I can't escape.'

'You would miss a last opportunity to dine with your wife—' I begin. I cannot help myself. When he uses endearments I am always suspicious because it is not in his nature.

'I have no choice.' He opens his palm and raises his shoulders, widening his half-undone shirt and showing me the coarse black hairs on his chest that are oily with sweat. 'What would you have me do?'

'Be it so,' I say. 'But I will take my farewell now, for as I have said I'm departing early in the morning.'

'As you wish.'

Reaching for my hand, he raises it to his lips. 'Estella,' he murmurs, fluttering his lashes at me.

I believe he thinks he is being provocative. Sadly, in this area, he has much to learn and in a number of ways I am grateful for this enforced separation.

*

The journey home is long and tiring. It is one thing to travel for enjoyment; it is quite another to travel when one is anxious and desirous of reaching one's destination without delay.

Apart from changing trains and crossing the English Channel by boat, Matilda and I remain in a swaying carriage and watch the world go by outside the window. She tries to interest me in a game of whist, but my mind dwells steadfastly at Satis House. I envision the scene, try to recreate what might have occurred. I see Miss Havisham upon the hearth, sitting hunched forward in her moth-eaten chair, her hands upon her stick, staring fixedly into the fire. I imagine an ember floating free and lighting upon her ragged gown. Catching and flaming. She rises up, she shrieks, and a whirligig of fire blazes all about her and soars above her head.

Who was with her? Who came to her rescue? The scene fades to black and I try to sift through the darkness to find Miss Havisham's rescuer, but all that remains are sooty ashes and smut that drift up towards the ceiling and then shower down around her, and I am left pondering.

After what seems like an eternity, but is in fact a couple of days, we arrive in the village. The day is almost gone, and I pay a fare for a coach to take Matilda and me and our luggage to the house. Most of the traders have shut up shop already for the evening, and we pass along the deserted high street in silence. Reaching the gates of Satis House, we alight and, while Matilda rings the bell, I gaze around. The bare-limbed trees stand like sentinels in the forsaken garden. A line of rooks perch along the wall, inspecting me, and higher up a clamour of them turn and swirl in the dusky air. Their black wings stretched wide, they ride on some invisible current as if they are Valkyries. If this is an omen of matters to come, it is altogether unsettling.

It is a shock to see Miss Havisham. Covered in white cotton sheeting, she lies upon her bed with her mass of grey hair festooned about her head. Her bed has been placed upon the great table where once the ravaged wedding cake stood, where often she would strike her stick and say, 'Here I will lie one day.' All detritus of the cake has been cleared. All the silken dresses have been packed up, all the withered blooms and desiccated flowers swept away, the room cleaned for perhaps the first time since the fateful day on which the clocks stopped.

Miss Pocket and I take it in turns to sit with Miss Havisham. She has been wrapped in cotton dressings and sedated. The surgeon calls in once a day to check on her. He administers morphine to help her cope with the pain and I assist him to change her dressings. The first time he wanted to do so he begged me to leave the room. He said it was not fitting for me to witness such sights, but I advised him that I had no intention of departing and that he should simply get on with it. He was taken aback. I softened my voice and said that I would please like to learn how to change the dressings. He acquiesced then and did not argue further.

As a consequence, I have learnt a great deal about burns. Changing Miss Havisham's dressings is by no means a pleasant task; the stench of burnt flesh is something I have not smelt hitherto, and it is acrid. It becomes embedded in one's olfactory senses like an unwelcome and recalcitrant house guest. It is, however, intriguing to note how the body reacts to such trauma: how the skin splits and lifts and oozes fluid; how the wounds are blackened and charred; how in other places they are the colour of bone, denoting the flesh and all feeling is dead. The surgeon informs me that it will be the shock to Miss Havisham's aging body that will most likely be the cause of her eventual death. We must endeavour to keep her warm, he instructs, since so much of the skin that holds the body heat in has been mutilated. As a result, the fire in the grate is kept constantly alight and Matilda does her best to bring in fresh supplies of logs daily.

Miss Havisham's body has been burnt, but her hands, old now and wrinkled, have escaped and oft times I sit at her bedside and hold one or other of them. What with my weariness from the journey and my vigil at her bedside, I fall asleep alongside her in the first few days that I am home, my head on her coverlet. I am awoken by her voice—

'Pip,' she is saying. 'Pip.' It is clear, there is no mistaking it. Then she says, 'I forgive her. I forgive her. Take the pencil and write under my name, *I forgive her.*'

I am bewildered. Of whom does she speak? Whom does she forgive, and what has Pip to do with this? It would be a different matter if she were saying, I forgive *him*—meaning the lover that jilted her all those years ago. But it is not him, it is her. *I forgive her.*

I draw Sarah Pocket to one side when she takes over from me in the late afternoon and ask if Pip was here, and with some reluctance she tells me that indeed he was.

'Pip?' I repeat, should she have misheard me.

'Yes, Pip,' she says. Her dried rosebud of a mouth is stiff, as if it pains her to mention his name. 'You know the boy.'

'I do,' I say. 'What was he doing here?'

'I do not know. I only know that he had a note from Miss Havisham asking him to see her *on a little matter of business.*'

How puzzling, I think. 'Do go on,' I say.

'Well, he was here. That is all there is to it. And at the moment when Miss Havisham caught fire, he had returned to the room to bid her goodnight. He wrapped her in his coat and held her down, for I believe she struggled to escape, and when I came upon the scene she was insensible upon the floor—'

'And Pip? Was he unharmed?'

'No—'

'No?' I interrupt. 'Why are you only telling me this now?'

'You did not ask. How was I to know—'

'Never mind that, go on. How is he? What are his injuries?'

'I believe his hands and, to some extent, his arms were burnt. But I do not know for certain.'

'So he returned to London?'

She shakes her head and screws up her mouth. Her little face is as crinkled as a walnut these days. 'I have no idea,' she says.

I return to my room. One of the rooms upstairs that I was afraid to enter as a child has been cleaned and dusted and my bed from near the kitchen brought up. I would not sleep in the bed that was there, the bed that from my childhood I remember as smelling of the deceased. All this is so I am closer to Miss H. I sit at the dressing table and pull paper, pen and ink from a drawer.

Dear Pip, I begin.

I stop. The thought of my dear friend being in pain disturbs me greatly. I scratch that through, crunch the paper up into a ball and turf it into the fireplace. I have never addressed him as *Dear Pip*, there has never been formality between us. Why should it start now?

I try again. *Pip, I understand you were here when Miss H—* But I pause once more. My tone is wrong; it is too formal. And this letter feels like the most arduous thing I have ever had to write. Is it because I have not seen him for such a long time? Is it because ever since my marriage to Bentley he has been avoiding me? And who can blame him? Once upon a time it was the easiest thing in the world to talk to Pip. Why is it all of sudden so hard now?

Talk to? Well, yes.

This is what I am doing, dear Pip. What I have been doing ever since Sarah Pocket told me you were here, dear Pip. Talking to you in my head. Why were you here? How badly are you hurt, and are you in pain? Oh, how I long to see your kind face. How I yearn for your good-natured company, your friendship. Your sweetness. Your vivid blue eyes. I know if you were beside me now, you would have something kind to say, something of comfort. If you were here beside me, this would all be so much less difficult to bear.

If you were beside me, I would want to lay my head against your chest. I would want you to hold me. If you were beside me, it would be *me* asking you for a kiss of consolation and not the other way around. It would be me seeking to hold your hand in mine. For you are the only one who knows my history, who might understand what is going on in my heart.

I weep then, for what could have been and what might have been, and what I threw away. I weep for the man that I did not marry because of pride. And in my state of self-pity, my letter to Pip is never written.

*

A week, maybe two, perhaps even three go by—I forget the time—before Miss Havisham dies.

It is still a shock, for in the last few days of her life she rallies. She recognises me and is lucid and present for short periods of time.

As it happens, I am with her on one of those occasions when she opens her eyes. She looks at me and murmurs, 'Estella. Oh, Estella.'

'Yes, Miss H, I am here,' I say gently.

'Estella,' she moans.

'Are you in pain, Miss H? Do you need something?'

She shakes her head. She closes her eyes once more.

'Forgive her,' she says again. 'Forgive her. Write under her name *I forgive her.*'

'Who, Miss Havisham? Of whom do you speak—?'

A wild idea occurs to me. 'Is it my mother?'

'Your mother?' Her voice is faint.

'Yes, my mother. Do you talk of my mother?'

'Oh, child,' she says. Almost imperceptibly, she shakes her head.

I squeeze her hand and, with the lightest of pressures, she squeezes back. 'Pip,' she says, 'I forgive her.'

I wonder then if she intends for *Pip* to forgive her. Is this what she means? It makes sense, I think. I remember the last time I saw him, he said it had been cruel of Miss Havisham to prey upon him and torment him through the years, but that he believed she had not once reflected on the gravity of what she was doing, that in her own suffering, in the endurance of her own trial, she forgot his.

And I remember that my attention was distracted, for she put her hand on her heart and held it there and looked between Pip and me and was moved. And I remember thinking that at last something other than her own predicament had moved her.

This is what she means then, when she says *I forgive her.* She wants Pip to forgive her! And I believe he does, for his nature is kind and generous. I believe—

My thoughts are interrupted by an agitated movement of her hand in mine and I glance up.

'What is it?' I say.

'Oh, what have I done?' she murmurs.

Her eyes open then and she stares directly at me. Her expression is awful, her anguish discernible.

Her head falls gently to one side then, and her mouth gapes open.

'Miss Havisham,' I cry, rising from her side.

But she has gone.

Try as I may, I cannot find her pulse.

The room feels empty and desolate. The room feels as if some great wind came through and lifted Miss Havisham's papery body and swept everything hurly-burly in its path out onto the roof and into the heavens above.

I feel abandoned. Deserted. Lonelier than ever.

A chapter has closed. I must rely on myself and my wits to get me through the next one, for I cannot rely on Bentley.

God speed, Miss Havisham, I think.

You were unhappy in life, and it is my earnest wish that you find some respite for your soul. Rest in peace.

33

Mr Jaggers assembles me and Miss Havisham's relatives all in London to read out the will. A clerk by name of Wemmick ushers us into his small room. It is a dreary place, lit only by a weirdly pitched skylight. There are some odd objects about: a rusted pistol, an ancient sword in a scabbard swinging from a hook on one wall, and on a shelf two dreadful casts, their faces eternally screwed up in horror. Horror is the right word.

Mr Jaggers sits across from us in a high-backed chair with rows of brass nails around its edges, as if it were a coffin, the likes of which I have so recently seen bearing Miss Havisham's remains and being lowered into the gloomy depths of the muddy earth. It was raining on the day she was buried and we huddled silently around her grave. Afterwards, I bade all the Pockets who were there good day, and hoped I would never see them again, and yet here we are. I am not in a good frame of mind; this is no surprise. The Pockets are here—Sarah and Camilla and Georgiana and Raymond—but not Mr Matthew Pocket nor his son, Herbert.

The majority of the property has been left to me, with some small amounts to the cousins. Nothing unexpected there. The surprise is that an amount of four thousand pounds, a generous stipend, has been left to Mr Matthew Pocket. This rattles the cousins. Although I am seated at the back of the room, I see indignation rising in the spines of their backs. Raymond, who is not provided for, demands to know when this could have been settled upon? Mr Jaggers informs him that Miss Havisham wrote out a codicil a day or two before her accident. He picks up a piece of paper and waves it provocatively in front of Raymond and I recall that Sarah Pocket told me Pip was at Satis House at that time on *a little matter of business*, and I wonder if this codicil and this generous stipend is his doing?

'Now,' Mr Jaggers says, pushing back his coffin-like chair, 'Estella and I have one or two issues to discuss, if you will excuse us?'

The Pockets rise from the chairs that were hastily brought in for us to sit upon and, after a glance at me, depart. As Sarah leaves the room, she says with some degree of triumph, 'And what about the boy, he got nothing!'

Pip may well have received *nothing*, but at least he has the satisfaction of knowing that as a result of his recommendations, Mr Matthew Pocket has been adequately provided for.

'Mr Jaggers,' I say.

'Yes, Estella.'

'Can you ... Did you ...?' I start again. 'Are you at liberty to now tell me who Pip's benefactor is?'

'I am not.'

He bites at his forefinger again.

I am half expecting him to quibble over my choice of words, to say that he *is* at liberty to tell me, but that he is not *free* to do so, which are two different issues, and which is it?—and I am only half hearing what he is saying.

'And ...?'

'Are you not listening, Estella. I am *not*. Now,' he says. 'What are you going to do?'

'How do you mean, what am I going to do?'

'Are you going to live at Satis House—?'

'God forbid.'

'Well, then, what are your plans?'

'I have no plans for the moment. I do not wish to sell it; I do not wish to let it. For now, Satis House is to remain as it is.'

'Are you certain?'

'Yes,' I tell him.

I have my own reasons for doing this, reasons which I do not intend to discuss with Mr Jaggers. Well, not yet at any rate.

He nods at me and shuffles the papers on his desk. 'Then there is nothing more to be said, is there, Estella?'

'There is nothing more to be said,' I reiterate. I rise from my chair. 'Good day, Mr Jaggers,' I say.

There *is* something more to be said, something more I would like to know, something more I *dearly* want to know, but this is not the time.

I walk from Jaggers's room, and out into the front office, and the clerk called Wemmick glances up and looks at me. His face is rather square and officious, but not unapproachable, and I think surely he knows of Pip, and of Pip's current whereabouts?

'Pip?' I say.

'What of him?' Wemmick responds.

'Are you in touch with him? Is he well?'

'I have been, and no. He has not been well, but I believe he is on the mend now.'

'Where—' I am on the point of asking Wemmick where I can find Pip, since I know he is no longer at the same address where I once wrote to him. But a man with one eye and a dark, shadowy opening where the other should be appears in the doorway, off the street, and I break off.

The man is dressed in a greasy velveteen suit and is wiping his nose on his sleeve. 'I have to see Mas'r Jaggers,' he declares.

'Now, Mike,' Wemmick says, turning to him, 'that won't do.'

'I've found one,' Mike says, sounding hopeful.

Sounding hopeful, but sounding, in addition, as if he is suffering from a perennial cold. He wipes his nose again, this time on his fur cap. 'I've found one arter a deal of trouble, Mr Wemmick. One as might do.'

'What is he prepared to swear?'

'Well,' says Mike, twisting his cap in his hands, 'in a roundabout way 'most anythink.'

Mike glances at me with his one eye for the first time then, and Wemmick remembers that I am still in the room.

'Mrs Drummle, was there something further you wanted?'

I shake my head. 'It is nothing,' I say. 'Good afternoon.'

Mike steps aside and I go out the door.

I walk without knowing where I am going. Blundering into a man selling thimbles on a wooden tray. Sidestepping—in time—a sooty chimney sweep. Then recalling that it is good luck to come across a chimney sweep and wanting to turn back and grab the man's hand, wanting to ensure some of that luck rubs off on me. But of course I do not. I walk until I see the great black dome of St Paul's bulging at me from behind a grim stone building that I recognise as having seen with Pip, which seems like a hundred years ago. In a carriage, we were, on our way to Richmond. Pip, so anxious to please me, so affectionate, so kind-natured.

Newgate Prison. I follow the high wall of the jail and find the roadway covered with straw to deaden the noise of passing vehicles, and it is not until a woman with blackened and broken teeth stops me to beg for a coin that I come to my senses. A woman who could be my mother for all I know.

*

I reach our dwelling in Hyde Park and Matilda meets me in the hallway and informs me that Mr Drummle and Jarvis have returned from abroad in my absence.

Matilda was greatly pleased to be reunited with Albert when we returned from Satis House, but it must be clear from the expression on my face that I am not enamoured by Bentley's arrival. There could be no greater contrast between the two of us.

'But he went out directly, leaving a message that you are not to expect him until the morning, miss.'

I cannot help the half-groan that escapes me as I peel off my gloves, finger by finger. I know what this is about. I made the mistake of writing and telling Bentley that I was to see Jaggers this afternoon for the reading of the will. Bentley assumes he is coming into a windfall and has gone out, not only to pay off his arrears and celebrate, but to rack up more gambling debts. Oh, what am I to do with the man!

'Would you like coffee, miss?' Matilda tilts her head to one side to observe me. She appears concerned by my appearance. She still calls me *miss* for all that I have been married for almost a year.

'Yes, please, Matilda,' I say, handing her my gloves and hat. 'I will take it in the library.

'Oh, and Matilda,' I say, as she turns from me, 'I am going out again.'

'As you wish, miss,' she says.

*

Mr Jaggers's house in Gerrard Street, Soho, is a surprise. I have expected something not quite so dark and dreary. Or sombre. It is a dignified house, yet it is in dire need of painting and brightening up. The windows are blurry with dirt and the flagstone porch is plain and dim and clearly little used.

The housekeeper, a tallish older woman with a pale face and a great deal of hair bundled up behind her head, opens the door to me. She seems altogether startled to see me, but I tell her that I know Mr Jaggers and whilst he is not expecting me, he will not mind my being there. 'I do not have an appointment,' I tell her, 'but if it is convenient, I will wait until he comes in.'

She does not reply, only steps aside to let me through. My presence seems to set her all aflutter, for her hand clutches at her throat. She takes me through the hall and up a murky staircase and I hear her breathing hard as if we are running a mile like athletes, rather than ascending stairs.

She leaves me in a sepia-coloured room with a dining table at its centre and garlands looped on the panelled walls and an unlit fire in a cold grate. I pull out a chair and sit down to wait. Only I cannot sit still. I keep thinking of what it is I am here for, and how Mr Jaggers will no doubt attempt to fob me off, and how I must be firm.

The table is laid with four places, nothing ostentatious, the cutlery is plain. A dumb waiter with various bottles and decanters of spirits and wines on it stands to the side of one chair. Smells of cooking waft up the stairs and I distract myself by imagining what it is the housekeeper is cooking. Mutton? A bird of some kind? Fish? Or all three? A bookcase stands against one wall, but from the backs of the tomes it is clear they are all law books—criminal law, trials, Acts of Parliament and so on. Deadly dull. The furniture is solid and reliable like the man himself, nothing fancy. In one corner, on a small table of papers, is a lamp with a shade and I imagine that Mr Jaggers might sit here and work further on a case after dinner.

I do not have to wait long. I have risen from the chair and begun to pace the floor when I hear a key turning in a lock and the rattle of the door being opened downstairs. Shortly afterwards, the low murmur of the housekeeper's voice, obviously announcing my presence, reaches me.

Mr Jaggers comes directly upstairs.

'I did not expect to see you soon again,' he says from the doorway. 'To what do I owe the honour?' He takes my hand, the fragrance of scented soap being immediately discernible.

'I find that I have a question after all,' I tell him, coming straight to the point, believing that my directness will work in my favour.

'Everyone has a question at some point,' he tells me, going over to the dumb waiter, 'but whether they will receive the answer they want is quite another thing. Drink?' he asks. 'I can give you a glass of sherry.'

I shake my head. 'No, thank you. I do not desire to take up your time unnecessarily.'

He turns to pour something from a decanter into a glass, then stands on the hearthrug with his tumbler, his back to the fireplace, and looks at me.

I open my mouth. I am about to frame my question when he says, 'You know, of course, that you may not get the answer you want, only the answer you need?'

I do wish he would not interrupt and give me time to arrange my thoughts! But try as I might, there is no other way to ask.

'Who is my mother?' I blurt out.

He *must* know who my mother is. He was the one who took me and gave me to Miss H. Surely he knows my origins? But will he tell me?

'Ah, Estella,' he says as if I have queried how the world began. He pauses, raises the glass and knocks back the golden liquid. 'Why don't you ask me something that I *can* answer?'

'Why can't you answer this?'

'Now, now,' he says, chastising me. 'I *can* answer it.'

He turns to the decanter to pour another and I must wait until he resumes his position on the hearthrug, and says, 'But I must not.'

'You must not?'

'I have sworn not to give away the identity of your mother.' Here he bites at his forefinger in his old habit. 'And I have given my word.'

'But what if ...' I begin. 'What if I am asking, *pleading*, in fact, for the knowledge because I mean to do good with it?'

'Ah, but you see, my dear, already we are at odds. For your interpretation of *do good* may not align with mine. Who is to say what the exact interpretation of such a phrase is, and whether that interpretation is the correct one?'

'Mr Jaggers, *please*.'

'Estella, my dear, let me ask you this. Is this information required for your own peace of mind?'

'Yes—although that is not all of it, only part—'

'So you are only thinking of yourself here?'

'No, no, of course not.'

'Because this information may give *you* peace of mind, but in my imparting it I am at risk of destroying any peace of mind your mother has. Have you considered that?'

I sigh. I can see Mr Jaggers is immovable on this topic. 'Would you at least tell me,' I ask with a heavy heart, 'is ... is my mother still alive?'

He sips from his glass and looks steadily at me.

'She is,' he says. 'But do not attempt to find her. She has given strict instructions that there is to be no contact. If I find that you are attempting to locate her, I will be suitably and severely harsh. Do you understand?'

I nod. 'As you wish,' I say.

'It is not as *I* wish, it never is. It is what other people wish. There is a difference.'

'Quite so,' I agree.

There seems little else for me to say. 'And now I will leave you,' I tell him. 'Thank you,' I say.

I have not sat down during our entire time together and I turn for the door. Mr Jaggers makes to come down with me, but I tell him there is no need, that I can find my own way and let myself out, and leaving him standing on his hearthrug, sipping at his drink, I make my way downstairs.

I slip out of the garden gate.

It is dusk now and a man on a ladder is lighting the gas lamps. One minute they are dark balls and the next they flare into brilliance and glow like small planets. I have the strangest feeling that I have been here before but, for the life of me, I cannot remember when or with whom I might have been. Pip? It seems unlikely.

I have it in my mind to walk to the corner and from there hail a hackney, when I hear the squeak of the gate and footsteps gaining on me. Perhaps I have forgotten something. My gloves? No, they are in my hand.

I stop and turn.

It is the housekeeper. Her sleeves are rolled up and she is still wearing her apron.

She is all atremble again. Her right hand, quivering violently, is up near her mouth as if the idea of speaking to me is causing her great agitation. She pauses in front of me and I notice that it is not only her hand that quavers, but her whole body. I wonder what ails the woman.

'What is it?' I say.

'Miss,' she starts.

I nod encouragingly. 'Yes.'

'Miss ... miss, I know your mother—'

'My mother?' I am so astonished it is all I can do to repeat her words.

She nods. 'I can give a message for you if you want. I can tell her that I seen you and what a fine lady you are.'

I open my mouth, but the words will not come. Not that I know what it is I want to say.

She nods at me. 'Would that be agreeable to you, miss?'

I am weak with shock. I put my hand on her arm to try to pull myself together, and feel the warmth of the woman's flesh and how she quivers beneath my touch.

'Olivia?' She cocks her head to one side.

I look at her blankly.

'The name don't mean anything to you, miss?'

I shake my head. 'No. Should it?'

In answer, she covers the top of my hand briefly with her own—a caress and the sensation of both warmth and roughness—and says, 'Thankee, miss'. Her eyes are shining.

Then she is gone, slipping away from me back the way she has come, and I have not said another word.

34

I do not see Bentley until noon the following day, when he rises. Clearly, the night before, he was out drinking, for he comes to the dining table and the midday meal clutching his head and looking positively green about the gills.

'The money,' he says to me without so much as a greeting, 'the money from Miss Havisham. Have you got it?'

I shake my head. 'I only went to the reading of the will yesterday.'

He pulls out a chair and collapses into it. 'Well,' he demands agitatedly, and screws up his eyes with pain. No doubt his head is pounding. 'When will you have it? I need it as soon as possible.'

I put down my knife and fork. 'How much do you need?'

'What do you mean, how much do I need? I need it all. Isn't that obvious, woman?'

'I will give you some of my inheritance from Miss Havisham,' I say, 'but only if you stipulate a sum—'

'The deuce take you!' He bangs his fist upon the table so that the crockery jumps.

I lift my knife again and cut into a piece of ham and spear it with my fork, but when I raise it to my mouth I cannot eat; my jaw is clenched tight.

I rest my cutlery on my plate and look out of the window. Beyond the glass, the leaves of the trees are shaking and shimmering in the breeze. They are bright green, but soon the season will change, soon the leaves will turn rusty-coloured and shrivel and fall from the branch. Winter is coming.

'Estella? Estella, look at me.'

I do not wish to look, but I must. My husband leans across the table. He smirks. His teeth are yellowed, no doubt because he has not yet brushed them, and the reek of his breath makes me feel ill.

'Mr Jaggers,' he says, 'is my friend. He'll tell me precisely how much you have inherited from the old crone, and then we'll talk again. Hah!' he says.

He leans forward. With one hand, he smacks first one of my cheeks and then the other. I believe the staff are all currently downstairs and thankfully not present to see his treatment of me.

He pushes back his chair and rises. He belches. He walks, nay sways, across the room.

I am about to leave the table, too, and go to my chambers, for under the circumstances I cannot consume a morsel, when Jarvis appears from the staircase below.

The stealth with which he emerges—no sound of his footsteps on the stairs—tells me he has been on the treads all the time, listening. The expression on his face, part amusement, part gloating, confirms it. He does not like me, that much is clear.

'What is it, Jarvis?' I ask, aware that my cheeks are burning.

'I am looking for Mr Drummle,' he says, gazing down his overlarge nose at me.

'He has gone to his quarters.'

'Did he need me, Mrs Drummle? I thought I heard someone clapping,' he says, deadpan.

'You must be mistaken,' I tell him. 'Nobody was clapping.'

'My apologies,' he says.

He turns and goes back down the stairs. I hear him whistling. I have never heard him whistling before. I think it is Tchaikovsky's *1812 Overture*. I believe it is no accident that he whistles this tune. He is sending me a not so subtle message.

*

I am not concerned about Bentley and Mr Jaggers. Bentley forgets that Jaggers is a man who does things by the book. Client confidentiality is one of the hallmarks of his existence. But all the same, I take care to be out of the house for the next few days, returning only in the late afternoon, by which time Bentley has given up on me and gone to his club.

It is a temporary reprieve.

Three days later, he knocks at my door at five in the morning. 'Estella,' he bellows.

For fear he will wake the servants and the neighbours, I am about to rise and let him in when he opens the door without permission.

Bleary with lack of sleep and drink, he sits on the edge of my bed. He puts his head in his heads. 'I am sorry, Estella,' he mumbles, as if it pains him to apologise, 'but I require those funds. If I don't gain access to them by twelve today, I am in hot water.'

'Let us agree on a sum, Bentley,' I say gently, for fear of irking him, 'and let us agree that you will stop gambling—'

'Stop gambling?' He shakes his head. 'Are you mad, woman? My luck is about to change, I know it!'

'It is out of my hands, then. I cannot give you anything unless—'

'You cannot give me anything *unless*?' He laughs harshly.

Rising from the bed, he walks across to the door to lock it. Then he returns to me, flings back the covers and stares down at my body.

Later that morning, I put on a long-sleeved dress and, hobbling with pain, visit the bank. I have yet to receive my inheritance, but I transfer a sum from my savings into Bentley's account.

*

Bentley and I, and James and Eliza, married now, are all invited to the same party.

When I notice them amongst the guests, I am perturbed that Eliza will rebuff me yet again, but I am overjoyed to find that perhaps absence has made her heart grow fonder, for she—and James—appear gladdened to renew their acquaintance with me. Perhaps they have had time to reflect on their original decision to cut me out of their lives. On the other hand, it may simply be that we are at a social gathering and certain niceties must be upheld, but I am being cynical.

I am immensely pleased to clasp her hands again and see her happy face—it has been too long—but the presence of James is sobering, reminding me of that day he carried the dreadful news of Laurence's death to me, and I cannot look at him without feeling distressed.

The four of us spend some time together conversing and this appears to help smooth matters over, for a week later Eliza invites us to Waverley to stay for a few days. I suspect the invitation is the work of Eliza, and purely for my benefit, but I am elated that Bentley agrees we should go.

I have the opportunity, then, to contrast my life with Eliza's, and see that marriage can be a happy and fulfilling union, for Eliza and James flirt with one another, they make jokes and laugh and constantly discreetly and tenderly touch each other. I think, nay I *know*, that Pip was right—I have flung myself away on a brute.

It is odd, but the presence of the happy couple and the atmosphere they live in seem to have an effect upon Bentley. He is kind and courteous over the weekend. Even—dare I say it?—loving. Up to a point.

Eliza is expecting their first child and glows with health and happiness. Her fair curly hair seems shinier, her eyes brighter, and she is prettier than ever, which doesn't escape even Bentley's notice. On our last but one evening, when he and I are preparing for bed, he says a little worriedly, 'You are not yet with child, are you?'

I shake my head.

'Are you concerned?'

'No,' I shake my head again. 'Everything in the fullness of time.'

He frowns. 'What do you mean?'

'That it will happen when the time is right.'

'I see. There's nothing you can do to make it happen now?'

'Perhaps,' I say.

'Well, please look into it.'

He pauses for a moment at the side of the bed to look at me. Our eyes meet. I half-expect him to tell me to remove my gown but he does not.

Once I am under the covers, I take up my book and turn away from him towards the light. I have just commenced a paragraph on surgery during hypnotism when his finger runs up my spine.

'Estella,' he murmurs. 'I want to make a little Bentley.'

This is original. Has he been learning things from James? For Bentley's habit is not to speak, not to ask, but simply to act.

'You'll have to excuse me for a moment,' I say, throwing back the covers.

He clutches at my hand and pulls me back. 'Why?'

'I need to relieve myself.'

'But surely you relieved yourself earlier?'

He takes my hand and guides it under his nightgown to his engorged member—he is quick to rise to the occasion. Then he closes his eyes. 'Estella,' he murmurs.

'I need to go again,' I tell him.

'I don't think you do. Come,' he demands, pushing me flat upon the bed and lifting my nightgown, 'let us make a little Bentley.'

'*A little Bentley*?' I cannot help it but I laugh.

He raises his face from my breasts. He has gone bright red. 'What? You would laugh at me?' And reaching for my hands he grips them tightly above my head.

'I try to be civil,' he mutters, 'and this is how you reward me.' Lowering himself onto me, he begins to thrust his stiff and swollen organ between my closed thighs. 'Open!' he demands.

'I will not. Do you want to burst my bladder!'

'Very well!' He flings himself backwards in a fit of pique. 'Go! But do not be long.'

Sometimes when he lies comatose upon me after the act, his hairy limbs sprawled across my body, I feel that he really *is* a spider. I have discovered that an arachnid known as a flower spider injects digestive juices into its prey and sucks out the internal tissues, leaving only a body husk behind. I wonder, is this what he is doing to me?

*

Eliza takes up the subject of confinement with me, too. The men have gone riding, and we stroll arm-in-arm, as we once did, but this time in the Waverley Manor's rose garden. It is late afternoon and one of those near perfect autumn days: absolutely still and not a breath of wind. The sunshine bathes the trees, the flowers, with a thick and golden honeyed hue. The sky is pale blue and a fingernail of moon is suspended above the horizon.

'You are not yet expectant?' she asks.

I shake my head. 'And happy not to be so,' I add.

She pauses to turn and look at me with surprise.

'Come, Eliza,' I say, 'let's be frank. You are aware of the kind of man I married.'

'But why?' she asks, continuing to walk. 'Having a child will change him into a better person, don't you think?'

'I doubt it,' I say.

Perhaps it is the fact that our friendship appears to have been restored that I let my guard down. 'It is difficult for me now,' I murmur. 'Imagine how much more difficult it would be if I had a child.'

Eliza looks puzzled. 'But how …?'

'There are ways and means.'

She giggles nervously. 'Oh dear,' she says, 'I am in the dark here.'

'Naturally,' I say. 'You are happily married. Why would you even think of such matters, let alone be interested?'

'But I *am* interested, Estella,' she persists. 'Pray tell me?'

I lower my voice. 'There is a device called a cup, a type of sponge that you insert, and that is easily removed by the pulling of a string. That is the most reliable method I have found,' I say, remembering that I only just managed to achieve this the previous night. 'In addition, I keep an eye on the calendar and my menses cycle and feign a headache when I am at my most fertile. Then there is douching straight afterwards, but that is inclined to be unreliable and I do not recommend it.'

I do not tell Eliza that feigning a headache with Bentley never works. He will have his way. Nothing, in fact, as I have illustrated, deters him except the sight of blood, and on occasion I have been forced to go down to the kitchen and find a tomato, remove the pips and mash the flesh with the juice until I have the right consistency.

Pausing to bend down to the flowers and use the tips of two fingers to avoid the thorns, I pluck a rose, pretty and full-blown and pink.

'Here,' I say, handing it to Eliza. 'A beauty for my dear friend. Now, who is the most beautiful?'

She smiles at my teasing tone and admires the bloom. 'No competition,' she says. 'You are.' She takes my hand again and the moment is forgotten and we pass on to some or other subject.

The truce between Bentley and me does not last long. The fact that I am without child becomes his new criticism, for naturally it is all my fault. I do not mind this fault-finding because I know the reason for my failure to conceive, but my complacency seems to goad him. It seems he is not happy unless he leaves me close to tears, and he reverts to this modus operandi.

Then, one evening after nine, when Bentley is at his club and I am in the drawing room and have put away my knitting and begun preparations for retiring, Matilda comes to me in near hysteria.

One of her hands is up near her mouth and it seems she cannot speak for distress. I gently take her hand and pull it from her face, and notice that her lovely nails are bitten down to the flesh; the cuticle of one is even bleeding.

'What is it, Matilda?'

'It's—it's Albert,' she says, managing to get the words out between sobs. 'He has sent word—word—that he has been taken by the police.'

'By the police? For what reason?'

'I don' know, miss,' she says, and falls into a renewed bout of crying.

'Matilda,' I say, 'you must have some idea?'

'It is probably Jarvis,' she says, sniffing. 'He's a cunning one, miss.'

'You mean he's deliberately done something to put Albert in the frame?'

'It's possible, miss.'

From what I know of Jarvis, I do not like the man. I have already said this. Owing to my insistence on retaining Albert, and perhaps wary that he might hold a grudge, I have steered clear of Jarvis—apart from the occasions I have already mentioned. If Bentley and I were happily married, I would no doubt by now have had a great deal more to do with Jarvis, but Bentley and I lead separate lives.

I give Matilda a handkerchief from my pocket and, with my hand reassuringly on her arm, tell her to dry her tears.

I walk across the room, deep in thought, turn and walk back again.

There is nothing for it, I think. It must be done, and the sooner, the better.

I turn to Matilda.

'Get our coats,' I say.

'Our coats, miss?'

'Yes, our coats. We are going out.'

35

We pause outside the house on the south side of Gerrard Street, Soho. The dwelling is in darkness.

I do not pay the coachman; I tell him to wait. Matilda and I slip through the gate and approach the door.

I try some gentle knocking—I do not wish to wake the whole neighbourhood—but there is no response. Nobody stirs.

'Here, miss, let me do it,' Matilda says.

She gives the wood an almighty beating. A dog barks somewhere and, above the porch, a window opens and a head sticks out. 'What the devil?' Mr Jaggers says.

'It's me, Estella.' I step backwards onto the path where he can see me better.

The window closes again and, after a minute or two, he comes down to let us in. We troop up the dusky staircase into the murky brown room with the dining table at its centre and the garlands looped on the panelled walls. A fire has been burning in the grate, but is practically out, and Mr Jaggers puts on another log and stirs it into life with the poker.

I do not pull out a chair.

'This is Matilda,' I tell him. She does a little curtsey. She has gone from crying to being as pale as a candlestick. 'She is my maid and has been with me since I first came to London.'

Mr Jaggers, at the dumb waiter, is pouring some liquid into glasses and does not respond. I wait until he turns and hands us each what appears to be a tumbler of sherry.

'And?' he says. He is in his dressing gown and his bushy black eyebrows are awry from sleep.

'She is married to Albert, who works for Bentley and me.'

Jaggers sips at his drink. 'Go on.'

'Bentley has a manservant by the name of Jarvis who has taken a dislike to Albert. You should know that I had to press hard to retain Albert. You should know that Jarvis is constantly trying to undermine him. Matilda, this evening, came to tell me that her husband has sent word he has been taken into custody by the police—'

'For what reason?'

'She has no idea.'

'And you want me to do something, now, in what is practically the middle of the night?'

'Yes, please.'

'Hmph,' Mr Jaggers says. He downs the remainder of his drink. 'Wait here,' he instructs.

We wait. We finish our sherries. Matilda pulls out a chair for me, but I shake my head. 'I don't think he will be long,' I whisper.

He is not.

Out in the street, I am relieved to see the horses and carriage are still waiting. The coachman no doubt wants his fare.

We do not converse on the journey. The bridles of the horses jingle in the damp night air and their hooves clip the cobblestones. Matilda sits bolt upright at my side and every now and then I reach for her hand and squeeze it. At one point, I say to Mr Jaggers, 'What will you do?'

'I won't know until I get there and find out what the charge is,' he tells me.

We arrive at the mournful and forbidding-looking building that I know to be Newgate Prison. It remains much as it was the first time I saw it with Pip—stained by the elements, here and there hung with fetters and chains—only this time there are no dismal and dreary-looking people loitering outside it.

'Wait here,' Mr Jaggers says again, getting out.

'On second thoughts'—he puts his head back in the doorway—'perhaps you had better come with me, Estella. So you can point this Albert fellow out to me.'

I squeeze Matilda's hand one last time and alight. I instruct the coachman to wait, and to take care of my maid, and then I follow Mr Jaggers.

He is already at the gate, talking to the night watchman, who has a truncheon at his side and is in a great coat and swings a lantern. After some discussion, which I am too late to overhear, the watchman opens the gate and we follow him inside.

'Stay close to me,' Mr Jaggers instructs.

I do not need a second warning; I cling to the man like I am his shadow.

We cross a flagstone courtyard and arrive at a second gate and a turnkey who is very much half-asleep. Rising from his chair, he stretches his arms and yawns copiously. He blinks. He shakes his head as if seeing a ghost and is immediately bright-eyed and all attention.

'Mr Jaggers, sir!'

'A man called Albert—' Mr Jaggers murmurs. 'Estella,' he turns to me, 'what is his last name?'

'Findlay.'

'Albert Findlay,' Jaggers says. 'I understand he was brought in this afternoon. What is he charged with? I need him to be released. I will settle bail in the morning.'

The turnkey draws a ledger towards himself and runs his finger down a column of names. 'Here,' he says, at last. 'Albert Findlay. Pickpocketing.'

'Pickpocketing? Who laid the charge?'

The turnkey now runs his finger across the page. 'A Mr Fagin, says here.'

'And what was taken?'

'A gen'leman's wallet.'

'Hmph,' Jaggers says. 'Was it recovered?'

'Yes.'

'Small fry,' Jaggers says. 'Lead the way,' he tells the man.

The turnkey reaches up and takes a light from the sconce upon the wall, and we follow him down a thick stone-walled passage. Here and there, set into the stone walls, are more sconces with lights. The floor underfoot is hard and bumpy and wet in places. The smell is putrid, a mixture of urine, sweat and unwashed bodies. The odour claws at the back of my throat and I cover my mouth with my gloved hand.

We stop suddenly in front of another great iron gate and I almost walk into the back of my companion. The clinking of keys, the grind and groan of the gate swinging open and being securely locked behind us once more, and we pause in a long narrow room. High up on the walls, barred windows let in what little outside light there is.

There are humps and lumps upon the floor. Bodies. Prisoners. Some sleep on, others raise themselves from their filthy coarse blankets to stare at us. Their faces are grimy and hopeless-looking.

'Albert Findlay?' the turnkey calls, holding the flaring light high above his head.

One of the lumps close by, barefoot and dressed in nothing more than rags, rises from the ground. 'Yessir?' he says, 'I be Albert.'

'He may well be Albert,' I whisper to Mr Jaggers, 'but he's not our Albert.'

Mr Jaggers shakes his head at the turnkey and we proceed further into the room. I am mindful of where I put my feet, and my eyes, for my gaze lights upon a face and its expression of despair is almost more than I can withstand. I look hurriedly away, but not before the prisoner has reached for the hem of my dress and tugged upon it.

'Miss—?'

I look down. Two oddities strike me about the man. On the fourth finger of his left hand he wears a tarnished but ornate ring. A snake of some type. The second is that he has an ulcerated sore in one corner of his mouth. I have read about this and I know how to treat it.

'Albert Findlay?' the turnkey calls again and the man drops his hand as Mr Jaggers and I pause and gaze around us.

At the end of the room, another man rises. Dishevelled, he looks about him in bewilderment.

'Albert!' I exclaim.

When we emerge outside the prison gates, Matilda springs from the carriage and, with a cry, flings herself into her husband's arms.

They request to sit together in the front with the coachman, which I understand, and Mr Jaggers and I ride in comfort inside.

'I'll need him to come by in the morning,' he tells me as we head back to the Hyde Park house. 'Nine o'clock sharp, my office. And to report to Wemmick. Understood?' He nods at me.

'Yes,' I say. 'And thank you. I don't know what I would have done without you.'

'Where's that husband of yours?' he asks, biting at his forefinger.

I shake my head and say nothing.

'Oh, it's like that, is it?' he says.

I turn my head from Mr Jaggers and gaze out of the window. I have no desire to discuss Bentley.

As I step from the coach, his parting words are, 'You have remembered what I told you regarding your mother?'

'I have.'

'Good. Mind you continue to do so.'

Of course I have remembered what he told me regarding my mother. Not a day goes by when I do not recall Jaggers's housekeeper and her promise. I have imagined the woman going to my mother and telling her what a fine lady I am.

I am a lady, this is true, but there are times when I am not convinced about the fineness.

*

The matter is settled out of court in the morning. I don't accompany Albert and Matilda to Mr Jaggers's office and do not know what he says to or offers the plaintiff, only that Mr Fagin withdraws his charges.

When Albert and Matilda return, I call them into the library and talk to them quietly behind the locked door. Albert tells me that he and Jarvis were sent by Mr Drummle to collect an amount of coin, winnings from a horse race. He believes they were sent together to ensure the money came back in its entirety.

'Are you saying that Mr Drummle does not trust Jarvis, either?' I ask Albert.

He nods. 'It's possible. Why else would he send me to accompany him?'

Albert goes on to say that, while he and Jarvis were in the queue, Mr Fagin, who was ahead of them, emptied his pockets and declared that his wallet had been taken. As Albert was standing directly behind him, the man accused him of stealing it.

'I shook me head, miss,' Albert says. 'I said, not me, for why would I do such a thing? Then Jarvis pipes up to say he believes I have the wallet on me person, and next thing I know he produces it from me back pocket.'

I, too, shake my head for it sounds like a contrivance. I advise Albert that under no circumstances is he to take up his grievance with Jarvis. I say that we cannot trust the man, that he will be looking for any opportunity to pin something on Albert again, and until such time as I have worked out a plan, he is to lie low. At least, to keep out of the man's way.

'Yes, miss,' Albert says. 'Thankee, miss.'

After they have left the room, I cannot help thinking of the prisoner who remains incarcerated in Newgate Prison. The man with the face of despair who reached for my hem. I wonder if he is still there, and whether he has a wife, and what his fate is to be? Try as I might, I cannot escape thinking of him.

I have bad dreams again in the night. I, myself, am imprisoned in Newgate. For some reason, I am disguised and dressed in men's clothing—or I am a man, I know not which. But I am left there for days, amongst those rank and vile bodies, with no hope. Nobody, not even Mr Jaggers, comes to rescue me. I eventually wake myself with my sobbing and I am sick to my core with horror.

But it gives me an idea.

36

For the first time in a long time, I am animated.

I am not thinking selfishly about myself and my plight, but about someone else.

For I begin to see how I might shape my life, what I might do with it and what its purpose might be, and the thought fills me with hope and with warmth.

I said earlier that Miss Havisham once told me the meaning of my name was *Star*, and I comprehend how I can be true to my name, how I can be like a light shining in the dark once more.

'Matilda,' I say at breakfast, eating alone as is customary and finishing my coffee, 'can you tell Albert that I am going out this morning shortly before ten, and that I will need the carriage, please?'

'Yes, miss,' she says, pausing with my dirty plate in her hands.

I have to talk hard and fast with Albert when I meet him and the carriage in the yard, but he is grateful to me for my recent assistance and it does not take long to convince him of my plan. Particularly when I tell him that if I do not reappear outside

Newgate Prison within the hour, he is at liberty to call upon Mr Jaggers for help.

Newgate. For, yes, that is where I am going.

Albert drops me around the corner from the main gate. The arrangement I have with him is that he will wait with the horses until my return.

The throng of dismal and dreary-looking people I have witnessed before at the prison's gate is still there, but because of who I am and how I am attired, they part before me so that I find myself at the front. The only person ahead of me is a woman, and she turns to see who has come up behind her as if I might be going to steal from the cloth-covered wicker basket that she carries. Her face is lined, her grey hair bundled up under a tartan scarf, and a number of hairs sprout untidily from a mole upon her chin.

'After you, miss,' she says, stepping aside.

'No, you were ahead of me,' I say. 'You must go first,' I insist.

'Thankee,' she says.

But the guard turns the woman away. She is not best pleased and argues her case, but over and above the noise of newspaper boys, trotting horses, vendors selling their wares from their trundling barrows and the clamour of people behind me, I cannot hear what he says to her. 'Good luck to ye,' she mutters as she departs.

'Prisoner's name?' the guard says, without taking his attention from the newspaper he has opened before him.

'I do not know the prisoner's name,' I say, shocking him into looking up, open-mouthed. The man is heavily built and as warty as a toad and he gazes at me through fat, narrowed eyelids.

'That is … That is most uncommon, madam, if I may say so—'

'Mr Jaggers sent me,' I say, interrupting, or we might be here all morning.

'Mr Jaggers?'

'That is correct. You are to allow me access to the prisoners.'

'Very well, madam.' He lifts the keys from where they are chained to his belt and lets me through into the lodge.

The toady guard accompanies me across the yard to the second set of gates.

'What is your name, madam?' he asks on the way.

'Mrs Drummle,' I tell him.

'Mrs Drummle,' he announces to the second guard. 'Here to see a prisoner. Sent by Jaggers hisself,' he adds, in case the man is inclined to give me short shrift.

The second guard raises his eyebrows, but does not comment. He unlocks the gate and we set off along the mouldy fetid passage I traversed before, and this time I do not cover my mouth with my hand.

We reach the long gloomy room with the high windows, and the lumps, bumps and bodies upon the floor, and the guard turns to me.

'Prisoner's name?'

'His name doesn't matter,' I say. 'I know what he looks like.'

Ah, but do I?

I try to remember something about the man, apart from the sore upon his face, that might assist me to identify him, and I think again of how he reached for the hem of my dress and ... The ring! The ring he was wearing in the shape of a snake.

I walk forward. I recall where I had stood previously and, minding where I put my boots, move to that place and look down upon the man who sits nearest to me and study his hands.

Grubby hands, but empty of rings. I move along and look at the next man. The same. The next fellow withdraws his hands from under the warmth of his soiled blanket, holds them out for inspection, and looks up at me. Most of the prisoners are looking at me now because I am an oddity. I am a well-to-do woman out of place.

'What yer looking for, madam?' the guard asks.

'A ring,' I murmur, 'a snake ring.'

'Aah, why didn' you say so, madam? That'd be Sam Mulligan.' He raises his head. 'Sam Mulligan, where be you?' he calls.

The man who rises from the floor is in the same place where Albert previously sat. Strange. Maybe his logic is that there is something lucky about the position?

I make my way over to him and, by the time I reach him, he has sat down again, as if his legs will no longer hold him upright.

He looks with curiosity and suspicion at me this time. But I am convinced it is the same man, I do not need to check his left hand to confirm it, for there is the sore at the corner of his mouth and his face bears the despairing and hopeless look he wore before. As if the sun is not going to rise in the morning. As if he has been sentenced to hang and his hours are numbered. Perhaps he has, and they are.

'Wot you want?' he says.

'What are you in for?' I ask.

'Who wants to know?'

'A friend,' I murmur, crouching down on the floor alongside him. 'Mr Jaggers can get you out.'

'Mas'r Jaggers? I can' affor' no Mas'r Jaggers,' he says. His teeth are brown and stained and the ulcerated corner of his mouth weeps.

'Never mind that. What are you in for?'

'Loitering. Loitering with intent, if yer must know.'

'And your name is Sam Mulligan?'

He nods. 'Samuel Joseph Mulligan,' he states. He still has some pride in his name, then.

I ferret in my pocket for the small tin of ointment I have brought and slip it to him. 'Put some of this on that sore place at the corner of your mouth. It will help to heal it.'

He looks at the tin suspiciously, but nonetheless takes it from me.

'Who are you?' he says.

I rise from the floor. There is no need to say anything further, much less to respond to his query, and I return to the guard.

It is when we are leaving that I see him. *Her*? Far back against the wall. I do not know what gender it is. The hair is too long, the face too filthy and the clothes too raggedy for me to determine whether it is boy or girl. But I must assume it is a boy since I have seen no women in here. I do know, however, that prisoners—men, women and children—*are* sometimes mixed together. I have read it somewhere.

'Wait,' I tell the guard, touching him on the arm and pausing.

'Who is that? The child?' I add, when he looks back at me, puzzled.

'That'd be young Mick Saddler,' he tells me.

I have stopped to stare and the child notices. He is small and light enough that he can perch on a ledge on the wall, but it means he is elevated, can keep out of harm's way and can watch over everyone else. He is not dull-witted, then. He gazes back at me from under his overlong fringe and it is not exactly a friendly look. I would describe it as insolent.

'And what is he in for?'

'Shoplifting.'

'Very well,' I say. 'Thank you,' I say. 'We can go now.'

Outside, I make my way back to Albert and the carriage and horses. St Paul's is striking the hour and I have been less than thirty minutes.

'Home, Mrs Drummle?' Albert asks.

I shake my head. 'I wish to go to Mr Jaggers's office, please,' I tell him. 'It is only around the corner, as you know.' He nods. 'As you wish, Mrs Drummle.'

We are soon underway, heading for Jaggers's office, and the narrow and dirty street in Little Britain soon approaches. The offices with the door marked *Mr Jaggers* are in sight, and the door is open, to my relief.

I leave Albert and go inside.

Wemmick is behind his desk. There is no-one else in the room. The door to Mr Jaggers's office is open, but from the general air of silence, I assume it is vacant. I pray that it remains that way, for I do not wish to see the man. I have an instinct that he will not approve of my actions.

'What is it?' Wemmick asks without looking up, for the morning sun has caused my shadow to fall across the floor.

'I wish Mr Jaggers to do something for me,' I say.

Immediately, Wemmick glances up. 'Why, Mrs Drummle,' he says in surprise. 'Good day to you.'

He rises from his desk and comes forward while I begin to lay a quantity of notes upon the countertop.

'There are two prisoners in Newgate,' I tell him. 'One by the name of Samuel Joseph Mulligan; the other, who is but a child, is Mick Saddler. Mulligan is in for loitering with intent; the child has been incarcerated for shoplifting. I wish both of these prisoners to be freed and here are the funds that I am willing to pay for Mr Jaggers to represent them in court.'

Wemmick looks at the notes, then looks sceptically at me. 'I am not sure that Mr Jaggers would approve.'

'That is between me and Mr Jaggers,' I tell him.

'And what are these prisoners to you?'

I shake my head. 'I am merely trying to brighten their lives.'

He does not respond. He is counting the notes under his breath.

'If the funds are insufficient, I will be back tomorrow at the same time to make up the shortfall. And not a word to Mr Drummle, please.'

'As you wish, madam,' he says.

'Good day to you, sir,' I say, and sweep out of the room.

*

The following morning, Albert and I set off again for Mr Jaggers's office, arriving at roughly the same time as before.

But I have become cocky with my sense of goodwill and step into the office without first checking whether Mr Jaggers is in, and whether Wemmick is alone.

He is not.

The small boy called Mick Saddler is standing on tiptoes, trying to see over Wemmick's counter. They appear to be having some kind of argument.

Wemmick says, 'Get out now, you whippersnapper, or I'll be calling the police.'

'Not before yer telling who it were set me free,' the boy demands.

He turns, then, to see who is coming in the door and recognises me.

'What yer do that fer?' he says in a chatty tone of voice. 'Set me loose? I were happy in there, I was. Food and a roof over me head.'

He sticks his thumbs into the waistband of his raggedy trousers and surveys me, as if he cannot decide what to make of me and of the fact that he has been released.

'It's not the workhouse, yer know, miss, so I'd thankee not to go doing that again.'

As a parting shot he gives me another look of insolence, and then slips out of the door and scarpers down the street. Gone.

So much for that!

'Do I owe you further funds?' I say to Wemmick.

'Yes, Mrs Drummle, you do.' He has risen from his desk and come over. 'Two shillings. Not exactly a fortune. But two shillings is two shillings and, without two shillings, I am two shillings short.'

I open my purse and draw out the coins.

'It's as well you are here,' Wemmick says, 'for he wishes to see you.'

He?

Behind me I hear the creaking of Mr Jaggers's coffin-like chair as he rises from it. 'Estella, is that you?'

Mr Jaggers emerges to glare at me. He hooks his thumbs into his waistcoat pockets—a little like the urchin did—and surveys me, his beetle-black eyebrows twitching.

'*Brighten their lives?*' he says with sarcasm and almost snorts. 'What is the meaning of this?'

'Isn't it obvious?'

'Not to me, it isn't. The child is not grateful, and as for Samuel Joseph Mulligan, it will be a matter of hours before he is back in gaol. The man is a habitual offender. He cannot help himself. Very soon he will find himself being shipped off to Australia.'

'I see,' I say slowly, comprehending that my good deeds have come to naught.

'And you,' Mr Jaggers continues, extracting one hand and biting at his forefinger, 'have now wasted a considerable amount of money, in addition to my time. I hate to think of what Mr Drummle's opinion of your exploits would be—'

'Oh, please, Mr Jaggers. You will not tell him, surely?'

'Not this time, Estella. But if it happens again, I may be forced to. Is that understood?'

'Yes, Mr Jaggers,' I say meekly.

*

I return to the carriage. I am suitably chastened, and my head is lowered and I see only the ground in front of my feet.

I feel foolish, overwhelmed and inept. What is the point of my life if I cannot do something with it!

In due course, we journey back to the Hyde Park house, and when we turn into the driveway it is around eleven. Jarvis is in the yard, a mug of steaming tea at his feet. His tall and skeletal frame leans against the back wall and his arms are folded against his chest. He studies Albert through narrowed lids as he hops down from the box and opens the door for me to alight and, from the expression on Jarvis's face, I would say he is brooding. He is up to no good, I think.

I remember, then, that I undertook to think of some way to bring Jarvis and Albert together or, at least, to prevent the former from continuing to snipe at the latter, or worse.

And I have another idea, which I cannot claim all the credit for. I think it springs from Jaggers telling me that the man called Samuel Mulligan is a habitual offender, and from me reflecting on how little I knew, or suspected, and now realising that I know very little about Jarvis. In fact, I know next to nothing.

Perhaps, I decide, all is not lost for the day.

I go in and find Matilda in my quarters where she is making my bed and dusting and tidying.

'Matilda,' I say, 'can you bring me a set of Albert's clothes? His workday clothes, nothing special. It doesn't matter if they are dirty. In fact, it'd be better if they are soiled.'

'Albert's clothes?' Bewildered, she pauses with the wicker basket of soiled laundry in her hands.

I nod. 'Trousers, shirt, jacket. Braces—we'll need braces to hold up the trousers. An old cap would be good, too, if he has one he can spare.'

'Miss—?' she begins.

'Bring the clothes to my room, please, Matilda,' I tell her. 'I'll explain it all in due course.'

'As you wish, miss,' she says.

When she brings Albert's clothes to me later, I take them from her and outline what it is I plan to do. At first she is against it, but by degrees she comes around, particularly when I describe the way I saw Jarvis studying Albert. Between the two of us it is agreed that she will return to my room at around four-thirty and help me to dress.

At five-thirty, in the dusky light, and when Matilda has checked the coast is clear, I make my way out of the back door and slip across the road to the park. I wear my own pair of flat black boots and Albert's trousers with the hems rolled and braces keeping them up. I have on a filthy shirt and a rough and ready jacket that is patched at the elbows and fraying at the cuffs. Soot and ash are smeared around my lower jaw, disguising a lack of stubble, and my hands are none too clean. I went out into the garden and grovelled around in the earth to get dirt under my fingernails. It does feel strange to be dirty and yet I cannot say that I am revolted by it. But then the dirt is fresh and underneath it I am clean. It would be a different story if I were forced to don the same clothes and had neither washed for a month nor had an opportunity to brush my teeth and hair, as some poor and needy vagrants are obliged to live.

Matilda has bound up my hair using hairpins from the pretty little crystal dish, and she has arranged a shabby flat cap to hold my tresses firmly in place and cover most of my head.

I position myself under a tree. From here I can observe who is coming and going, both into and out of the house. It is a Wednesday and on Wednesday nights it is Bentley's habit to dine at his club and stay out until the small hours and, as a consequence, Jarvis finishes work at six. However, it is nearly eight and I am half-dazed with boredom and stiffness before a man with his trousers flapping about his legs emerges from the gloom of the house and exits the gate.

I follow Jarvis, keeping well back, to wherever it is he is going. It helps that he is hefting a carrier bag of sorts, the weight of which slows him down. The bag reminds me of his statement concerning Albert and stolen foodstuffs, and I wonder what exactly it holds. Jarvis's height is to my advantage, for he is easy to spot amongst the other foot passengers. Moreover, he has not the faintest idea he is being tailed. Here and there along the way, a gas lamp shows me the body of a sleeping vagrant in a doorway, and once or twice a beggar stops me. But mostly I am left alone. It is because I am slight and poorly dressed. No-one would believe that I had anything of value on me.

It is a low and poverty-stricken neighbourhood where Jarvis eventually pauses outside a set of stairs leading up to a door. The streets here are narrow and twisted, the walls of the ruinous houses blackened with dirt and soot. Underfoot the cobbles are slimy with effluent and the carcass of a dead dog in the gutter catches my eye. The people that I have seen look weary and despairing and the air carries the smell of putrefaction, but then we are not far from Smithfield and the meat market.

I have to admit it does all remind me of the time I went seeking my artist friend, Theo Whittaker. I wonder what became of the man? Whether he eventually managed to make a living from his art? I do hope so.

I pause on the corner and kneel, ostensibly to do up my bootlace, but I am watching Jarvis out of the corner of my eye. The establishment he has stopped outside, squashed between hovels of a similar kind, has a rickety wooden staircase leading up to an equally rickety ramshackle door. Someone wrote—it might have been Dickens—that every one of these darkly clustered houses encloses its own secret, and every beating heart in the hundreds of thousands of hearts in the vast city of London has its own secret … Jarvis and his secret is merely one of these.

I would guess that the dwelling probably once was a warehouse loft of some kind. The windows are shuttered and boarded up since the glass has long broken, and faint candlelight flickers through the wooden planks. I am guessing again, but I believe I know what kind of establishment Jarvis has stopped outside.

He mounts the stairs, knocks and the door is opened to him.

A sliver of light shows me the outline of an elderly woman. She wears a shawl, uses a stick and is hunched over. Jarvis steps in and she closes the door behind him, but not before I see him put his free arm around her shoulder and embrace her.

I am bewildered. This is not what I am expecting.

This is no fallen woman.

I have jumped to conclusions, inaccurate ones. The evidence I had hoped to gather and hoped to use against Jarvis is non-existent.

I glance around. Across the street, a newspaper boy is selling the late edition of the paper and I walk over to him.

'Whose dwelling would that be?' I ask in a gravelly voice, tilting my head towards the shabby building and handing him a coin for the paper.

'That'd be Ma Jarvis's place. She'd be an old hag but she ain't a bad 'un,' he tells me.

Jarvis's mother. And Jarvis displaying qualities of warmth and affection towards her, attributes I would never have guessed he had.

I do not need to see any more. I know the name of the street—Cock Lane—and will be able to identify the house again. Now all I need is to reach home safely.

I hail a chaise-cart, but until I show the driver I have the necessary fare and hand it over, I have a difficult time of it persuading him to take me back to Hyde Park.

St Paul's is striking the midnight hour by the time I reach home. Albert has been keeping a look out and lets me in. The master is not yet home, he tells me, and it is therefore safe for me to enter the house dressed as I am and go up to my quarters.

In the morning, I am slow to rise, but I have much to ponder.

After breakfast, I find Jarvis sitting in the scullery on a stool cleaning Bentley's boots and I close the door leading into the kitchen so that we are alone in the small room.

'Mrs Drummle?'

He pauses in his polishing to look across at me and gradually rises from his seat, one boot still clutched in his hand. I am gratified to see that, in spite of his height and my petiteness, he appears ruffled by both the closed door and my presence.

'Jarvis,' I say, speaking low-voiced, 'it has come to my attention that you have an elderly mother, would this be correct?'

His eyebrows shoot up.

'Yes, Mrs Drummle.'

'Does Mr Drummle know this?'

'No, missus.'

'No?'

He does not respond. It is clear he is reluctant to converse with me and I tilt my head to one side enquiringly.

'Mr Drummle does not interest himself in my personal affairs,' he tells me, looking down his nose.

I pull an envelope from my pocket and hold it out.

'Funds for you to buy your mother whatever she needs,' I say. 'Please use them wisely.'

He does not move to take the envelope. He looks at it askance.

'Why would you do this?' he says stiffly. 'What do you want from me?'

'I only want a happy household.'

I extend the envelope further towards him, and say, 'Can you do that for me, Jarvis? Can you make amends with Albert? Can you get along?'

I can see him considering my request, but, finally, he reaches out for the money, avoiding my eyes as he takes it. 'Thank you. I will endeavour to do so.'

'It will be much appreciated if you do,' I say. I do not mention the matter of the hefty bag. One issue at a time. But I pause, tucking a stray hair behind my ear. 'What is your mother's name, Jarvis?'

'Ivy.'

'And how old is Ivy?'

'Sixty-two.'

'Goodness! That's a good age,' I tell him. 'And how does she get on? Does she manage?'

'Not so well since my sister passed away last year,' he says. 'I try to visit as frequent as I can,' he adds.

'That is good of you,' I say. 'And Jarvis? If you need time off unexpectedly on your mother's account, be sure to take it up with me and not Mr Drummle. Do you understand?'

'I don't know, missus. Mr Drummle wouldn't like that.'

'I know he wouldn't,' I say. 'But leave him to me.'

Turning back to the door, I open it and leave the room.

We may not be allies yet, but it is a start.

37

Monday is one of the rare days that Bentley is up before nine, and I tell him at breakfast that Mr Jaggers has suggested I go down to Satis House.

I tell falsehoods to Bentley so freely now that the words roll off my tongue without any effort. However, it is my belief that he does the same with me—witness his reaction. He shakes his head.

'You know I cannot go with you,' he says, avoiding my eyes. 'I have far too much on my plate to leave town. But Estella—' he reaches for a piece of toast '—since you are going down, could you not think about putting the old place up for sale? We really could do with the capital.'

You mean *you* could do with the capital, I think, but I do not voice the thought.

'I shall see,' I say.

'Why does Jaggers want you to go down? Has he also advised you to sell?'

I shake my head. 'I don't know what Mr Jaggers thinks of selling. He has asked me to look at one or two matters that need attention.'

Bentley pauses with his hand on the butterknife. 'Estella, that will mean more money going out the door. Think about it. You cannot afford to throw funds at something not worth saving. I won't allow it.'

'Who said it's not worth saving?' I murmur.

'Pah,' he says, 'you can't be serious. That old place?'

I do not respond. I am not going to get involved in a protracted argument about Satis House. Which is still mine. Which is one of the few possessions that is still mine. Which I intend to cling onto for as long as I can. Instead, I reach for my coffee cup and raise it to my lips.

The truth is that I am rather fond of *that old place.*

The truth is that I rather miss that old place.

And yet, the truth is that Satis House makes me sad. When I am away from it, I miss it, and when I am there, I do not wish to be there. It is altogether odd.

*

I go down alone to the marshlands. Matilda has not been feeling herself—I wonder if she is with child?—and I tell her to take some time off while I am away and try to regain her strength.

I do not book a room at the Blue Boar. I have told no-one, but I intend to stay at Satis House by myself. Perhaps a foolish undertaking? But then I am given to doing foolish deeds.

I go down on the late morning coach and the best light of the day is gone when I arrive. Leaving my luggage at the Blue Boar with instructions for a boy to bring it over at his convenience, I walk the distance to the house.

I stop at the gate and gaze up at the house's seared red brick walls and boarded windows. Ivy crawls across the walls and, with its sinewy old arms of twigs and stems, embraces the stacks of chimneys like a possessive lover who never wants to let go. Rooks hover about the roofline, as before, and swing in the naked trees of the overgrown garden. But whereas previously the rooks were silent and filled me with foreboding, today they are raucous and carefree as if Satis House belongs to them and to them alone, and what a fine time they have been having of it.

I go in and cross the courtyard and cannot help but remember the boy with the vivid blue eyes that I first met here. It seems to me—nay, in my heart of hearts it does not seem to me, I *know* it—that I was unkind and said hurtful words and delighted in his discomfort. Oh, if only I could go back and undo what I did! But, as I have said before, this is my bed and I have made it and thus must lie in it.

In the passage, a stub of candle and the matches are still sitting in the nook where they always are. I light the candle and holding it aloft make my way towards the staircase. Ahead of me, a scurrying beetle slips under the skirting board and on the stairs lies the desiccated body of a large moth. The smell of Satis House is always the same: dusty and stale and the air, frigid. It appears unchanged from when I left it after Miss Havisham's death. Her room remains the same, the large table with her empty bed upon it and the clean sheets put to one side, the cold and empty fireplace. I recall the scattered dead blooms that I once knew, the brightly coloured silken dresses lying half unpacked in their trunk, the jewels upon the dressing table. And I remember the woman at its centre. Who even now might have been asking, *What ails you, Estella? You look like a weighty washing line on a wet Monday.*

All done, all gone!

When the boy comes with my luggage, I ask if he would gather wood and light a fire in the kitchen and he does so willingly. He tells me business at the Blue Boar is slow and he is glad of the opportunity to have something to do.

'Are you staying here, miss?'

'I am.'

'Oh, miss, yer brave. I would not do that. I would not do that for any amoun' of money.' He shakes his head. 'Have you not heard, miss, that Miss Havisham crosses the courtyard at night and walks the brewery staircase?'

'Indeed?' I say, raising my eyebrows, half inclined to laugh.

He nods sombrely. He looks up from snapping twigs of kindling into two and says, 'Begging your pardon, miss, but would yer be the daughter of Miss Havisham?'

'I am,' I say.

'Then I s'pose it's all right for yer to stay overnight. I don't s'pose Miss Havisham will bother yer, miss?'

'I don't suppose she will,' I say.

In addition to my luggage, the boy has carried across a tray of tea and, after I have poured a cup and drunk it, I take the clean sheets I have brought and make up my old bed downstairs.

I read for a long time in front of the fire. The Scotsman, Dr Simpson, has now published a paper on the anaesthetic properties of chloroform. He tested it on two of his medical friends, willing test subjects apparently, who were in the custom of trying new chemicals to ascertain whether they had any anaesthetic effect. They inhaled it and were initially filled with good humour and cheer, but subsequently collapsed and did not regain consciousness until the morning. It is a fine line apparently between having too much and an insufficiency.

Simpson is an expert on obstetrics and gynaecology, a word I am familiar with since it is from the French *gynécologie*, and has been advocating for the use of not only chloroform in childbirth, but the assistance of midwives.

It is hard to tear myself away from his words, but eventually I decide that I should retire. Although I am not sleepy, my eyes are tired and aching, and if I do not close my book now I will wake in the morning looking like a fright.

But I cannot sleep. I toss and turn, rearrange my pillows, force myself to lie still and count to an infinite number for minutes at a time, but it is all to no avail.

The matter that gnaws at my brain is that my attempts at doing something worthwhile with my life have failed.

What will I do with my life, with myself, and how am I to occupy my days?

It is almost dawn before a fragmented peace descends upon me and I sleep. In desperation I have thought of my mother, my true mother. This is not the first time that I have thought of her to lure me into sleep and I begin with considering what I can do to locate her, and how I can possibly do anything without raising the ire of Mr Jaggers. Then I move on to remembering Mr Jaggers's housekeeper, her warmth, her kind words and the touch of her hand upon mine, and I subsequently fall into oblivion. I do not quite follow how these thoughts all conspire to send me to sleep, but I am grateful.

The following day, the outside world is shrouded in thick fog, an unearthly haze that the marshland sometimes throws up at us to test our mettle. And I am distraught with disappointment, for there will be no walking on the marshlands in this murk. The boy from the Blue Boar arrives, shivering at the gate, to fetch my luggage and I lock up Satis House. I take the route along the high street in this ethereal atmosphere—not being able to see more than two feet in front of me—with the intention of meeting my transport back to London, and pass the saddler's, the coachmaker's and the tailor's. Only today, none of these establishments are visible, nor are any of these gentlemen to be spotted standing outside surveying one another. If I had not seen the lad from the Blue Boar this morning, I would be tempted to assume Armageddon had come and I were the only survivor.

Then I hear the *tap-tap* of footsteps approaching and a stranger looms out of the mist. Strangely, there is something familiar about this man, but I cannot for the life of me think what it is.

He stops. He is tall with a full moustache and he is nicely turned out in a high-collared long black jacket with a green cravat at his neck.

'Why,' he says, doffing his soft dark cap, 'if it ain't Miss Estella.'

It is the mud-splattered freckles, the gold-flecked green eyes and the ginger hair that now lies flat upon his head that give him away. That make me realise, finally, who he is. But I have a devil of a job recollecting his name.

'Is that you?' I ask, trying to buy myself time.

'It's me,' he says, smiling faintly. Well, it was a foolish phrase to use!

He is so much older and quieter than I remember him, however, that I can scarce equate this man with the boy who raised his eyebrows comically at me and gave me the giggles.

'How have you been?' I ask Trabb's boy. 'Are you still working for Mr Trabb?'

He twists his cap in his hands. 'No, miss,' he says, but he does not elaborate. And although he no longer works for Trabb, it is clear he has picked up a thing or two about dapper dressing.

'I'm a'getting married,' he blurts out and smiles. It is that old smile, the one I remember, mischievous and happy.

'What, this morning?'

'Yes, miss.'

I do not know what to say. It seems incongruous that an *audacious* boy like Trabb's boy can have grown up and be getting married. Is this what happened when one grew up? One turned serious and sombre? One lost one's spirit? Is this what has happened to me?

'That's splendid. I am so pleased for you,' I say at last, but it sounds artificial, like the Pockets pandering to Miss Havisham in the old days.

He lifts one hand in the air and gesticulates in the gloom. 'I'm ... I'm a'sorry about ... ' he starts, but his gaze shifts to his boots and he cannot say what he is sorry about. His face flushes with the effort.

'You mean you're sorry about the weather, the weather that day I was to meet you?'

He grimaces. 'Well, that, too,' he says.

Lifting his cap, he replaces it firmly on his head, pulling on its peak, and the act of doing that seems to give him courage.

'I'm a'sorry for the way I spoke to you,' he says.

'The way you spoke to me?'

'Yes. I had no right ... I was insolent.'

'Oh, for goodness' sake, Ted.'

Ted. The name emerges as if a little clerk in my brain has been methodically working his way through the files of the alphabet, stopping to scratch his head once in exasperation, but finally hitting upon the right letter. *T*.

Impulsively I reach for his hands with my gloved ones and take them into my own.

'You made me happy that day,' I say. 'I didn't have a friend and you were kind in what you said and in what you offered. I don't believe you meant any harm by it?'

He shakes his head. 'No, miss, I didn't. I were only having a bit o' fun.'

'Well, then,' I say.

He fixes his greeny gold-flecked eyes upon me and we regard one other and I wonder if he, too, is wondering what might have happened if we had met that day and gone for a *stroll*. Then he gently withdraws his hands.

'I'd best be getting along, miss,' he says. 'It's been good meeting like this. I'd always hoped ... I'd always hoped I would see you again.

He doffs his cap a second time. 'Good day to you, Miss Estella.'

Then he is gone.

He disappears along the high street.

He vanishes into the fog.

All I can hear is the sound of his boots on the cobbles fading into the distance.

38

I have been back from the marshes but a few days when I feel ill one morning, and have a violent urge to vomit as I rise from the bed. At first I think it is something that I ate, but within a couple of hours I feel completely well and manage to keep down a slice of toast without any effort. Then the same thing happens again the following morning, and I know it is not food-poisoning.

I am with child.

I do not know how far along I am. Bentley's visits to my chamber have become infrequent, and I have been distracted by my exploits and not paying attention to my calendar.

I am aghast. The thing that I did not want to happen, I have allowed to occur. Through sheer carelessness perhaps? I try to remember when last Bentley visited me in the night. I do have a memory of an occasion, but I was so wound up with my adventure as a man-boy it is all a bit of a haze.

I make up my mind then and there I am not going to tell my husband. It is more than likely early days and I have read that it is not wise to mention one's condition until one is certain one is safely past the first three months. For these are the months when something can go awry.

I do wish it *would* go awry! I stand unclothed in front of the mirror and look at my belly, but there is no marked difference from any other day. My breasts have changed, however. They are swollen and tender.

I carry this secret with me. First one week passes, then another. I continue to feel unwell first thing in the morning and have to conceal it from Matilda.

When I tell her that from now on I would prefer tea at breakfast and not coffee—the smell makes me bilious, of course—she asks, 'Are you not well, miss?'

'I am perfectly fine,' I say testily, 'only I am in the mood for a change.'

'What about eggs?' she wants to know. 'Would you like eggs this morning, miss?'

Shaking my head I reach for a piece of toast. 'No, thank you,' I say.

I remember that recently Matilda was not well, either, and that I suspected *she* was with child. She, no doubt, has her equal suspicions concerning me. Who am I fooling?

I wait until she has gone downstairs, then I get up, cross the floor to the window, open it and toss the toast out to the birds.

Matilda furrows her brow and glances at me in consternation when she returns not five minutes later. My plate is empty, but the knife that remains alongside the plate is clean. Clearly, I omitted to butter the toast before I ate it. What is more, I apparently also consumed it without any jam.

My brain is addled.

What is the point of all this? I wonder in the third week when I am still not well at breakfast, and still attempting to keep the secret from Matilda who has gone downstairs to fetch the teapot and remains puzzled by my reluctance to eat anything.

She returns and I blurt out, 'I am with child.'

I put my finger to my lips. 'But we are not going to tell Mr Drummle.'

'Oh, miss!' Her mouth falls open with delight, her eyes take on a shine. 'You and me together, miss.'

'Congratulations,' I say, smiling. 'I had my suspicions you were, Matilda.'

'Congratulations to you too, miss—' she begins, putting the teapot down upon the mat.

I shake my head. 'No,' I murmur. 'This child is not something I want.'

She straightens and looks curiously at me. 'Not something you want, miss?' she repeats. 'Begging your pardon, miss, but why is that?'

I purse my lips. How do I explain it to her?

'I don't think Mr Drummle wants an infant,' I whisper. 'He does not have the patience for children.'

I am lying, of course, for Bentley's latest advice is that I visit the physician to find out why I am not yet with child.

'Oh, miss,' Matilda says sadly. She lingers at the table. She smooths the breakfast cloth, straightens Bentley's cutlery and adjusts his placemat. 'But even so, miss,' she says. 'Even so. A child is something special, innocent and pure. How could anyone not love a child? Begging your pardon, miss, but you should not allow Mr Drummle's decision to influence you.'

'Is that so, Matilda?'

She colours visibly. I have cut her to the quick. Why am I so cruel?

'I am sorry, miss, if I have spoken out of turn, but that is what I believe,' she says with some spirit.

'Thank you, Matilda,' I say more kindly. 'I will certainly think on it.'

*

I do reflect on it. First thing in the morning, when I am feeling at my lowest, I sit with my hands across my belly and consider Matilda's words. *A child is something special, innocent and pure. How could I not love a child?*

I remember that once I was a child. I remember that once I was small and defenceless and innocent, and that my mother gave me away, not because she did not love me—Mrs Butters was always definite about this—but in order to give me a better life. What sort of mother does not love her own child? What kind of mother would not do anything—*anything*—for their little one?

The strangest thing happens. I begin to love this child. I begin to cherish this embryo growing deep within me. I begin to think of nothing else but this little life form who is even now creating its own fingers, toes and eyes within my womb.

This little mite.

This little treasure.

What shall I christen it?

Not Bentley, surely? God forbid I should have to call it Bentley!

I begin to plan where it will sleep and how I will decorate its nursery. I have my heart set on a rocking horse, and a sumptuous dolls' house—not like the one I had as a child. I read up in medical journals about my condition and what I should expect and when.

When I walk in the park across the road, I find myself studying other children, particularly if they are engrossed in sailing a boat or playing hopscotch. For when they are occupied they hardly seem to notice that I am there. Sometimes I will even talk to them. I am aware that I am not familiar with children and this needs to change.

At mealtimes, I look at Bentley across the table and wonder when the opportune time is to break the news. I am reluctant to do it too early, for if the truth be known, I far prefer the Bentley who ignores me to the Bentley who fawns over me. And I have a suspicion that once Bentley knows that I am bearing his child, my life will not be my own.

39

Bentley and I argue over finances at Satis House again. He continues to badger me to sell it. His funds are once more at a low ebb and he wants further amounts transferred into his account.

I refuse. It is all for horse-racing and gambling and, I am convinced, other women. I have not seen him with another woman, but as I have said, his visits to my chambers to satisfy his needs have been infrequent and, of late, he has not been near me. For which, in my condition, I am grateful. I must, however, assume that this is because his desires are being satisfied elsewhere. I have not yet told him about the infant. The three month period is only just up and I have been keeping the news as a trump card. When I am desperate, it is something I intend to use in my favour.

We are sitting at the dining table having a meal when an argument is initiated and he begins shouting at me. I rise from my chair, for I will not sit there and allow him to berate me.

Intending to make my way to my room, I pass the back of his chair in order to do so. Without warning he rises, knocking over his chair, and lunges at me.

The full force of his weight against my shoulder shoves me towards the window and the sill. And if that were not enough, he slips—because he is in his socks—and crushes me bodily against the woodwork and glass.

I fear the window might break with the force of both our weights against it. But it does not. In my anxiety, I have turned to fend him off and the brunt of his weight catches me in the belly. For a number of seconds, I am befuddled. I stand, clutching the windowsill at my back, panting heavily, such is the unexpected discomfort and the winding of my lungs.

Someone comes running up the stairs at the commotion. 'Miss!'

It is Matilda. She steps over Bentley, who has slipped to the floor and is struggling to rise, and for half a second I fear he may grab at her ankle and pull her down alongside him. 'Are you all right, miss?' she wants to know.

I cannot answer for a pain, a sharp and prolonged stab as if a screw is being turned deep within my flesh, is upon me. I clutch my hands to my lower abdomen and cry out.

'What is it, miss?'

'I don't know,' I manage to say.

Then I am aware of liquid, warm and sticky, between my legs. Of blood running down my inner leg and pooling on the floor.

I am bleeding. Only it is not the usual menses flow; it is much more copious than that.

There can only be one explanation: I am miscarrying the infant.

This little mite. This little treasure. This small and defenceless person.

Aah, God.

I slide down the wall and collapse onto the floor. I am speechless, stricken with distress.

Bentley gazes on in what is at first puzzlement, and then horror, as the blood continues to ooze out of me.

Slowly, the truth of the situation dawns on him. By degrees, he realises what is taking place and what he has done.

He sobs like child, then, calling out, 'Estella! Oh, Estella!'

As if I should comfort him.

*

In the morning I wake and lie in bed and gaze around at the four walls. I do not want to get up.

Matilda brings me a tray of scrambled eggs and toast, but I cannot eat. She sits at the side of the bed, heaps a forkful and brings it to my mouth, but I shake my head and push her hand away.

I do not want to eat and I do not want to live. I do not want to see my husband, either. In fact, I told Matilda to tell him that I am not in a fit state of mind to see him. The doctor came a second time after I issued that statement, but I informed him that I feared that if I saw Bentley, I would kill him. The doctor said, 'Surely, you joke, Mrs Drummle?' And I said, 'Do not count on it.'

I had something to look forward to, something that filled me with hope, and now that has been taken away from me.

Why did I marry Bentley when everyone warned me off him? Why did I not listen? Who did I think I was to believe that I could overcome all they said of him? How could I have been so wilful, so stubborn and so stupid?

I put the infant in danger. I knew of Bentley's bad temper and I did nothing to safeguard the little one. What was I thinking of by not telling him?

For I now believe that telling him would have made a difference. I think that he would have become caring and vigilant. I think he would have been most solicitous about my welfare, and driven me to drink while he was about it, at least until after the baby was born. But afterwards? Who knows?

I keep to my bed for a number of days. I do not want to, but I consider how I can extricate myself from my marriage.

One morning, I am sitting in the chair alongside my bed while Matilda fluffs up the pillows and straightens the sheeting and quilt. I watch her work and observe the slight bulge in her belly now. The slight swelling that indicates she is with child. A baby. A little one.

'Miss should get out,' she says to me.

She indicates the window and the sky beyond. It is not blue, it is grey. London's miasma of filth—the factories churning out smoke, the sooty towers of tall chimneys, the effluent in the Thames and the muddy, dung-filled lanes and dead ends. Oh, how I long for the mist on the marshes, the cows looming out at me, the drunken gravestones beside the churchyard and the smell of the wind!

I nod. 'I know,' I say. But I do nothing.

Later in the morning, Matilda reappears in my room and insists that I get up and dress. I comply. I am like a puppet in her hands. I have lost even the will to remonstrate.

She leads me by the hand and we go out across the street and into Hyde Park. Her hand is warm and her skin rough. She remarks that my hand is cold. She says it is stiff. She finds a bench for me and suggests that I sit. She leaves me there.

When she returns to fetch me and we go back to the house, I cannot tell her what I saw or whether I walked any further or spoke with anyone, but I do tell her I am hungry. For the first time in days, I tell her I am hungry.

I also pass Bentley in the passage. He is still in his dressing gown and slippers, but that is nothing unusual. I do not think I have ever seen the man brought down so low. He appears pale and haunted. And humbled. He makes to speak to me, but I put my finger across my lips. I will not talk with the man. I do not care how distressed he is, how contrite, I will not talk with him.

From then on, Matilda insists that I go out and into the park every day. It is as if we have swapped roles. She has become the mistress giving me orders, and I am the maid obeying without question.

On my walks, I find myself peering into perambulators I encounter. This is a new development and one which I appear to have no control over. One day when I am out, I come across a pram and a crying infant that appear to have been abandoned.

I stop and gaze around. But I am mistaken. I believe the mother is down at the Serpentine with an older child, feeding the ducks. She glances back at me and raises her hand as if to say, *It's my infant, I won't be long.*

The baby is crying uncontrollably, however, and try as I might I cannot walk away. I jiggle the pram a bit and say, 'There, there,' but it makes no difference.

In desperation, I lay my parasol down on the ground, and reach in and lift up the infant. For a moment, it ceases crying in fright—perhaps it can sense I am not its mother—then it catches sight of my unfamiliar face and breaks out into fresh paroxysms.

'There, there,' I say again, holding it to my shoulder and patting its back. I turn and bounce a little on my heels. The bundle of swaddling is warm and soft and the little one snuggles into my neck. It smells of something pleasant that at first I cannot find the words to describe. Something sweet? Or innocent? Something pure, at any rate. Odd, but that is how I think of it. Perhaps it is seeking food for it begins to bump its little chin against me.

'I am so sorry. I've nothing to give you—' I am saying, when the infant is abruptly wrested out of my arms.

'Thank you!' the mother says, glaring at me.

She has curly red hair, which is wild and free, and her anger has raised the freckles on her pale face to dark ugly splotches.

The older child, a boy, carries a striped spinning top wound with string and stares at me shamelessly in the way that children do.

I bend to pick up my parasol, hiding my face.

'My apologies,' I say, flushing. 'I did not intend to distress you. I did not intend—' But I cannot finish for the lump in my throat and my eyes filling with tears.

The mother will not acknowledge me.

She looks the other way; she calls to the other child. Holding the baby with one arm she shoves the pram forward, and all the while the little one continues to squawk.

I turn away from them and let the tears stream down my face.

I turn away and return to the house and take to my bed once more.

*

Bentley pens me a letter, since I will not speak with him, in which he apologises profusely and uses kind and compassionate words. At the letter's close, however, he writes, *If only you had told me, Estella, none of this would have happened. If you had told me, we would still have our little one. If you had told me, we would be planning for a bright future right now …*

It is clear, on the one hand, that at some stage Bentley has studied Aristotle and is familiar with employing repetition to drive home a point. On the other hand—hah!—it is also clear that he blames me. *He* blames *me*! For the loss of our child.

Days pass before I feel strong enough to walk in the park again. And two months go by in no time at all. Two months in which I begin to talk to Bentley again, but I will not allow him to raise the topic of the infant. The moment he does so, I leave the room.

He has also begun to knock on my door at night, but I take care to lock it these days. I cannot imagine how I will behave should he attempt to come into my bed.

In any event, I gird my loins. Part of the reason for doing so is that I must begin the search for alternative lodgings. I intend to leave Bentley, for once he knows Matilda is expectant, who knows what he might do? I am also no longer prepared to live with a man who is a bully and a brute.

My funds are depleted, however, thanks to Bentley's excesses. I need to be circumspect. I spend some days, and then a week, perusing the *Houses for Sale* followed by the *Houses to Let* columns in the newspaper, but everything in the right areas is beyond my means. I will have to look further afield, and it is then that I consider Richmond. There is no necessity for me to remain in London and I once resided contentedly in Richmond, so why not reside there again?

I ensure the following visit I make to the library coincides with a Wednesday, Dr Oliver's assigned day, my strategy being to discuss my plan of relocating to Richmond with the good doctor.

I set myself down at a table with a reading lamp and carry over a quantity of volumes to peruse, but although I am occupied for a good two hours, from ten until twelve, Dr Oliver does not appear.

'What do you know of Dr Oliver, has he been in today?' I ask the clerk when I check out my bundle of books. 'He is usually here on a Wednesday, is he not?'

The clerk glances up at me. 'Have you not heard, madam? Dr Oliver passed away last week. It was sudden, I hear—Madam!' he adds in alarm, rapidly rising from his seat for I believe I have gone quite pale and am clutching the countertop in an attempt to stay upright. 'Please sit yourself down.'

The clerk comes around to lead me safely to a chair and, in due course, brings me a glass of water. But it takes me a little while before I am steady enough on my feet to resume my journey home.

I write to Daisy, apologising for the long break in communications and offering my condolences. I ask if I may call upon her and Kitty the following week and, in addition, I write that news of Dr Oliver's death has only recently reached me and that it pains me that I am too late to attend his funeral.

I go down to post the letter. I have been endeavouring to do more errands myself so as to allow Matilda adequate rest, and while she tries her best to thwart me, I think that if the truth be known she is grateful.

Kitty writes back within a day. Daisy has taken Dr Oliver's death badly and is in no state for visitors, but Kitty would greatly appreciate it if I called upon her two days hence in the afternoon.

It is strange for me to travel back to Richmond after such a long time away, but everything appears largely unchanged, including the house next door to Kitty and Daisy's where I lived for many months.

'Oh, my dear, it's so good to see you!' Kitty takes both my hands and greets me at the door herself, such is her enthusiasm and her kindness.

We have tea in the library, and everything feels the same and yet it does not. The room remains warm and filled with books, but the furnishings are no longer so staid and old-fashioned and there are touches of femininity in the crystal cut bowls of roses upon the side tables, the lacy antimacassars and the China doll dressed in a sailor suit and perched upon the mantlepiece.

'In all likelihood it was his heart,' Kitty says of Dr Oliver as she pours the tea. 'He had been expecting it. We had all been expecting it. It is, in fact, a miracle that he lived to the age he did.'

'It is gratifying that they had the years together they did, then,' I murmur.

'It is indeed. I am grateful. Daisy, the poor child, is naturally decidedly distressed at present, but I believe she will find comfort and solace in her beloved books once more. It is only a matter of time.'

Kitty passes me my tea. 'And you, my dear, how are you?'

'I am well, thank you,' I say, taking the cup and saucer from her. I am not sure where to begin and how much to divulge to Kitty.

'Between you and me,' I start, 'I am in a little bother. Can I rely on you to keep my counsel?'

'Of course, my dear,' Kitty says, leaning forward to touch my hand. 'What is it?' she adds when I do not immediately speak.

'I intend to leave Mr Drummle,' I say, glancing at her. She does not ask why or appear surprised and I wonder if word of his ill-treatment of me has got around?

'I am currently looking for alternative accommodation and, to be honest, I have been struggling. It would not only be for myself, but for Matilda and Albert. Matilda is with child and I cannot leave her to her own devices.'

'Oh, my,' Kitty says.

'I was wondering,' I continue, 'about the house next door where we lived happily for many months. What is the situation there? Do you know if they have a vacancy?'

Kitty shakes her head. 'After I left and moved here, the house was sold and has new owners. A family with children, which makes that property sadly out of the question.'

She has picked up her cup and has been sipping at it, and without warning her eyes grow big.

'Of course!' She puts her teacup down where it rattles with excitement in the saucer.

'Why did I not think of this immediately! You must come and live here, my dear. We have plenty of space. In addition, we no longer have a driver for the horse and carriage because we had to let the last man go. He was unreliable. Albert would be most welcome to take over this role, and Matilda could continue to be your maid, but perhaps on restricted duties? The quarters alongside the stable that they once occupied are empty. Oh, my dear, I am so excited! What do you think? Please tell me this is a capital plan?'

'It is indeed,' I say, 'if you are quite positive Daisy would not object?'

'Daisy? Why, Daisy thinks the world of you,' Kitty says.

Thus it is decided that I, plus Matilda and Albert, relocate to Kitty and Daisy's, and the only uncertainty now, as I tell Matilda in the confines of my quarters when I reach home, is when we will move. I do not want Bentley to get wind of our plans.

40

I decide on a Wednesday in two weeks' time. Wednesday is Bentley's fixed day at the club whereas the other days, evenings and nights are undetermined. On Wednesdays he is routinely out of the house by four in the afternoon and does not return until the small hours.

Matilda and I surreptitiously begin to pack my possessions in the week and days leading up to Wednesday. If I am out, I take care to lock the room and leave Matilda somewhere in the vicinity doing some household task such as polishing the silver. The result of this is that we are practically ready to depart when Wednesday dawns. Of course, I am not at liberty to take anything in the house, which pains me for I brought back beautiful platters from our time in Rome and a number of other souvenirs. Over the years, Bentley has allowed me to put away some of his mother's artefacts and display my own, on the understanding that this is a temporary measure. It is too risky to remove, substitute or change anything now.

When the day dawns, I am so on edge that I feel sure he will not fail to notice how shaky my hand is when I reach for my water glass at the midday meal. But he does not. His head is in the newspaper, reading up, I believe, on the day's races.

'Satis House and the sale thereof,' he growls, for he has tired of being kind and compassionate and has reverted to form. 'Are you still unmoved?'

'I am,' I say. I force my hands flat to the tablecloth in an effort to keep them still, for my fingers are trembling. 'Why should I have changed my mind?'

'Indeed, why should you have changed your mind?' He raises his head. 'I'll tell you why, Estella.' He pauses to sniff. 'I am on the verge of giving Albert and Matilda their notice. We simply can no longer afford to maintain either of them.'

I attempt to appear shocked. I think that we have had a lucky escape. But I am ahead of myself, for we have not *yet* escaped.

'B-But,' I bluster. 'You can't do that.'

'I can and I will.'

He slouches back in his chair and kicks out his legs in front of him. 'But I'll tell you what, Estella. You bring me a letter addressed to Jaggers in which you unequivocally state that you wish to put Satis House on the market and that the proceeds are to be paid into my account, and I may think about changing my mind. Hmm? What do you think? By three-thirty this afternoon, before I leave for the club? I believe you will find that an easy solution.'

Oh, God.

So it is that I write to Mr Jaggers and *unequivocally* state that I wish to put Satis House on the market, and that all proceeds are to be paid into Bentley's account. I sign the letter and present it to Bentley at three-thirty, whereupon he reads it, grunts, and seals it in the accompanying envelope and tells me not to concern myself posting it, he will ask Jarvis to do so.

I hear him go downstairs, calling 'Jarvis!', but I do not hear what he says to the man.

I am not too concerned about the letter, for tonight, once we are safe in Richmond and before I go to bed, I will pen another missive to Jaggers and tell him that I have left Bentley and that the first letter was written under duress and that he must ignore it.

I position myself in a shaft of sunlight in the drawing room, trying to warm my trembling bones and so that the moment I hear Bentley leave the house, we can continue with our preparations. I take up my knitting, which seems the most mindless thing to occupy my restless fingers and my scattered wits. Matilda comes up more than once from the kitchen to check what the situation is, and I put my finger to my lips and send her away again.

Finally, I hear the creak of Bentley's boots as he passes the drawing room and the squeak of the front door as he opens and closes it behind him.

Throwing aside my knitting, I jump up from the sofa and go out into the passage to alert Matilda.

But the door opens again and Bentley glances in at me.

'I forgot my umbrella,' he says, frowning. 'It looks like rain. What's wrong with you, woman?' he demands, when I remain staring at him.

I seem quite unable to do or say anything, let alone move.

He reaches for the furled umbrella standing in the hallstand, and smacks it against his palm.

'Nothing,' I get out. 'Nothing. I am merely ...'

I raise a hand and twirl a finger in the air. I am merely *what?* I have no idea, although the wicked thought crosses my mind to say, *I am merely leaving you.*

He shakes his head as if I am an imbecile and he has no idea what to do with me, and leaves a second time, on this occasion banging the door behind him.

I tiptoe after him, open the door softly and gaze down the street. He shambles along in his usual spider-like manner, swinging the umbrella out in front of him like it has become a third leg, and does not look back.

Part of me wants to rejoice that this is the last time I will hear and see my bully of a husband leaving for his club, but another part of me is not convinced I am shot of him yet.

I find Matilda and we recommence finalising our packing, but there still remains the matter of Jarvis. Although I have broken the ice with him, and there have been no further incidents between him and Albert, I do not believe I can rely on the man to be my ally. We cannot leave the house until he sets off to see his mother, as is his habit. But I do think about suggesting he go earlier.

I track him down to Bentley's quarters, where he is tidying up after his master. The room is in an absolute pickle, discarded garments lying here, there and everywhere, and the bed unmade—a flurry of sheets and pillows lying askew. Honestly, I do not know how anyone can live in this state.

'Jarvis?'

'Yes, Mrs Drummle?'

'Why not take yourself off earlier this afternoon to see your mother? Do you remember we discussed the possibility of you taking time off, and I assured you I would take it up with Mr Drummle?'

'I do remember, madam, but I have not indicated to Mr Drummle that I wish to take time off this afternoon,' he says, folding his long frame in two to pick up a pair of trousers from the floor. 'I have not indicated that to my mother, either, for that matter,' he adds.

'How is your mother? How is Ivy?' I ask.

'She manages, madam. All things considered.'

'I see,' I say. 'Well, be sure to pass on my greetings to her and to let me know if there is anything I can do for her. Why not take something small from the kitchen for her?'

My suggestion is subtle. I do not know whether he will pick up on it and realise that I am aware he has been taking foodstuffs from the kitchen for her.

'Thank you, madam. I will.'

'And regarding your early absence this afternoon … My point is that it does not matter. If Mr Drummle finds out, I will settle it with him, you can be reassured of that.'

'But what about the room, madam?' He indicates the state of it.

'Matilda will do it,' I tell him.

'I cannot allow Matilda to do my work,' he says, shaking his head. 'Particularly when …'

I frown. 'When what, Jarvis?'

'When …'—he seems awkward—'when she is with child.'

'You have noticed, then?'

'I have indeed, Madam. I have also told Mr Drummle.'

'Oh.'

The man is poker-faced. I cannot decide where I stand with him.

If my husband is aware of Matilda's condition, I wonder why he has not mentioned it? His threat to fire both her and Albert is therefore doubly unkind, but nothing about him surprises me nowadays.

I do not know what else to say to Jarvis. Must I revert to monetary bribery as before?

He looks down his nose at me. 'When I have done the room, I will go, but not before,' he says.

'That is admirable of you,' I say. 'I will leave you to it then, Jarvis.'

I return to my quarters. Matilda has almost completed my packing. I tell her that I will finish what remains to be done, and for her to ensure her own and Albert's preparations for departure are complete. I also inform her of the arrangements I have made with Jarvis. We cannot, I stress, begin to ready the horses and carriage or ask Albert to convey our luggage to the back door until Jarvis has gone. We need to listen for the man leaving or we could be stranded here unnecessarily, and I ask her to go down and find Albert and tell him to keep a watch on Jarvis's movements.

I finish off my packing, close my trunks and do a last tour of the room, checking my drawers, inspecting my robe. I will not be sad to leave this house or my quarters, for my memories of this room are mostly painful ones.

It is after four, but still Albert has not been up with news of Jarvis's departure. I ring the bell in the dining room to order tea, but it takes Matilda an age to appear.

I do not speak for she appears flustered. 'He has just left, miss.'
'At last,' I say triumphantly.

Now Albert has to work with haste. He must get the horses bridled and hitched to the carriage. He must carry my trunks through the house and across the yard. We cannot help. I forbid Matilda to carry anything in her condition, and Albert will not allow me to carry anything, either. Oh, that I were a man and did not have to put up with this! I become immensely irritated sometimes by the fact that I am a woman—no, that is incorrect, not by the fact that I am a woman, but by the fact that women are not allowed to act as they see fit.

At last, as the church bells are striking a quarter past five, we are ready to depart. I leave a note and money for the cook in a place where she will see it, but she is the only one. I do not have much to do with the gardener, and the funds I originally gave to Jarvis were exceedingly generous and I do not intend to do so again.

Albert, in the driver's seat, is bringing the carriage out into the yard and Matilda and I wait upon the back steps. It is a raw evening. The rain that Bentley predicted would fall has not eventuated, but there is a chilly dampness to the air as well as the sour smell of the fog creeping in. I wear my flat-soled boots and my cape. My gloves are already on my hands, keeping them warm.

This moment is forever caught in time. I wake from bad dreams sometimes and know I have been here, revisited this time and this place, this memory. I fear it will never leave me.

Albert, sitting atop the box, halts the carriage. 'Easy,' he says to the horses. 'Easy.'

I take Matilda's hand. We step down onto the cobblestones and begin to cross. The fog has begun to sneak into the yard; it is unfortunate, for it will slow us down on our journey out to Richmond. I am determined not to be sad, however, and there is a spring in my step.

I glance away from the carriage, for out of the corner of my eye I notice one of the gates to the house swing open. It swings wide with such violence that it clatters and crashes against the side wall and judders on its hinges.

I hear Albert call out, but my brain is not working properly. I do not know what he has said, for I am fixated on the man storming through the open gate towards me.

In the dim half-light, it is not easy to recognise him, but his solid, squarish head and his overly long arms and legs that earned him the nickname of the Spider are all I need to know who he is.

'Quick, Matilda,' I cry, 'get in, get into the carriage!'

I fling open the door and push her bodily up the stairs, in spite of her protests, in spite of her agitation.

I follow closely behind. Leaning forward, I step in.

I have one foot poised over the carriage's entrance when Bentley grabs my hand and jerks me backwards, towards him. My boot slips from under me. I fall across the steps and entrance. My chin bangs to the floor. The taste of salty blood gushes into my mouth, for I must have bitten my tongue.

But my hand is free! My glove has come off in Bentley's hand.

'Quick, miss, quick,' Matilda cries, leaning down to help me up and inside.

But Bentley seizes one of my legs and pulls on my boot, dragging me across the entrance, yanking me towards him. I tied my boots on tightly, but still I wonder if my boot will come off in his hand? It will take a miracle and seems unlikely. Meanwhile, Matilda tightly clutches my right hand with both of hers while Bentley heaves on my foot and I feel as if I might be torn asunder when suddenly my leg goes slack.

Bentley has dropped my foot. I do not know why.

'Let me go, Matilda,' I cry and she does, and I crawl to my knees and lift my skirts and get inside the carriage and she slams the door shut behind me.

'Go,' Matilda shouts to Albert and bangs on the side panel of the carriage. 'Go!'

We lurch forward. The horses' hooves clip-clop across the cobbles. I remember the gate is only half-open and wail with distress, waiting for one of the horses to slam into the metal and rip out its chest, waiting for the carriage to come to a grinding halt.

But both gates must be open, for we careen out into the street. The wheels screech, the whip cracks across the backs of the horses and the floor jolts beneath us.

Getting to my feet, shakily holding onto the seat, I look out of the back window.

Two men are fighting in the fog. One has the other in a headlock and they stagger around the gloomy yard like they are drunk. One of the men is Bentley and the other has wide trousers that flap about his skinny legs. I think it is Jarvis.

Jarvis who was perhaps suspicious and fetched Bentley from his club?

Jarvis who has perhaps had second thoughts and has opened the other gate, and is keeping Bentley otherwise engaged so that he is unable to chase after us?

Jarvis has come to my rescue. Displaying attributes I clearly underestimated.

I believe my few kind words regarding his elderly mother were enough for this change of heart. And I believe that perhaps we have both been at fault. Each suspecting the other, each disliking the other, when all this time we could have reached an understanding and been not friends, but certainly of help to one another.

41

It has been a week and I think I can safely say we are settled in Richmond. My letter to Mr Jaggers, not only instructing him *not* to proceed with the sale of Satis House, but also advising him of my separation from Bentley and my change of address, was delivered. Mr Jaggers replied, by return, to the effect that he had no intention of following my original instructions until he had at least discussed the matter with me. He did not say anything about the last time he saw me and I believe he means to overlook that conduct for the time being.

I have a room at the side of Dr Oliver's house and, whilst it is not as attractive as the rooms I had in the house next door and I do not have my own sitting room, it is adequate. It does have a view out onto the garden. And once I set Miss Havisham's pretty little crystal dish containing my hairpins out on the dressing table, I began to feel more at home.

To my relief, Bentley has not made an appearance at our new abode. I have half expected him to show up on the doorstep to drag me back to London, but he no doubt has no idea where I have gone and is too idle to make the necessary enquiries.

Matilda is none the worse for her ordeal and appears to be well. I am keeping an eye on her condition and she is progressing as she should be. I am attempting to ensure I am aware of all the stages of her confinement by reading all I can on the subject.

For my part, I am recovered from my recent injuries—outwardly, at any rate.

I found Daisy in the library of the house on my second day. We embraced one another with tears in our eyes. 'He was a good man,' I murmured, and Daisy nodded. I gathered she did not feel capable of talking about her husband yet. I understood. Just as I am not capable of talking about the loss of my child. These matters take time.

At breakfast, Kitty tells me that she has accepted an invitation to cards at Wright House and that the invitation includes me.

'I would be delighted if you would accompany me, but I also understand if you do not feel up to it,' she says.

I am taking the top off a boiled egg and am quiet for a moment, peeling back the shell and thinking. I would like to see the Wrights and the Hathaways—but do they want to see me?

Kitty reaches a hand across the table to me. 'I think it will do you the world of good, my dear. In addition, there will be the benefit of people seeing for themselves that you are well and recovered, and you can confirm—if they ask—that you have separated from Mr Drummle. What do you think?'

Put like that, it is hard for me to refuse.

I nod. 'Yes, I will come with you,' I say. 'And thank you.'

We are driven out to Wright House by Albert at three, as before. It is almost the middle of winter and a cold and frigid day and we huddle under the blanket together as before, only this time my companion is not so talkative and I am subdued. I am also apprehensive, to be honest. It is not common for married couples to separate and live apart, and I will be viewed as something of an anomaly. A hurdle I must overcome.

The willows lining the driveway have lost all their leaves and their bare arms sweep the cold ground, but there is still the sense of them curtseying before us. Stately Wright House remains the same, though perhaps the mullioned windows do not twinkle quite so brightly in the meagre afternoon sunlight. The lawns are yellowed with frost damage and no roses bloom in the garden around the lake. It is depressing. But I must try not to let that further affect my mood.

The Hathaways, the couple I met before at cards, are in attendance, plus Mr and Mrs Wright, and because we are six we sit at one table and play gin rummy.

I have to say that both the Hathaways and the Wrights do their best to make me feel welcome and comfortable. There is no reference to my past with Bentley. It is as if none of that ever happened and I am still single. It is generous of them, and I am most grateful.

'Lady Waverley sends her best wishes,' Mrs Wright says in an aside to me while Kitty deals out a fresh hand. 'I did invite them to join us, but they had a prior engagement.'

'Oh,' I say. 'Thank you. And how is Lady Waverley?'

'She is well, my dear. She is kept entertained with Eliza's two—'

'Eliza now has two children? Forgive me, I have been otherwise distracted and had no idea.'

'Oh, yes. They are little darlings, of course. So sweet natured, like their mother and father. And they have been of great comfort to Lady Waverley in her grief.' She raises one finger. 'I must not forget. She specifically asked me to say that you are welcome at Waverley Manor at any time.'

'How kind,' I murmur, reaching for my cards and spreading them across my hand.

'She is very fond of you, if you must know.'

'Indeed?' I say, 'I cannot think why that would be.'

'The way you conducted yourself at Laurence's funeral left a great impression, not only on her, but on everyone else.'

Kitty clears her throat then, hinting that we should cease talking and play. It is as well, for I fear if I begin thinking about Laurence again, it will do me no good. I have tried my best to put the Captain from me, for I cannot reflect upon the man without being overwhelmed by guilt and sorrow. What a fool I was! How nasty and calculating. Am I ever to forgive myself?

We play another round, which I win again, and everyone groans good-naturedly.

'You have not lost your touch at cards, then,' Mr Wright says, winking kindly at me.

Lucky at cards, unlucky in love, I want to say.

We begin another game and the afternoon passes. When we break for refreshments, Mrs Wright joins me on the settee. 'I am so sorry to hear of your separation from Mr Drummle,' she murmurs.

'Don't be,' I say. 'I am better off without him.'

'I did hear that he used you with great cruelty,' she whispers.

I do not respond. What is there to say, apart from agreeing with her? And I do not wish to make more of the subject. Instead, I pick up my cup and sip at my tea.

'What will you do?' she asks.

'I will lie low and wait for him to divorce me,' I say, 'and after that, I do not know. Perhaps ... Perhaps, I will run away to China,' I suggest, glancing at her.

She laughs and pats my hand affectionately. 'I would not put that past you, my dear,' she says.

My heart has had little to be glad of, of late, but it is glad of the warmth of my friends and of Mrs Wright's interest and concern.

*

Days later, Kitty, Daisy and I are all in the library. It is a chilly and bitter morning. The fire has been lit and maintained since before breakfast, and the library is the warmest room in the house, apart from the kitchen.

Matilda enters and comes directly to my side. I look up from my book. I am reading of Florence Nightingale and the work she has been doing, and am in complete admiration of the lady. She is an unmitigated inspiration.

'Mr Drummle is here to see you, miss,' Matilda says, low-voiced.

'Mr Drummle?'

'Yes, miss.'

I put my bookmark between the pages to mark my place and put the book on the little table at my elbow. I will have to face Bentley and tell him in no uncertain terms that he is not to come here again, or he will keep returning. He will continue to harass me until he gets what he wants. It is not me he wants, of course. It is money.

I rise from my chair, but am stopped short. Bentley has appeared in the library doorway. He appears to have forgotten his manners altogether, for not only has he entered without permission, but his gloves and his hat are still on.

'Estella!'

Startled by the tone of his voice, Kitty and Daisy glance up. Matilda, for her part, does not leave the room and remains by my side.

'Estella, you are to come home forthwith!' Bentley says.

I shake my head. 'I will not be returning. This is my home. I am here now and I intend to stay.'

'We will see about that.'

Bentley shambles towards me, but pauses, for Kitty's book falls from her hands and clatters to the floor as she rises from her chair.

She steps forward. Matilda and Daisy follow suit.

'What the devil,' Bentley mutters, for to get to me he will have to get past them.

'I think you should leave, Mr Drummle, and leave now,' Kitty says.

'Out of my way, woman,' he blusters, throwing his arms out.

'No.' Kitty blinks and crosses her arms across her chest.

I do not take my eyes off Bentley, for he is unpredictable in this mood, but out of the corner of my eye I see Matilda slip to the fireplace to pick up the poker.

Bentley notices, too. 'You would not dare to use that on me,' he says to her in a mocking tone.

'Wouldn't I?' Matilda says. For all her bravery her voice is shaking.

I have forgotten how intimidating Bentley is, how hairy, how long and untidy his limbs. He really does resemble a spider. A tarantula. Biding his time, waiting to pounce.

Then, out of the blue, taking him by surprise, Matilda lifts the poker and rains it down upon him.

Bentley cries out in fright. But he has quick reflexes and snatches the instrument out of her hands, flinging it to one side.

'You little minx!' He spits at her feet.

'Estella, come!' His face is florid with agitation.

I shake my head again.

He brushes Kitty aside, then darts forward and raises his hand, slapping me across the face with his open palm.

And I fall to the floor, such is the violence of the blow.

Stunned and in a state of vagueness, I am aware of clamouring and shouting. I gaze up to see Kitty and Matilda and, yes, even Daisy, all beating Bentley with their raised fists and the man attempting to fend them off.

He covers his head; he lumbers backwards. Then he turns and stumbles from the room with them following at his heels.

When at last Kitty, Daisy and Matilda return, the latter bringing me a cold washcloth for my face, they are jubilant and victorious.

'You ought to have seen him run for the gate,' Kitty tells me. 'It was quite something, Estella.'

I am sore and embarrassed and feel sorry for myself, but I cannot help smiling. What good friends I have. How kind they are. What warmth and support they have shown me.

We station Albert at the front door for the next ten days as a precaution, but Bentley does not make another appearance.

Tarantula, incidentally, is from the old Italian *tarantola.* Named for the seaport Taranto, the name was originally given to the wolf spider and was once thought to be the cause of a disease in which the victim wept and skipped about before falling into a wild dance.

Bentley did not weep, but he did skip about and I do not think it is stretching the truth to describe his retreat as a wild dance.

42

I gather that Matilda has no idea when her baby was conceived. She *believes* it is due in early spring, but she is uncertain. She also believes it is a girl, but I have no notion on what basis she makes this decision.

I ask her one day, when I am writing at my escritoire and she is dusting my room, what arrangements she has made to have the child, and she puts her hand up to her mouth.

'No,' I say, mimicking her gesture, shaking my head and smiling.

She lowers her hand, and smiles at me in return. She knows what I am saying. I do not have to voice it.

'Arrangements for the baby?' I repeat when she remains looking at me, but is without words.

'Oh, miss,' she says at last, beginning to blush.

'Go on,' I say, when again she stalls.

She lowers the feather duster. 'Miss knows how miss is always reading medical books?' she says.

'Yes?' I say again.

'Well,' she draws out the word, 'I were wondering if miss knew anyone who could help? Help with the baby's delivery, that is,' she adds.

I believe I understand what Matilda is saying in her roundabout way. I am taken aback, amused and flattered. All three. She has seen me reading up on her condition; she knows I am more than a little interested. In addition, I have said to her more than once that the medical books say this or that should be happening to her about now, and asked if indeed it is?

Matilda clearly thinks that I, having never delivered a baby in my life, am capable of doing so.

Am I?

Furthermore, is this something I want to do? And what will Kitty and Daisy say? Or think?

I have been wanting for so long to do something meaningful and worthwhile with my life and here is an opportunity and I am worried about what people will think.

For God's sake, Estella!

'I will reflect on it,' I say to Matilda, and return to my letter. 'And let you know,' I add.

'Thank you, miss,' she says.

But, despite the gleam that must be obvious in my eye, I am deeply concerned about the risks, for they are great. Not only for the baby, but for Matilda. A recent report in *The Times* stated that one in eight women is currently dying in childbirth. This is a high statistic. If something goes wrong, if the baby is in the breech position and I cannot help it out, if Matilda haemorrhages and suffers from prolonged bleeding, if ... if ... There are so many issues that can go awry. Do I actually want to be held responsible for the lives of both mother and child?

We have about three weeks until early spring and I waste no time in finding Daisy and asking her if she still has the details of the doctor who attended Dr Oliver the first time he became ill. She does, but she tells me that as far as she knows he no longer practises. I have an idea, then. I place an advertisement in the paper, stating a midwife is required, and asking one to please call upon our address.

Then I talk to Kitty and Daisy at breakfast. I am always discussing concerns with them at breakfast, but it is the one time of the day when we can rely on us all being together at the table. Strangely, it is Kitty who is averse to the idea of becoming involved in the birth of Matilda's infant, and not Daisy. Kitty thinks it is unbecoming of us and it would not do for word to get around.

'How is word going to get around if we do not say anything?' I ask, putting my coffee cup down in its saucer.

'Yes, Mama,' Daisy says. 'Surely we can keep this to ourselves? Who needs to know?'

'I am not convinced,' Kitty says in a firm voice.

'I am,' Daisy says, reaching for the marmalade. 'And I know that Dr Oliver would have been firmly behind us and, since this is his house, I think we should respect that it is something he would have wanted us to do.'

'Well said, Daisy,' I say. She blushes at my approval.

'Hmm,' Kitty says, clearly not best pleased.

'You will simply have to guard your tongue, Mama,' Daisy tells her.

I want to laugh at the thought of Kitty standing sentinel over the lively thing that so often runs away with her, but I do not.

'What can I do to help, Estella?' Daisy wants to know.

'For the moment, I think I have everything under control,' I say, 'but thank you.'

After breakfast I draw up a list of what we will need: sheets, towels, face cloths, nappies and nappy pins, swaddling blankets, nightgowns for Matilda, clothes for the baby, clean rags and bowls, and set about ordering what we are lacking.

Sadly, only one midwife calls. She is a short, portly woman of little cheer with a carpetbag hooked over one arm. She produces several letters of recommendation, however, tells me her fee and seems confident in her manner. She asks to see the patient and I take her across the courtyard to Matilda and Albert's quarters adjacent to the stables, where Matilda is resting.

I have never been inside Matilda and Albert's quarters and am surprised by how sparsely furnished and plain they are, and yet at the same time everything is neat and tidy. There are no pictures upon the walls. A single bed is pushed up against one wall. There is a fireplace, and one armchair, one small table, a small cupboard and a bowl for washing. Above the bowl is a shelf holding a couple of items, including two mugs. I remind myself that this room was originally intended for a single man and not a married couple, but why is it that I never made it my business to discover the kind of room Matilda was being allocated when Dr Oliver agreed to her sharing Albert's quarters?

The lighting is not good. There is a single curtained window alongside the door and a candle in a holder upon the little table, but that is all.

If Matilda is embarrassed by my appearance in her quarters, she does not show it. In the dimness of the room, her eyes appear wide with unease. I receive the impression she is far more anxious about the midwife's presence than she is about anything else.

The midwife feels all over Matilda's belly as I have been doing, but says little.

'And?' I say, when at last she turns from the patient.

She nods and tilts her head indicating we should step outside, and when we do she murmurs, 'Her first?'

'As far as I am aware,' I say.

'It won't be easy, madam,' she continues and wobbles her outstretched hand to indicate uncertainty, 'but on the other hand it may pop out. I seen plenty that appear difficult, but end up surprising one.'

Clearly, the woman is hedging her bets.

'I see,' I say. 'So you will take her on?'

She nods. 'The bed will have to be moved to the middle of the room, madam,' she says. 'I need space to get around. And we will be requiring more light. Then we will be needing sheets, towels and so forth: the usual,' she says.

I nod. 'I have that in hand already. Anything else?'

She ferrets in her copious bag and produces a sheet of paper with an address on it. 'If I'm not here, someone will know where to find me. But I's a busy woman and it may be that I cannot get to your girl immediately and there will be a delay of sorts.'

I nod. 'I will bear that in mind,' I say.

The time until the baby is expected passes slowly. I keep myself busy by literally keeping an eye on Matilda. I do not want to trouble or alarm the poor girl by insisting upon an examination every day, but I do give her a long hard stare every morning to see if I can tell whether anything has changed. This analytical interest in her condition helps me to focus on her and her baby, and prevents me from dwelling on myself and the child I lost.

She comes to my room every second day and lies upon the bed and lets me prod and feel. Sometimes the baby kicks and we smile at one another with delight. 'Did you feel that, miss?' she asks. 'I most certainly did,' I say.

Lately, it has seemed to me that the infant is now lying not so high up in her belly. The books I have been referring to say that it is normal for the baby to move down towards the birth canal in the last few days. Can it be long now? I wonder.

I make frequent visits to the library to obtain whatever reading material I can on the subject and, one morning, an elderly gentlemen stops me on the stairs outside. He is tall and well-dressed and a refined-looking man. I have noticed him before at one of the desks inside and, although we have not been introduced, we are aware of one another. Recently, he was at the counter checking out his books at the same time as I was. He walks with a limp and uses a cane and is a regular like Dr Oliver was.

'Good day to you,' he says, lifting his hat and peering at the books in my arms. 'What are you taking out today? Forgive me, but I couldn't help noticing the other day what you were reading.'

'More books on childbirth and confinement,' I say.

'You are intent on becoming a doctor?'

'No,' I say, smiling. 'I have been asked to assist at a childbirth and I am preparing myself by finding out everything I can.'

'I see.' He nods politely. 'I am Dr Vincent,' he tells me. 'I have retired from medicine, but if you need to know anything, please do not hesitate to ask.'

'I am Mrs Drummle,' I say extending my hand, which he takes. 'How kind of you. If it is not too impertinent, I already have something in mind.'

'You do?'

'Yes. I will come straight to the point. Where can I obtain ether?'

'Ah, a good question.' He responds and taps his stick upon the stairs. 'I could give you the name and address of a druggist, but I doubt that he would hand the substance over without a script of some kind.'

'I see,' I murmur.

'Have you used ether before?'

I shake my head.

He tut-tuts and looks anxious. 'I would not recommend it,' he says. 'I know it has been administered to Queen Victoria, but that does not mean it is suitable for every Tom, Dick and Harry.'

'I see,' I say again.

He tilts his head to one side and studies me, and I feel myself beginning to blush. This is not the first time where I feel that my looks give me a certain advantage over other plainer women.

'Why don't we,' he suggests, 'visit the druggist together? I will obtain the ether for you and you will, in turn, promise me that you will not use it unless you are placed in a dire situation?'

'You have my word,' I say. 'And I am much obliged.'

*

We take a horse and carriage to an address on the Strand.

The premises of the druggist are dismal and drab. The building is low-roofed with dirty mullioned windows, although several glass jars containing liquids of varying hues can dimly be made out standing on shelves.

'May I accompany you?' I ask.

'If you wish,' Dr Vincent says. 'I see no harm in it.'

The druggist himself comes out to the front counter to greet the doctor. They are obviously acquainted, but I stand in the background and am not mindful of their conversation. Instead, I am entranced by my surroundings. The liquids in the bottles: verdant green, cobalt blue and vermillion. The coriander seeds in jars and the bunches of dried lavender. Ceramic urns are marked with various names of balsams, and on a shelf beyond the counter is a sealed bottle containing leeches. Below the counter, an array of bullets is for purchase and the smell of tobacco permeates the air.

In the carriage, Dr Vincent hands me the small brown bottle containing the ether and I put it safely away in the pocket of my cape.

'How much do I owe you?'

He shakes his head. 'Never mind,' he says. 'Remember, you only need a small quantity. Use a silk handkerchief if you have one.'

Once we are returned to St James's Square, we part company with, naturally, many and repeated thanks on my part.

But here is a strange occurrence. The next time I am at the library, I make a point of going past Dr Vincent's desk and of greeting the man and smiling at him.

He appears reluctant, however, to acknowledge me or converse, and I believe that he is perhaps concerned about what his colleagues will think. I would not be speaking out of turn if I said there is a general feeling among men that it is not a woman's place to meddle in their professions, and it may well be that he does not want to be seen as having assisted me. Strange are the ways of men.

In addition to my reading, I keep myself occupied with my knitting. I have advanced to making infant's bootees and matinee jackets, in white naturally. I keep my efforts rolled up in muslin when I am not knitting and I am pleased with my progress.

Kitty and I receive a further invitation to Wright House for cards, but I decline, for I do not want to leave Matilda for any lengthy period, and Kitty goes alone. 'What shall I tell them?' she wants to know before she sets off. She means regarding my absence. 'Tell them I have caught a chill and do not wish to make it worse by being out in the cold,' I say. 'But that would be telling an untruth,' Kitty says. I shrug. 'Kitty, in all honesty, have you never fibbed before?' 'Well, perhaps,' she admits, biting her lower lip, 'once or twice.' 'This will make it three times, then,' I say.

It is as well that I decline to go, for shortly after Albert has driven away with Kitty in the carriage, Matilda appears at my door. She holds her overlarge belly with both hands and looks distraught.

'My waters have broken, miss,' she says. 'And—and—' She breaks off as a grimace of pain sweeps over her features '—the contractions—the contractions have started.'

We return to her quarters, Matilda waddling slowly across with her hands on her hips. I get the fire burning more brightly in the grate, light the extra candles I have provided and help her to change into one of the nightgowns. One of her fair braids has come loose and she lets me plait it again and tie them both out of the way. Albert has already moved the bed into the centre of the room and I cover it with old sheeting. Matilda wants to help, but is caught up with another contraction. Bending over, she clutches onto the side of the bed. 'Oh, miss,' she groans.

It passes and she raises her face. I am alarmed by how pale she is, how white her fingertips grasping the sheet.

'Sit,' I tell her, indicating the chair. 'Rest while you can.'

Matilda has barely sat down when another contraction comes and she rises to lean over the side of the bed again, gasps for breath and cries out.

My instructions to Albert were not to wait for Kitty but to return to the house directly he had dropped her off, and I keep reassuring myself he will soon make an appearance and can be sent with all due urgency to fetch the midwife.

As a precaution, I warned the cook to keep a plentiful supply of water on the boil, and she staggers in with a full pail and leaves it alongside the fire. I know I was sceptical when the midwife said that sometimes infants *pop out*, but it is better to be prepared for all eventualities. The cook, incidentally, who has always been a little odd, has already made clear her opinion on the matter; she will assist by providing boiling water etcetera, but that is as far as her help will extend. I do not like to probe, but I fear her reluctance to become involved stems from a bad experience. Whether her own or someone else's, I do not know.

The frequency of Matilda's contractions are happening more rapidly than I expected, and they are intense. Unnerving and unsettling me. Where is Albert? What is he doing? I do wish he would turn up.

I leave Matilda as she grimaces and shudders with pain once more against the bed, and rush across the courtyard to fetch Daisy. Another safeguard. If I have to deliver this baby on my own, I will need all the help I can get.

'Daisy,' I call sharply at the library door. 'I need your assistance. Please come across to Matilda's room and bring all the towels and what not. You will find them on the floor of my bedroom.'

'What, now?' she says faintly.

'Yes, now,' I tell her.

I get back to Matilda. Her face is flushed and she is holding onto the side of the bed and rocking back and forth. She groans with pain. 'Miss,' she says, 'I think the baby's coming now.'

'Nonsense,' I say, 'that is way too quick.'

But I think about it. If Matilda thinks the baby is coming now, surely it is? Surely she knows what is happening to her body better than I do?

'Matilda,' I instruct, 'I need you to get up on the bed. I need to see what is happening. Please!'

'I can't, miss—' She breaks off to cry out. Her skin has gone from pale to bright red with exertion. Her face is contorted with pain and perspiration beads her hairline. I do not believe it is because the room is too warm.

I move to her side and put my arm around her to comfort her. Her body is rigid.

I lift her skirt tentatively up to her waist. A trickle of blood slides down one leg and her legs are wide apart as if she is going to deliver this baby here upon the floor. Now!

Daisy comes in then with towels and the bundle of linen. I do not know if she is going to be of much use to me since she takes one look at Matilda and turns as white as the sheets she is carrying.

'Daisy?' I say crisply.

She shakes her head and, pushing the bundle of linen into my hands, bolts from the room.

A merry pickle I have got myself into!

43

I am in the midst of yet again encouraging Matilda to get up on the bed when Albert bursts in the door. Clearly, he has been informed of the situation by either Daisy or the cook. And catching sight of Matilda bent over the bed groaning, he blanches visibly. 'Matilda, love,' he cries.

'What happened?' I demand. 'Where've you been?'

'Tell you later, miss. Address for the midwife? Let me go right now, miss.'

'There's no time for that, Albert. The baby is on its way. Quick,' I say, 'I want you to run upstairs to my room. In the top drawer of my dresser you will find a silk handkerchief and a little brown bottle marked *Ether*. Bring both to me now, please. And Albert, do be careful. Do not on any account drop the bottle.'

As soon as he has left, I wash my hands thoroughly a second time and put my hand down between Matilda's legs and finger the swollen and warm flesh. I find the gap and insert my fingers. If I am not mistaken, I can feel the top of the baby's head. I pause then, as another wave of pain surges through Matilda and she trembles violently against the bed and cries out in anguish.

Albert bursts in the door a second time and carefully hands over the bottle. 'This the one, miss?'

I nod.

'Albert,' I instruct. 'I want you to put your arms around Matilda, support her from behind. I am going to give her a little of this and she is most likely going to go limp and we don't want her to fall. We need to get her onto the bed.'

Taking the folded silk handkerchief, I place it over the little brown bottle's opening and quickly invert it. I have no idea how much is needed, only that too much can be disastrous, and too little of no use at all.

I do worry about what I am doing. It is all so new and untrialled. And I worry about my promise to Dr Vincent, but I believe that I am in a *dire situation*. At present, with Matilda bent over the bed and steadfastly refusing to budge, I feel that I have little option. I *need* to see what is happening. I cannot do that in her present position.

It happens slower than I expect—from the time that I open the silk hanky and spread it across her nose—that her body goes slack. Albert takes the bulk of the weight while I lift her legs and between the two of us we hoist her onto the bed.

I push up her nightgown then, prop open her legs, and at last I can see.

And not a minute too early.

The head, with a mat of dark brown hair, is emerging. It is covered with a whitish substance I know to be *Vernix caseosa*. From the Latin, meaning 'cheesy varnish'.

Matilda's body is propelling the baby out at its own, albeit hectic, pace.

'Don't push, Matilda!' I call out. 'Do not, under any circumstances, push.'

And she responds to me. Clearly the ether is wearing off. 'Yes, miss,' she groans, blowing out air. 'I'll try not to. I'll try—' She breaks off to moan in agony again.

The mother's desire to push is strong. In her haste, she can tear the skin around the aperture. Matilda's flesh is already stretched and shiny with tautness since the infant is arriving with such haste, and it will not take much to split it.

The head protrudes, so now for the shoulders, which are more difficult. I find myself holding my breath as one appears and edges forward.

'How is Matilda?' I call to Albert who is with his wife. 'Is she coping?'

'Yes, miss.'

'And how about you, Albert? Are you still with us?'

'Yes, miss. I think so, miss.'

'The shoulders are coming out now,' I call excitedly. I have to stop myself from trying to ease the little bumps out into the world, one after the other.

'Don't tell me, miss,' he says, gulping. 'Please.'

Then, in a sudden rush, the whole baby slides out.

An entire infant with two arms and two legs and a perfect little face lies glistening between Matilda's legs.

'Oh, my goodness!' I cry. 'Albert, it's a boy! It's a boy!'

I cover him with a towel and wipe the cheesy substance from his rosebud of a mouth and his little nose, clearing his airways, and he opens his lips to take his first big breath and cries out.

And, oh, what a sweet sound it is.

'Oh, miss,' Matilda calls. 'Oh, miss!'

I find a shawl and bundle him up tightly, taking care not to entangle the cord, and place the parcel into Matilda's arms.

'You have a little baby boy,' I tell her.

'The baby has come, miss? And it's a boy?' She seems confused. Perhaps it is the ether muddling her senses. 'Are you sure, miss?'

'Yes, I'm sure,' I say, smiling at her. Smiling at them both.

Later, I cut the umbilical cord with the reference book open on the sheet beside me for guidance. The baby—Charles, apparently—lies quietly on the towel while I complete the necessary steps, but his arms flail the air as I reach across to put down the scissors.

I encounter a little fist. I prise open his hand and he clutches onto my index finger, enclosing it tightly in his entire small hand and gazing at me with unfocused eyes. He holds on as if he has reached the shore after swimming for long hours, as if he has no words with which to thank me for taking his hand. He holds on as if I am all he has got. All of a sudden, I begin to cry. To sob. As if the world has ended. As if something inside of me has been wrenched apart and opened the floodgates.

'What is it, miss?' Matilda raises herself on her elbows to look at me.

I shake my head. 'It's nothing,' I say, pulling myself together and wiping my eyes. 'Nothing.'

I wrap Charles up a second time in clean swaddling and pass him over to her, and distract myself by beginning the job of cleaning up.

But it is not nothing.

For when Kitty has arrived home, seen the baby and been euphoric and incredulous over the whole business, wanting every last little detail (I omit the bits regarding Daisy's failure to be of any assistance), and we have toasted Charlie's health, and eaten a meal that the cook half-burnt in her delayed excitement, and gone through the particulars of where and when I obtained the ether, and I have at last excused myself and gone to bed, I cry again. I weep.

I weep for what could have been. I weep for what I lost. Not only recently, but in the past. I weep, for it feels as if the advent of this small child has touched something deep inside of me, something that was forcibly enclosed behind walls for many years and shuttered and bolted, and now that I have confronted it, unbarred it and let it loose, there is no end to my emotion.

It sets me to ponder, too, on the old Estella, and how heartless she was. How cold and unfeeling, and I am ashamed of the person I was and embarrassed by my insensitivity.

Oh, Pip!

I believe it is not too late, though, to make amends, to become a better, kinder person.

44

Less than two weeks after little Charlie is born, I receive a letter from Eliza. *Dear Estella,* she writes. *Please forgive me for being so long out of touch. You will have heard that James and I now have two little ones, with a third on the way, and what with the estate and the children we are kept occupied. Rest assured, however, that I have thought of you often, my dear friend, and wondered how you are. I heard, naturally, that you had separated from Bentley and, while I was relieved, I was also sad that you were alone again.*

I am writing to ask you a favour. I have heard from Mama, who needless to say heard it from Kitty—I pause here to laugh, so much for Kitty guarding her tongue!—*that of late you were instrumental in successfully delivering a baby. I was at first quite shocked, but then I thought you have always been full of surprises, why should this be any different? And Kitty confirmed to Mama that you have long been interested in medicine. What I am saying, in my roundabout way, my sweet friend, is that I would very much appreciate your care and attention during my confinement. I believe the infant is due in the next three or four months, and I am at home most days now if you would care to call by when it suits you.*

I can't tell you how much I am looking forward to seeing you again, and to renewing our friendship. I remain, your true friend, Eliza xx

So it begins. Eliza's letter is the first. And I think that *this* is perhaps what I was put on earth to do, and that it may be I have at last found a worthy cause to pursue. I have lost a baby of my own, but there is no reason why I cannot atone for that by helping to bring little ones safely into the world.

I am also grateful that Eliza has sought me out, and that although we have not been much in touch of late, she continues to think of me as her friend.

I give instructions to Mr Jaggers to sell a number of pieces of my jewellery—those cold pieces which only bring back memories best forgotten—and from the funds raised, I am able to buy forceps, a stethoscope, a number of other midwifery essentials and a sturdy leather bag to accommodate them.

I assist at Eliza's birth, which follows the traditional pattern: I have an array of maids at my beck and call, her husband waits for news beyond the birthing room in the passage, and everything goes smoothly. Naturally, it helps that it is Eliza's third and that we once were close friends. Later, James insists upon payment of a fee and a substantial one at that, for which I am grateful. He no doubt has his suspicions regarding my financial situation.

It does concern me, however, that while Matilda's and Eliza's births have gone well, what will the consequences be the minute I am involved with an infant who becomes lodged in the birth canal? Or where I am responsible for a birth that does not turn out well? Or, and I can hardly bring myself to think it, where I have a situation where both mother and child perish? This latter question does not bear thinking about.

45

Not much later, a letter arrives one summery morning from an acquaintance of Eliza's who has heard of my talents and wishes to engage me. Mrs Peel apologises for the late notice, but she believes her infant is due in less than ten days' time. She writes that she engaged another midwife, but was not entirely happy with the woman and would be grateful if I would call upon her as soon as possible. I reply by the evening's post saying that I will call upon her the following afternoon and trust that this arrangement will suit. However, the next morning I am scarcely out of bed when Matilda comes to tell me that a certain Mr Peel is on the doorstep and wishes to speak urgently to me.

'Forgive me for the early intrusion, Mrs Drummle,' he says when I come to the door in my dressing gown. He is much older than I expected. At a guess, he is in his forties whereas I have anticipated someone who is Eliza's age. He is clearly in a state of distress, however, tapping one hand in agitation against his thigh and speaking in a staccato-like manner.

'My wife is in labour. It began shortly before midnight. Her mother had intended to assist with the birth, but has been taken ill. The family doctor indicated some time ago that he did not wish to be involved. Could you accompany me now, this minute, to assist her? It would be greatly appreciated.'

I dress in haste. On the way, the man fills me in on a few details. It is their first child. Mrs Peel—Fanny—has not been well with the confinement.

'Let me be frank, Mrs Drummle,' Mr Peel says. 'Fanny is much younger than I am. She is my second wife—sadly, my first died in childbirth—and she has suffered from both nausea and fainting spells. In addition, she is far too thin in my opinion. She has also not endeared herself to the staff. She can … She can be difficult. This is partly the reason why she finds herself in the predicament she does. With no-one to come to her aid. You understand I cannot force the servants to help her. I am not that kind of man.'

This sounds neither positive nor encouraging and I begin to grow anxious.

Mr Peel's abode is an opulent dwelling much the same as Wright House or Waverley Manor, but with an orchard of bright red apples on the slopes of the grounds. I am hastily ushered in and relieved of my coat and gloves. A maidservant takes me upstairs while Mr Peel remains below, pacing the entrance hall. Before the maid can abandon me at the chamber door, which she seems intent on doing, I stay her with my hand. 'Please bring up a pail of warm boiled water, a bowl and clean towels and sheets. Ask someone to assist you, if need be.'

The maid nods, but does not speak. She looks alarmed by events and I do not think I can count on her to offer me any further assistance.

Mrs Peel is alone in the darkened bedchamber, lying on her back. My first impression is of the smell—fetid—for the room is much too warm. In spite of the summery temperature outside, a fire is burning in the grate.

'Good morning,' I say brightly. 'I am Mrs Drummle, Eliza's friend.'

A low moan is given in response and my spirits sink still further.

I move quickly, opening the curtains and the windows, letting in the sunlight and the fresh air. I wash my hands using the clean jug of water and the bowl I find upon the washstand, then I inspect the patient.

Mrs Peel is a slight and slender woman, hardly more than girl, and she appears to be half-unconscious with pain and exhaustion. She lacks even the energy to converse with me. The baby is lying low in her huge and distended belly and, although the contractions are frequent and severe, all good indications, there is no sign of the infant emerging as yet.

I administer ether using the silk handkerchief, a small dose for she looks as if she weighs next to nothing, and for a time she is comfortable. The waves of contractions continue, but there is little indication that her body is ready to give birth and my anxiety heightens.

The maid brings up the water and the clean sheets and, at my request, assists me to remove the soiled sheets from under Mrs Peel and make up the bed with fresh ones. We also remove Mrs Peel's nightgown and dress her in a fresh one. With closed eyes, almost as if she does not want to be here and is trying to absent herself, the woman puts her arms up obediently like a doll when we ask her to. The end result, however, is that the room begins to smell a little less unpleasant. I ask the maid to use a cloth to wash Mrs Peel's face and wipe down her perspiring and clammy body, but she is so fraught with nerves that she says she cannot. I am not best pleased, but perhaps she is aware that Mr Peel's first wife died in childbirth and is terrified of the same thing happening again?

It is nearly noon when I dash out to relieve myself and find not only a tray of tea together with a plate of sandwiches outside the door, but Mr Peel. He looks up at me sharply.

'Forgive me,' he says, 'I am going half-mad downstairs. Is there anything I can do to help?'

'Yes,' I say. 'I would be grateful.'

I take him to his wife's side, hand him the washcloth and ask him to do what the maid could not.

'Of course,' he says, 'by all means. Fanny?' he murmurs to his wife. 'Fanny, my love.'

I am pleased then, that Mr Peel is older and appears practically minded and has no qualms about being in the birthing room.

I leave him administering attentions to Mrs Peel and return to the passage and the sandwiches, for I have not had breakfast and my stomach is rebelling. I bite into one and consider my options. The patient by my reckoning has now been in labour for over twelve hours, she is weary and growing weaker by the minute, and I cannot see the baby's head at all. If I do not do something, I will lose the infant. I may even lose the mother as well. And how will I break that news to Mr Peel? He has already lost one wife and child, how will I tell him that he might be about to lose another?

I start to cough and, before I know it, I have regurgitated my food into my palm, the bread coming up slimy and stodgy. Clearly, I am much too anxious to eat.

Have I brought this upon myself with my fears of having an infant lodged tight in the birth canal? I am not superstitious and I do not think so. Surely, it was bound to happen at some point?

I put down my unfinished sandwich. I lean against the wall and take a shuddering breath.

What am I to do?

What *can* I do?

I have my own forceps, but I have never used them before and, in all honesty, I am afraid. I have read such ghastly stories regarding them. Stories in which the only way to save the mother's life and remove the dead infant is to work from the outside in and cut it away piecemeal.

I could run away, but I am not a person who deserts another in their time of need. I am also not a person who gives up readily. Besides which, if I give up now, what does that mean for my future as a midwife? I do not want a reputation as someone who flees a sinking ship. I have undertaken to do this and I am not going to let it defeat me!

Think, Estella. Think!

We need a doctor, and we need a doctor urgently, that much is clear—

Dr Vincent, I think. Dr Vincent. He may well refuse, but it is a chance I must take.

I return to Mr Peel.

'I need you to fetch a certain Dr Vincent with all due haste,' I tell him as he rises, frowning, from his wife's bedside.

'A doctor?' he repeats.

'Yes, a doctor. I believe that a doctor is required. You will find Dr Vincent in the London Library in St James's Square. If he is not there, you should ascertain his address from the clerk at the desk and fetch him. Urgently.'

I want to add that it is a matter of life and death, but I do not want to scare the wits out of the man.

'Of course,' he says. He is already halfway out the door and I believe he can tell it is a matter of life and death. 'Consider it done,' he calls over his shoulder.

His footsteps retreat rapidly down the passage. I am alone again. Except for Mrs Peel lying comatose upon the bed, and the baby, of course. The baby!

'Please, little one,' I say, 'can't you do something to hurry things along?'

Time crawls. I vacillate between despair and hope. I look out of the window to see if can spot Mr Peel returning, but the window has a southern aspect over a rose garden and is no use to me. I pace the floor and wring my hands and make promises that I will never do this again, never again assist without a doctor being available to come to my aid, and gaze out of the window once more. The roses are past their bloom and wasted petals of yellow, cream and white lie strewn upon the ground.

I return to Mrs Peel. 'Mrs Peel?' I say, but she does not respond. She is still breathing, for I can see her chest rising and falling, but her face is ashen. Her long fair hair, which should have been tied up, is limp and damp with perspiration. I wonder what colour her eyes are? I use two fingers to palpitate her belly and the skin is as taut as a ship's full-blown sails.

In the late afternoon, to my intense relief, I hear footsteps in the passage at last and Mr Peel arrives at the door with Dr Vincent at his heels. The former resumes his place at his wife's head. 'Fanny, my love, Fanny,' he murmurs.

The doctor has already been stripped of his gloves, coat and cane. He puts down his bag, begins rolling up his shirtsleeves, and raises his eyebrows enquiringly at me. 'Mrs Drummle?'

'I am so glad to see you, you have no idea,' I say all in a rush. 'Mrs Peel is weak with pain and fatigue. The baby does not appear to be moving down the birth canal. I gave the mother a small amount of ether some time ago to relieve the pain, but nothing since.'

'I see,' he says, quickly washing his hands.

Dr Vincent does not speak while he examines the patient, although his moustache twitches as if he is deep in thought. He presses down, on and around her belly, then widens her legs and inspects between them before glancing up at Mr Peel.

'Could you kindly come up this end, sir? I need these legs lifted and propped open. There is some movement down there now, Mrs Drummle,' he says to me. 'But we are going to need the Simpson forceps. In my bag,' he says.

I retrieve them for him and he demonstrates how to insert them. He places his fingers around the blades and gently manoeuvres them into the opening, at the same time cradling them around the infant's head. It is clearly something that comes with experience.

'The skin is thin, the skull weak, and one must be careful not to be too rough or hurried, or damage can be sustained.'

He talks to me as he works, which I find of comfort. How lucky I am to have found such a man who is not only willing to help me but to share his knowledge!

He locks the forceps into place and it seems to me that he times the work of the instrument with the mother's contractions, for only as one surges through the body does he gently tug. I have read that this is how it is done, but it is the first time I have seen it in practice. It does not look like an easy task. In fact, the sight of it makes my toes curl up.

'Mrs Drummle, could you press down gently upon the belly?' Dr Vincent asks. 'Mrs Peel,' he calls, 'I need you to push, please. Could you do that, Mrs Peel? Could you push?'

'Fanny, love,' Mr Peel calls. 'Are you hearing this? Please push, my darling. Push!'

Mrs Peel moans. She pants and heaves and gasps as she tries her best, but she is clearly exhausted.

We all have our jobs to do and we do them as best we can. Mine is to press down upon the belly and prop up one leg. Mr Peel's is to do the same with the other leg, while Dr Vincent is bent over between us, intent on his task.

Little by little the top of the head appears between Mrs Peel's legs, then the face. The face is scratched from the forceps and streaked with blood. One eye is shut and bruised, one ear clogged with blood. But I can scarcely believe it. I thought this was an impossibility, and that I would not see this infant. Certainly, that I would not see it alive.

The tears start to my eyes, for I seem to cry easily these days.

Finally, the baby slides out. Immediately, she takes a breath of air and wails with all her might. Yes, it is a little girl. And, yes, it has been a rough entry into the world. No wonder she is howling with distress. Dr Vincent removes the forceps, puts them to one side and rubs his fingers gently over the red marks left on the sides of the baby's face.

'It's a little girl,' Mr Peel is saying excitedly over the baby's wails. 'Fanny, it's a little girl! Is she in good health, doctor?'

'I believe so,' Dr Vincent says as he begins to clean the baby's mouth and face.

'Well, I'll be,' Mr Peel says. He seems overwhelmed and there is awe in his voice. 'Faith,' he announces. 'She will be called Faith.'

Faith is not so little, in fact, and appears well nourished, and I understand from Dr Vincent that infants often take all they require from the mother and, if she is not eating sufficiently or well, it is the mother who will be left weak and undernourished. 'As has happened here,' he murmurs.

Mrs Peel manages to prop herself up on her elbows, look at her daughter and smile wanly, then she falls back against the pillows.

Dr Vincent cuts the cord. I swaddle Faith and put the little bundle into Mr Peel's arms and at last she ceases her crying. Mr Peel gazes down at his baby daughter adoringly and she looks earnestly back up at him—it is quite the picture. A day ago, I did not know this man; he was a stranger. Now he practically feels like family. Not that I know how that feels, not really.

'Fanny,' he says to his wife. 'Fanny, look.' But Mrs Peel is clearly in no state to acknowledge her daughter.

Her husband stops to thank Dr Vincent for his help, telling the doctor that when he is ready to depart, the carriage for his return trip awaits him at the front door, then leaves the room carrying little Faith. I suspect that he is on his way to the kitchen to make enquiries from the staff as to the whereabouts of a wet nurse.

Before he goes, Dr Vincent attends to Mrs Peel, retrieving the placenta and ensuring she is comfortable. He works quietly, but his bedside manner is faultless.

'She needs rest and nourishment, in that order,' he tells me before he leaves. 'Could you ensure that Mr Peel understands?'

'I will,' I say. 'Thank you. I am exceedingly grateful for your help. I cannot adequately express my gratitude.'

'It was my pleasure, Mrs Drummle.'

As he wipes the forceps and returns them to his bag, he smiles kindly. 'If you must know,' he says, 'I rather enjoyed it.'

*

It is after midnight when I return home. Much later, I conclude that to safeguard myself I must ensure that a doctor is notified and is able and prepared to come to my aid if the infant or mother gets into difficulties.

I make a trip to the London Library to talk with Dr Vincent. Remembering his previous reluctance to talk in front of his peers, I leave a note for him with the clerk, asking him to meet me in a well-known coffee house in the Strand.

He seems pleased to see me and happy to converse, which confirms my suspicions and, after some discussion, he tells me that as a special favour he will assist me if the need should arise. He says it is hard to say no to me. He says it is especially hard because I am an educated woman and not your everyday midwife. By this stage, I have gathered that midwives as a whole do not have a good reputation. I ask Dr Vincent about this and he smiles and says that he could tell me some horror stories, but probably the less I know, the better.

We begin a business relationship of sorts. I send him a list with the names and addresses of the forthcoming births I have been requested to assist with and keep him regularly updated as to their progress. Consequently, I am much happier about continuing with my role of midwife.

Suffice to say, I am kept occupied. And the resulting funds prove useful, since I can no longer consider myself to be wealthy, thanks to Bentley.

46

I am in the library with little Charlie at my feet and we are playing with his building blocks. I have got into the habit of spending an hour or so with him in the mornings to enable Matilda to get some of her housekeeping duties done.

Charlie is the sweetest little boy with dark hair like his father and deep brown eyes, and already at two years of age he has a remarkable vocabulary. I build his blocks up into a castle and he knocks them down again with much chortling. It is a game we play almost every day and neither of us seems to tire of it. The dexterity with which he picks up the blocks in his chubby fingers and attempts to make his own tower engrosses me. He often fails. Sometimes he announces, 'Oh dear!', but he is never deterred.

On occasion, I even get down on all fours and crawl around the floor with him, less frequently now he is walking. Sometimes I allow him to clamber onto my back and I jog around the room until he is paralytic with laughter and I am breathless. He brings me a great deal of delight and compensates for the fact that I have no offspring of my own. I believe I am particularly fond of him because I helped to bring him into the world. He was the first.

You never forget the first, Miss Havisham once told me, though she was not talking about babies.

Oh, Pip!

Matilda appears in the doorway, carrying a letter. Charlie cries 'Mama' with joy and lifts his arms for her to pick him up, and she takes him away to give me peace while I open my mail. It has come post-haste and I wonder who it is that requires my services so urgently.

The letter is dated today. It is short and succinct. *Dear Estella, Regretfully I must advise that your husband, Bentley Drummle, was killed late yesterday afternoon as a consequence of an accident with his horse. I will be in touch again soon with further details. Regards, Jaggers.*

Slowly, I put down the letter and stare into the distance. I ought to feel something other than relief, but I do not. I once said to Pip that our marriage was one of convenience and that Bentley and I would be useful to one another. I did not know then, of course, that this usefulness would be unequal and heavily weighted in Bentley's favour.

I have become that person that I derided and belittled many years ago: I have become a widow. What did I say about widows? That nobody wants to marry them; that they do not fit in at cards or other social gatherings because they are single; that they are in a class, and a lowly class at that, of their own unless they are exceptionally wealthy; that they are spare parts.

How unkind I was. How ungracious. How proud, arrogant and presumptuous I was back then.

I go up to London that day. I cannot wait. There is a part of me that does not believe Bentley is really gone and I need confirmation from Mr Jaggers. I take a chance, for I do not have an appointment, but I am fortunate and the man is in. He rises from his chair to kiss my hand. 'Estella.'

'Mr Jaggers.'

'I did not think you would wait,' he says, 'and I was right, but then I am seldom wrong.'

I sit in the office where I have sat before, with the cask faces filled of horror, with the rusted pistol and the ancient sword in a scabbard swinging from a hook, with Mr Jaggers in his nail-embedded, coffin-like chair, and I wonder how many years I have ahead of me until I, too, will be in a coffin.

He finishes shuffling some papers on his desk. He looks up and gazes quietly at me. He says, 'Amongst his acquaintances, Bentley had become quite renowned as a compound of pride, avarice and meanness. How you withstood him for so long is beyond me.'

I shake my head. 'Let us not talk of that. How did it happen? I am curious.'

'I understand that he died of injuries consequent of his ill-treatment of his horse. He was about to mount when his horse kicked out, without warning apparently, and caught him in the stomach. He fell to the ground in agony. The animal delivered another swift blow, this time to the head, and he was gone in minutes.'

'At least his death would have been quick,' I say.

'Which is no doubt more than he deserved,' Mr Jaggers murmurs.

I have witnessed Bentley seizing his horse's mane and mounting in his brutal and blundering manner and do not forget that many was the time he shared my bed. I would say that his treatment of his horses and of me was not too dissimilar. Naturally, I do not voice this opinion to Mr Jaggers.

'You are at liberty to visit the house in Hyde Park to collect anything that belongs to you. Are there things you wish to retrieve, Estella?'

'There are some things,' I tell him, 'platters and so on, but I will not be able to look at them without thinking of Bentley and they are therefore better off remaining where they are.'

Mr Jaggers nods. 'There is, of course, no money left,' he says. 'He ran through everything he had and then some. I trust you were not counting on monetary benefit of any kind?'

I shake my head.

The big man pushes his chair away from the desk and fixes his dark eyes upon me, and for the first time ever I see something in his expression that could be construed as compassion.

'You are committed to remembering what I said about your mother?'

'I am.'

'And that other foolishness, the less said about, the better? You have quite given that up?'

'I have.'

'And Satis House. How do you wish me to proceed?'

'I will advise you in due course,' I tell him. 'You can see now why I held off selling for so long?'

'I can,' he says. 'It was a considered move, Estella,' he adds, and I believe this is the highest praise I have ever received from the man.

He bites at his forefinger in his old habit then, and says, 'I do not think there is anything further.'

I take that as my cue to depart and get up from my chair. We bid farewell to one another in the usual manner, but it seems to me that his eyes remain on me for longer than usual.

On my way out, Wemmick, who was absent when I came in, rises from his desk to gaze at me over the countertop.

'Mrs Drummle. Good day to you.'

'Mr Wemmick.'

He seems to stare for an inordinately long time. As if the woman he sees before him is not the woman he once knew.

47

In due course, I advise Mr Jaggers that I wish to sell the house and the sale happens more quickly than I expect. Apparently, a wealthy landowner wishes to set up a country retreat in opposition to the Blue Boar and has had his eye on Satis House and its grounds and established trees for some time.

Subsequent to the sale, I decide to visit the old place again before all trace of it is extinguished, as it is my understanding that the house and outbuildings have already been demolished. There is more than one reason for this: although I have been kept occupied, I have been restless and low. Eliza and James have kept in touch, sending letters of condolence on Bentley's death, but they have their own lives to lead and are occupied with their families and households. To be honest, we no longer move in the same circles, for I am a working woman now.

I have my occupation and, at one point, I believed it would be enough. I believed that this plain and honest working life had nothing in it to be ashamed of, but offered me sufficient means of self-respect and happiness ... But all in one moment, some fleeting remembrance of Miss Havisham and my past falls upon me like a destructive missile and scatters my wits. Scattered wits take a long time picking up and, often before I have got them well together, they are dispersed in all directions by another stray thought. The truth is my work does not wholly satisfy me and quell my unquiet spirit. For I am like Oliver Twist, I think, being so bold as to want more. *More. Please, sir, I want some more.* Always yearning for ... I know not what.

The change of scenery, the fresh air and a walk on the marshes will do me good, I believe.

I book a room at the Blue Boar and go out on the first coach of the morning, and arrive before noon and find the aforesaid establishment to be much the same as Mrs Butters pronounced it in my childhood. Dear Mrs Butters. Sleeping beside a hedge, however, is not an option, much as I might prefer it.

I take myself off as soon as I can and make for the lowlands. I reach the churchyard and stand in the lee of the vestry and remember a man I met here, a man with whom I was infatuated. I was young and inexperienced and thought it was love, but it was not. I remember another man who ties me to this place and who has been the only constant in my life, but he may as well be lost to me, for I have no idea where he is, only that he is abroad.

I walk out amongst the gravestones overgrown with nettles and pause beside the five little stone lozenges that are arranged in a row. Each is about a foot and half long and sacred to the memory of the five male infants with the family name *Pirrip*. I know this to be Pip's last name, but I have never reflected on whether these babes who lie here are his brothers. I suppose they must be. The thought saddens me. I have lost one child; imagine losing five.

Pip's mother and father lie here, too. Philip and Georgiana Pirrip. Pip is the only one of his siblings who carries the name of his father. It strikes me that I have spent a great deal of time thinking about my mother and the name Olivia which Mr Jaggers's housekeeper mentioned. Who is Olivia? And is that my mother's name, and what kind of woman is she? Or *was* she, because for all I know she may be dead by now. I have rarely given a thought, however, to my father. Who was my father, and where is he now? Do I resemble him in any way, and will I ever know the answers to these questions?

I attempt to shift the one gravestone that has dipped precariously forward back into alignment with my hands, but it is bogged in the earth and I give up finally and brush the dirt from my gloves and walk still further afield to where the cattle graze.

The grass is long and my skirts rustle amongst it, startling the birds that fly up at my approach. Across the dark flat wilderness, the scattered cattle pause to gaze at me, jaws working and tails flicking. The river is a low leaden line ahead of me, the light soft and hazy. *Otherworldly*, some might call it. It is a pleasant day, sunny, with a slight breeze, but not a whiff of salt-laden air, imagined or otherwise, and perhaps this accounts for the lack of atmosphere because, try as I may, I cannot recapture the sense of exhilaration and freedom that the landscape once brought me.

But that is the way of life, for the experiences which intoxicate us in our youth are never the same when we grow up. In our youth, we spend half our time longing to be older and in our maturity we ache to be young again.

I stay out until the evening's damp settles upon the marsh grasses and hangs from blade to blade like spiders' webs. When I pass through the graveyard, it is wet and clammy. I think of returning via Mr Gargery's forge, Pip's old home, and of seeing the blue shadows of the flames leap upon the walls, but the absence of Pip will make me sadder than ever. As it is I return, at last, to the Blue Boar with an even heavier heart than I set out with.

This will not do, Estella, I tell myself.

I cannot bear the thought of retiring so early to my rooms, which are dismal and dreary. Instead I make my way to Satis House. No matter if I go again in the morning.

The evening is settling in when I reach the place where Satis House once stood. A cold silvery mist veils the dusk and one or two stars hang in the sky and glimmer through the queer half-light. The moon will be up soon.

I go through the gate, it and the wall being the only constructions remaining, and meander through the grounds. Everything—the disused brewery, the disintegrating beer casks, the rusted staircase, the house itself—is gone, knocked down and removed, although here and there small heaps of rubble still remain. The old ivy has struck root anew in one or two of them, and I think of nature and how it seldom gives in and how it is always searching for ways to renew itself, and what a survivor it is.

I stand, lost in thought in the gloom, toeing at the rubble with my boot for some lost memento, some fragment of china from Miss Havisham's room, *anything* to bring back the past, when the gate creaks and I glance up.

But it is only the evening breeze making the gate sway. There is no-one here. No-one but me.

And I know who it is I have expected to see, who I want to see, desire to see—*long* to see—although it has taken me an eternity to realise this.

Oh, I have been so blind. So ignorant.

So foolish!

Without realising precisely how it happens, I find myself leaving the poor deserted grounds of Satis House and slipping down the high street in the gloom, my hood over my head. I know where I am going. I do not fight it.

Once there would've been a time when I fought it, but that time is over.

The forge is in darkness, the wall where I cowered and where Pip drenched my boots with a bucket of dirty water still standing. Unchanged, too, is the little wooden house with the mullioned windows and the warm glow behind them.

My tap at the door is answered by a woman who is perhaps a little older than I am. She is plump and kindly-looking with bright brown eyes, reminding me of Mrs Butters. I recall then that Pip told me at some point that his sister had passed on. This must be the blacksmith's new wife.

'Miss!' she says, startled.

'Forgive me,' I say, 'is this the home of the blacksmith'—it pains me but I cannot remember his name—'the man to whom Pip was once apprenticed?'

'It is,' she says. She widens the door. 'You would be Miss Havisham, wouldn't you?'

I nod.

'Biddy,' she tells me, introducing herself. 'Come in, miss,' she says, stepping aside. Over her shoulder she calls out, 'Joe?'

The name comes to me, then, and Mr Joe Gargery is rising from his place beside the chimney when I enter the small but homely kitchen. A child with dark hair like the blacksmith clutches one of his big hands.

'Why, miss,' Mr Gargery says. 'Miss Havisham?'

'You presume correctly. Good evening, Mr Gargery. I am sorry to intrude. I was in the area and ...' I trail off.

All three are looking at me with curiosity and there is nothing for it but to spit it out.

'Pip,' I say. 'Do you have news of him? Do you know where he is, where he finds himself?'

'He's in the Middle East,' Mr Gargery says. He glances at Biddy. 'What's the name of the place, love?'

'Cairo,' Biddy says, nodding. 'He's in Cairo, working with Mr Herbert. Mr Herbert Pocket, that is.'

I nod. 'I know Herbert. He was Miss Havisham's cousin.'

I pause and in the quiet I hear what I recognise as the snuffling of a baby. A crib is in the corner of the kitchen, I see now, a wickerwork crib and, as I watch, a little fist rises from beneath the swaddling and bats the air.

'Don't mind her, miss,' Biddy tells me, smiling. 'She's merely settling down. Pip,' she says to the small child who has crept further forward, all the better to see me, 'go talk to your sister, would you? Tell her I won't be long.'

'I won't keep you,' I say. 'Do you have an address for Herbert? A place where I could write to him?'

Biddy nods. 'It's simple, miss. It's Clarriker & Co—Clarriker with two r's—Cairo. They don't need a formal address for a letter, miss, they are that well known. We write to Pip all the time, don't we, Joe? And he's always receiving our letters.'

'Thank you.' I turn to go, but remember something else, something that is difficult to ask, but must be asked.

'He—he hasn't married, has he? Pip?'

'No, miss.'

'And you won't tell him, will you, that I was here or what I asked for?'

'No, miss. If that is your wish, we won't do that.'

I nod. 'It is my wish,' I say.

I thank them again and bid them both goodnight.

Very soon, I am walking back towards the town and the Blue Boar. The moon has risen, lighting my way forward, and this time there is a spring in my step and a lightness in my heart.

48

I travel by train to Marseilles, thus avoiding a lengthy sea trip and the infamous swells and storms of the Bay of Biscay. Crossing the Mediterranean by boat to Malta, I continue my journey on a P&O mail ship to Alexandria on the continent of Africa, and from thence I travel to Port Said on yet another boat, finally arriving in Cairo in the late afternoon.

It is quite the adventure, but I keep to myself for the journey. I am polite, but I do not engage with the other passengers. I am preoccupied with what I will find. In fact, I have my heart set on what I will find and, like a planet, I cannot veer from my trajectory. I have no wish to make new acquaintances, to engage in discussions regarding why I have made the journey and what I hope to achieve.

I have this fear that if I give my thoughts wings, if I discuss my hopes and dreams, they are so fragile they will either be crushed or fly away and never return.

Cairo is unlike any other city I have visited. It is not the noise, for the streets of London can be deafening. It is the combination of the gaudy colours and pungent smells together with the heat that are an assault to the senses. I stand on the deck of the boat, squinting into the sun and fanning my face, when we dock in Port Said. A guide has been sent to meet me, a man wearing a turban, a long sand-coloured robe and sandals upon his brown and bare feet. How Ali finds me in all the bustle I do not know. I understand from him that I and my luggage will be conveyed by donkey cart, but when we reach Cairo, he suggests that we alight and walk along the dusty streets to the hotel because it is quicker. People in colourful robes jostle against me. The sun beats down upon my head in spite of my parasol, and I hear the sounds of a low melodic language that I do not understand.

I stay at lodgings recommended to me by Herbert. Miss Havisham's cousin owes me nothing, but he has been most welcoming and kind in his correspondence—in stark contrast to the last time I saw him. It is not a hotel, but Herbert assures me that it is far preferable to the establishment the tourists use, which is frequented by loud Americans and boorish English.

I have travelled alone, which is most unusual, but again it was Herbert's suggestion. He wrote, too, that it was Clara's experience that once I am here, I will have no need of a maid. (Clara is Herbert's wife, apparently, and he assures me that she counts Pip as a dear friend and is greatly buoyed by my intention to visit.) There are men and boys that do the duties of maids, Clara says, and do them equally well if not better. If Ali is any indication of this, I am well satisfied.

I am tired by my journey, but my anticipation and excitement cannot be quelled. My room is spacious and ornately furnished with bronze urns and artefacts and richly patterned, tasselled cushions and rugs. It has high ceilings and thick plastered walls with long narrow openings that let in what breeze there is. There is a view out to a courtyard with a fountain at its centre, and one can hear the sound of tinkling water. A number of green-grey palm trees are fanned out against the wall and shimmer in the heat. They are majestic, but nothing like the trees I am accustomed to. They make a statement with the rustle of their fronds and the bright yellow fruits at their centres.

Behind a partition in the far corner of my room is a washstand and a copper jug filled with cool water. After I unpack, setting out Miss Havisham's pretty little crystal dish with the hairpins upon the dresser where it looks both out of place and at home, I refresh myself and change into lighter garments. I put up my hair, taking it off my neck.

Shortly before six, I leave the key on one of the hooks behind the desk in the small entrance hall as I have been instructed to do and close the door behind me. Apparently, the night concierge will come on duty later and be here to let me in on my return.

Outside, the heat has abated and the sky has paled with the onset of evening. One lone star hangs in the heavens as if tacked to a piece of parchment. I have been told to expect a long twilight and that it will not be dark for some time.

I walk down another dusty laneway, following the instructions Herbert sent. On either side, there are gated dwellings with high stuccoed walls, and the aromas of cooking and spices waft through the warm air. It is much quieter than when I arrived, although I still have to step aside to allow a camel laden with bulging hessian sacks to pass, and then a man with bare feet and several rugs rolled up and hoisted upon his shoulder.

'*Ahlan wa sahlan*,' he says to me with a folding gesture of his hands. *Peace be with you.* I heard this from one of the passengers on the boat, and am grateful I know what it means. It seems a gracious thing to say.

I pause around a corner to gaze up at a solid square-shaped building with an upper storey that is open to the stars. Herbert told me that every evening after work, he and Clara, and sometimes Pip, can be found here for a short while at least. A number of people, locals and Europeans, are seated at tables, talking or laughing or drinking, but I cannot see the Pockets. Not from where I stand. I will have to go up the stairs.

I cross the open space with my head lowered and reach the building's outside stairs, and pause for a moment.

I pause because my heart is fluttering wildly out of control, my legs unsteady beneath me. After all this time, I have a desire to bite my fingernails. *God forbid!* I cannot remember when last I have been so anxious, so jittery. What if this is all for nothing? What if I am too late?

Slowly, I mount the stairs.

I reach the upper storey and scan the guests. At first, I do not see Herbert. Then a man dressed in an oatmeal-coloured suit seated at a table catches my eye. Is it Herbert?

No, it is Pip.

Surely, it is Pip!

He is older, but his hair and sweet face are unchanged. He is talking animatedly to a woman, a woman dressed like I am and, as I watch, he reaches across the table for her outstretched hand.

Oh, Pip!

I feel quite faint.

I lean back against the wall to recover my breath, and perhaps it is the movement that distracts him because Pip turns away from the woman to look at me.

Our eyes meet.

It is a moment of significance.

Everything I have ever done, every breath I have ever taken, has been leading towards these seconds of crystal clarity. How could I have been so ignorant for so long? So unaware of what lay in my heart?

I am giddy with emotion.

For, of course, it is Pip.

It has always been Pip.

I know this in my heart of hearts.

I know that pride has prevented me from acknowledging my feelings for him.

Pride and haughtiness. Scorn and derision. A capricious nature.

Before I know what I am doing, I have turned on my heel and fled.

I thought I was sure of myself. I thought I was prepared for this moment, but with this new-found knowledge it is clear I am not.

In the semi-dark, I plummet back down the stairs. Down, down and down. Pausing at the bottom, I look left and right, and then I dash across the street.

'Estella?'

His voice stops me in my tracks.

I turn and gaze back over my shoulder. I gaze at the man who descends the staircase and walks steadily and surely towards me.

'Estella?' he says again in a tone of incredulity.

I swallow. I appear to have lost my voice.

'Pip,' I say at last.

My eyes start with tears as he draws near.

'What are you doing here?' he asks.

I stretch my hand out to him and he takes it and holds it between both his own and brings it to his lips.

He is still handsome. The lock of fair hair still falls over his forehead and his kind, brilliant blue eyes are unchanged.

'I am greatly altered,' I say. 'I wonder you know me.'

'I would know you anywhere, Estella. Besides which,' he says, smiling faintly, 'we are all greatly altered.'

He pauses, his eyes upon me. 'How did you find me?'

'The blacksmith, Mr Gargery, and his wife—'

'Biddy? You visited Joe and Biddy?'

'I did.'

'And how are they?'

'They are well. They were very kind—'

'They are always very kind,' he murmurs.

'I heard of Bentley's death,' he says, still holding my hand. 'I am so sorry.'

'Don't be,' I say.

'Pip? Am I too late? Are you with another?' Desperation makes me blurt it out.

'Another?'

'The woman with you, upstairs—'

'Clara?' He smiles. 'Clara has announced she is with child. We are celebrating.'

'Oh.'

I am conscious of the light but warm pressure of his fingers enveloping mine. The action may be absent-minded but it gives me hope.

'Pip—'

'I thought you had gone from me forever, Estella,' he murmurs.

I shake my head. 'I have never gone from you, Pip, not truly. It may have seemed that way, but you were always with me. *Are* always with me. I think of you often, and I have thought of you much of late.'

'Estella—'

'Wait,' I say. 'Let me talk, Pip, let me say my words before I lose my spirit. Please?'

He looks at me with such intent, with such blue-eyed wide-eyed trust, it is a wonder I can manage to talk at all.

'There was a long hard time when I kept the memory of you at bay, Pip, the remembrance of what I had thrown away when I was ignorant of its worth. But suffering has been a strong teacher.

It has taught me to understand what you underwent, what your heart used to be—'

'Estella,' he says, rebuking me softly. 'Let's not talk of the past—'

'I must,' I tell him. 'For how can we have a future if we don't clear the misdeeds of the past? For I am utterly sorry, Pip, for the way I behaved towards you, and without my apology, without my admission that I did you a grave injustice, you and I—*us*—it will mean nothing!'

'Us?' he murmurs.

'I have been bent and broken by suffering, Pip, but I am a better woman now than I ever was …'

He clutches me to him then, and cradles my head against his chest because the tears are falling freely from my eyes, and I am sobbing like a child.

'Don't,' he tells me, 'don't cry, darling Estella. I cannot bear it. I have forgiven you, if ever there was anything to forgive.'

He takes out his handkerchief and tenderly dabs at my face and bends to gaze steadily at me, to satisfy himself my tears are all gone, and I raise my lips to his and kiss him.

Never was a kiss so sweet or so heartfelt. Or so equal in depth of feeling. Or so giving of our hearts one to another.

We break apart and I look up at him, and his blue eyes remain unwaveringly fixed on my own.

'Estella,' he murmurs. 'Can I hope …?'

'Yes, dear Pip, you can. I have been yours for a long time, perhaps as far back as when we were children. I could not … I could not acknowledge it.'

I think about blurting out that I blame this on Miss Havisham, on my upbringing, but that time is over. I, and I alone, take responsibility for myself now.

He takes my hand and we go back up the stairs. But before we reach the landing and Clara and Herbert, he pauses to look down at me again. As if he cannot grasp the fact that I am here, that we are together, that there are no barriers between us.

'I have so much to tell you,' he says. 'I will hardly know where to begin. And some might say that I should not discuss these matters with you, but I believe you deserve to know them. I believe you desire to know them.'

He says no more and we turn and go up the stairs.

Pip introduces me to Clara. She is a slight but becoming woman with dark hair and big, dark eyes containing a hint of mischief. I congratulate her on her forthcoming confinement, and she thanks me and says that she is looking forward to showing me around Cairo. She wants to know if tomorrow is too early for a tour of the pyramids and again I thank her and tell her it is not.

Herbert appears to spend much of the time not saying a great deal, but looking earnestly at me. I believe he is trying to tell me that I am to be kind to Pip and that he will not stand for any high-handed nonsense. Fancy myself once thinking that the fight between him and Pip in the yard of the brewery was about me. How vain I was, then. How ignorant. Herbert does not know that I am no longer the person I once was. I long to tell him that Pip and I have reached a new understanding, but it is Pip's news to impart and not mine, and in any event Pip no doubt does not wish to take away from Clara's joyful news, not this evening at any rate.

In due course, Herbert and Clara take their leave of us, the latter promising to call around in the morning, and I tell Clara that I am greatly looking forward to it. I believe we are going to be firm friends, for she takes my hand, holds it with such warmth and looks at me with such feeling.

'Pip,' I blurt out once they have gone. I cannot wait any longer. 'You said you have so much to tell me. What do you know of my mother? I have long wanted to know who she is and Mr Jaggers refuses to divulge the information. Please, will you tell me?'

He reaches across the table for my hands and holds them. 'Yes, I will tell you for I believe you mean only to do good with the information—'

'That is precisely what I wish, dear Pip—to do good. Now, please go on.'

'Your mother is Molly, Mr Jaggers's housekeeper—'

'Mr Jaggers's housekeeper?'

I am in shock. For Jaggers's housekeeper is the woman who was all aflutter and came after me in the street and told me that she knew my mother and would tell her what a fine lady I was. The woman who covered the top of my hand briefly with her own warm one, whose eyes were shining.

She is my mother? Not some friend of hers as she said, but she, herself. She is my mother.

I have found my mother. I can scarcely believe it. Then something occurs to me.

'Olivia,' I murmur, frowning.

'Olivia?' Pip repeats. 'Her name is Molly.'

'Then who is Olivia? She asked me if the name meant anything to me?'

Pip purses his lips. 'Perhaps it is your name, the name she gave you as a child?'

'My name?' I question. 'The name she gave me as a child? Oh,' I say, understanding dawning. '*Olivia*. I believe it may be Latin but I am not certain of its precise meaning ...'

'Nor I,' he says.

'And that was why she asked me, to see if I recalled it?'

'Yes, presumably.'

'And my father? What do you know of my father?'

'Steady, Estella. Is not one revelation enough for today?'

ESTELLA

'No, I must know. I have waited too long. Please, Pip?'

'Your father ...' He pauses as if he is not quite certain how to form the words, or how much to tell me. 'Your father was my benefactor—'

'*No!*'

'It is a long story, Estella, and I wonder if we should leave it for another time? Two revelations are quite enough for today, don't you think?'

'Probably you are right,' I say, for I do feel overwhelmed. But I am also strangely excited. I have a mother and she lives!

'Only tell me,' I add, 'Was ... Did ...?'

I begin again. 'Did he, my father, once stay at your place at the Temple? Only ... Only I visited you once and you were not in. The caretaker told me you were out. It was at that time when you were avoiding me, when every time I saw you, you looked troubled. There was someone at your house that day, a figure who stood in the shadows of the stairwell and watched me. And I wondered who the man was and why he hid himself—?'

'There were reasons why he hid himself, dear Estella. Reasons why I was troubled. I will come to them over the next few days. And, yes, that sounds much like him, like dear Magwitch.'

'You were fond of him?'

'I was indeed. He was ... He was a true—'

'*Was?*'

Pip nods. The anguished expression upon his face is almost more than I can bear.

'I am sorry to tell you he passed away, Estella. But ... But before he left me, I told him of you. I reminded him that he had once had a child that he loved and lost and he remembered—he remembered you. And I told him that you had been adopted and were now a lady, and that you were very beautiful.'

I smile wryly at this.

'And I told him that I loved you. It was the last thing I said to him and I believe it made him happy.'

'Oh, Pip,' I say, for the tears have started to my eyes.

I gaze up. It is still light. Above my friend's head, the heavens are clear and open and immense.

'Look,' I say.

I point to the same lone star I saw earlier. How it glitters and glimmers and shimmers in all that vastness. And I recall again Miss Havisham telling me that I came into her life at a time when she was in darkness. *I* have been in darkness, but is it possible that I have emerged now to shine, and to shine steadfastly?

'The first star,' Pip says.

He gazes from the heavens back to me and there is wonderment in his eyes, and happiness.

'I still love you, Estella,' he says. 'I have always loved you. I have never stopped loving you.'

The haunted look in Pip's eyes that I saw all too often has gone. And whatever my dear friend has to tell me about my father, I can bear—for my mother lives.

There are no shadows of any further partings between us. There is no darkness ahead. There is nothing to mar our happiness, and at last I am at peace.

Author's Note

This is a work of fiction based on another work of fiction, and while I attempted to be as factual as possible it was sometimes tempting to allow the former to overrule the facts. For instance, *The Pickwick Papers* was not published until after 1936 and therefore not technically in print at the time mentioned here, but I couldn't resist the irony of using Dickens's name. I therefore claim all errors as my own.

Readers may be interested in the books I read in preparation for the writing of *Estella*:
- *Great Expectations* by Charles Dickens
- *The Mystery of Charles Dickens* by AN Wilson
- *Charles Dickens* by Jane Smiley
- *The Victorian City: Everyday life in Dickens' London* by Judith Flanders

Acknowledgements

For most writers there is a magical spark that compels one to write a novel. I first read *Great Expectations* at school, but it wasn't until I went to university late in life and studied the novel in depth that I really understood and appreciated the work. It was then that I fell in love with Dickens's vivid descriptions and his intriguing array of often zany characters, and *Great Expectations* made its way onto my top ten list of great reads. Quite possibly the fact that it's never far from my thoughts was the catalyst for writing the enigmatic Estella's story. Hopeless romantic that I am, I have never been satisfied with Dickens's finale. In my opinion, both Pip and Estella go to hell and back and deserve better, deserve happiness, and I saw that with the writing of *Estella* there was a way to change that ending. The person, therefore, I am the most deeply indebted to is of course Charles Dickens—although he may not approve of what I have done!

I am also deeply indebted to the lovely Nicola Robinson, who was my initial commissioning editor at HQ, and who is also a huge Dickens fan and was so supportive and encouraging of my idea, inspiring me to write the best version of *Estella*. To my new publisher, Jo Mackay, and the team at HQ including Rochelle Fernandez, Sherryl Clark and Pauline O'Carolan, as well as all those who work so tirelessly and enthusiastically behind the scenes, thank you for taking me on and for believing in *Estella*. As before, it has been a pleasure and an honour to work with you all. Louisa Maggio, huge thanks for a haunting and evocative cover which captures the essence of my girl and blows me away every time I look at it.

Sincere thanks to my dear friend Merryl for reading early drafts, giving feedback, offering encouragement, and allowing me to rabbit on about writing at any time and any place. To my English cousin, Rosemary, thank you for taking me to Charles Dickens's haunts so long ago and for your willingness to answer all my questions, not to mention your enthusiasm.

Sincere gratitude to Sharyn Pearce. Your assistance as a reader is invaluable and I have come to rely upon your keen editorial skills and, quite frankly, this book would not be the same without you!

Thanks, as always, to my writerly mates: Andrea Baldwin, Laura Elvery, Mirandi Riwoe, Emma Doolan, Les Zig, Rebecca Jessen, Jodie How, Linda Brucesmith and the Dishevelled Little Owl. And the Brisbane Writing Crew—you know who you are—thank you for the support you give so effortlessly and so kindly.

Thanks to my agent, Sally Bird, for continuing to be on my team. Thank you for your steady presence, your friendship, your wisdom, and your ESP. Thank you for reacting so positively and so pleasingly to *Estella*.

To the Kimberley Girls High class of '73, big hugs. I was overjoyed by your response to *Sargasso* and I hope that you love *Estella* as much, and perhaps even more.

And, finally, to my dear family. My deep appreciation for your support, love, and understanding when I'm particularly ditzy. Especially Tim, who holds my hand in my dark moments, and reassures me, who believes in the work and in my ability to succeed and celebrates every little milestone with me. Thank you for letting me follow my dreams, sweetheart.